KUMA KUMA KUMA BEAR 3

STORY BY Kumananano ART BY Sergei CHAR. DESIGN BY 029

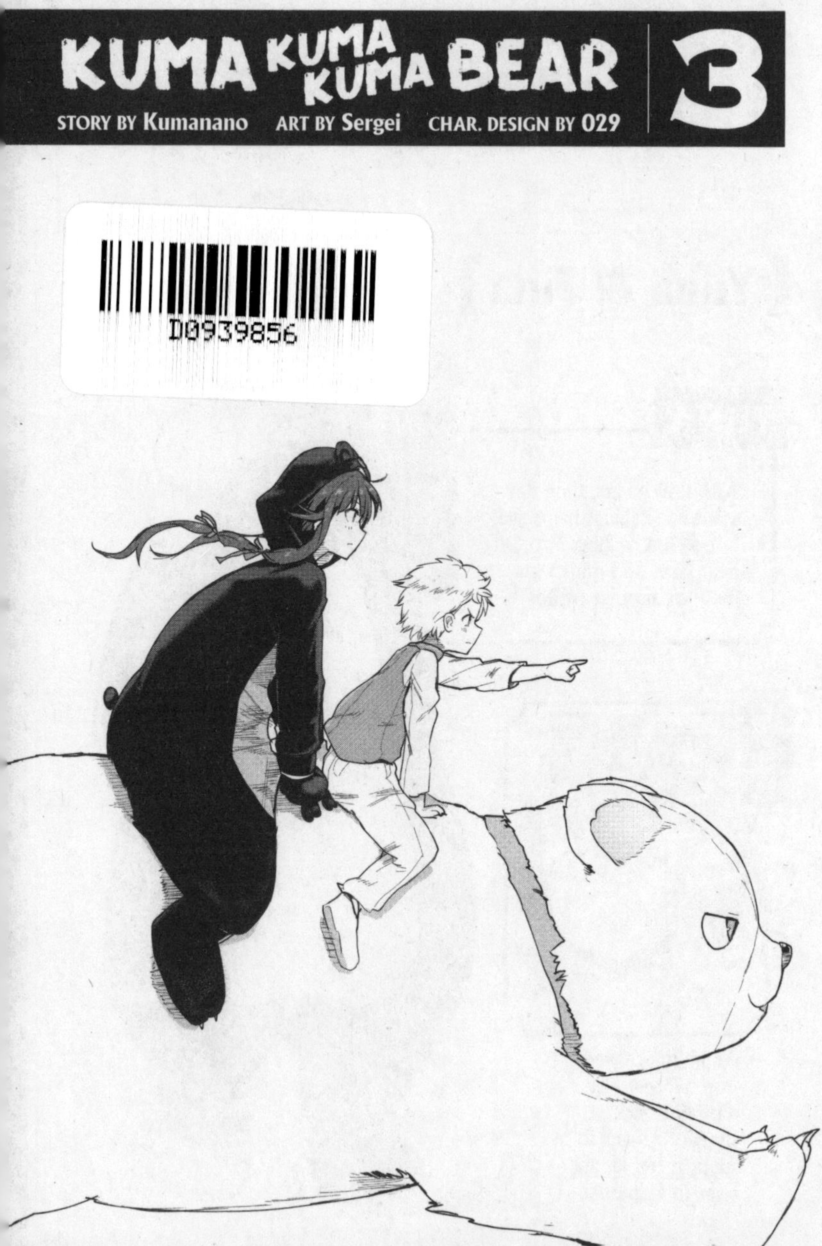

CHARACTERS

【 Yuna & Fina 】

YUNA

A shut-in gamer. One day someone calling themselves "God" forces Yuna into OP bear gear, and transports her into another world!

FINA

A girl Yuna saved from wolves. Her mother is sick, so she works hard to support her family. Lives in Crimonia.

【Fina's Family】

TIERMINA

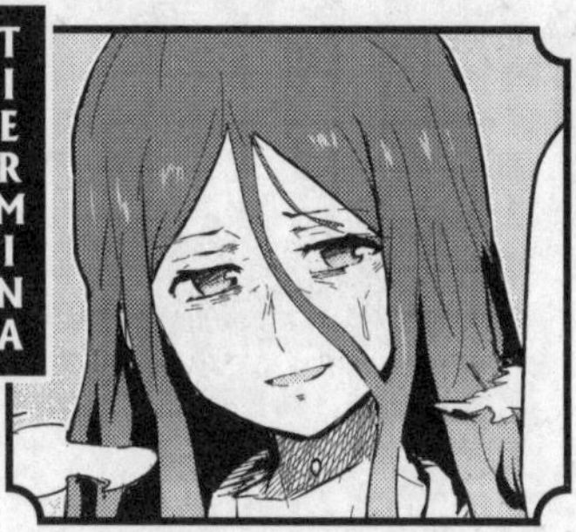

Fina and Shuri's mother. She's been bedridden since her busband passed away.

SHURI

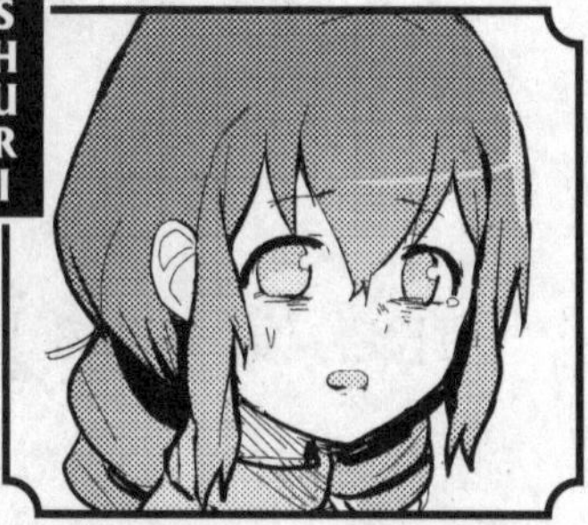

Three years younger than her sister, Fina. Lives with her sister and mother.

【Adventurers' Guild】

GENTZ

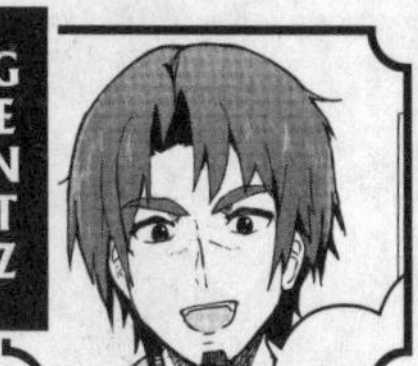

Nice guy who runs the Adventurers' Guild trading post.

HELEN

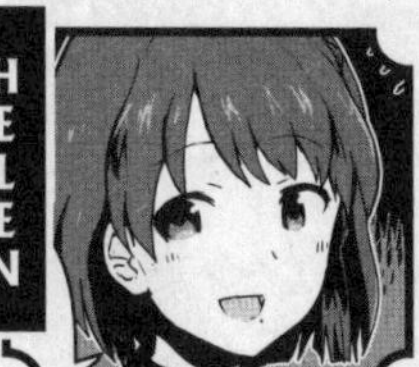

Adventurers' Guild receptionist. Yuna's overseer.

LAROC

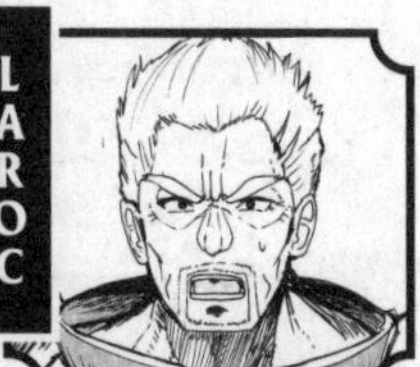

Guild Master of the Adventurers' Guild in Crimonia.

【Yuna's Bear Summons】

KUMAYURU

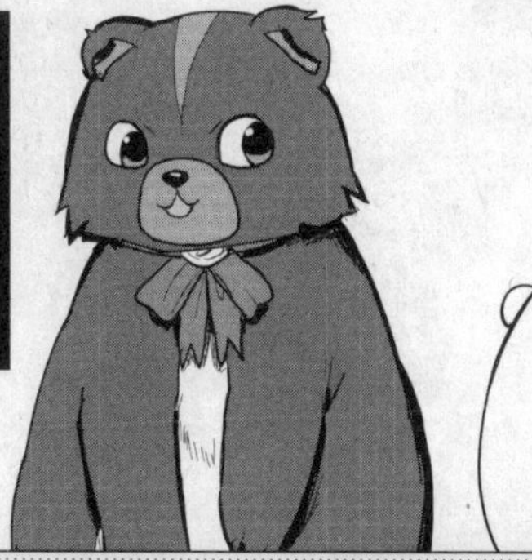

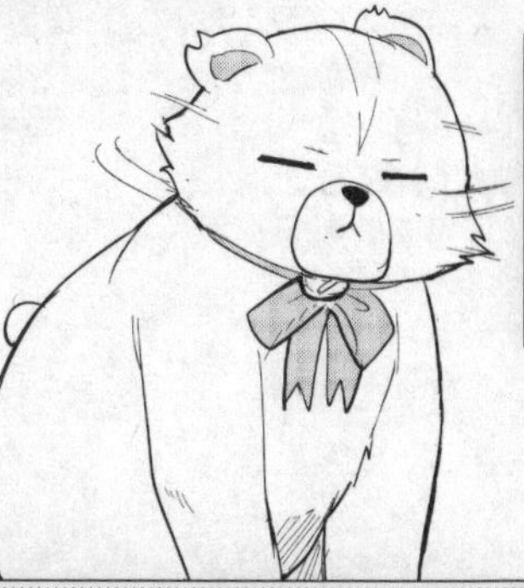

KUMAKYU

CONTENTS

STORY

Recluse gamer girl Yuna was given OP bear gear and then transported to another world. Yuna is settling into her new life in a fantasy town when Fina appears, distraught and begging for help. Her sick mother, Tiermina, has taken a turn for the worse...!

KUMA KUMA KUMA BEAR
VOLUME.3

Chapter 21

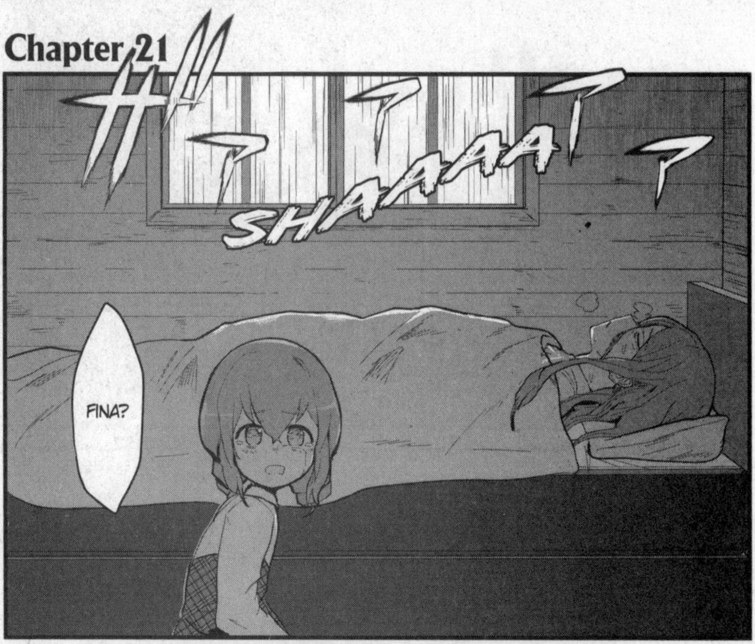
SHAAAAAT
FINA?

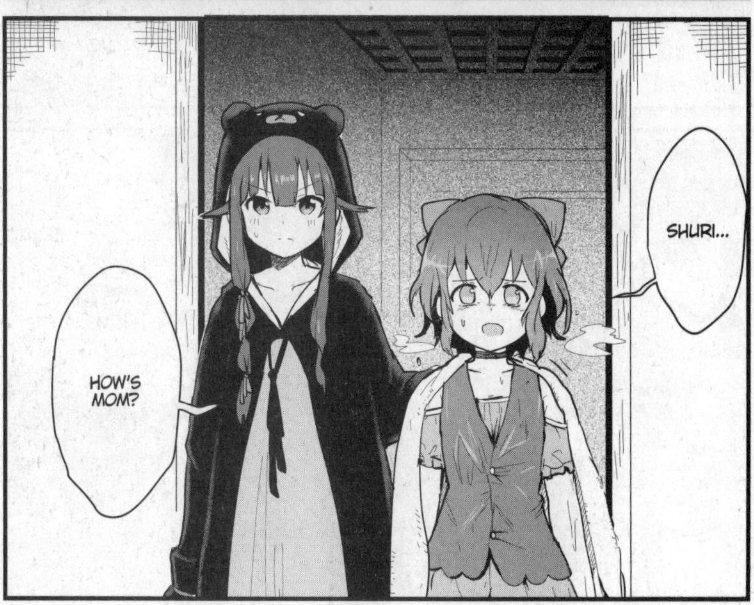
SHURI...
HOW'S MOM?

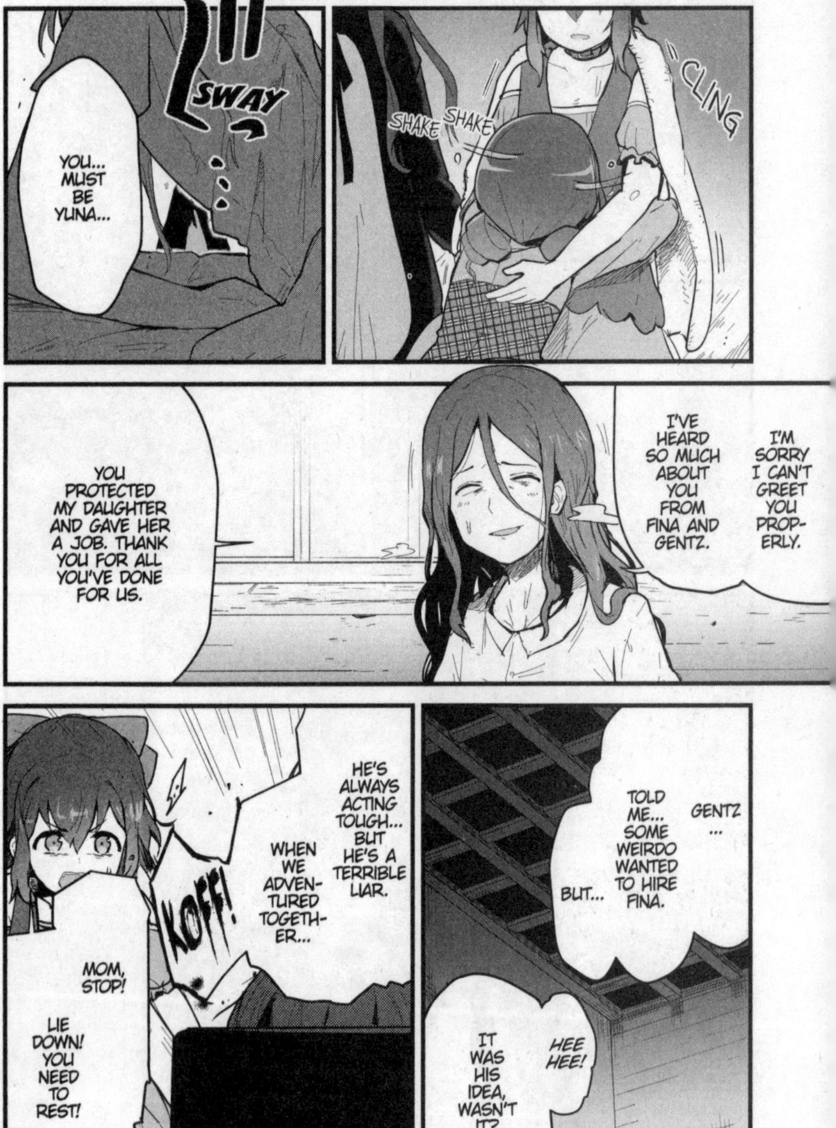
SHAKE SHAKE
CLING
SWAY
YOU... MUST BE YUNA...
I'M SORRY I CAN'T GREET YOU PROPERLY.
I'VE HEARD SO MUCH ABOUT YOU FROM FINA AND GENTZ.
YOU PROTECTED MY DAUGHTER AND GAVE HER A JOB. THANK YOU FOR ALL YOU'VE DONE FOR US.
GENTZ...
TOLD ME... SOME WEIRDO WANTED TO HIRE FINA.
BUT...
HEE HEE!
IT WAS HIS IDEA, WASN'T IT?
HE'S ALWAYS ACTING TOUGH... BUT HE'S A TERRIBLE LIAR.
WHEN WE ADVENTURED TOGETHER...
KOFF!
MOM, STOP!
LIE DOWN! YOU NEED TO REST!

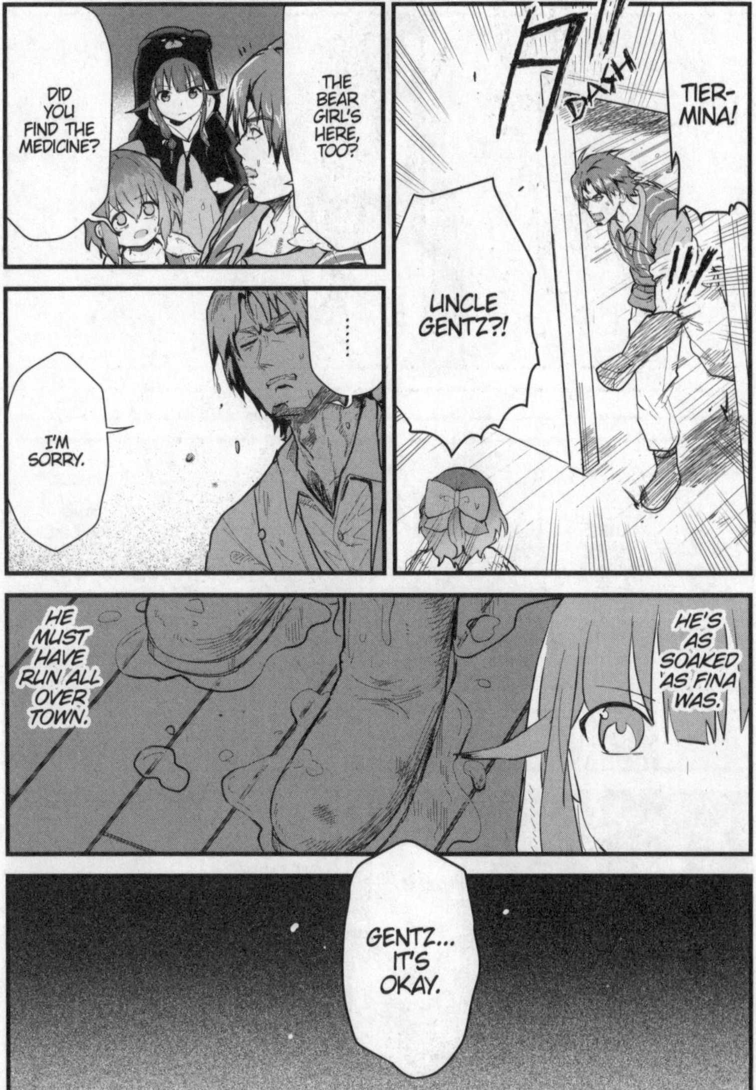
TIER-MINA!
DASH
UNCLE GENTZ?!
THE BEAR GIRL'S HERE, TOO?
DID YOU FIND THE MEDICINE?
......
I'M SORRY.
HE'S AS SOAKED AS FINA WAS.
HE MUST HAVE RUN ALL OVER TOWN.
GENTZ... IT'S OKAY.

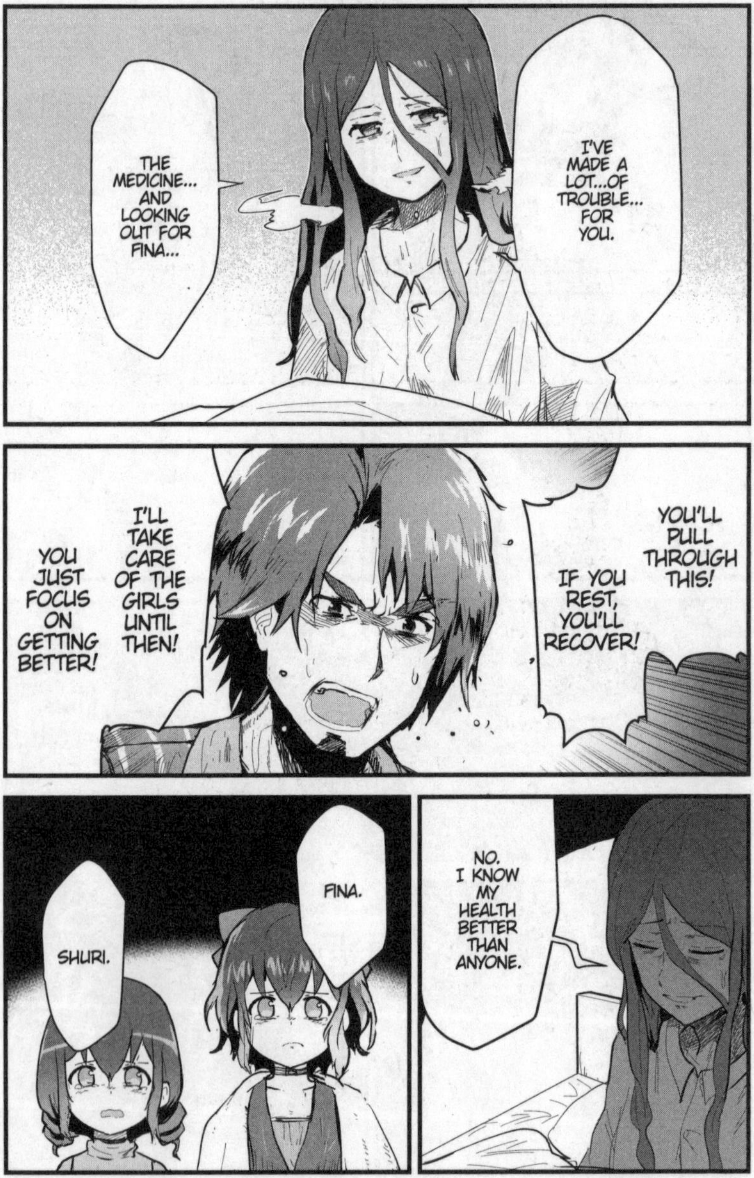
I'VE MADE A LOT...OF TROUBLE... FOR YOU.
THE MEDICINE... AND LOOKING OUT FOR FINA...
YOU'LL PULL THROUGH THIS!
IF YOU REST, YOU'LL RECOVER!
I'LL TAKE CARE OF THE GIRLS UNTIL THEN!
YOU JUST FOCUS ON GETTING BETTER!
NO. I KNOW MY HEALTH BETTER THAN ANYONE.
FINA.
SHURI.

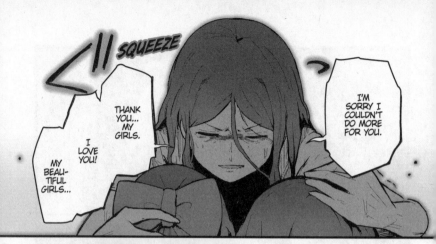

SQUEEZE
I'M SORRY I COULDN'T DO MORE FOR YOU.
THANK YOU... MY GIRLS.
I LOVE YOU!
MY BEAUTIFUL GIRLS...
N-NO...!
I... HIC! I'M SORRY...!
HIC! I COULDN'T... HELP YOU! UHHN!
WAAAH!
WAAAH! MAMA!
GENTZ... I HATE TO ASK FOR MORE, BUT...
PLEASE TAKE CARE OF MY DAUGHTERS.
I'M NOT GOING TO AGREE TO THAT, TIERMINA!
YOU'RE GOING TO RECOVER AND RAISE THEM YOURSELF!
FLOP
MOOOOOM!

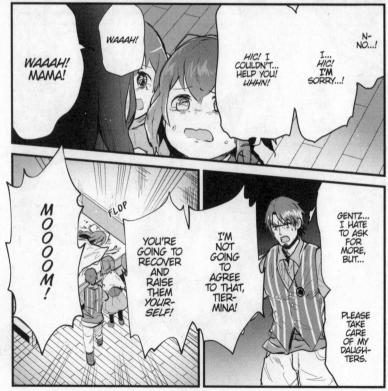

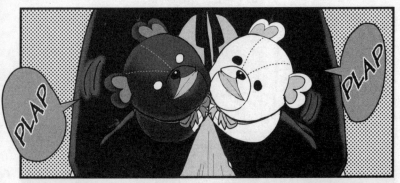

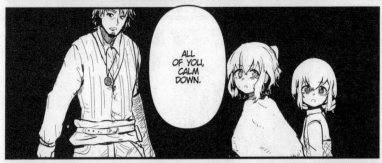

PLAP
PLAP
ALL OF YOU, CALM DOWN.
I'LL TAKE A LOOK AT HER.
BUT I CAN'T PROMISE ANYTHING.

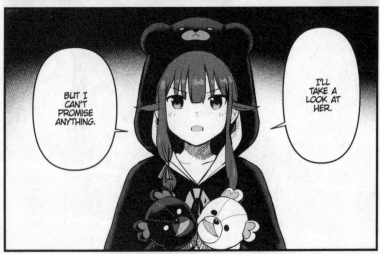

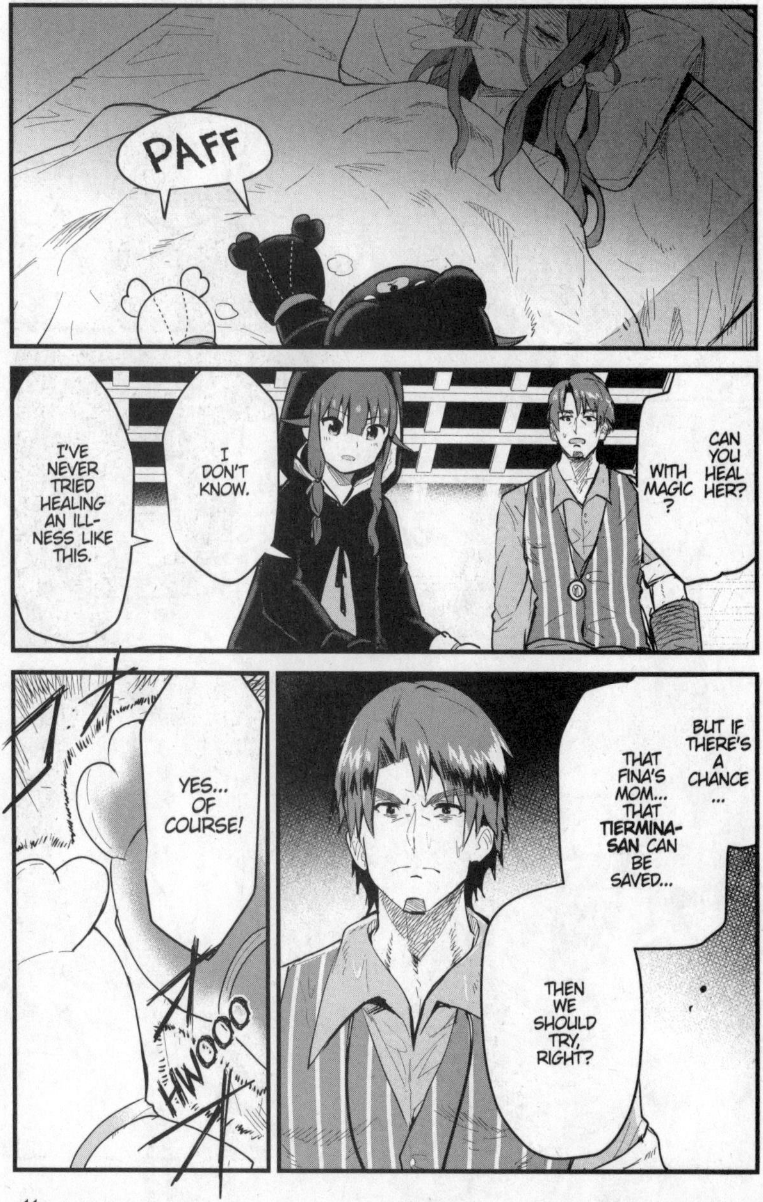
PAFF
CAN YOU HEAL HER?
WITH MAGIC?
I DON'T KNOW.
I'VE NEVER TRIED HEALING AN ILLNESS LIKE THIS.
BUT IF THERE'S A CHANCE...
THAT FINA'S MOM... THAT TIERMINA-SAN CAN BE SAVED...
THEN WE SHOULD TRY, RIGHT?
YES... OF COURSE!
HWOOO

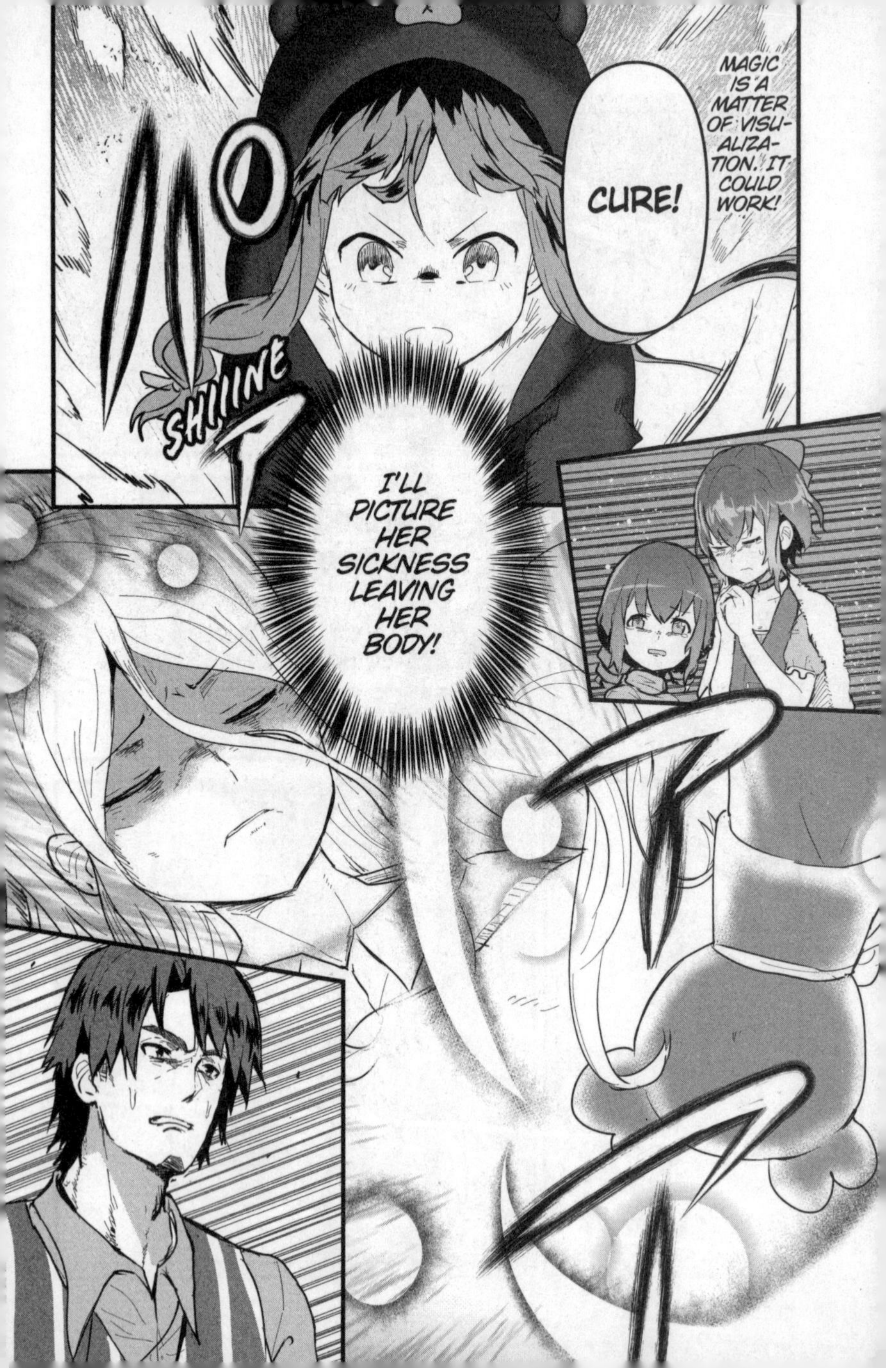
MAGIC IS A MATTER OF VISU-ALIZA-TION. IT COULD WORK!
CURE!
SHIIINE
I'LL PICTURE HER SICKNESS LEAVING HER BODY!

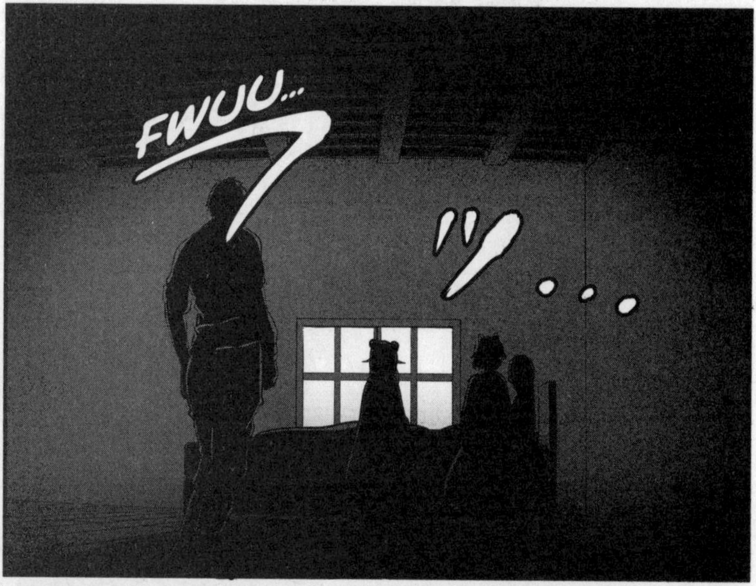
FWUU...

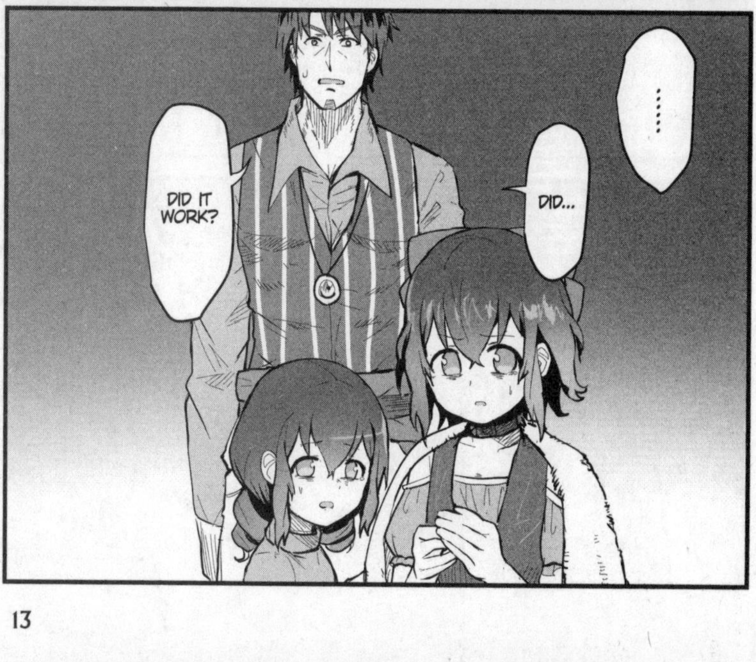
......
DID...
DID IT WORK?

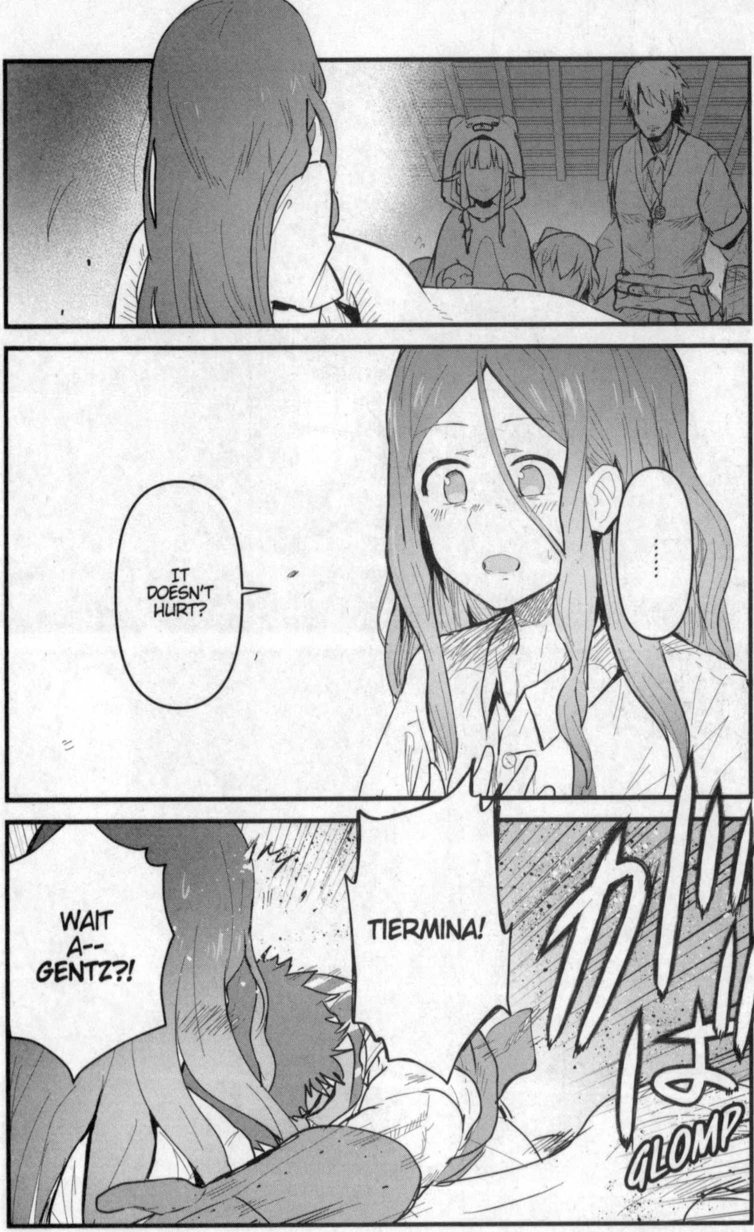
......
IT DOESN'T HURT?
TIERMINA!
WAIT A-- GENTZ?!
GLOMP

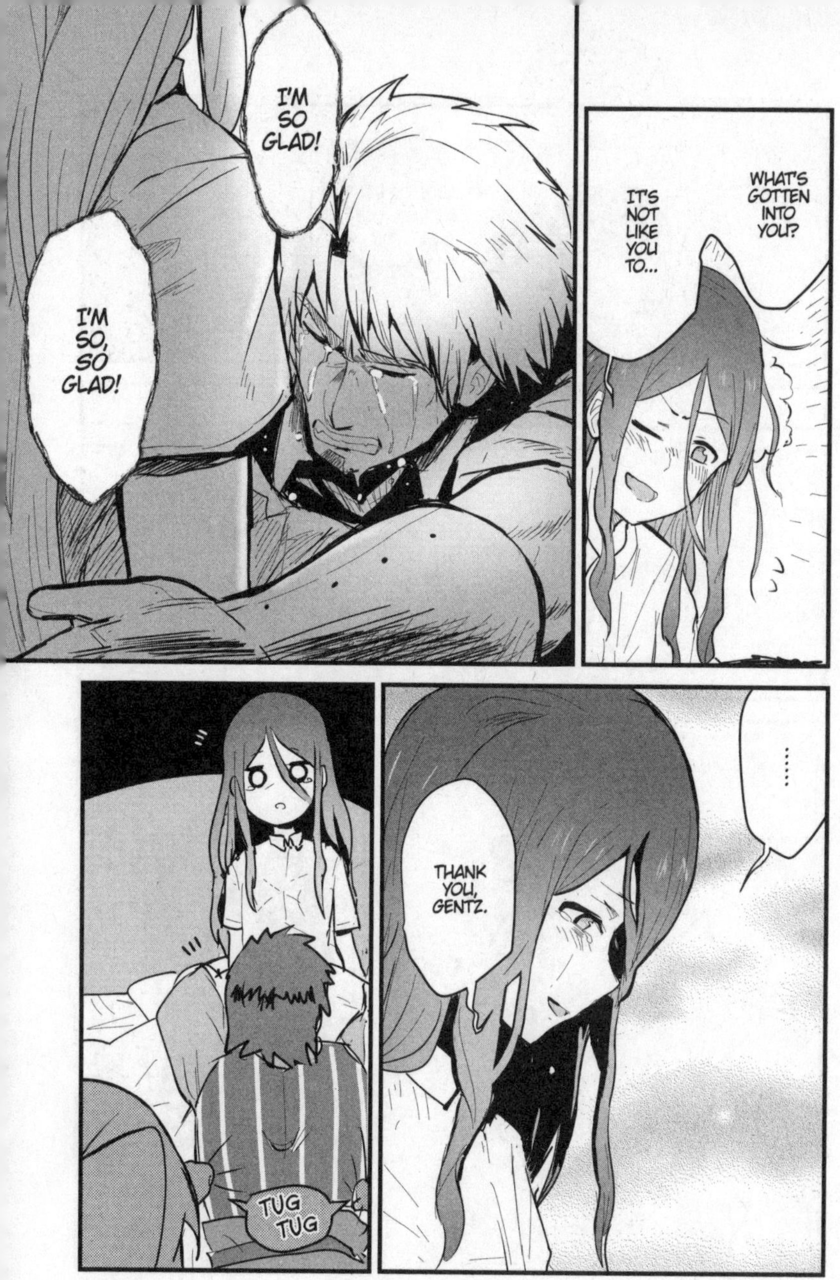
WHAT'S GOTTEN INTO YOU?
IT'S NOT LIKE YOU TO...
I'M SO GLAD!
I'M SO, SO GLAD!
......
THANK YOU, GENTZ.
TUG TUG

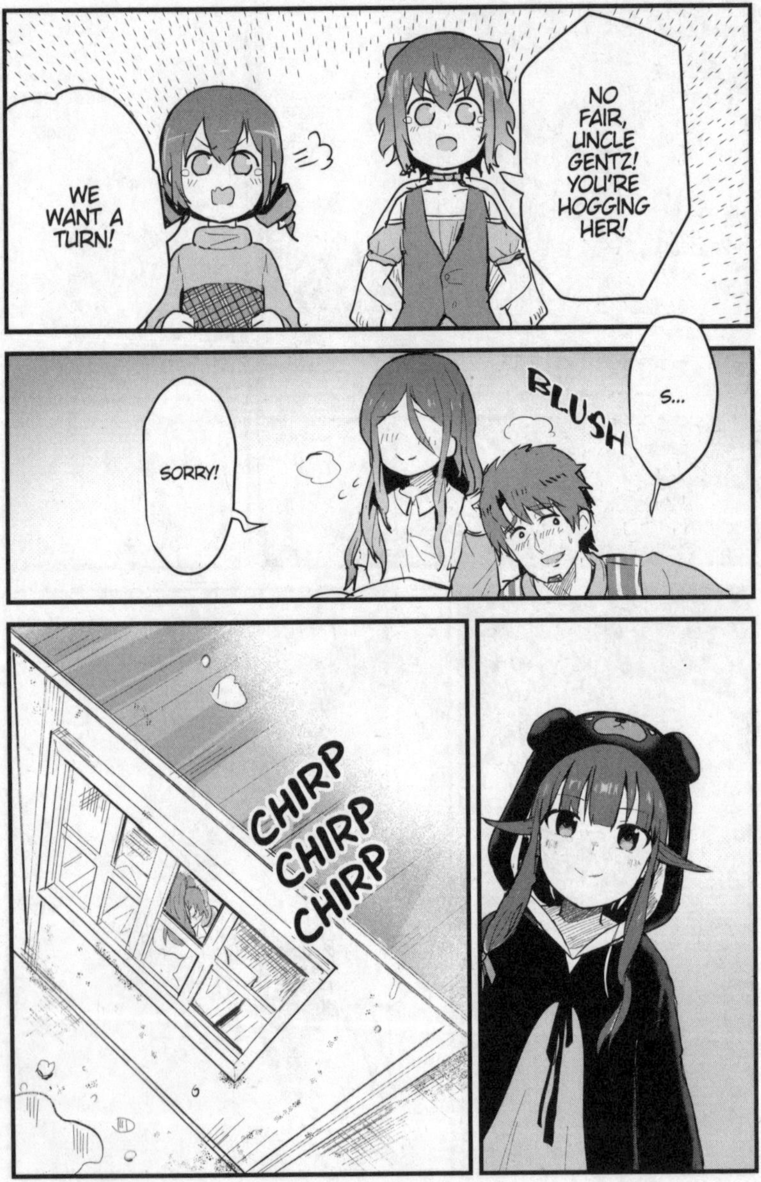
NO FAIR, UNCLE GENTZ! YOU'RE HOGGING HER!
WE WANT A TURN!
S...
BLUSH
SORRY!
CHIRP CHIRP CHIRP

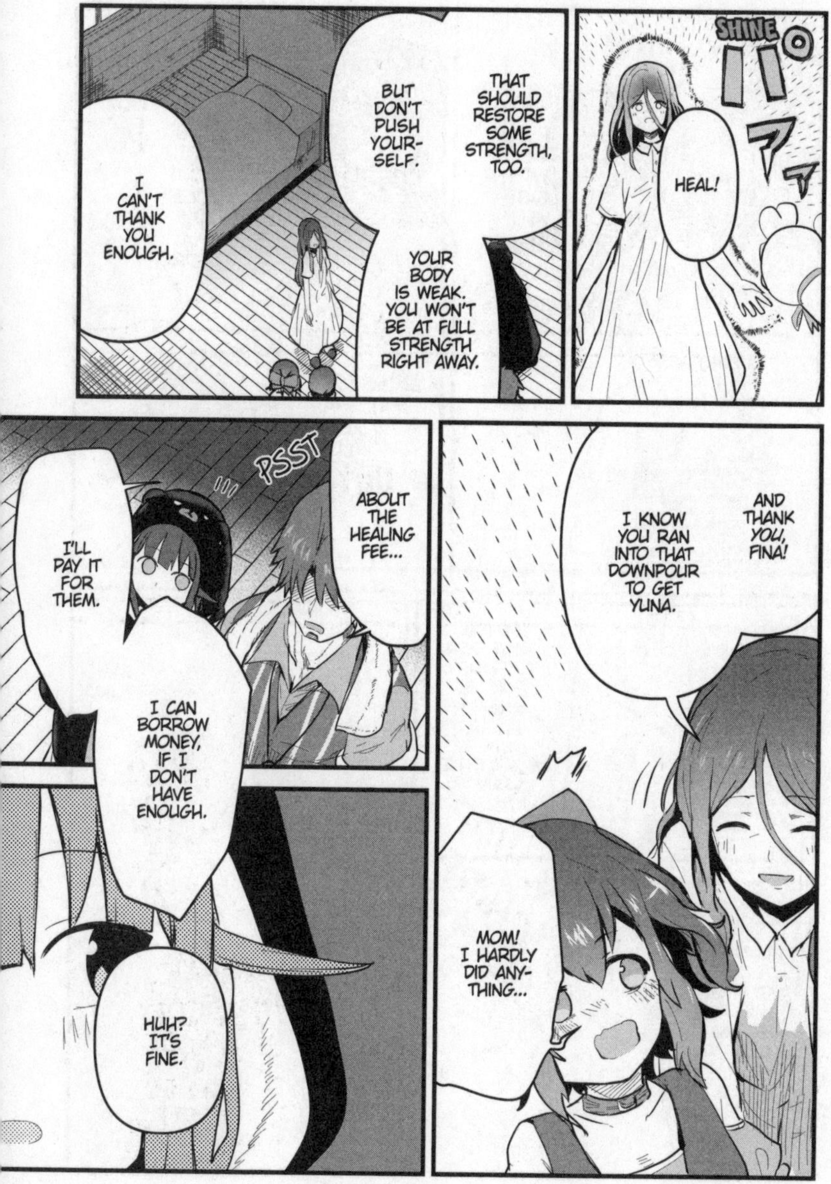
SHINE
HEAL!
THAT SHOULD RESTORE SOME STRENGTH, TOO.
BUT DON'T PUSH YOURSELF.
YOUR BODY IS WEAK. YOU WON'T BE AT FULL STRENGTH RIGHT AWAY.
I CAN'T THANK YOU ENOUGH.
AND THANK YOU, FINA!
I KNOW YOU RAN INTO THAT DOWNPOUR TO GET YUNA.
MOM! I HARDLY DID ANYTHING...
PSST
ABOUT THE HEALING FEE...
I'LL PAY IT FOR THEM.
I CAN BORROW MONEY, IF I DON'T HAVE ENOUGH.
HUH? IT'S FINE.

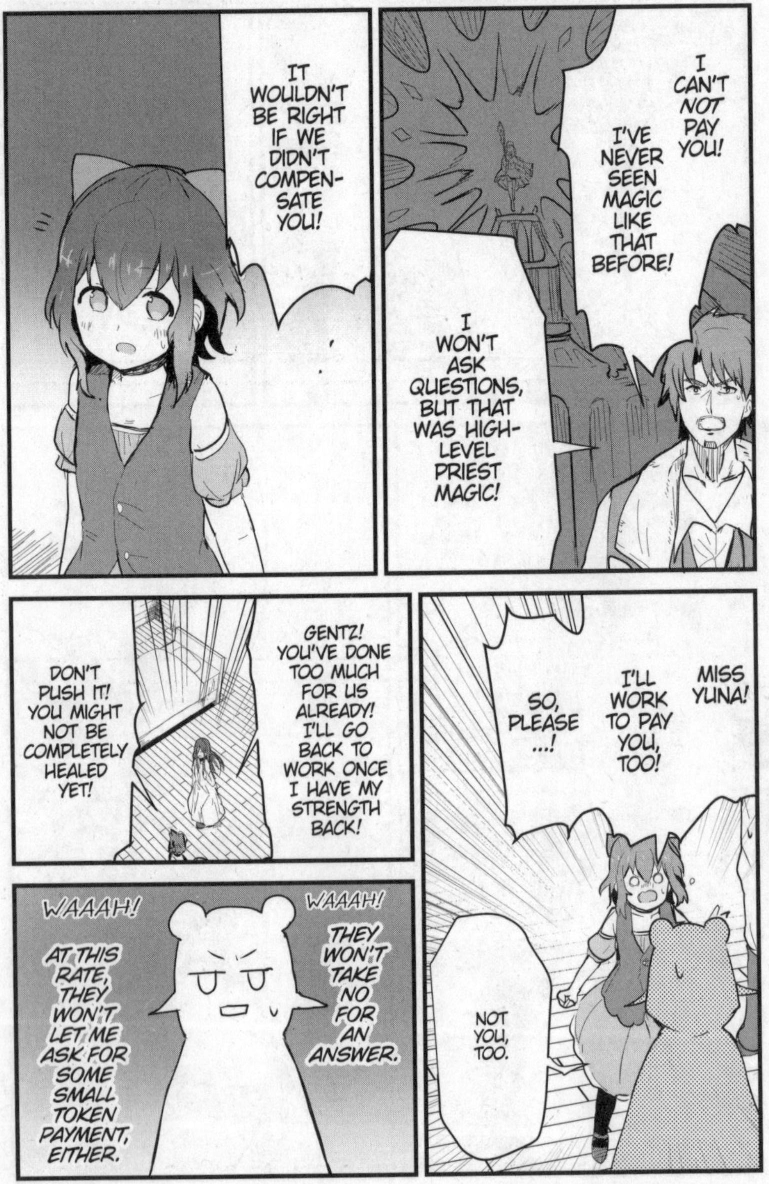
I CAN'T NOT PAY YOU!
I'VE NEVER SEEN MAGIC LIKE THAT BEFORE!
I WON'T ASK QUESTIONS, BUT THAT WAS HIGH-LEVEL PRIEST MAGIC!
IT WOULDN'T BE RIGHT IF WE DIDN'T COMPEN-SATE YOU!
MISS YUNA!
I'LL WORK TO PAY YOU, TOO!
SO, PLEASE ...!
NOT YOU, TOO.
GENTZ! YOU'VE DONE TOO MUCH FOR US ALREADY! I'LL GO BACK TO WORK ONCE I HAVE MY STRENGTH BACK!
DON'T PUSH IT! YOU MIGHT NOT BE COMPLETELY HEALED YET!
WAAAH!
THEY WON'T TAKE NO FOR AN ANSWER.
WAAAH!
AT THIS RATE, THEY WON'T LET ME ASK FOR SOME SMALL TOKEN PAYMENT, EITHER.

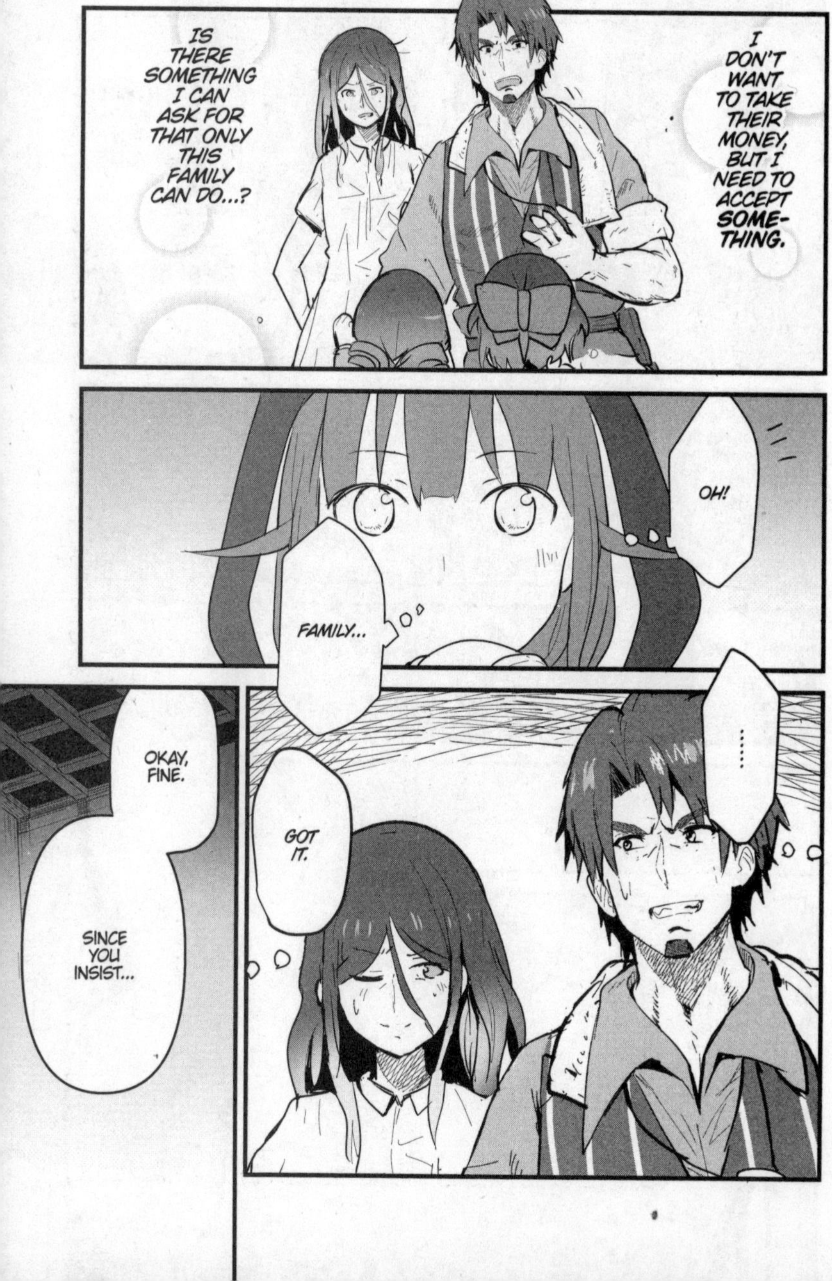
I DON'T WANT TO TAKE THEIR MONEY, BUT I NEED TO ACCEPT SOMETHING.
IS THERE SOMETHING I CAN ASK FOR THAT ONLY THIS FAMILY CAN DO...?
OH!
FAMILY...
......
GOT IT.
OKAY, FINE.
SINCE YOU INSIST...

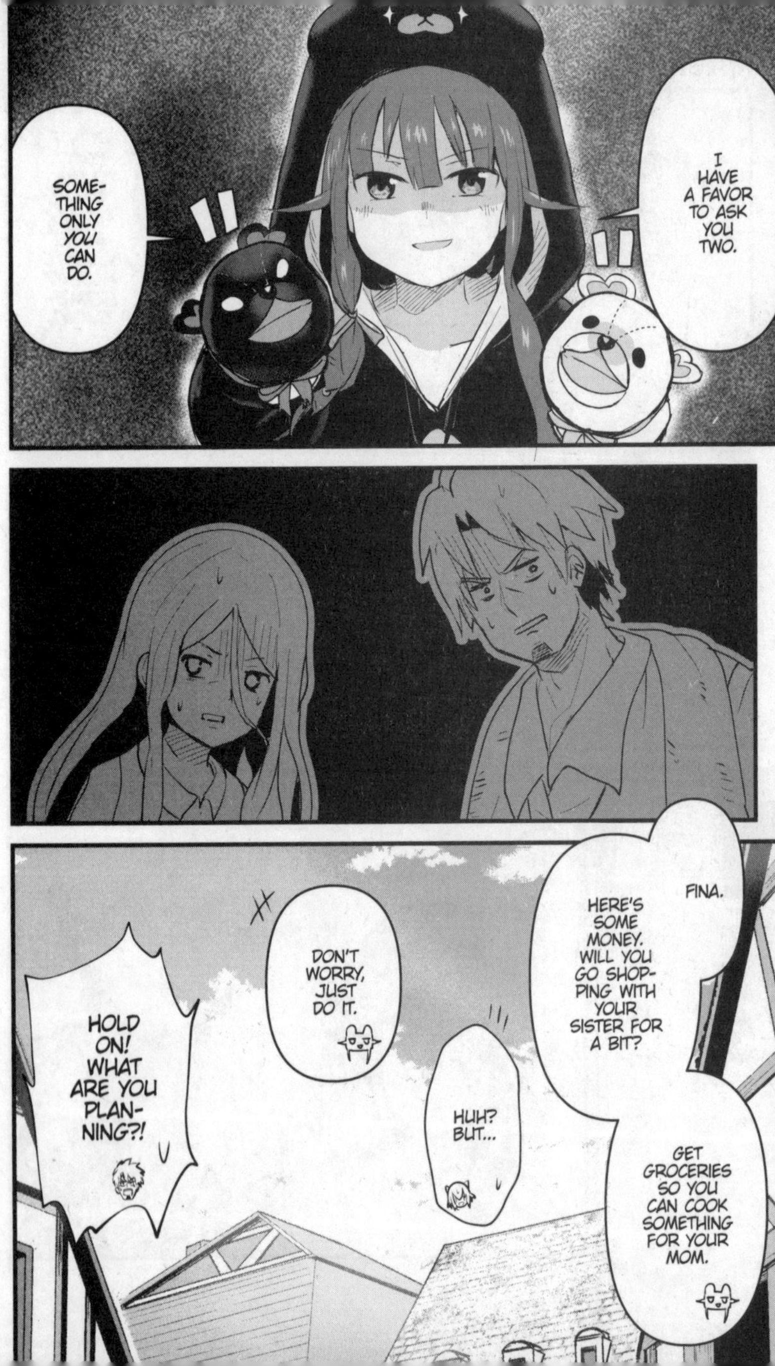
I HAVE A FAVOR TO ASK YOU TWO.
SOMETHING ONLY YOU CAN DO.
FINA.
HERE'S SOME MONEY. WILL YOU GO SHOPPING WITH YOUR SISTER FOR A BIT?
GET GROCERIES SO YOU CAN COOK SOMETHING FOR YOUR MOM.
HUH? BUT...
DON'T WORRY, JUST DO IT.
HOLD ON! WHAT ARE YOU PLANNING?!

Chapter 22

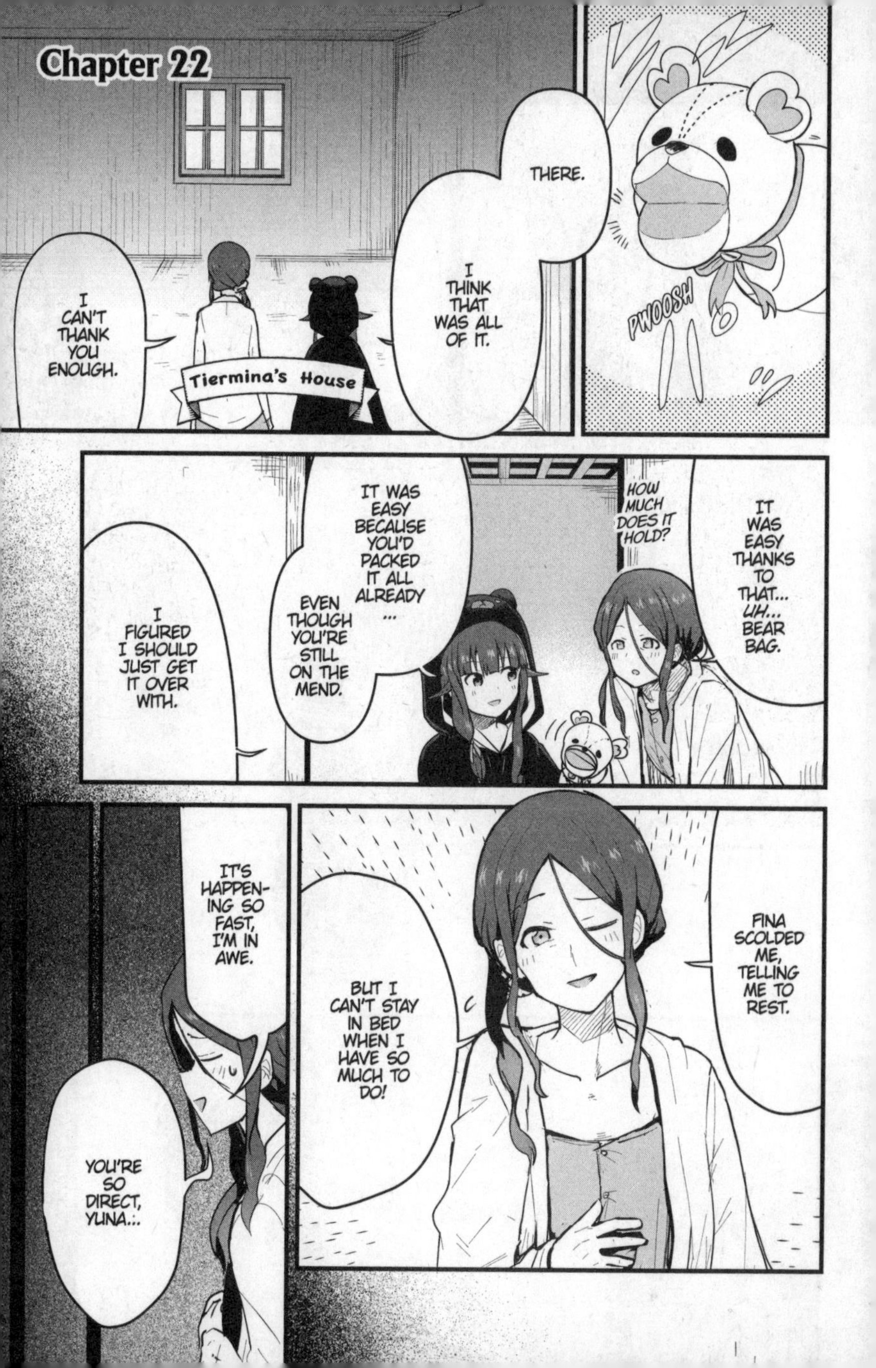
PWOOSH
THERE.
I THINK THAT WAS ALL OF IT.
Tiermina's House
I CAN'T THANK YOU ENOUGH.
IT WAS EASY THANKS TO THAT... UH... BEAR BAG.
HOW MUCH DOES IT HOLD?
IT WAS EASY BECAUSE YOU'D PACKED IT ALL ALREADY...
EVEN THOUGH YOU'RE STILL ON THE MEND.
I FIGURED I SHOULD JUST GET IT OVER WITH.
FINA SCOLDED ME, TELLING ME TO REST.
BUT I CAN'T STAY IN BED WHEN I HAVE SO MUCH TO DO!
IT'S HAPPENING SO FAST, I'M IN AWE.
YOU'RE SO DIRECT, YUNA...

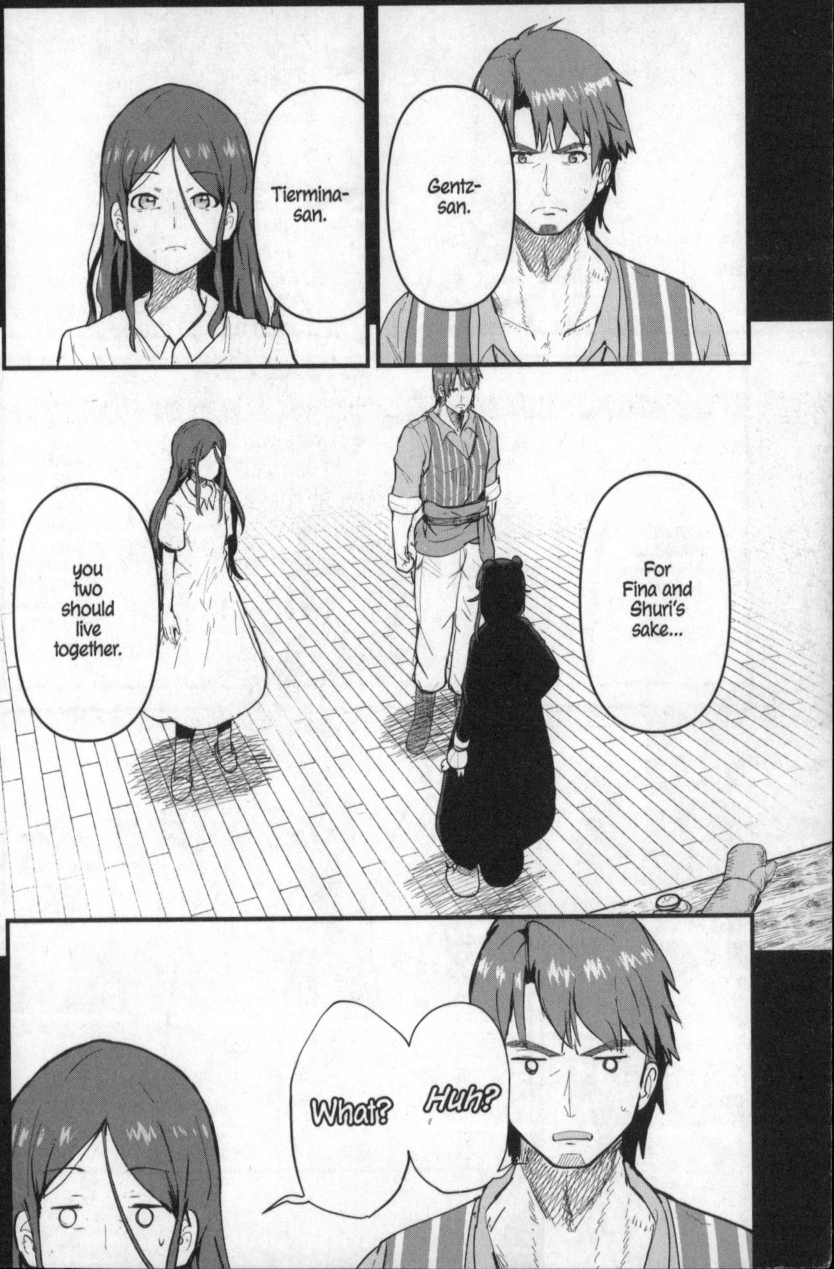
Gentz-san.
Tiermina-san.
For Fina and Shuri's sake...
you two should live together.
Huh?
What?

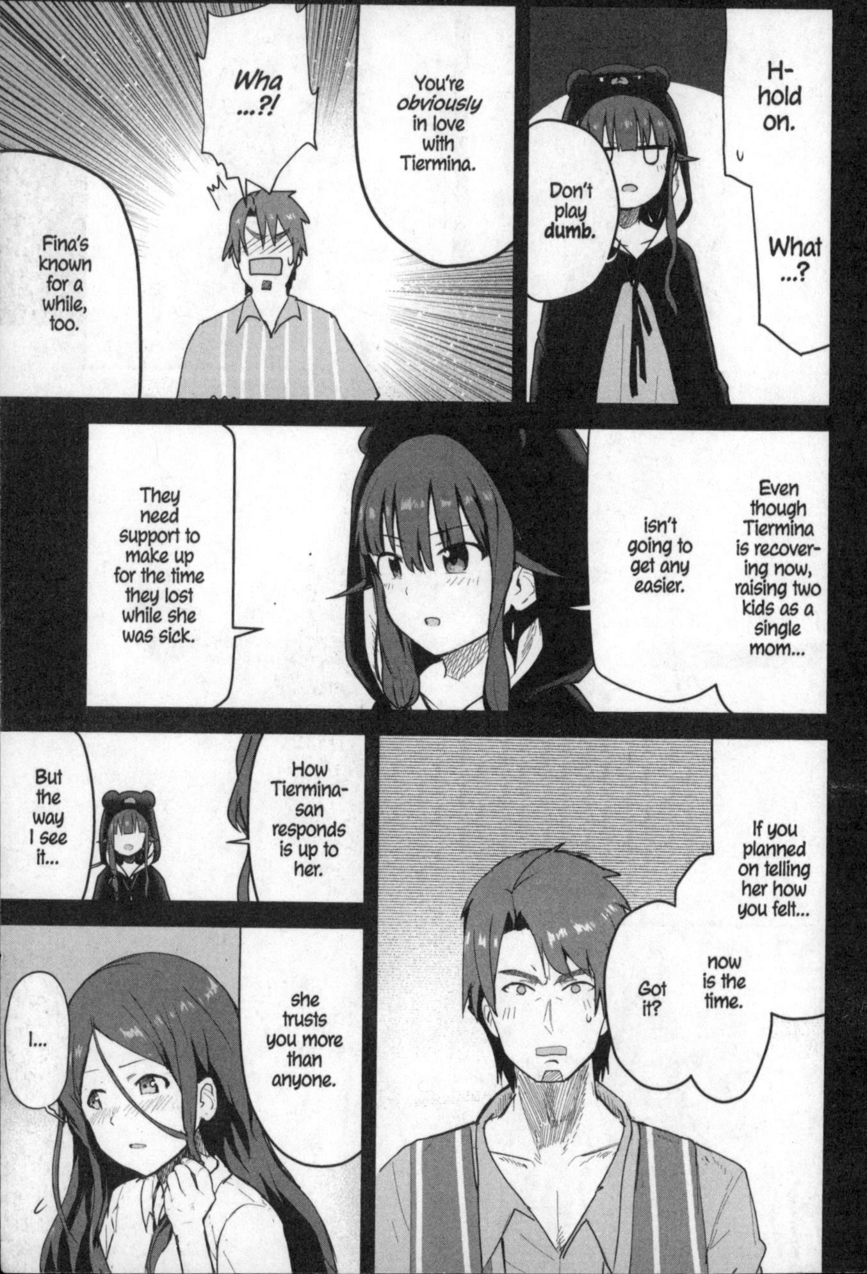
H-hold on.
What...?
Don't play dumb.
You're *obviously* in love with Tiermina.
Wha...?!
Fina's known for a while, too.
Even though Tiermina is recovering now, raising two kids as a single mom...
isn't going to get any easier.
They need support to make up for the time they lost while she was sick.
If you planned on telling her how you felt...
now is the time.
Got it?
How Tiermina-san responds is up to her.
But the way I see it...
she trusts you more than anyone.
I...

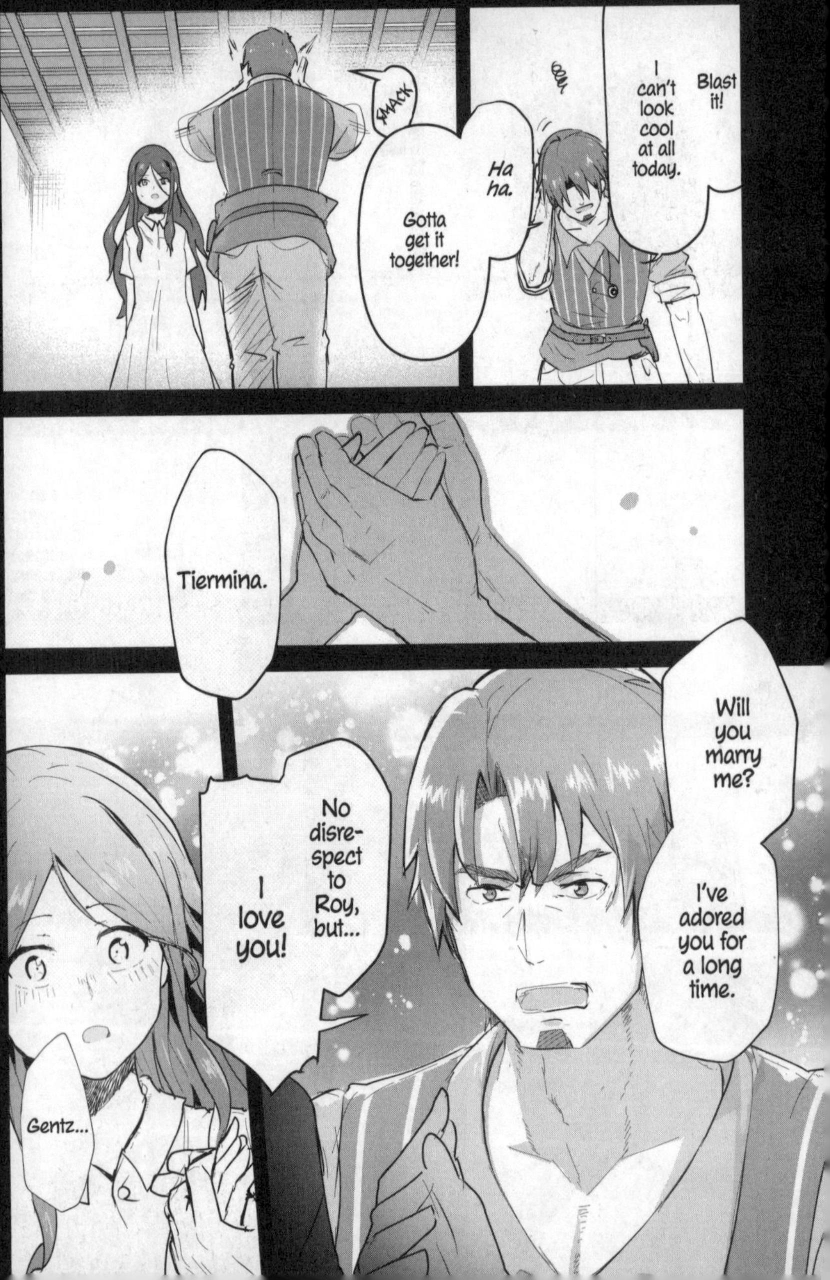
Blast it!
I can't look cool at all today.
Ha ha.
Gotta get it together!
SMACK
Tiermina.
Will you marry me?
I've adored you for a long time.
No disre-spect to Roy, but...
I love you!
Gentz...

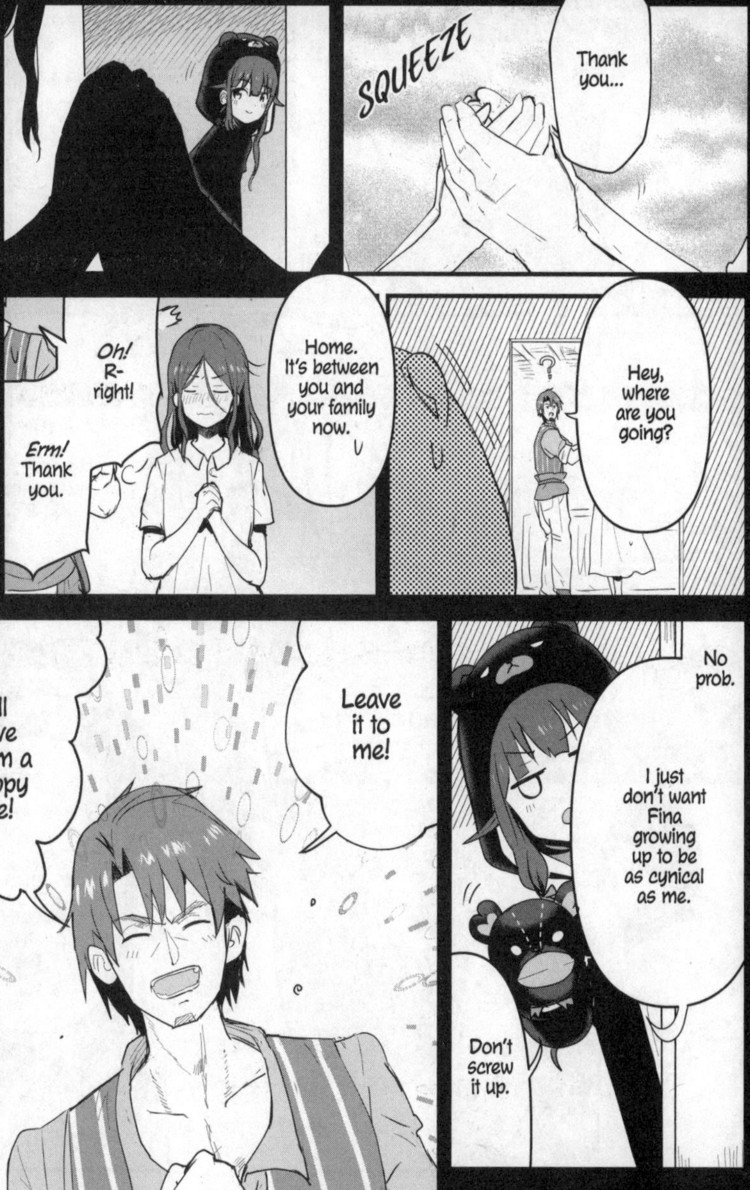
Thank you...
SQUEEZE
Hey, where are you going?
Home. It's between you and your family now.
Oh! R-right!
Erm! Thank you.
No prob.
I just don't want Fina growing up to be as cynical as me.
Don't screw it up.
Leave it to me!
I'll give them a happy life!

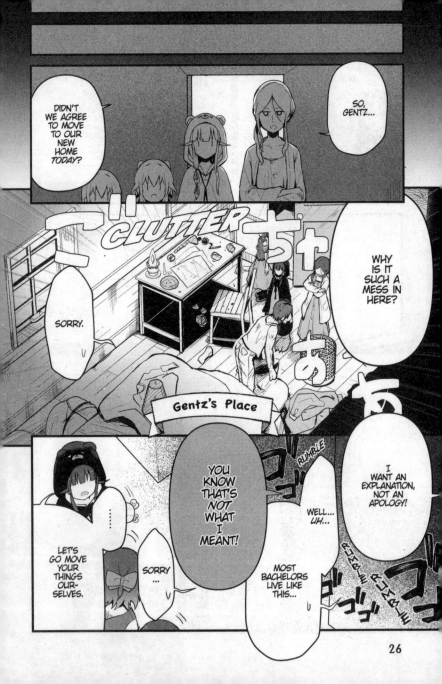

SO, GENTZ...
DIDN'T WE AGREE TO MOVE TO OUR NEW HOME *TODAY*?
WHY IS IT SUCH A MESS IN HERE?
CLUTTER
SORRY.
Gentz's Place
I WANT AN EXPLANATION, NOT AN APOLOGY!
RUMBLE
RUMBLE RUMBLE
WELL... *UH...*
MOST BACHELORS LIVE LIKE THIS...
YOU KNOW THAT'S *NOT* WHAT I MEANT!
SORRY ...
......
LET'S GO MOVE YOUR THINGS OUR-SELVES.

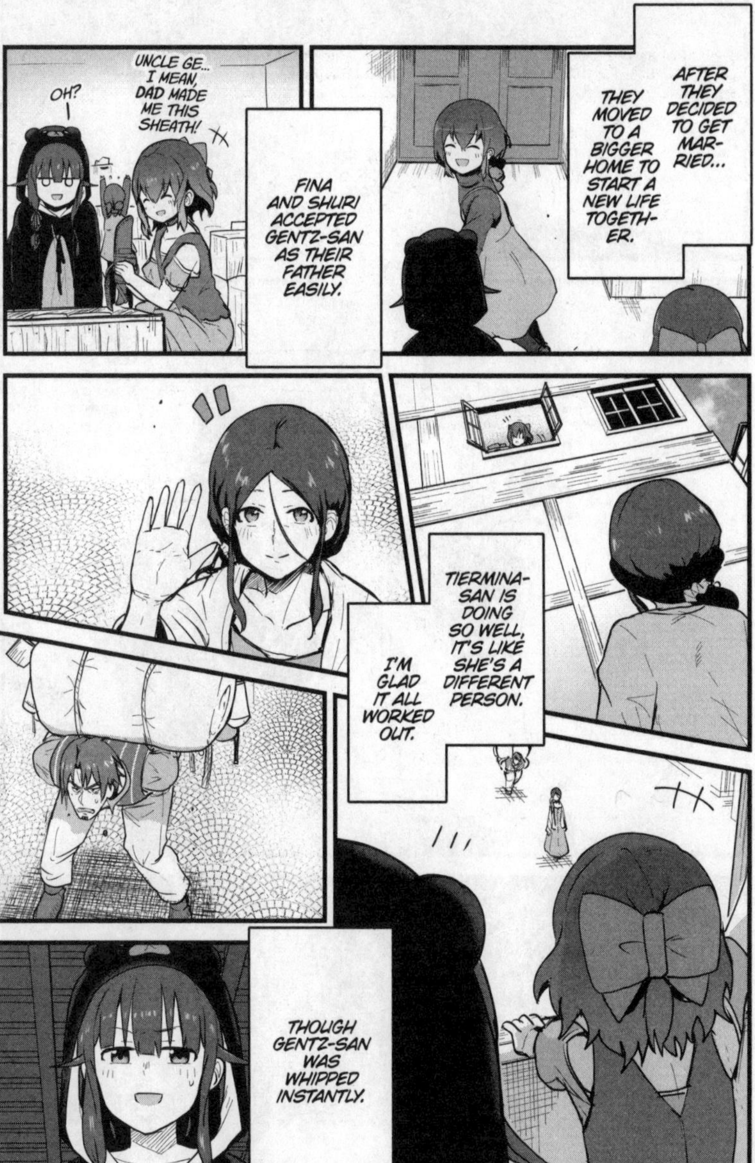
AFTER THEY DECIDED TO GET MAR-RIED...
THEY MOVED TO A BIGGER HOME TO START A NEW LIFE TOGETH-ER.
FINA AND SHURI ACCEPTED GENTZ-SAN AS THEIR FATHER EASILY.
UNCLE GE... I MEAN, DAD MADE ME THIS SHEATH!
OH?
TIERMINA-SAN IS DOING SO WELL, IT'S LIKE SHE'S A DIFFERENT PERSON.
I'M GLAD IT ALL WORKED OUT.
THOUGH GENTZ-SAN WAS WHIPPED INSTANTLY.

I'M SO SORRY, YUNA.

FIRST YOU HELP US MOVE, NOW WE'RE ALL STAYING THE NIGHT.

KEEP STILL!

COOKING TIME! ♪

IT'S NO BIG DEAL.

SORRY...

IF SOMEONE HAD BEEN READY, WE COULD HAVE BEEN UNPACKED ALREADY.

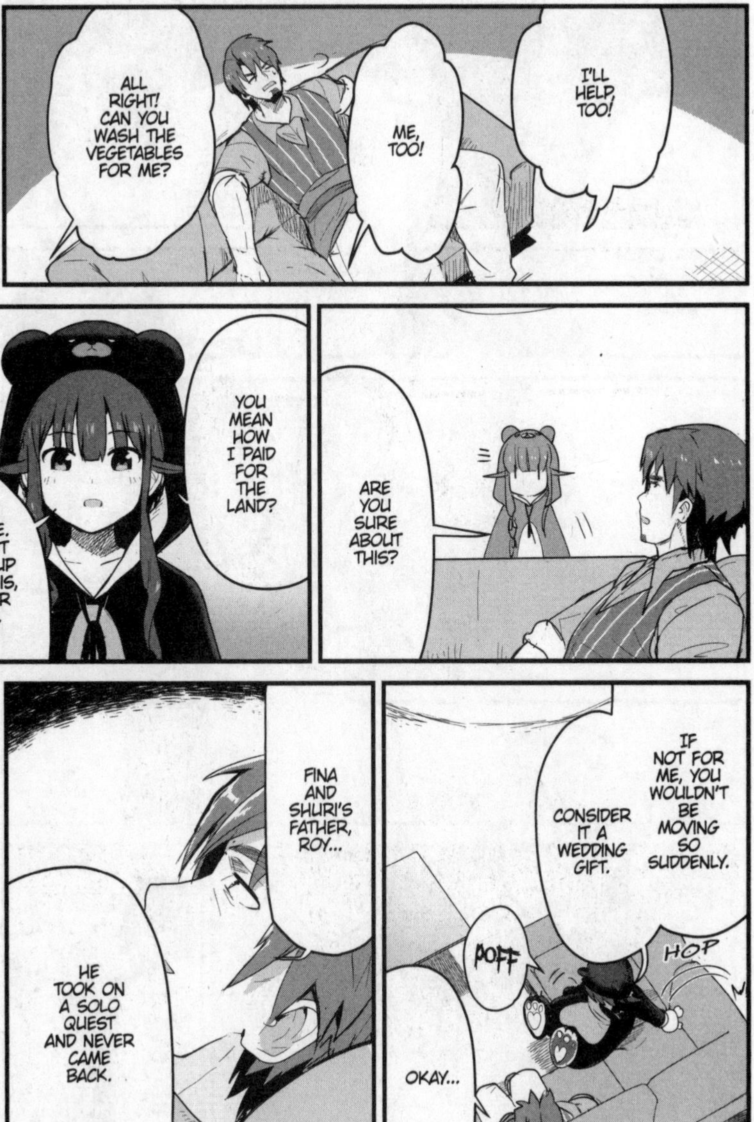
I'LL HELP, TOO!
ME, TOO!
ALL RIGHT! CAN YOU WASH THE VEGETABLES FOR ME?
ARE YOU SURE ABOUT THIS?
YOU MEAN HOW I PAID FOR THE LAND?
I'M SURE. I PUT YOU UP TO THIS, AFTER ALL.
IF NOT FOR ME, YOU WOULDN'T BE MOVING SO SUDDENLY.
CONSIDER IT A WEDDING GIFT.
HOP
POFF
OKAY...
FINA AND SHURI'S FATHER, ROY...
HE TOOK ON A SOLO QUEST AND NEVER CAME BACK.

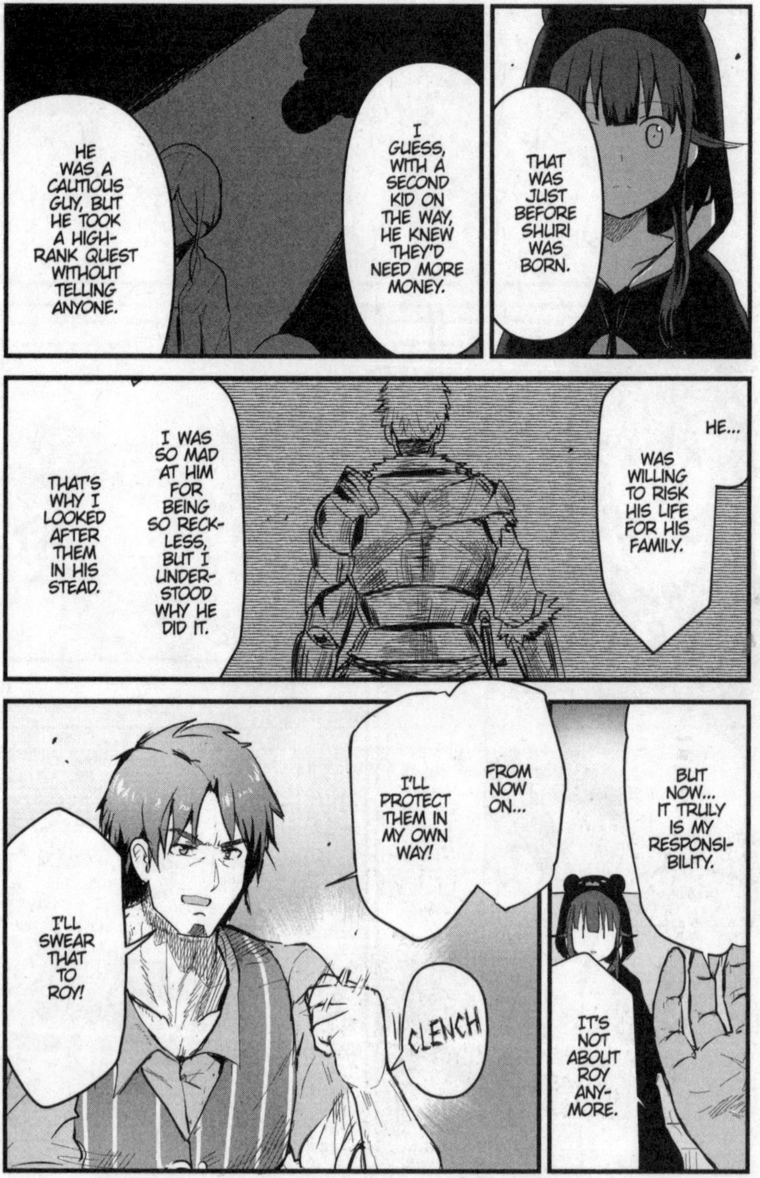
THAT WAS JUST BEFORE SHURI WAS BORN.
I GUESS, WITH A SECOND KID ON THE WAY, HE KNEW THEY'D NEED MORE MONEY.
HE WAS A CAUTIOUS GUY, BUT HE TOOK A HIGH-RANK QUEST WITHOUT TELLING ANYONE.
HE...
WAS WILLING TO RISK HIS LIFE FOR HIS FAMILY.
I WAS SO MAD AT HIM FOR BEING SO RECK-LESS, BUT I UNDER-STOOD WHY HE DID IT.
THAT'S WHY I LOOKED AFTER THEM IN HIS STEAD.
BUT NOW... IT TRULY IS MY RESPONSI-BILITY.
IT'S NOT ABOUT ROY ANY-MORE.
FROM NOW ON...
I'LL PROTECT THEM IN MY OWN WAY!
CLENCH
I'LL SWEAR THAT TO ROY!

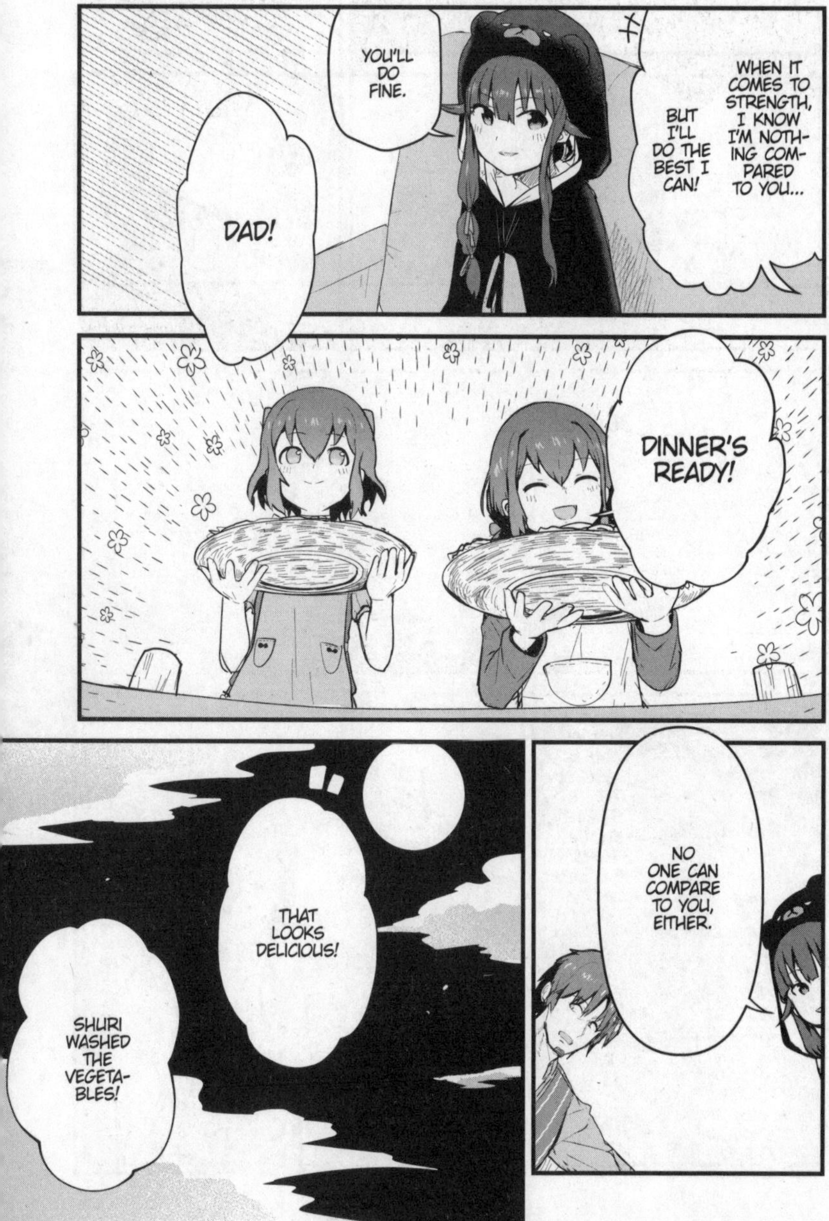
WHEN IT COMES TO STRENGTH, I KNOW I'M NOTHING COMPARED TO YOU...
BUT I'LL DO THE BEST I CAN!
YOU'LL DO FINE.
DAD!
DINNER'S READY!
NO ONE CAN COMPARE TO YOU, EITHER.
THAT LOOKS DELICIOUS!
SHURI WASHED THE VEGETABLES!

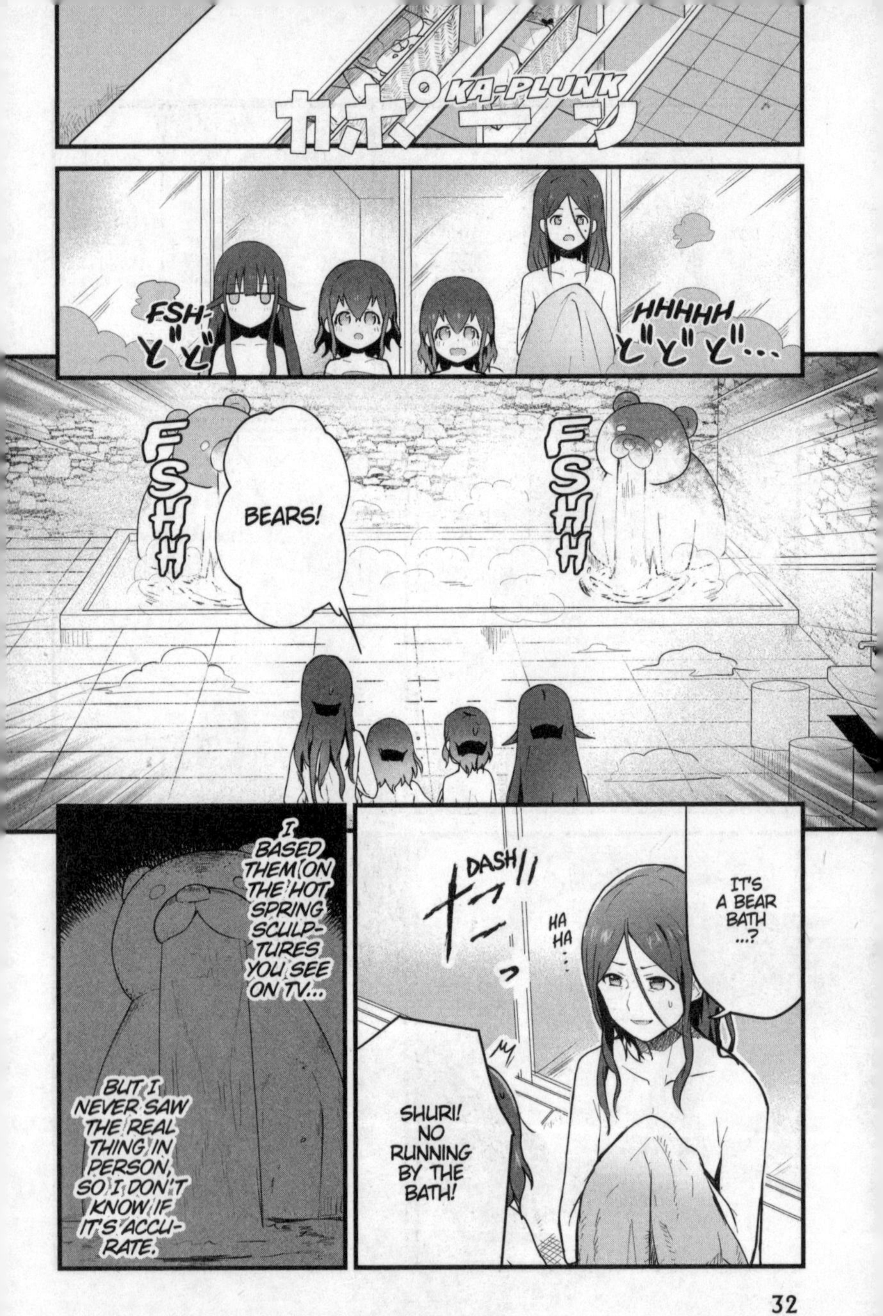
カポーン
KA-PLUNK
HHHHH
ど゛ど゛ど゛…
FSH-
ど゛ど゛
FSHH
BEARS!
FSHH
IT'S A BEAR BATH ...?
HA HA ...
DASH
SHURI! NO RUNNING BY THE BATH!
I BASED THEM ON THE HOT SPRING SCULPTURES YOU SEE ON TV...
BUT I NEVER SAW THE REAL THING IN PERSON, SO I DON'T KNOW IF IT'S ACCURATE.

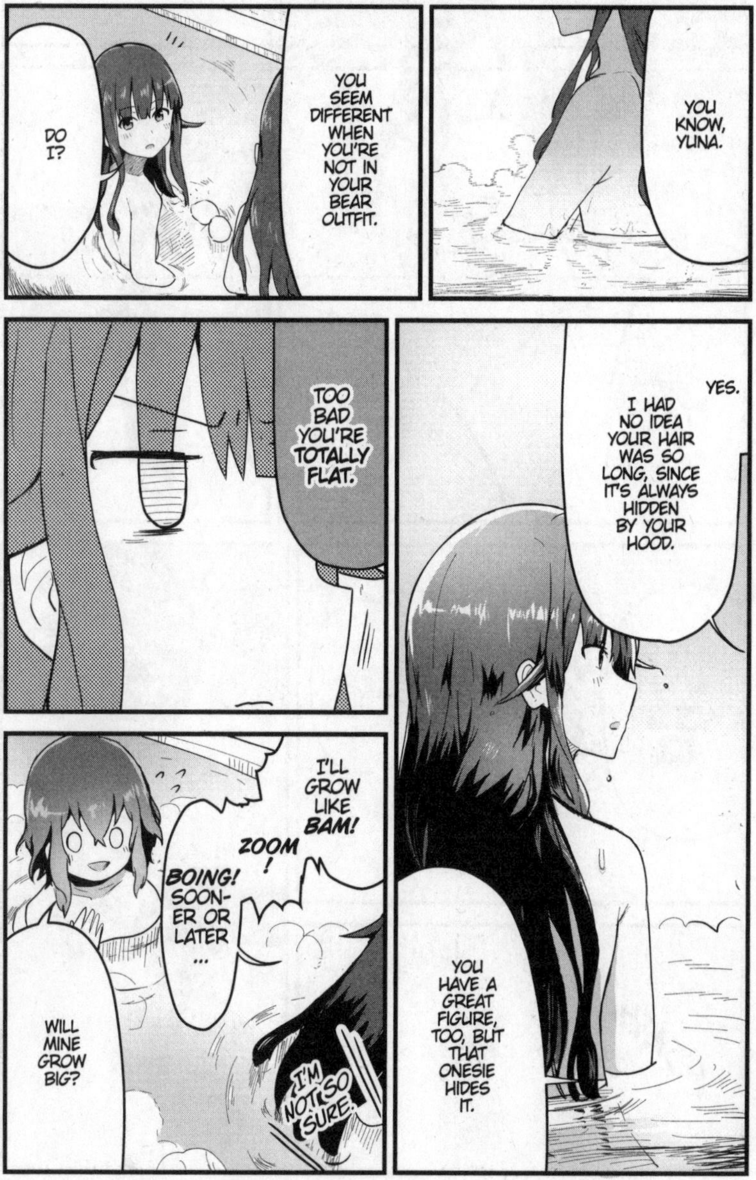
YOU KNOW, YUNA.
YOU SEEM DIFFERENT WHEN YOU'RE NOT IN YOUR BEAR OUTFIT.
DO I?
YES.
I HAD NO IDEA YOUR HAIR WAS SO LONG, SINCE IT'S ALWAYS HIDDEN BY YOUR HOOD.
YOU HAVE A GREAT FIGURE, TOO, BUT THAT ONESIE HIDES IT.
TOO BAD YOU'RE TOTALLY FLAT.
I'LL GROW LIKE BAM! ZOOM! BOING! SOONER OR LATER...
WILL MINE GROW BIG?
I'M NOT SO SURE.

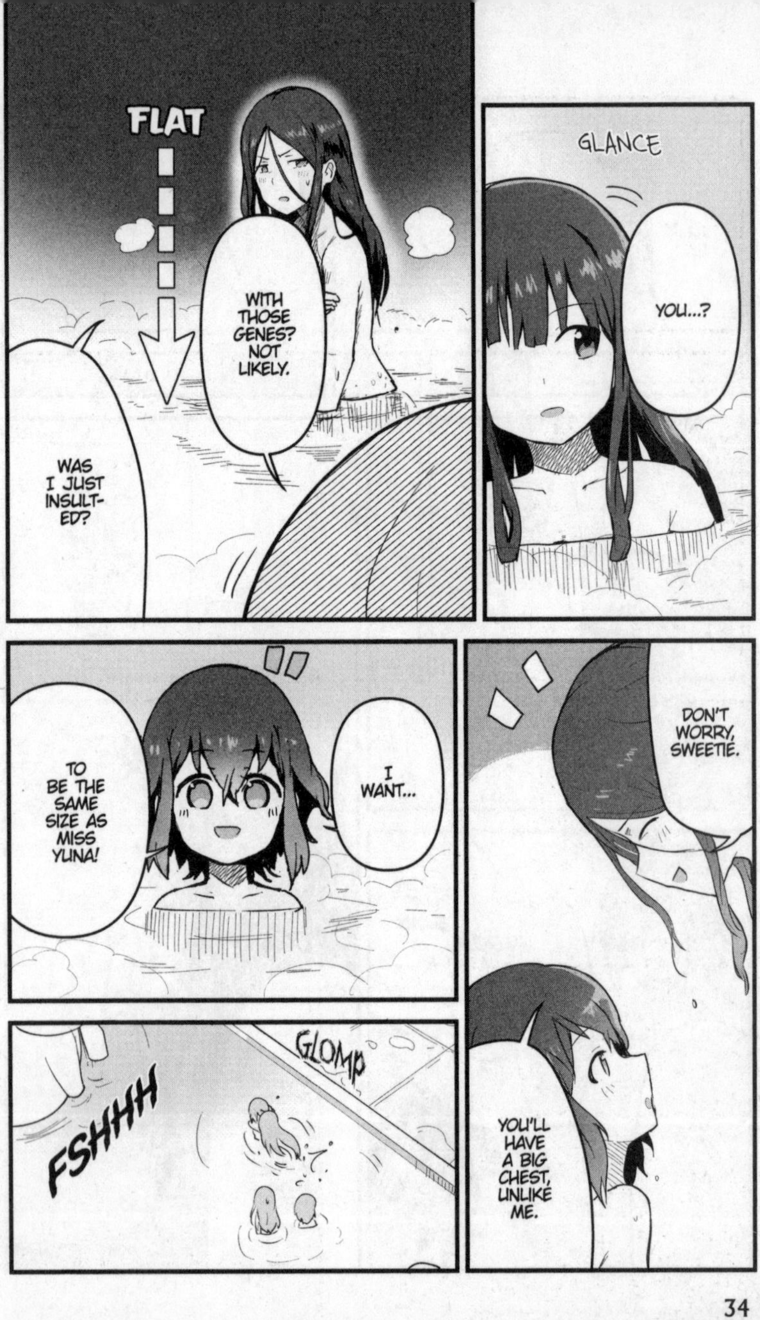
GLANCE
YOU...?
FLAT
WITH THOSE GENES? NOT LIKELY.
WAS I JUST INSULTED?
DON'T WORRY, SWEETIE.
YOU'LL HAVE A BIG CHEST, UNLIKE ME.
I WANT...
TO BE THE SAME SIZE AS MISS YUNA!
GLOMP
FSHHH

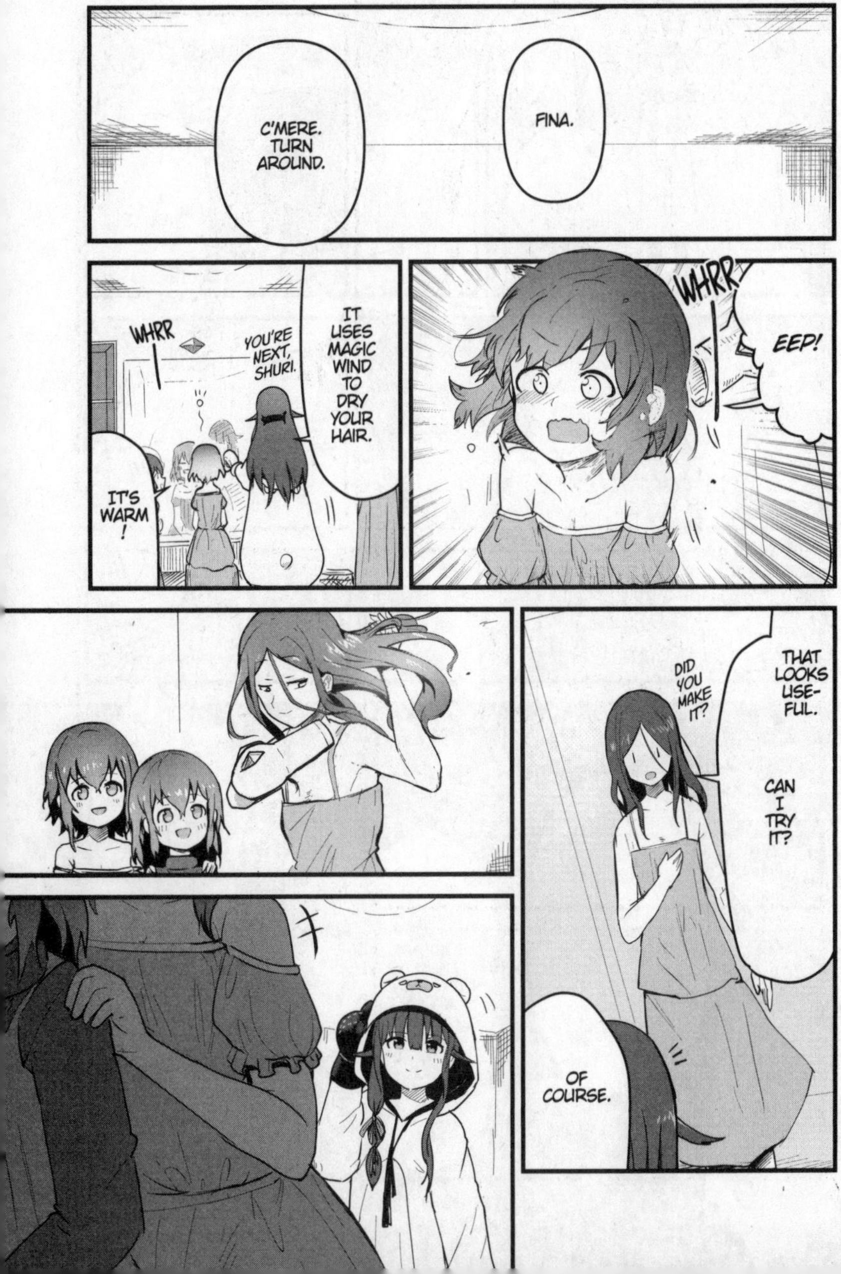
FINA.
C'MERE. TURN AROUND.
WHRR
EEP!
IT USES MAGIC WIND TO DRY YOUR HAIR.
YOU'RE NEXT, SHURI.
WHRR
IT'S WARM!
THAT LOOKS USE-FUL.
DID YOU MAKE IT?
CAN I TRY IT?
OF COURSE.

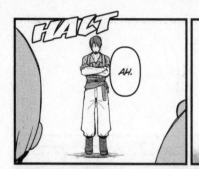

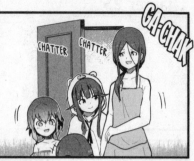

GA-CHAK
CHATTER
CHATTER
HALT
AH.
SHEESH!
YOU GIRLS TOOK FOR-EVER!
I COULD HEAR YOU GIGGLING HAPPILY THE WHOLE TIME!
SORRY.
WE AREN'T USED TO YOU BEING AROUND, SO WE FORGOT ABOUT YOU...
DON'T BE SO MOPEY.
I AM NOT MOPEY!

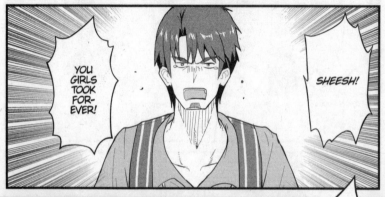

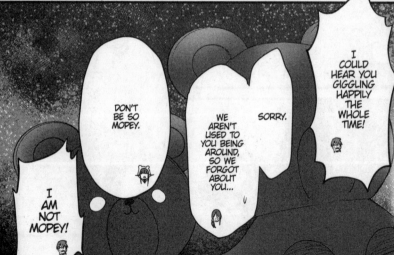

Chapter 23

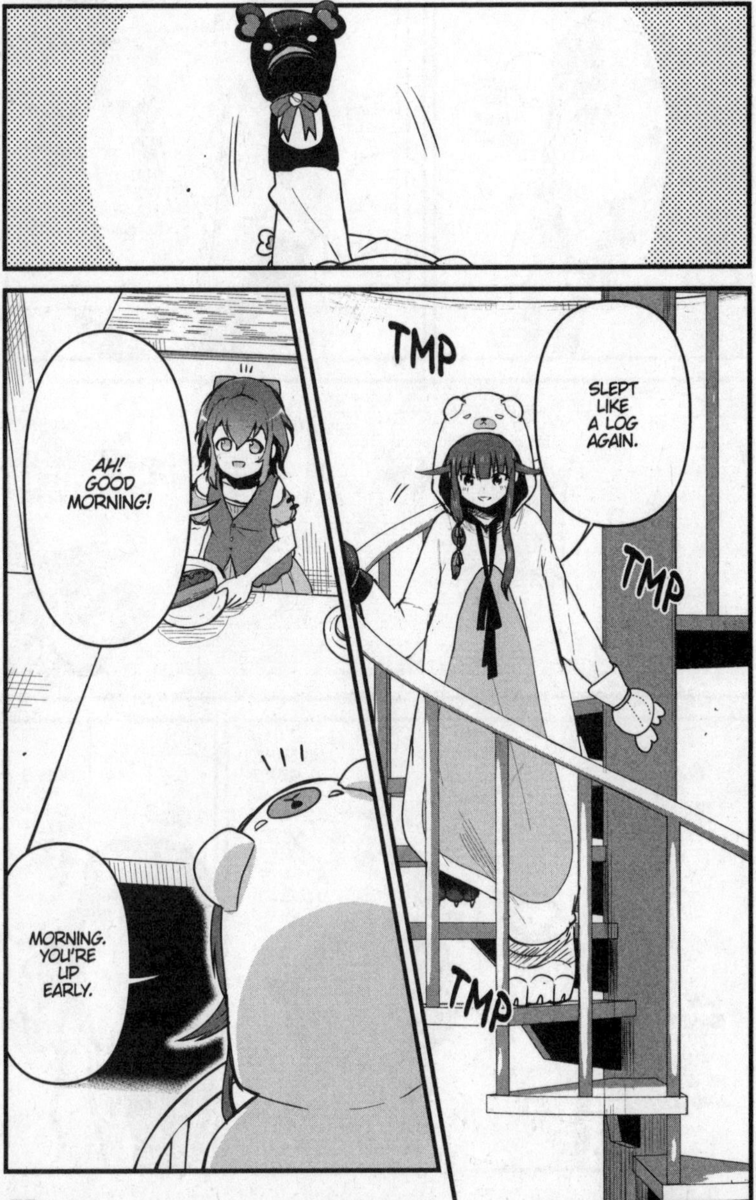

TMP
SLEPT LIKE A LOG AGAIN.
TMP
TMP
AH! GOOD MORNING!
MORNING. YOU'RE UP EARLY.

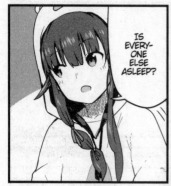

I ALWAYS COOK BREAK-FAST, SO...
I HOPE YOU DON'T MIND THAT I USED YOUR KITCHEN.
I'LL REPAY YOU FOR WHAT I USED.
DON'T WORRY ABOUT IT.
I'LL HAVE SOME, TOO.
IS EVERY-ONE ELSE ASLEEP?
SHURI AND MOM ARE ASLEEP.
UNCLE GE...
DAD ALREADY LEFT FOR WORK.
HE TOLD ME TO THANK YOU.
GUESS HE STILL NEEDS TO WORK.
NOM
I HAVEN'T HAD SAND-WICHES LIKE THIS SINCE I CAME TO THIS WORLD.
AN EGG SANDWICH ON THIS BREAD WOULD BE **AMAZING.**

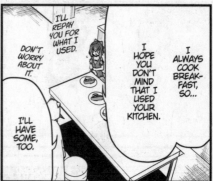

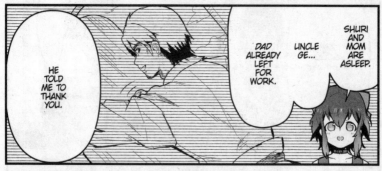

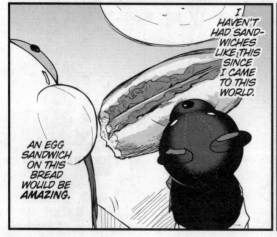

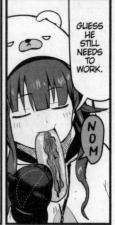

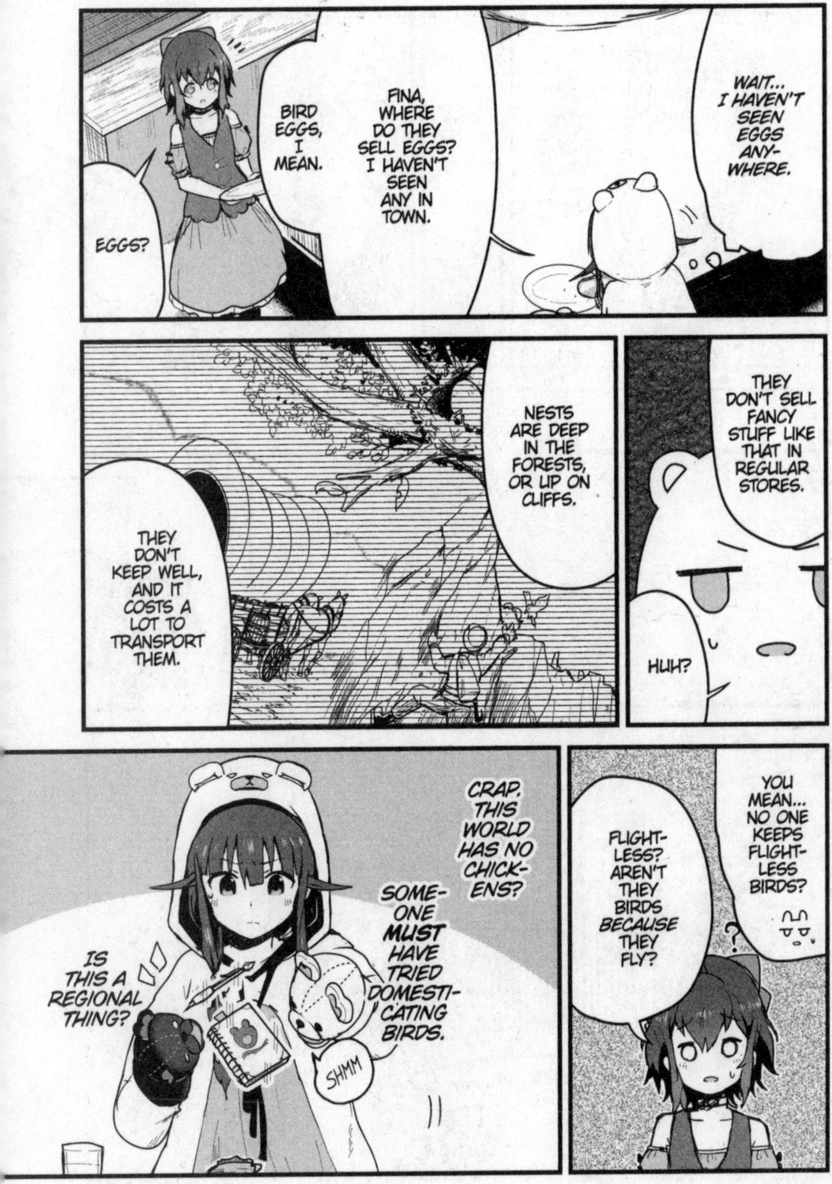
WAIT... I HAVEN'T SEEN EGGS ANYWHERE.
FINA, WHERE DO THEY SELL EGGS? I HAVEN'T SEEN ANY IN TOWN.
EGGS?
BIRD EGGS, I MEAN.
THEY DON'T SELL FANCY STUFF LIKE THAT IN REGULAR STORES.
HUH?
NESTS ARE DEEP IN THE FORESTS, OR UP ON CLIFFS.
THEY DON'T KEEP WELL, AND IT COSTS A LOT TO TRANSPORT THEM.
YOU MEAN... NO ONE KEEPS FLIGHTLESS BIRDS?
FLIGHTLESS? AREN'T THEY BIRDS BECAUSE THEY FLY?
CRAP. THIS WORLD HAS NO CHICKENS?
SOMEONE ***MUST*** HAVE TRIED DOMESTICATING BIRDS.
IS THIS A REGIONAL THING?
SHMM

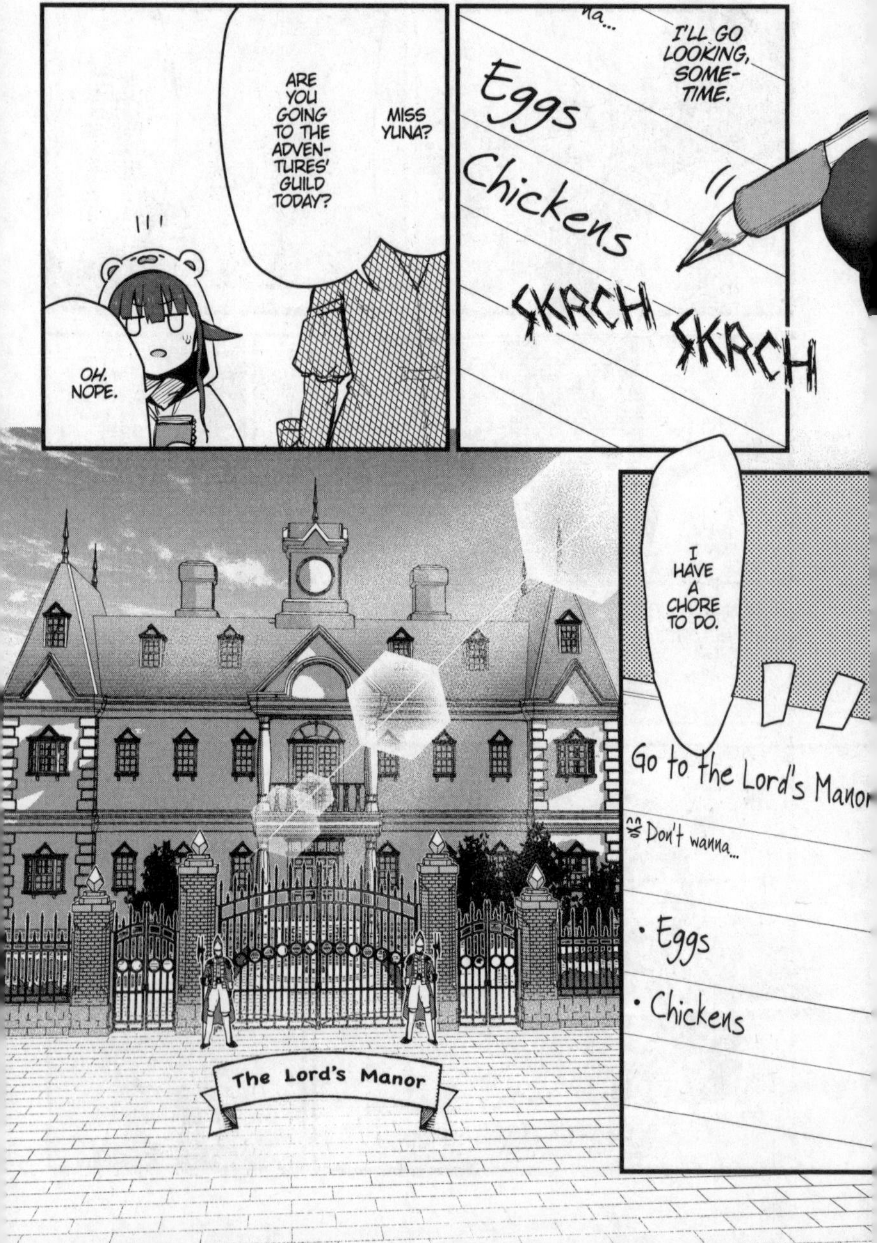
na...
I'LL GO LOOKING, SOME-TIME.
Eggs
Chickens
SKRCH SKRCH
MISS YUNA?
ARE YOU GOING TO THE ADVEN-TURES' GUILD TODAY?
OH. NOPE.
I HAVE A CHORE TO DO.
Go to the Lord's Manor
Don't wanna...
• Eggs
• Chickens
The Lord's Manor

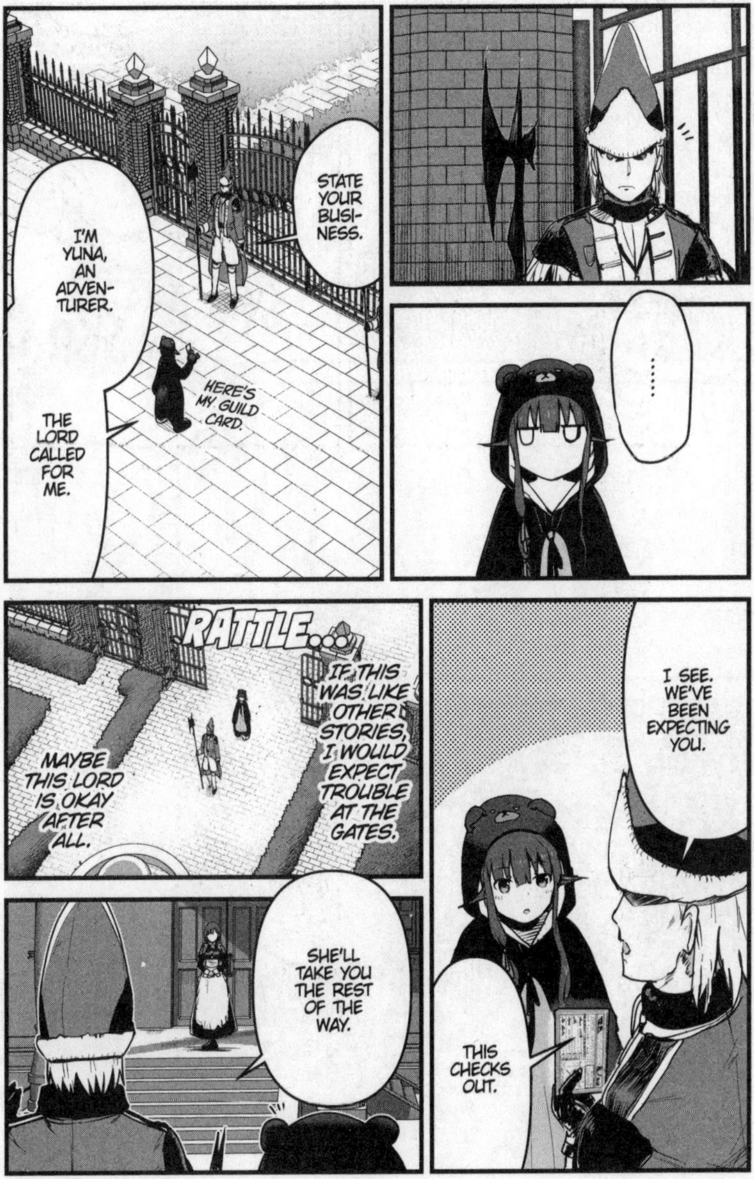
……
STATE YOUR BUSI-NESS.
I'M YUNA, AN ADVEN-TURER.
HERE'S MY GUILD CARD.
THE LORD CALLED FOR ME.
I SEE. WE'VE BEEN EXPECTING YOU.
THIS CHECKS OUT.
RATTLE...
IF THIS WAS LIKE OTHER STORIES, I WOULD EXPECT TROUBLE AT THE GATES.
MAYBE THIS LORD IS OKAY AFTER ALL.
SHE'LL TAKE YOU THE REST OF THE WAY.

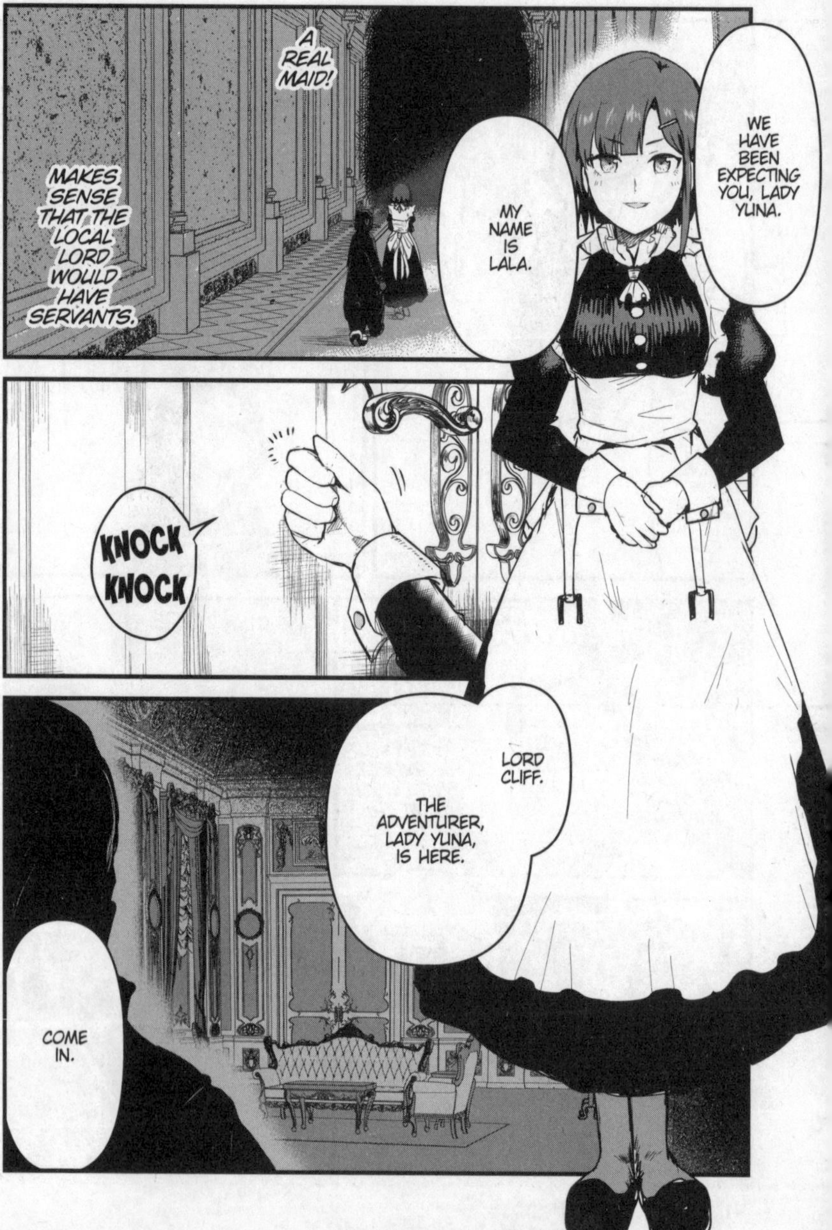
WE HAVE BEEN EXPECTING YOU, LADY YUNA.
MY NAME IS LALA.
A REAL MAID!
MAKES SENSE THAT THE LOCAL LORD WOULD HAVE SERVANTS.
KNOCK KNOCK
LORD CLIFF.
THE ADVENTURER, LADY YUNA, IS HERE.
COME IN.

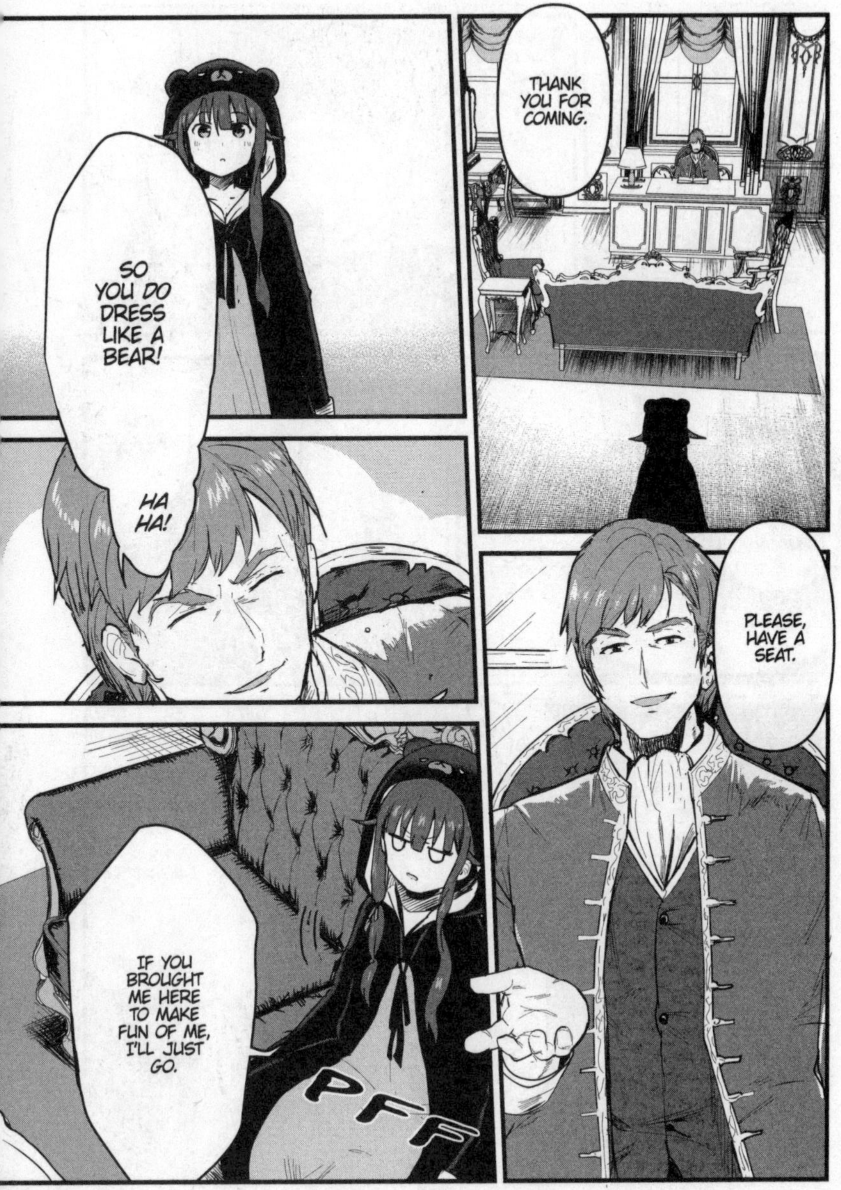
THANK YOU FOR COMING.
SO YOU DO DRESS LIKE A BEAR!
HA HA!
PLEASE, HAVE A SEAT.
PFF
IF YOU BROUGHT ME HERE TO MAKE FUN OF ME, I'LL JUST GO.

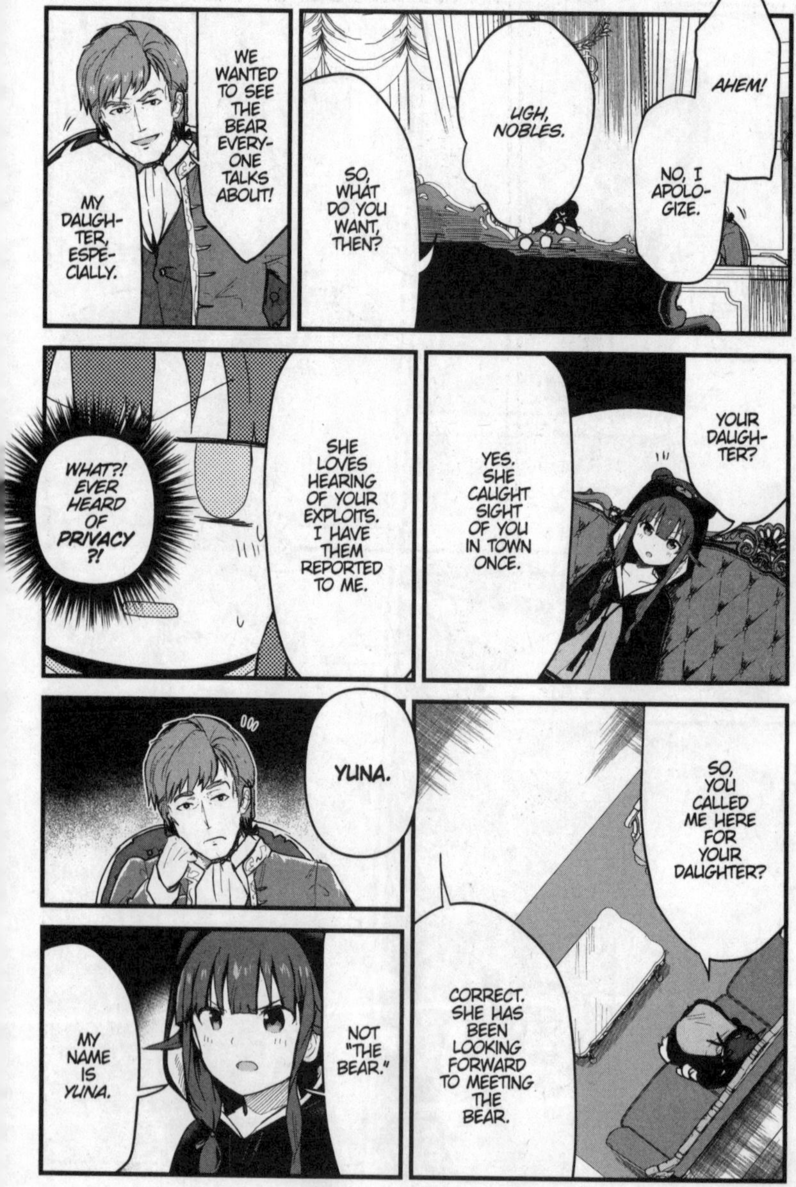
AHEM!
NO, I APOLOGIZE.
UGH, NOBLES.
SO, WHAT DO YOU WANT, THEN?
WE WANTED TO SEE THE BEAR EVERYONE TALKS ABOUT!
MY DAUGHTER, ESPECIALLY.
YOUR DAUGHTER?
YES. SHE CAUGHT SIGHT OF YOU IN TOWN ONCE.
SHE LOVES HEARING OF YOUR EXPLOITS. I HAVE THEM REPORTED TO ME.
WHAT?! EVER HEARD OF PRIVACY?!
SO, YOU CALLED ME HERE FOR YOUR DAUGHTER?
CORRECT. SHE HAS BEEN LOOKING FORWARD TO MEETING THE BEAR.
YUNA.
NOT "THE BEAR."
MY NAME IS YUNA.

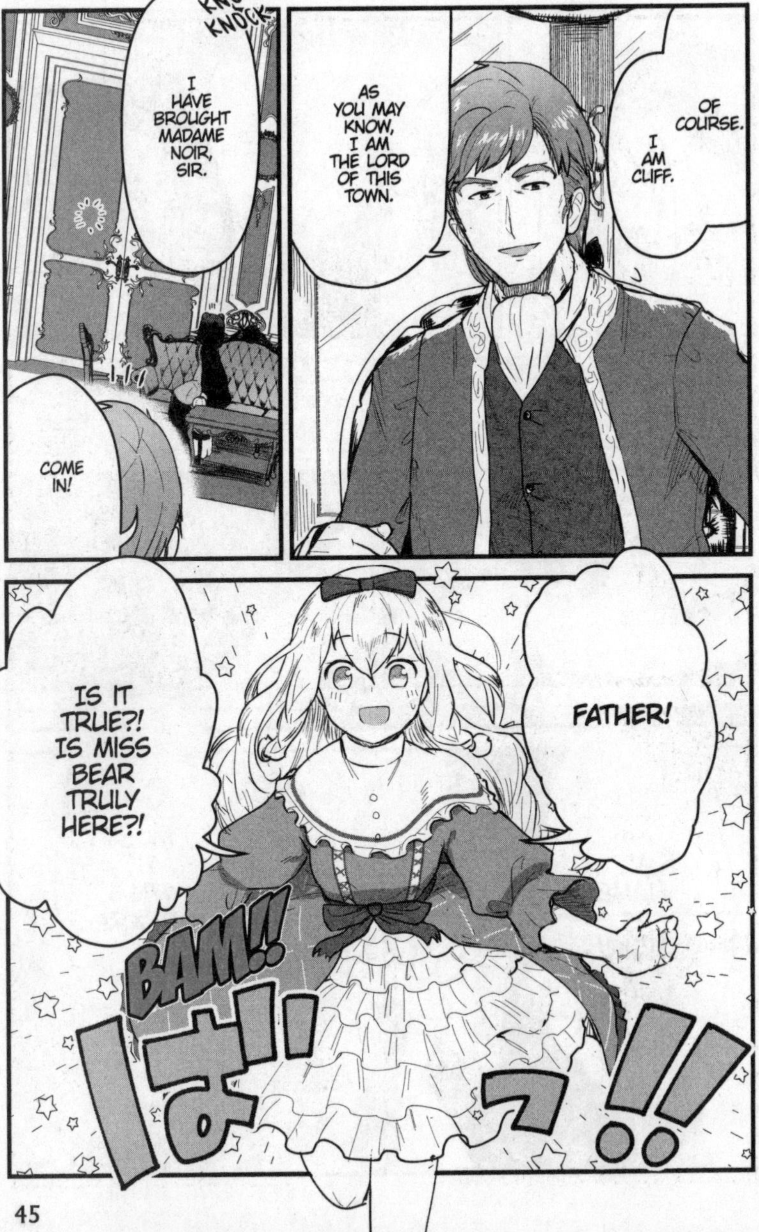
OF COURSE. I AM CLIFF.
AS YOU MAY KNOW, I AM THE LORD OF THIS TOWN.
KNOCK KNOCK
I HAVE BROUGHT MADAME NOIR, SIR.
COME IN!
FATHER!
IS IT TRUE?! IS MISS BEAR TRULY HERE?!
BAM!!
ばっ!!

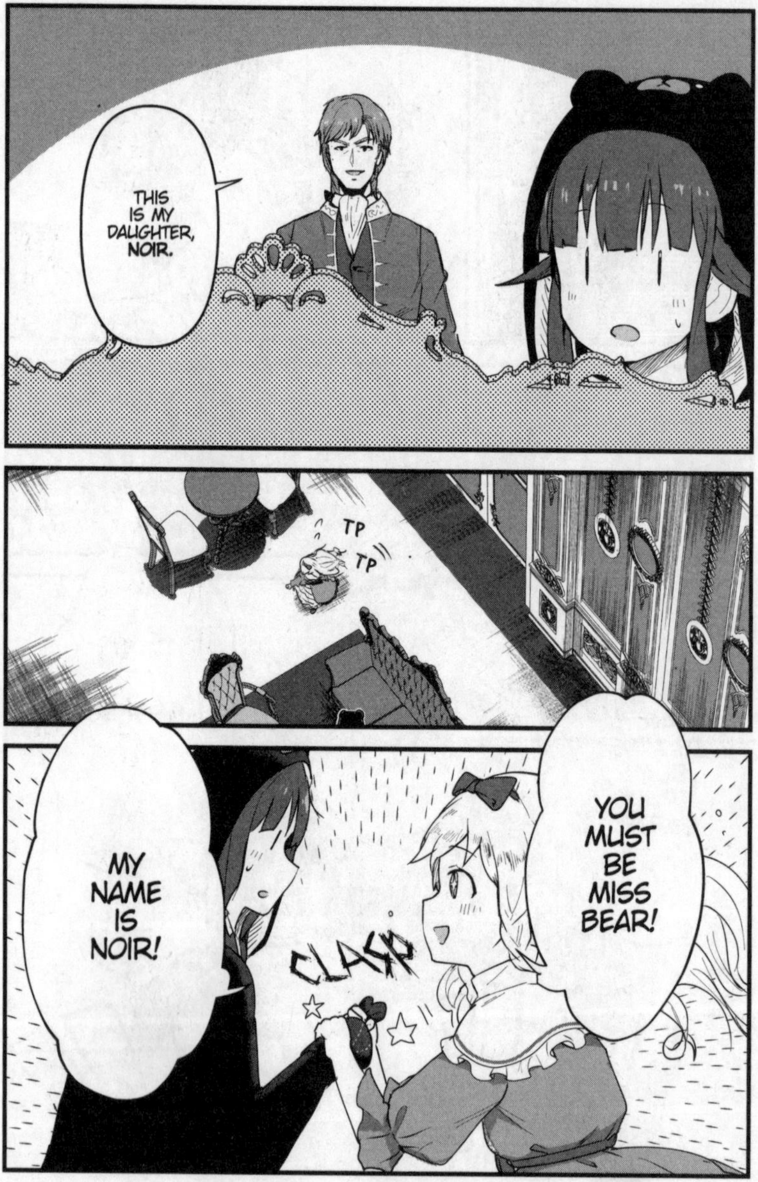
THIS IS MY DAUGHTER, NOIR.
TP
TP
YOU MUST BE MISS BEAR!
MY NAME IS NOIR!
CLASP

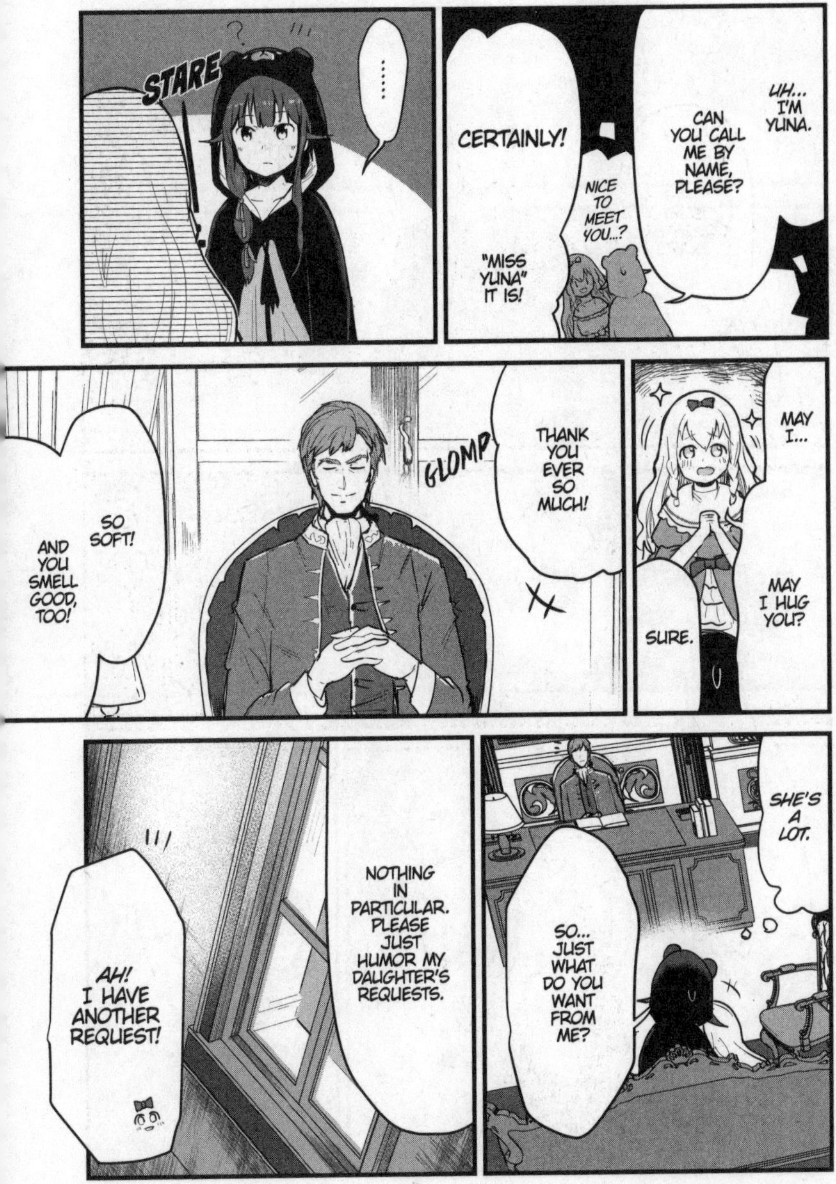
UH... I'M YUNA.
CAN YOU CALL ME BY NAME, PLEASE?
NICE TO MEET YOU...?
CERTAINLY!
"MISS YUNA" IT IS!
......
STARE
MAY I...
MAY I HUG YOU?
SURE.
THANK YOU EVER SO MUCH!
GLOMP
SO SOFT!
AND YOU SMELL GOOD, TOO!
SHE'S A LOT.
SO... JUST WHAT DO YOU WANT FROM ME?
NOTHING IN PARTICULAR. PLEASE JUST HUMOR MY DAUGHTER'S REQUESTS.
AH! I HAVE ANOTHER REQUEST!

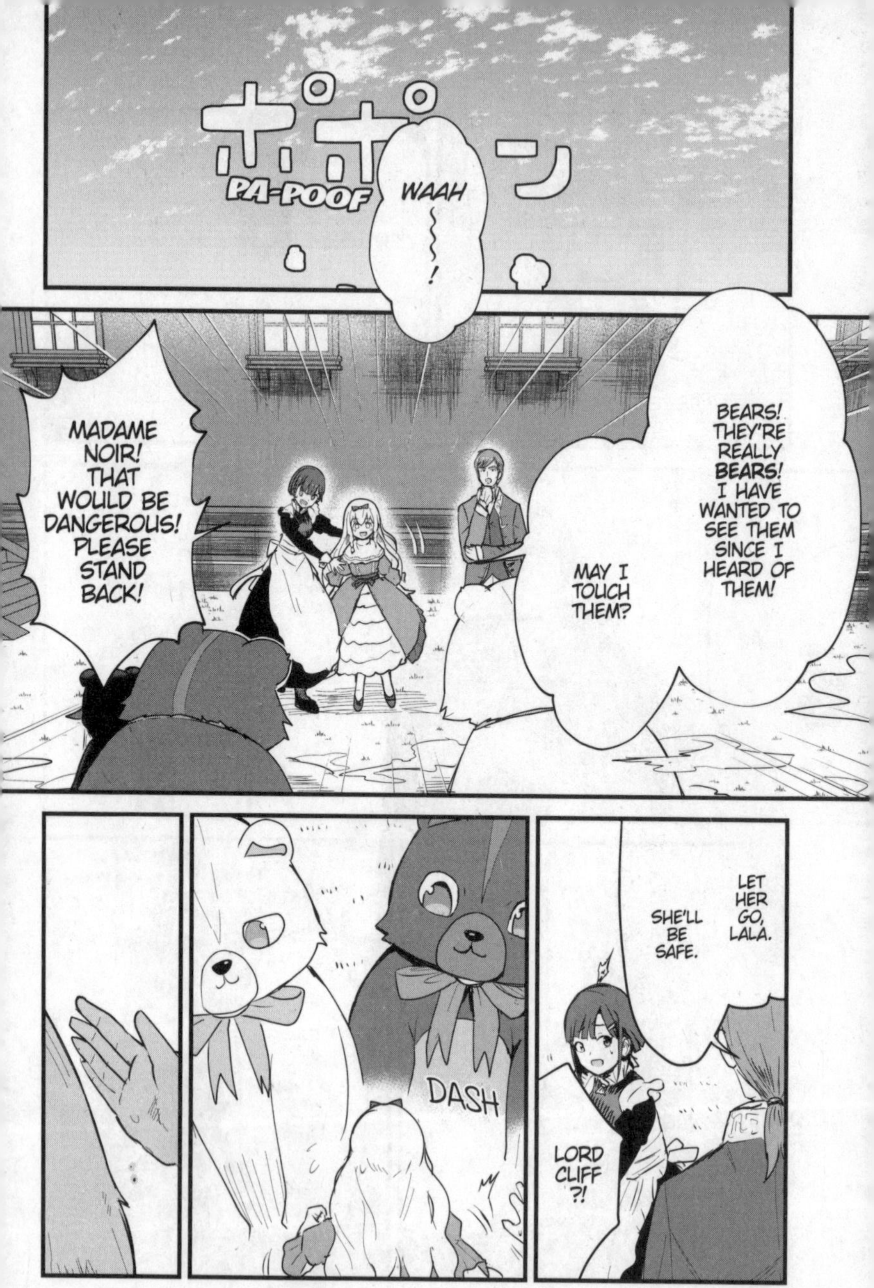
ポポーン
PA-POOF
WAAH~~~!
BEARS! THEY'RE REALLY BEARS! I HAVE WANTED TO SEE THEM SINCE I HEARD OF THEM!
MAY I TOUCH THEM?
MADAME NOIR! THAT WOULD BE DANGEROUS! PLEASE STAND BACK!
LET HER GO, LALA.
SHE'LL BE SAFE.
LORD CLIFF ?!
DASH

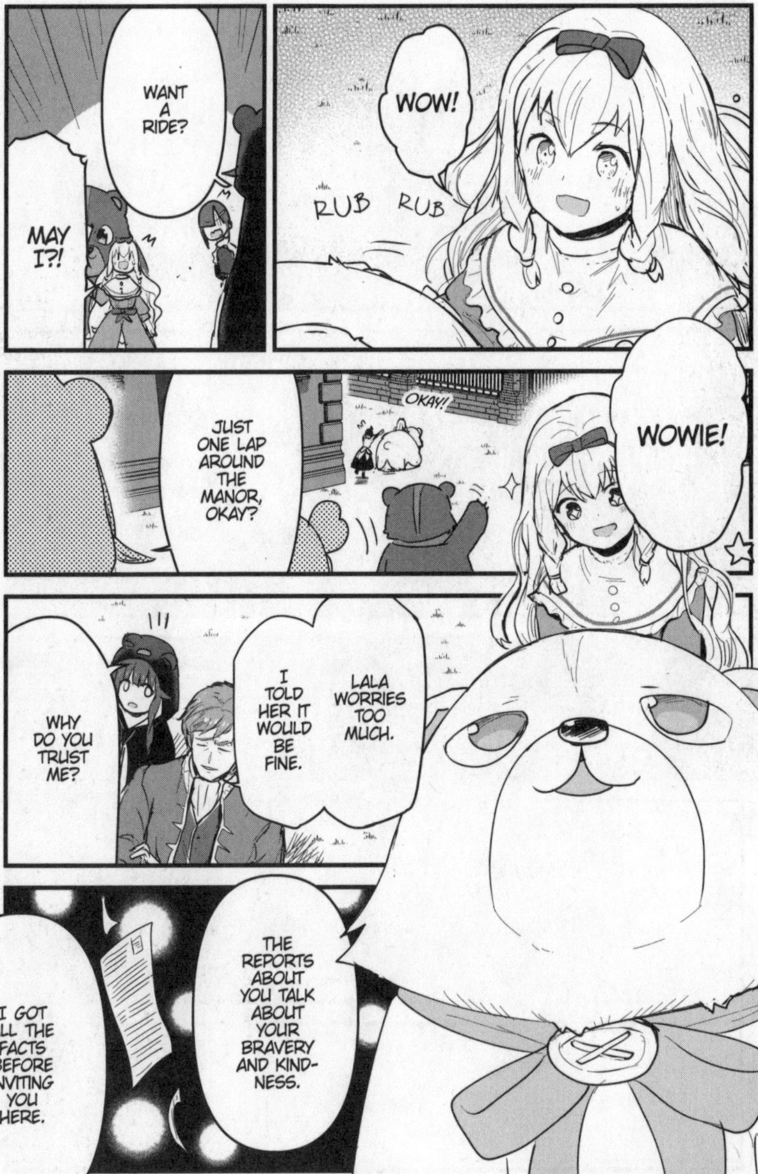
WOW!
RUB RUB
WANT A RIDE?
MAY I?!
WOWIE!
OKAY!
JUST ONE LAP AROUND THE MANOR, OKAY?
LALA WORRIES TOO MUCH.
I TOLD HER IT WOULD BE FINE.
WHY DO YOU TRUST ME?
THE REPORTS ABOUT YOU TALK ABOUT YOUR BRAVERY AND KIND-NESS.
I GOT ALL THE FACTS BEFORE INVITING YOU HERE.

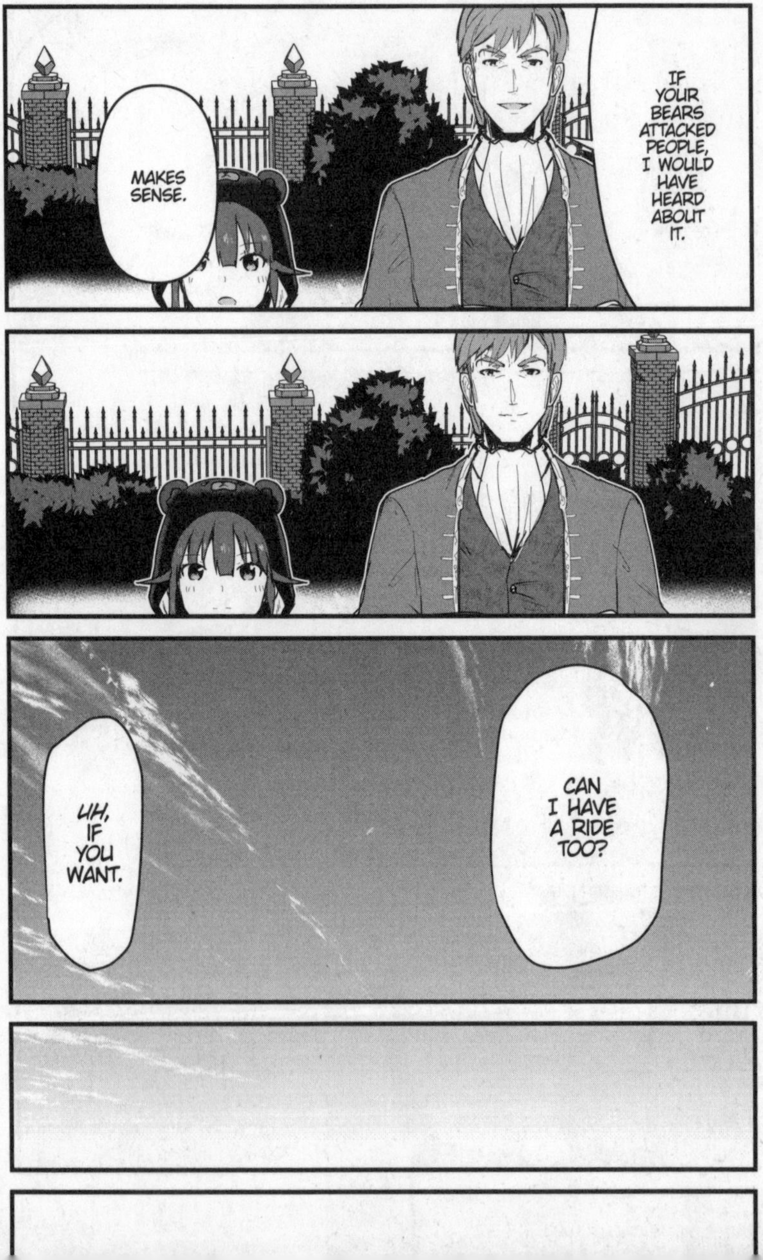
IF YOUR BEARS ATTACKED PEOPLE, I WOULD HAVE HEARD ABOUT IT.
MAKES SENSE.
CAN I HAVE A RIDE TOO?
UH, IF YOU WANT.

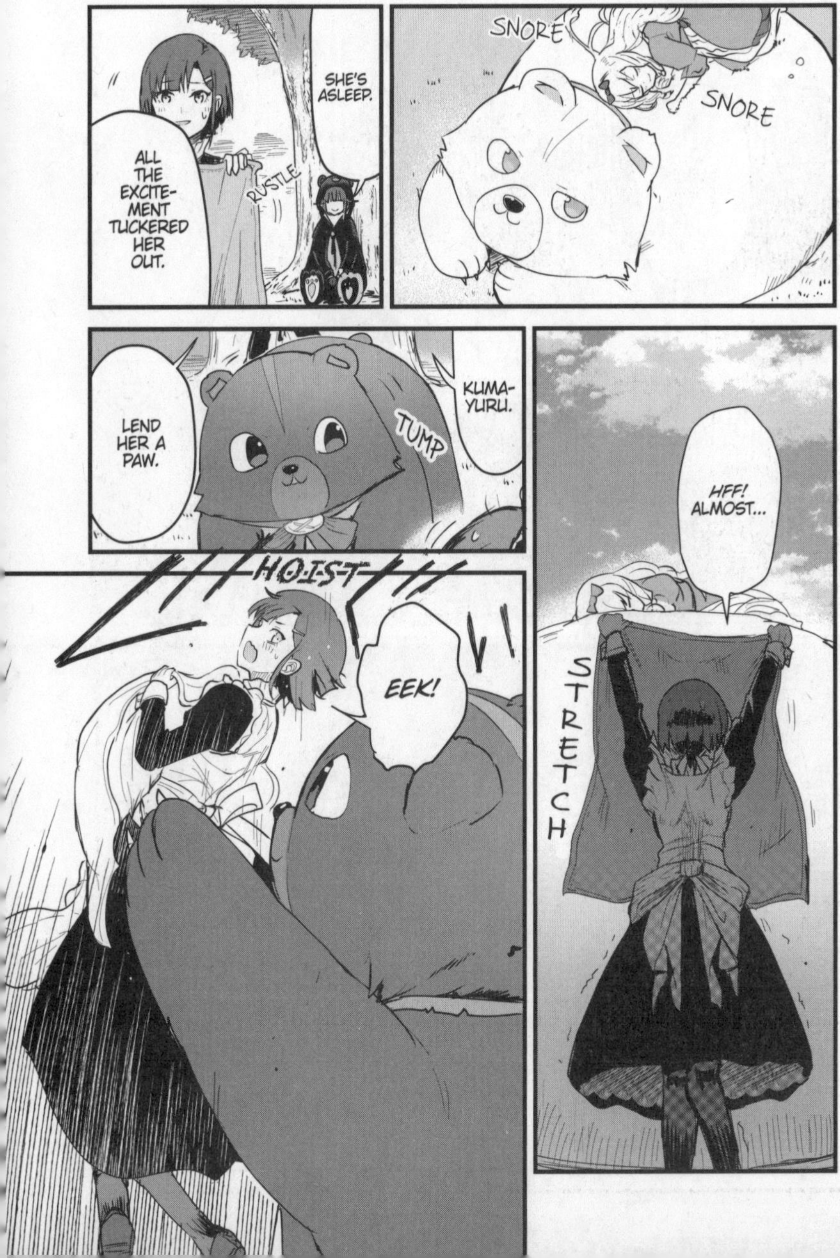
SNORE
SNORE
SHE'S ASLEEP.
RUSTLE
ALL THE EXCITE-MENT TUCKERED HER OUT.
HFF! ALMOST...
STRETCH
KUMA-YURU.
TUMP
LEND HER A PAW.
HOIST
EEK!

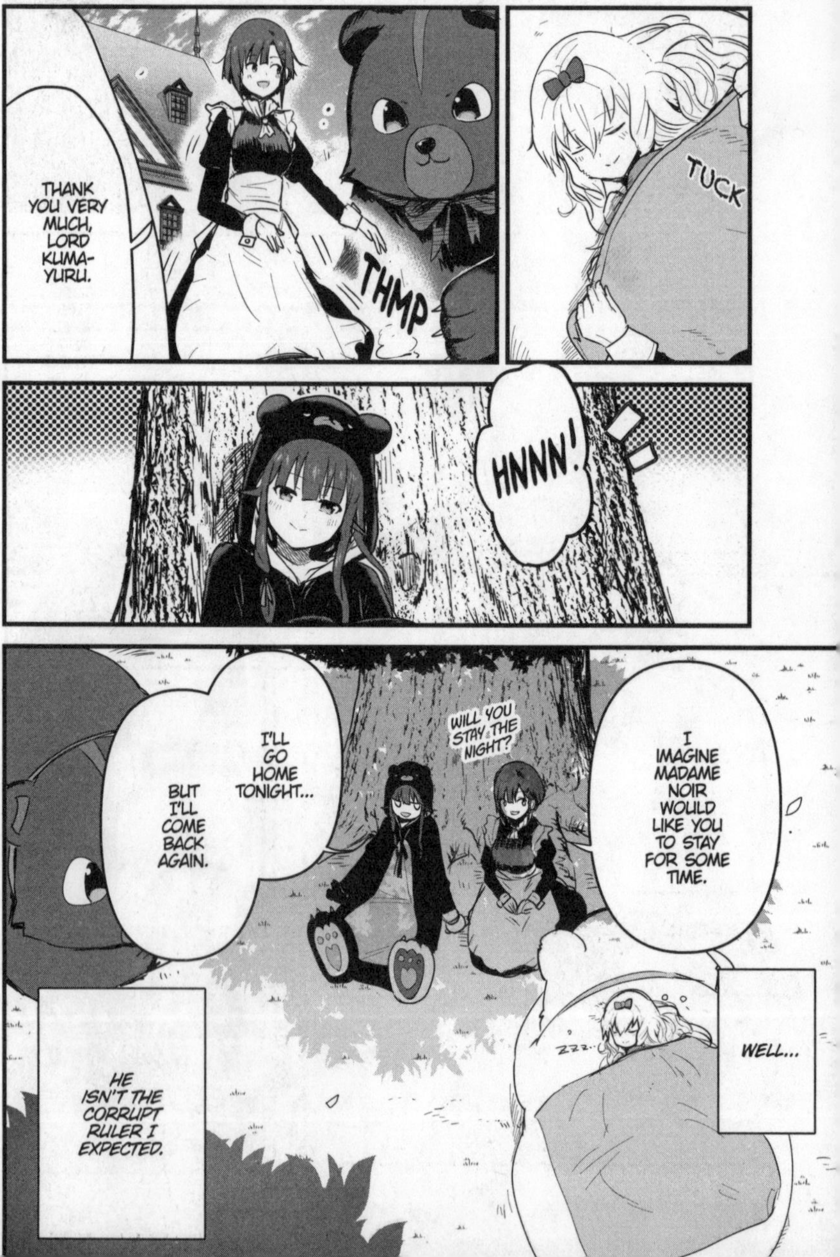
TUCK
THMP
THANK YOU VERY MUCH, LORD KUMA-YURU.
HNNN!
I IMAGINE MADAME NOIR WOULD LIKE YOU TO STAY FOR SOME TIME.
WILL YOU STAY THE NIGHT?
I'LL GO HOME TONIGHT...
BUT I'LL COME BACK AGAIN.
WELL...
ZZZ...
HE ISN'T THE CORRUPT RULER I EXPECTED.

Chapter 24

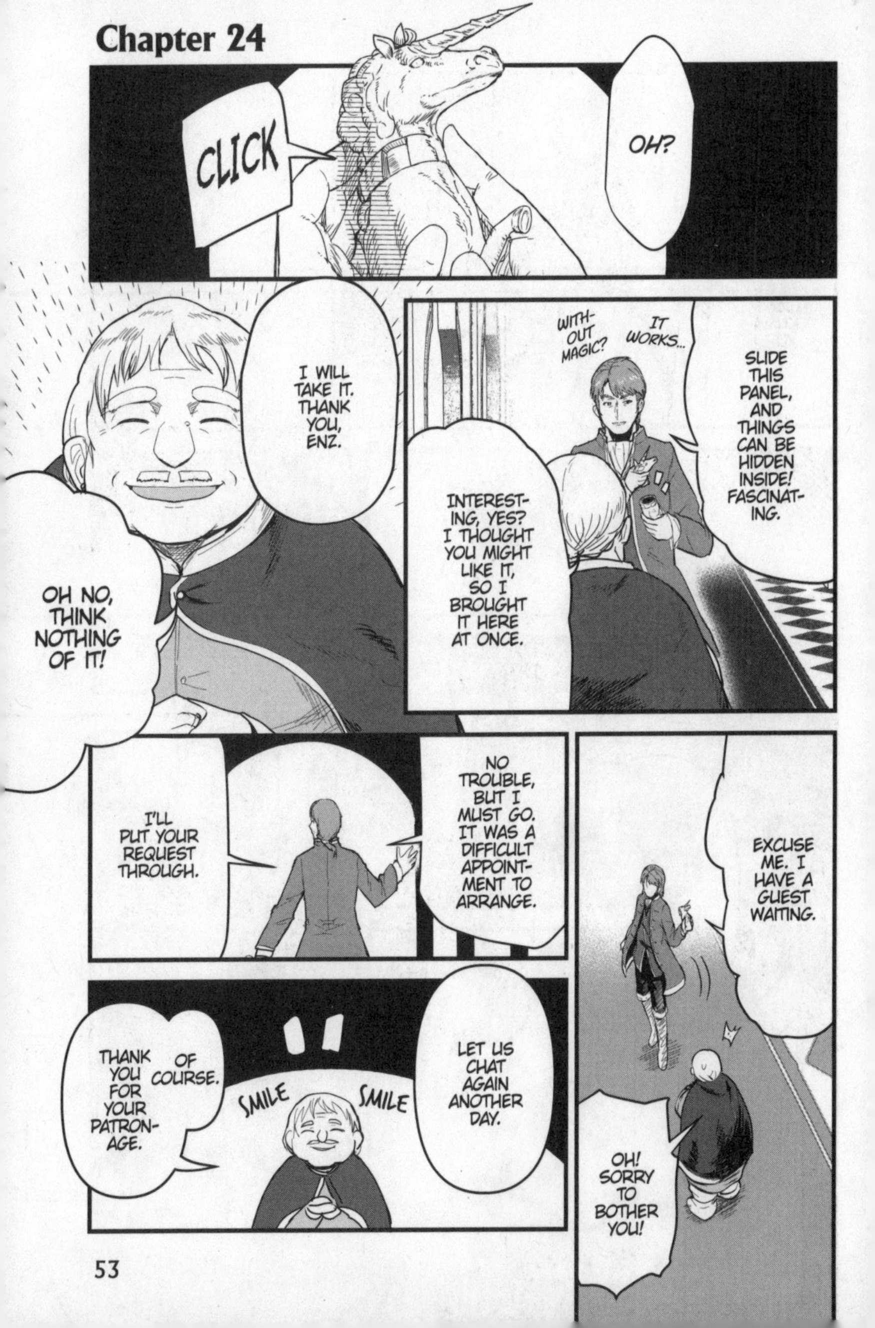

CLICK
OH?
I WILL TAKE IT. THANK YOU, ENZ.
OH NO, THINK NOTHING OF IT!
WITH-OUT MAGIC?
IT WORKS...
SLIDE THIS PANEL, AND THINGS CAN BE HIDDEN INSIDE! FASCINAT-ING.
INTEREST-ING, YES? I THOUGHT YOU MIGHT LIKE IT, SO I BROUGHT IT HERE AT ONCE.
I'LL PUT YOUR REQUEST THROUGH.
NO TROUBLE, BUT I MUST GO. IT WAS A DIFFICULT APPOINT-MENT TO ARRANGE.
THANK YOU FOR YOUR PATRON-AGE.
OF COURSE.
SMILE
SMILE
LET US CHAT AGAIN ANOTHER DAY.
EXCUSE ME. I HAVE A GUEST WAITING.
OH! SORRY TO BOTHER YOU!

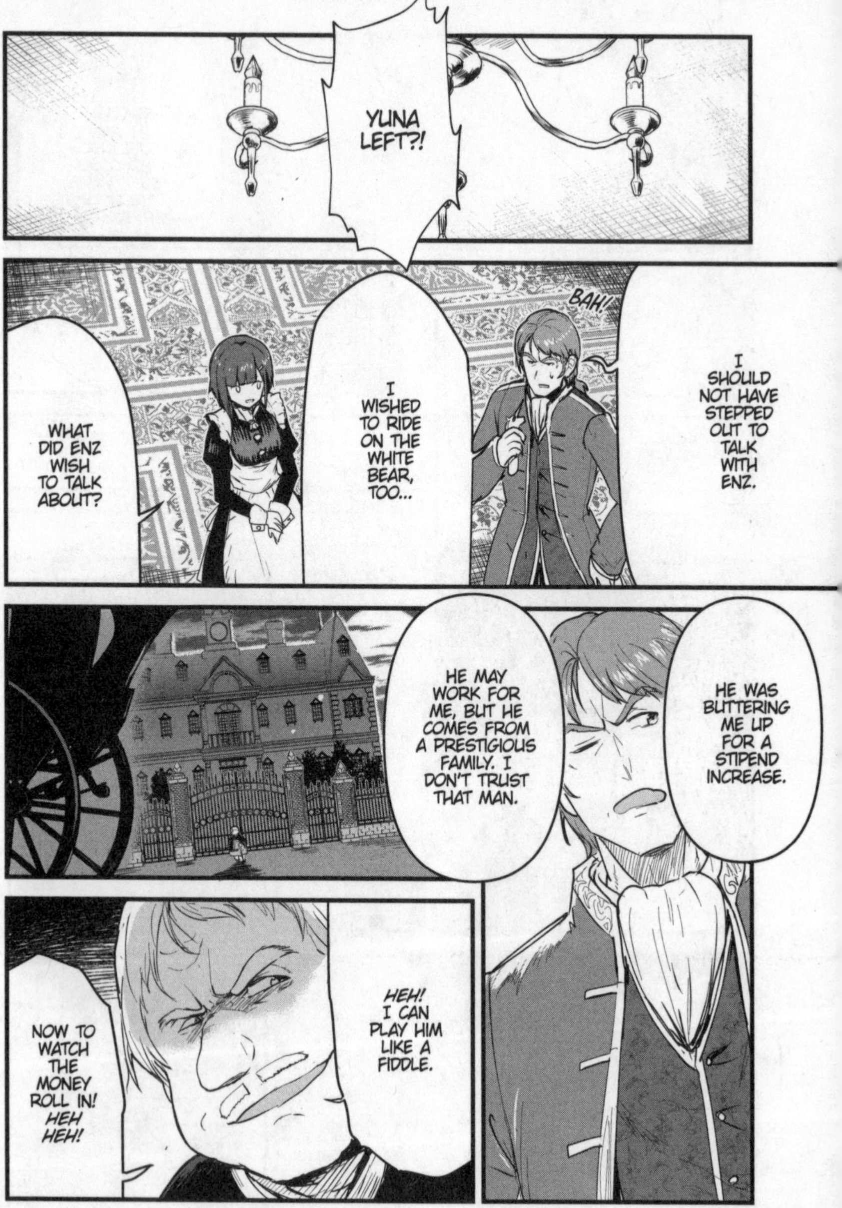
YUNA LEFT?!
BAH!
I SHOULD NOT HAVE STEPPED OUT TO TALK WITH ENZ.
I WISHED TO RIDE ON THE WHITE BEAR, TOO...
WHAT DID ENZ WISH TO TALK ABOUT?
HE WAS BUTTERING ME UP FOR A STIPEND INCREASE.
HE MAY WORK FOR ME, BUT HE COMES FROM A PRESTIGIOUS FAMILY. I DON'T TRUST THAT MAN.
HEH! I CAN PLAY HIM LIKE A FIDDLE.
NOW TO WATCH THE MONEY ROLL IN! HEH HEH!

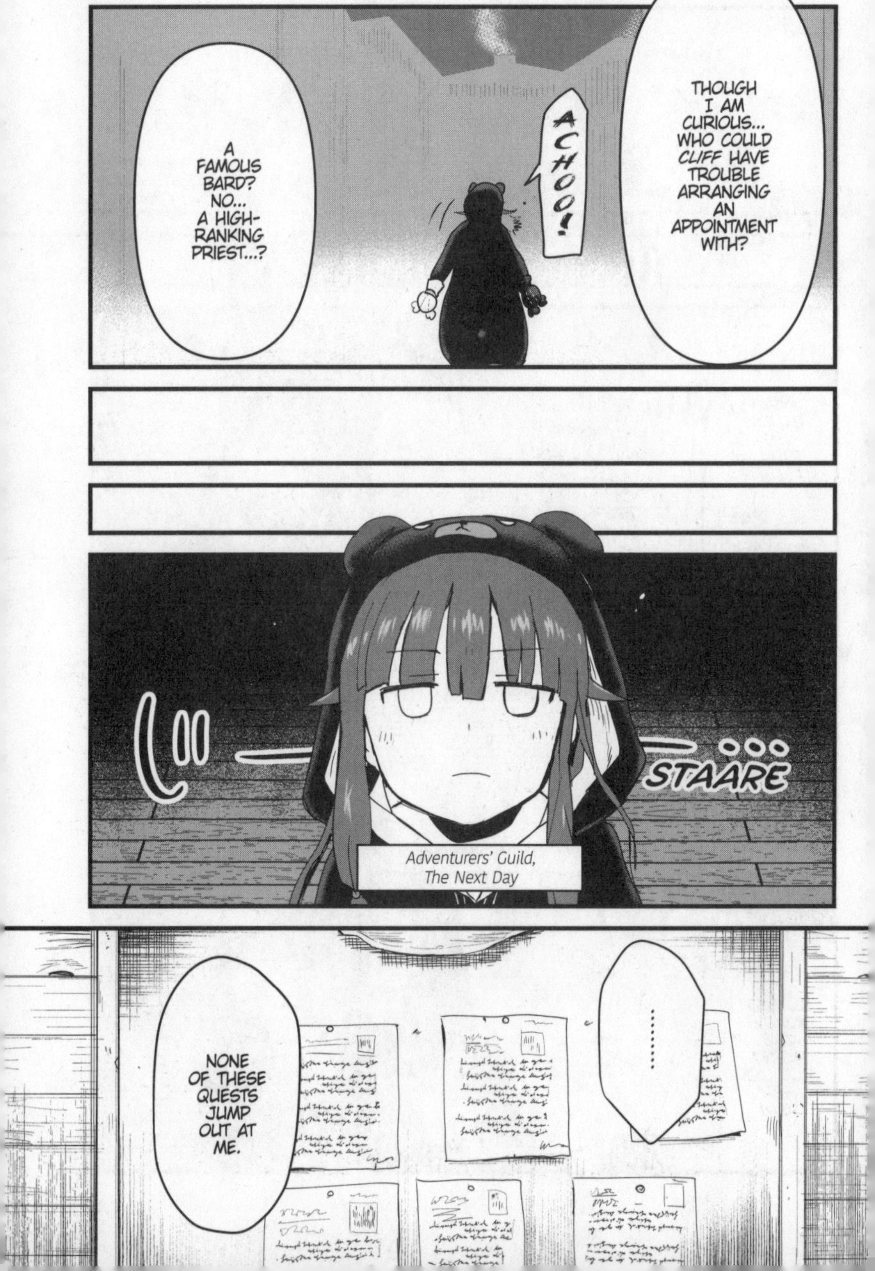
THOUGH I AM CURIOUS... WHO COULD CLIFF HAVE TROUBLE ARRANGING AN APPOINTMENT WITH?
ACHOO!
A FAMOUS BARD? NO... A HIGH-RANKING PRIEST...?
...
STAARE
Adventurers' Guild, The Next Day
......
NONE OF THESE QUESTS JUMP OUT AT ME.

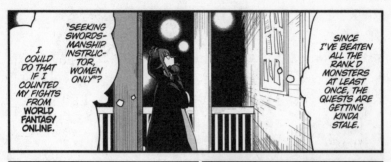

SINCE I'VE BEATEN ALL THE RANK D MONSTERS AT LEAST ONCE, THE QUESTS ARE GETTING KINDA STALE.
"SEEKING SWORDSMANSHIP INSTRUCTOR, WOMEN ONLY"?
I COULD DO THAT IF I COUNTED MY FIGHTS FROM WORLD FANTASY ONLINE.
THE RANK C QUESTS ARE ALL FAR AWAY, OR IN PLACES I DON'T KNOW.
HUH?
Wyvern Hunt
WYVERNS ARE DRAGONS, RIGHT?
I'D LIKE TO CHECK IT OUT, BUT THEY DON'T KNOW THE PRECISE LOCATION...
WHY WON'T YOU HELP?!

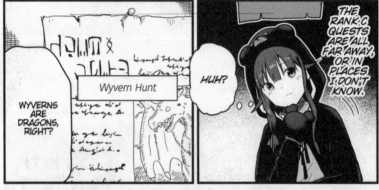

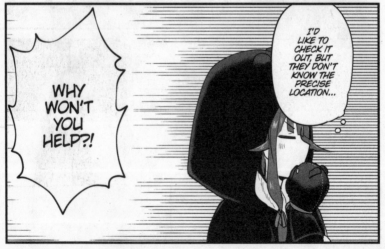

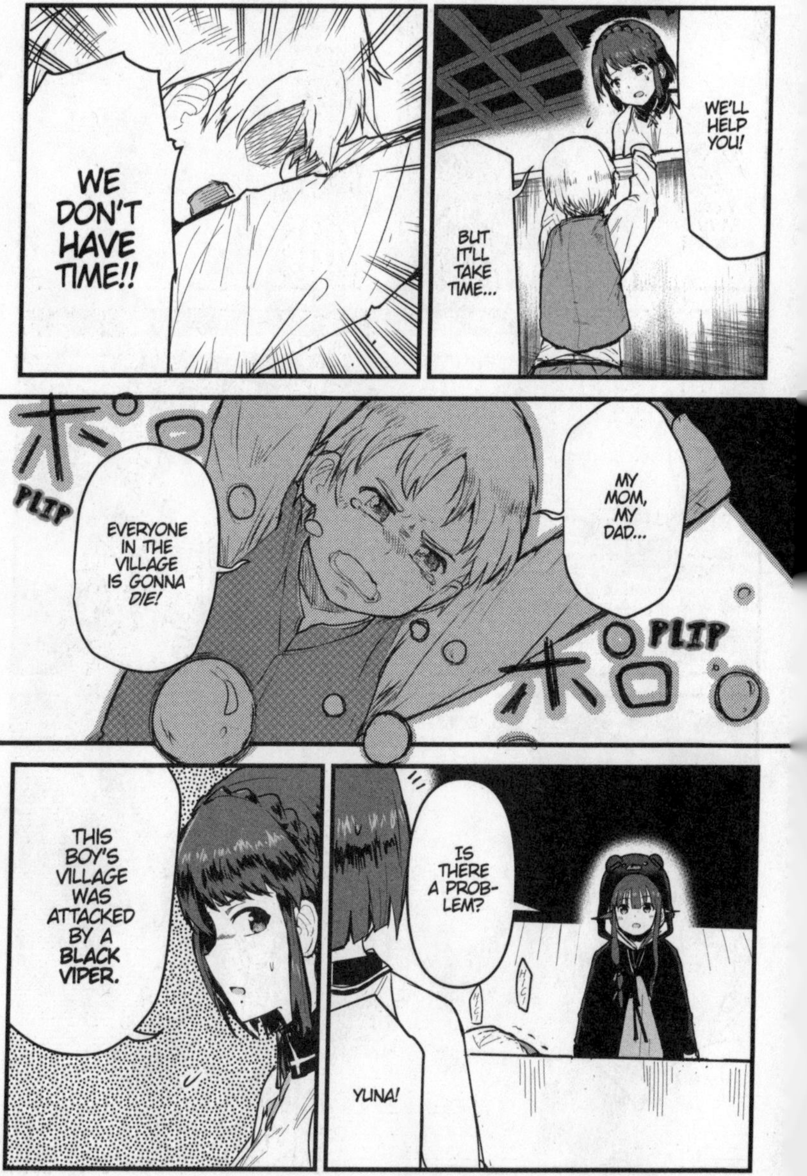
WE'LL HELP YOU!
BUT IT'LL TAKE TIME...
WE DON'T HAVE TIME!!
MY MOM, MY DAD...
PLIP
EVERYONE IN THE VILLAGE IS GONNA DIE!
PLIP
IS THERE A PROB-LEM?
HIC!
HIC!
YUNA!
THIS BOY'S VILLAGE WAS ATTACKED BY A BLACK VIPER.

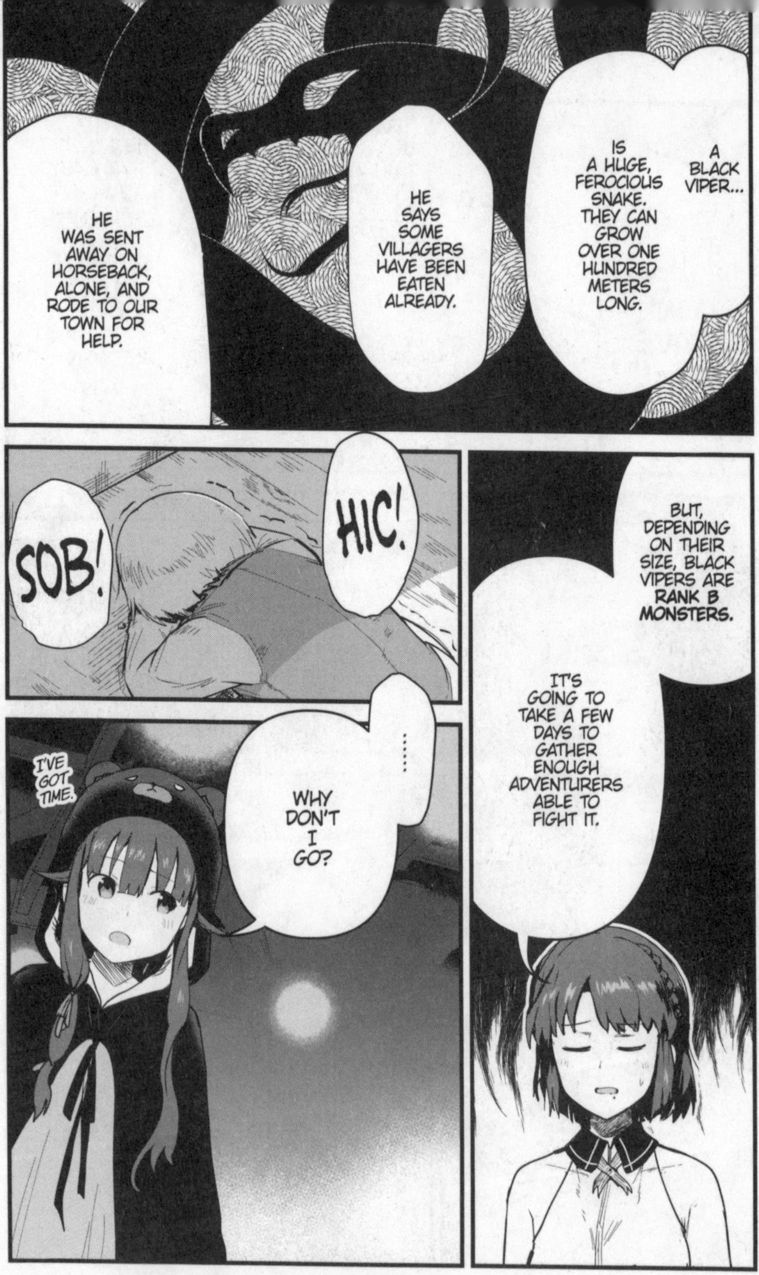
A BLACK VIPER...
IS A HUGE, FEROCIOUS SNAKE. THEY CAN GROW OVER ONE HUNDRED METERS LONG.
HE SAYS SOME VILLAGERS HAVE BEEN EATEN ALREADY.
HE WAS SENT AWAY ON HORSEBACK, ALONE, AND RODE TO OUR TOWN FOR HELP.
BUT, DEPENDING ON THEIR SIZE, BLACK VIPERS ARE RANK B MONSTERS.
IT'S GOING TO TAKE A FEW DAYS TO GATHER ENOUGH ADVENTURERS ABLE TO FIGHT IT.
HIC!
SOB!
......
WHY DON'T I GO?
I'VE GOT TIME.

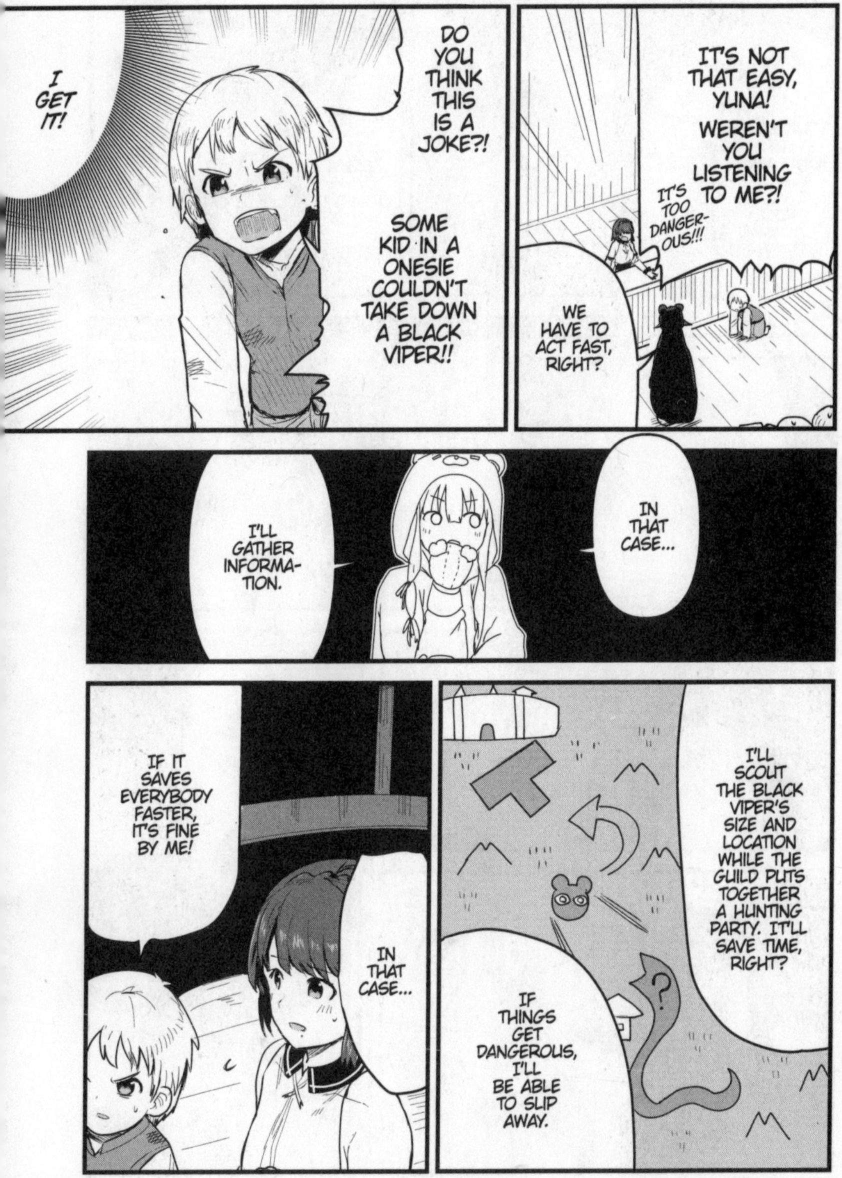
IT'S NOT THAT EASY, YUNA!
WEREN'T YOU LISTENING TO ME?!
IT'S TOO DANGER-OUS!!!
WE HAVE TO ACT FAST, RIGHT?
DO YOU THINK THIS IS A JOKE?!
SOME KID IN A ONESIE COULDN'T TAKE DOWN A BLACK VIPER!!
I GET IT!
IN THAT CASE...
I'LL GATHER INFORMA-TION.
I'LL SCOUT THE BLACK VIPER'S SIZE AND LOCATION WHILE THE GUILD PUTS TOGETHER A HUNTING PARTY. IT'LL SAVE TIME, RIGHT?
IF THINGS GET DANGEROUS, I'LL BE ABLE TO SLIP AWAY.
IN THAT CASE...
IF IT SAVES EVERYBODY FASTER, IT'S FINE BY ME!

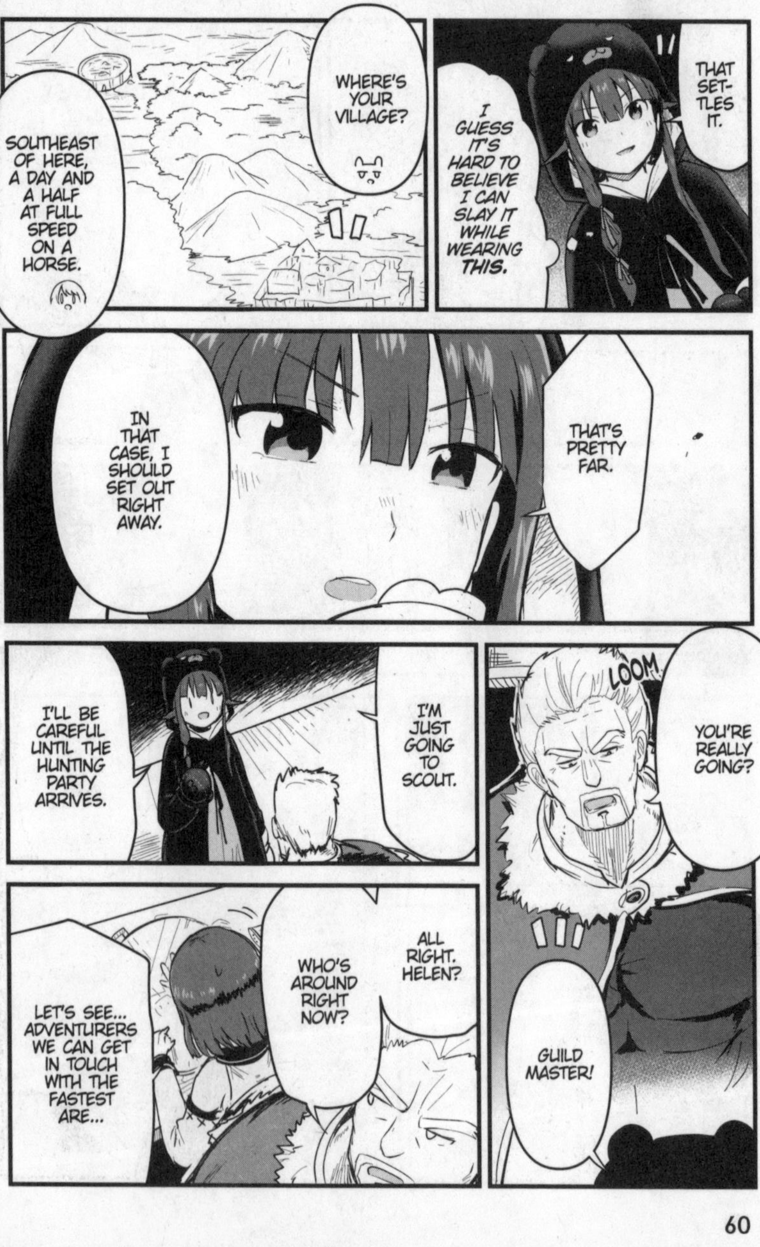
THAT SET-TLES IT.
I GUESS IT'S HARD TO BELIEVE I CAN SLAY IT WHILE WEARING THIS.
WHERE'S YOUR VILLAGE?
SOUTHEAST OF HERE, A DAY AND A HALF AT FULL SPEED ON A HORSE.
THAT'S PRETTY FAR.
IN THAT CASE, I SHOULD SET OUT RIGHT AWAY.
LOOM
YOU'RE REALLY GOING?
I'M JUST GOING TO SCOUT.
I'LL BE CAREFUL UNTIL THE HUNTING PARTY ARRIVES.
GUILD MASTER!
ALL RIGHT. HELEN?
WHO'S AROUND RIGHT NOW?
LET'S SEE... ADVENTURERS WE CAN GET IN TOUCH WITH THE FASTEST ARE...

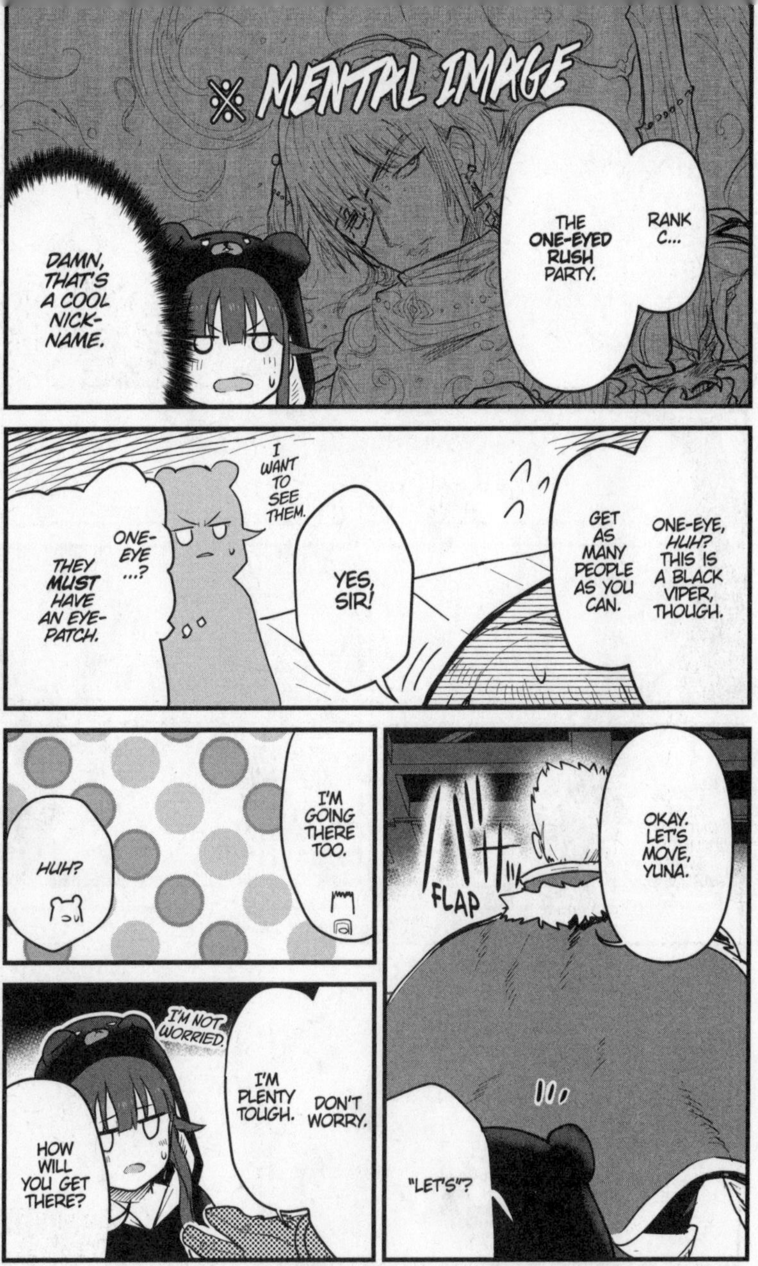
※ MENTAL IMAGE
RANK C...
THE ONE-EYED RUSH PARTY.
DAMN, THAT'S A COOL NICK-NAME.
ONE-EYE, *HUH?* THIS IS A BLACK VIPER, THOUGH.
GET AS MANY PEOPLE AS YOU CAN.
YES, SIR!
I WANT TO SEE THEM.
ONE-EYE ...?
THEY **MUST** HAVE AN EYE-PATCH.
OKAY. LET'S MOVE, YUNA.
FLAP
"LET'S"?
I'M GOING THERE TOO.
HUH?
DON'T WORRY.
I'M PLENTY TOUGH.
I'M NOT WORRIED.
HOW WILL YOU GET THERE?

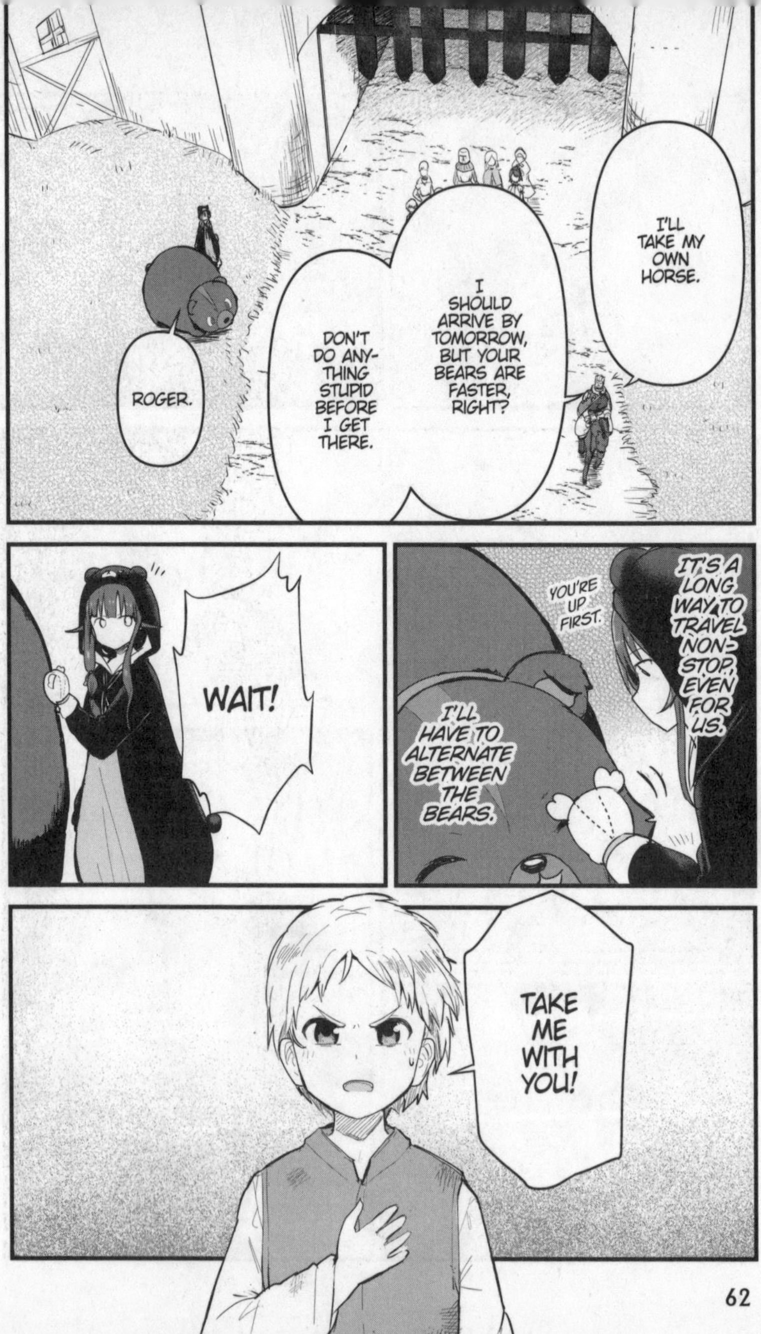
I'LL TAKE MY OWN HORSE.
I SHOULD ARRIVE BY TOMORROW, BUT YOUR BEARS ARE FASTER, RIGHT?
DON'T DO ANY-THING STUPID BEFORE I GET THERE.
ROGER.
IT'S A LONG WAY TO TRAVEL NON-STOP, EVEN FOR US.
YOU'RE UP FIRST.
I'LL HAVE TO ALTERNATE BETWEEN THE BEARS.
WAIT!
TAKE ME WITH YOU!

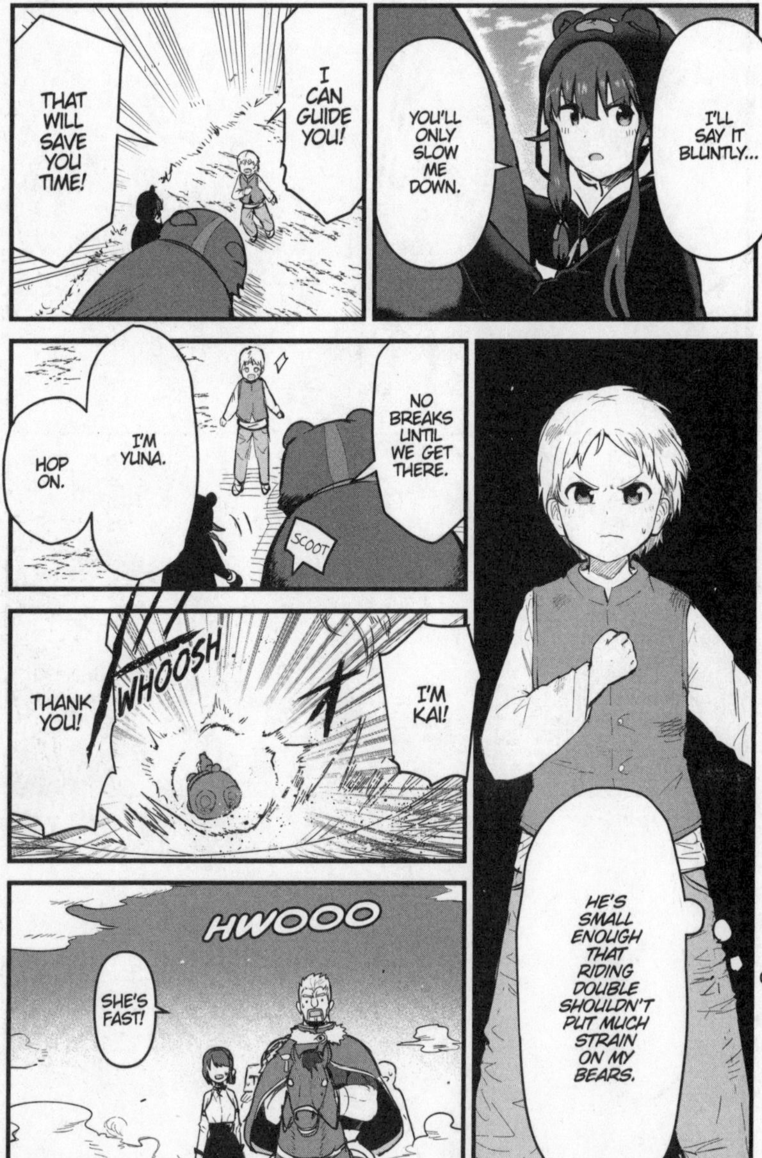
I'LL SAY IT BLUNTLY...
YOU'LL ONLY SLOW ME DOWN.
I CAN GUIDE YOU!
THAT WILL SAVE YOU TIME!
HE'S SMALL ENOUGH THAT RIDING DOUBLE SHOULDN'T PUT MUCH STRAIN ON MY BEARS.
NO BREAKS UNTIL WE GET THERE.
SCOOT
I'M YUNA.
HOP ON.
I'M KAI!
WHOOSH
THANK YOU!
HWOOO
SHE'S FAST!

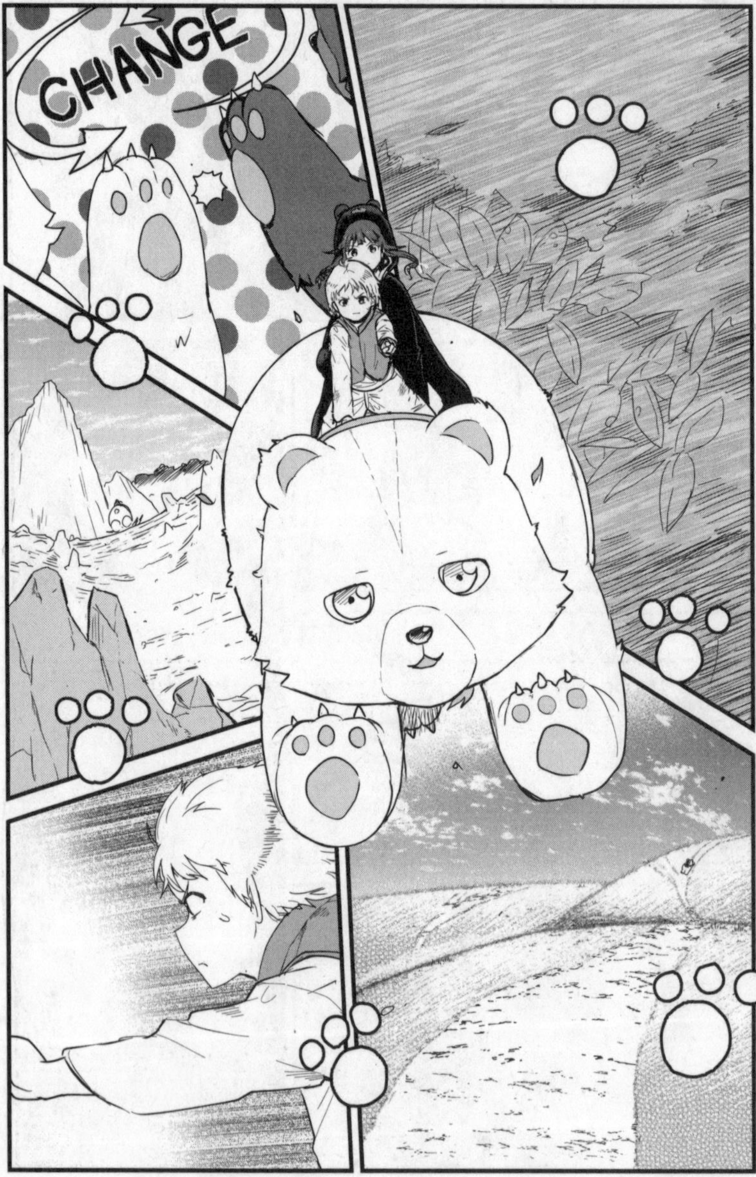
CHANGE

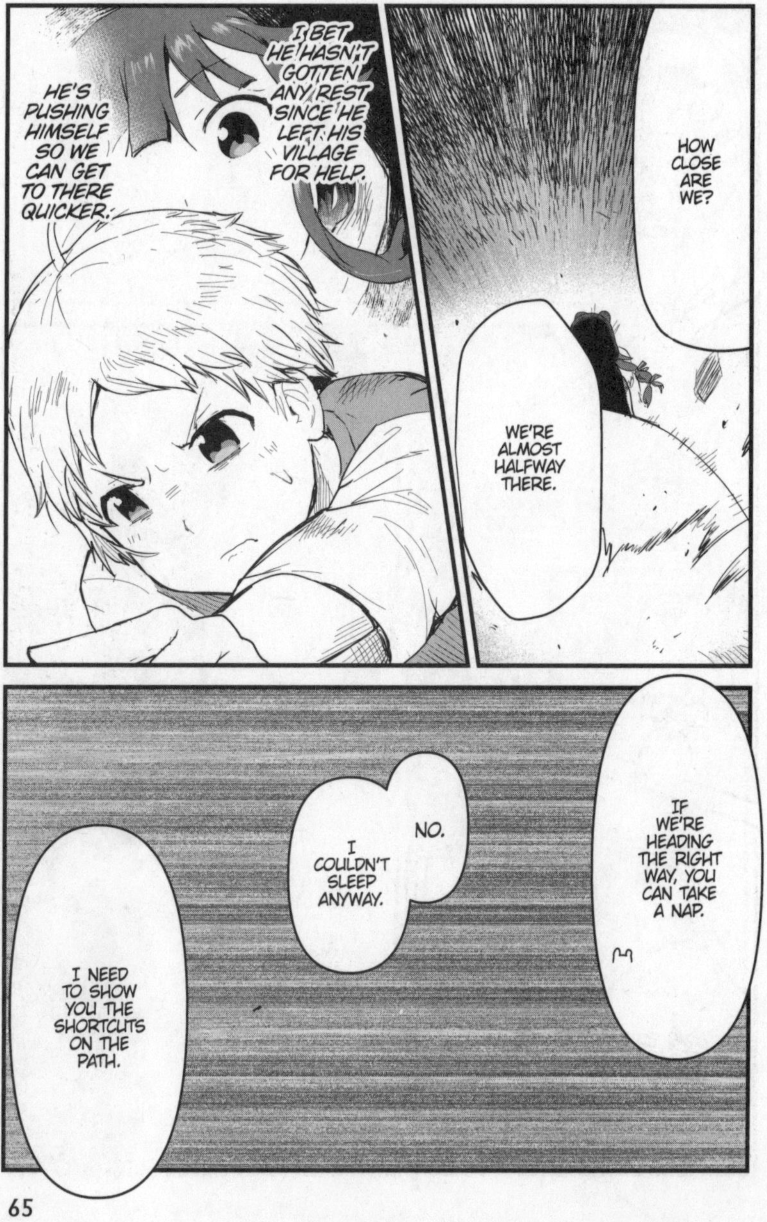
HOW CLOSE ARE WE?
WE'RE ALMOST HALFWAY THERE.
I BET HE HASN'T GOTTEN ANY REST SINCE HE LEFT HIS VILLAGE FOR HELP.
HE'S PUSHING HIMSELF SO WE CAN GET TO THERE QUICKER.
IF WE'RE HEADING THE RIGHT WAY, YOU CAN TAKE A NAP.
NO.
I COULDN'T SLEEP ANYWAY.
I NEED TO SHOW YOU THE SHORTCUTS ON THE PATH.

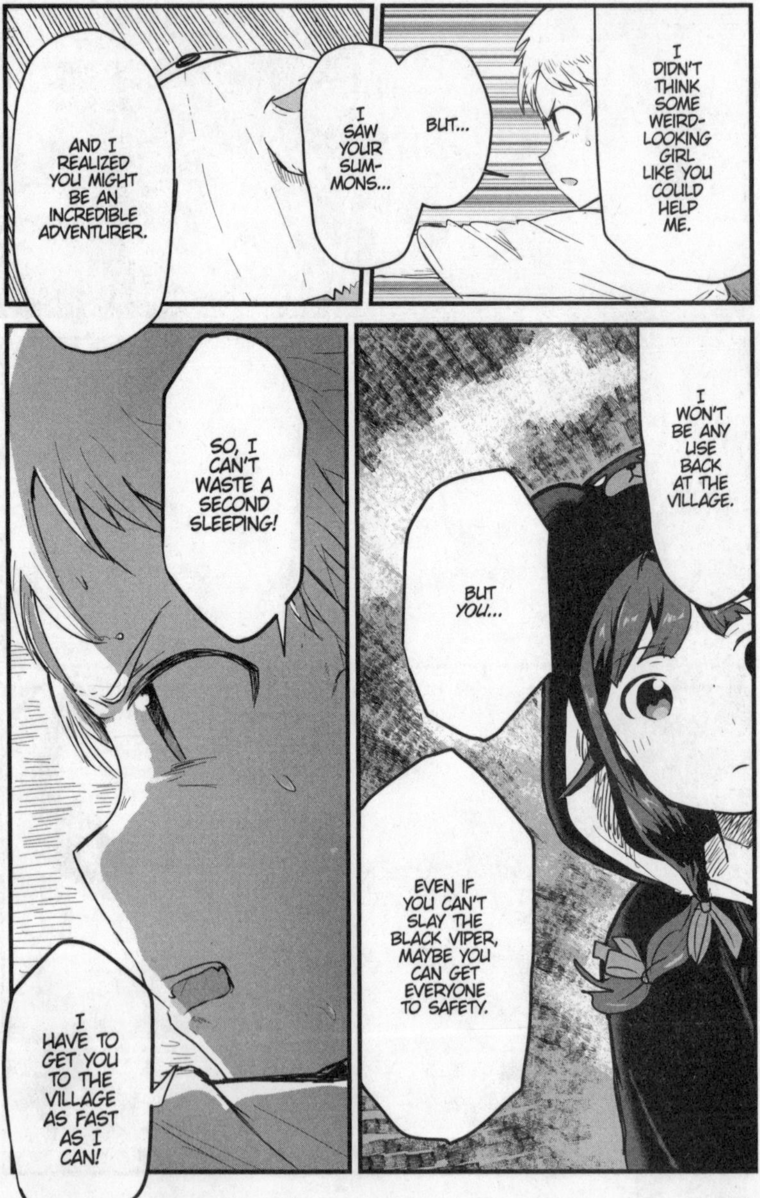
I DIDN'T THINK SOME WEIRD-LOOKING GIRL LIKE YOU COULD HELP ME.
BUT...
I SAW YOUR SUM-MONS...
AND I REALIZED YOU MIGHT BE AN INCREDIBLE ADVENTURER.
I WON'T BE ANY USE BACK AT THE VILLAGE.
BUT YOU...
EVEN IF YOU CAN'T SLAY THE BLACK VIPER, MAYBE YOU CAN GET EVERYONE TO SAFETY.
SO, I CAN'T WASTE A SECOND SLEEPING!
I HAVE TO GET YOU TO THE VILLAGE AS FAST AS I CAN!

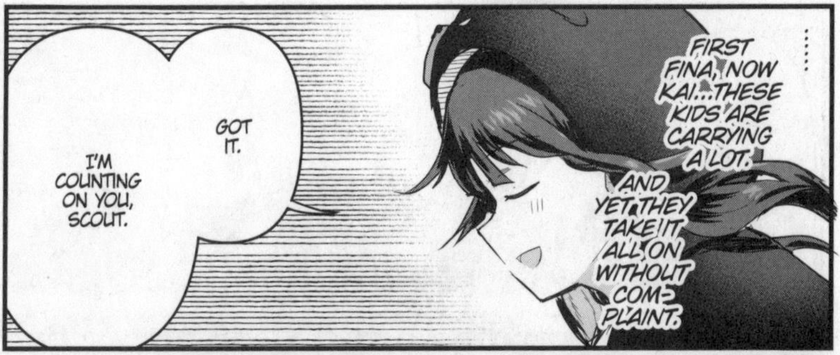
……
FIRST FINA, NOW KAI…THESE KIDS ARE CARRYING A LOT.
AND YET THEY TAKE IT ALL ON WITHOUT COM-PLAINT.
GOT IT.
I'M COUNTING ON YOU, SCOUT.
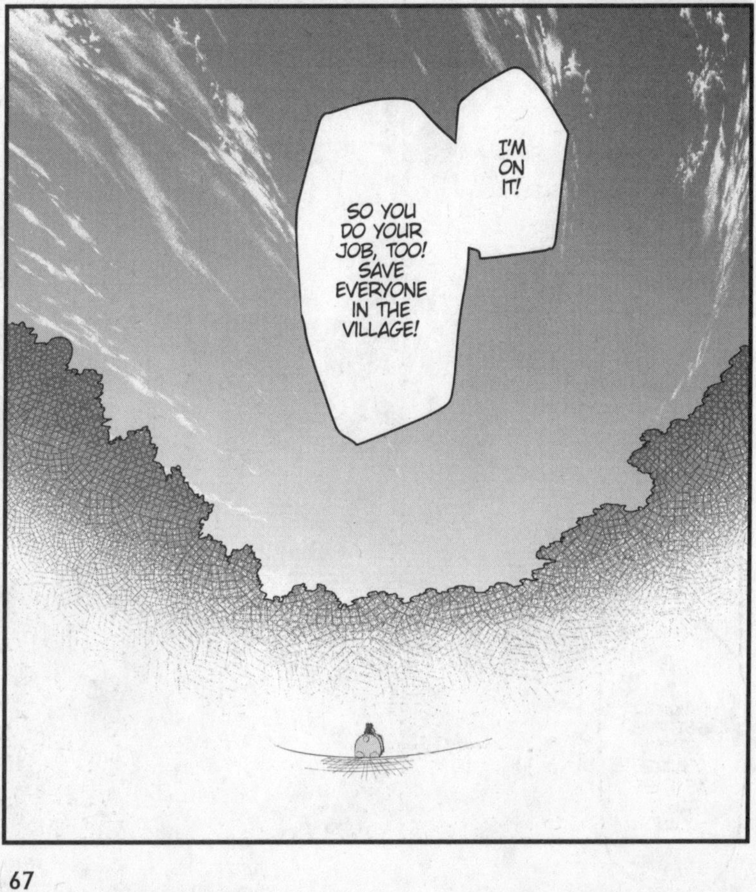
I'M ON IT!
SO YOU DO YOUR JOB, TOO! SAVE EVERYONE IN THE VILLAGE!

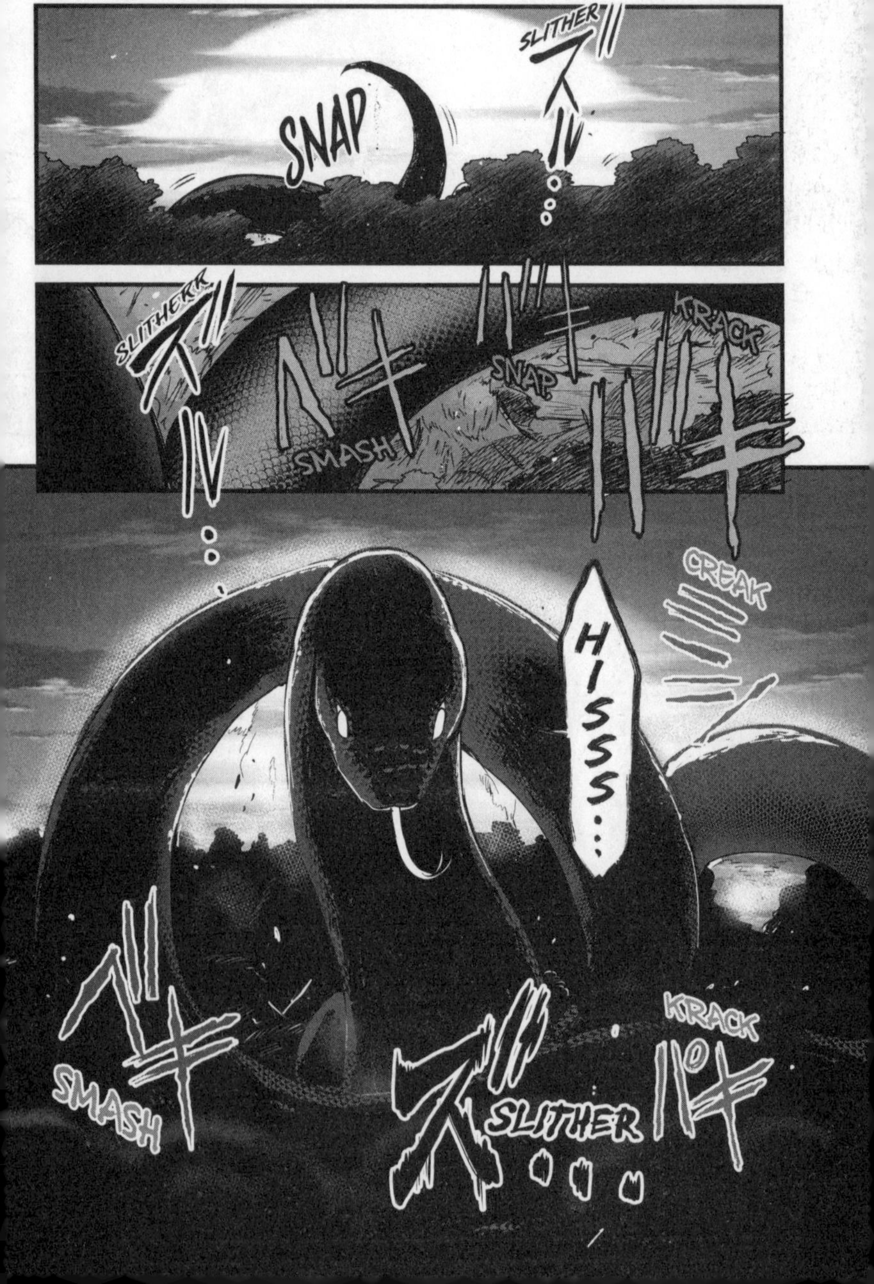
SLITHER
SNAP
KRACK
SNAP
SMASH
SLITHERR
CREAK
HISSS...
KRACK
SLITHER
SMASH

Chapter 25

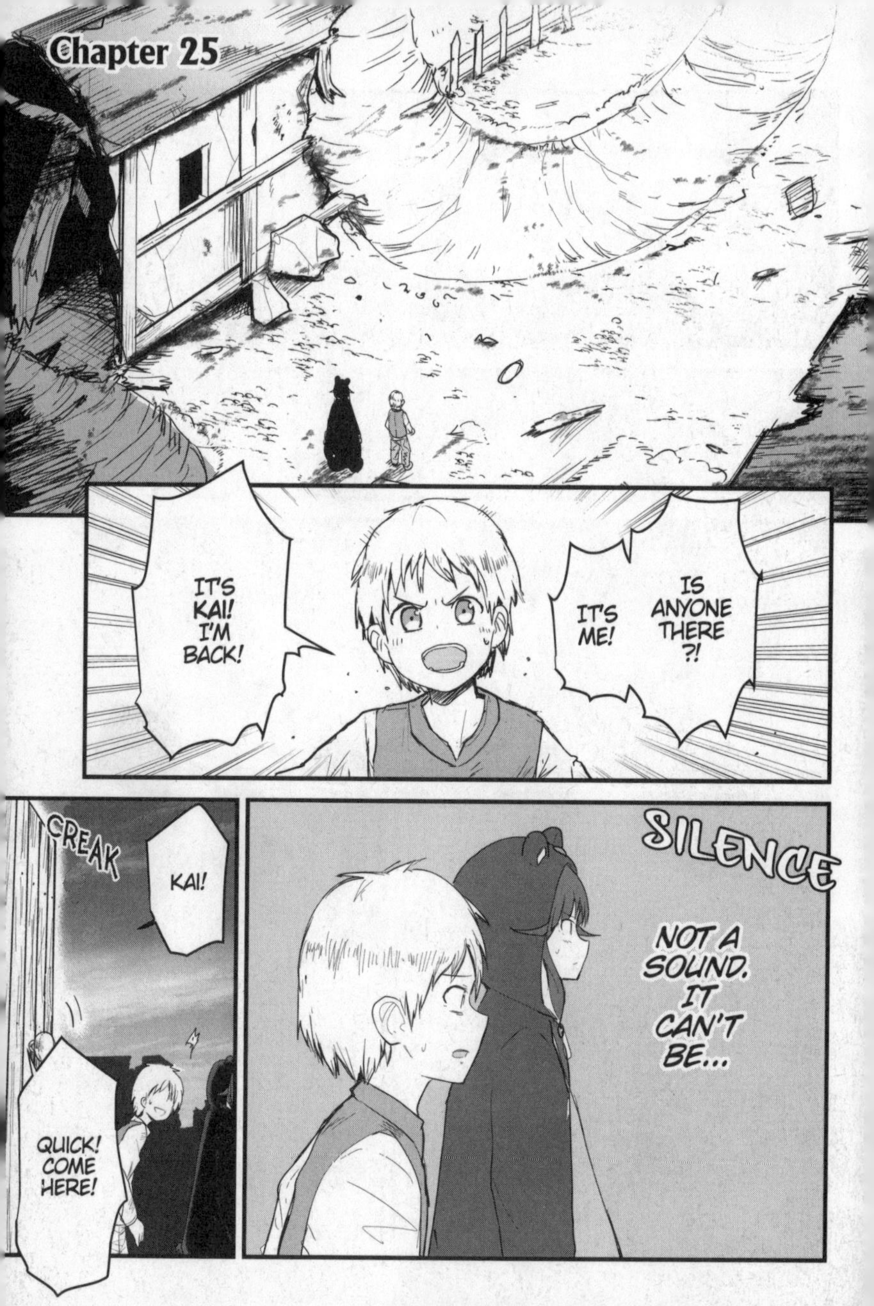
IS ANYONE THERE ?!
IT'S ME!
IT'S KAI! I'M BACK!
SILENCE
NOT A SOUND. IT CAN'T BE...
CREAK
KAI!
QUICK! COME HERE!

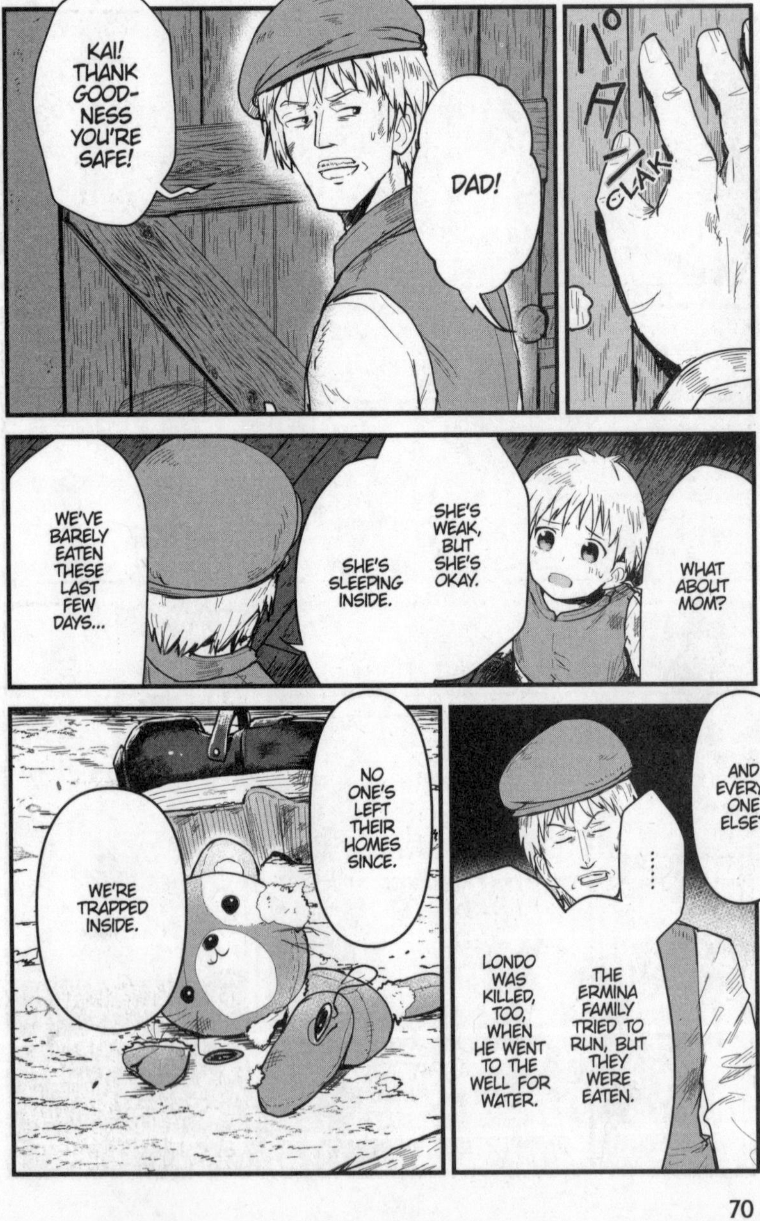
CLAK
DAD!
KAI! THANK GOODNESS YOU'RE SAFE!
WHAT ABOUT MOM?
SHE'S WEAK, BUT SHE'S OKAY.
SHE'S SLEEPING INSIDE.
WE'VE BARELY EATEN THESE LAST FEW DAYS...
AND EVERYONE ELSE?
......
THE ERMINA FAMILY TRIED TO RUN, BUT THEY WERE EATEN.
LONDO WAS KILLED, TOO, WHEN HE WENT TO THE WELL FOR WATER.
NO ONE'S LEFT THEIR HOMES SINCE.
WE'RE TRAPPED INSIDE.

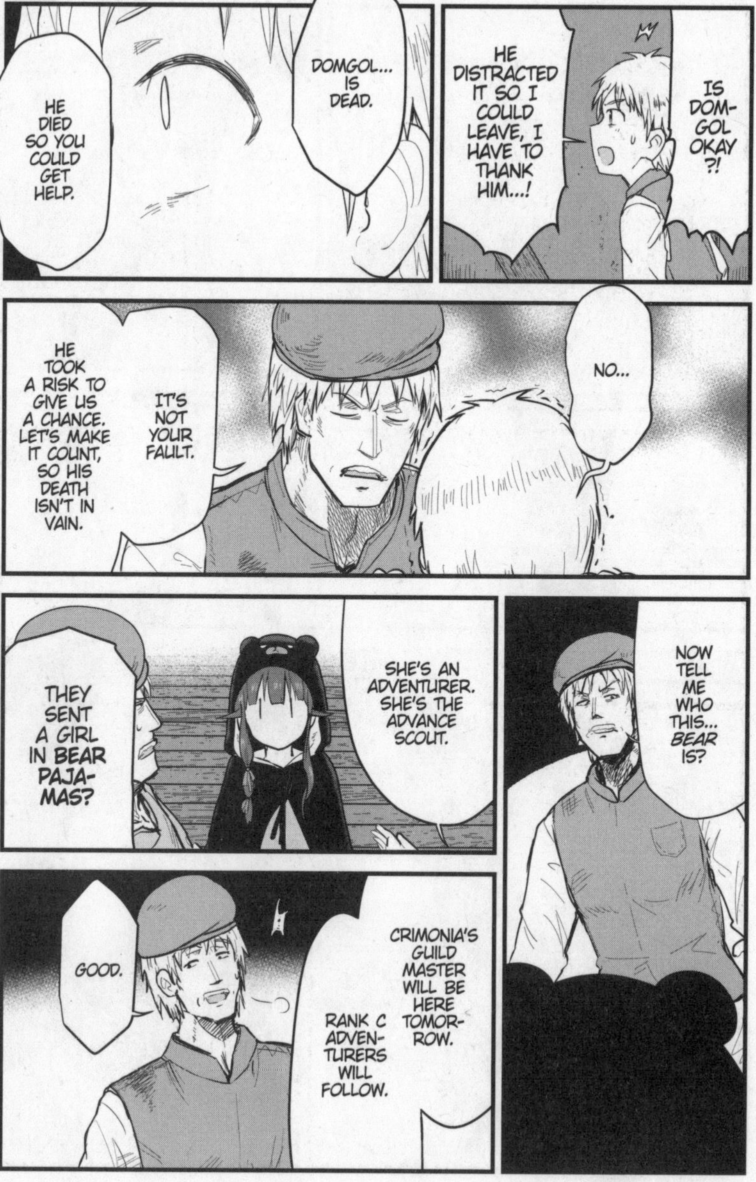
IS DOMGOL OKAY?!
HE DISTRACTED IT SO I COULD LEAVE, I HAVE TO THANK HIM...!
DOMGOL... IS DEAD.
HE DIED SO YOU COULD GET HELP.
NO...
IT'S NOT YOUR FAULT.
HE TOOK A RISK TO GIVE US A CHANCE. LET'S MAKE IT COUNT, SO HIS DEATH ISN'T IN VAIN.
NOW TELL ME WHO THIS... BEAR IS?
SHE'S AN ADVENTURER. SHE'S THE ADVANCE SCOUT.
THEY SENT A GIRL IN BEAR PAJAMAS?
CRIMONIA'S GUILD MASTER WILL BE HERE TOMORROW.
RANK C ADVENTURERS WILL FOLLOW.
GOOD.

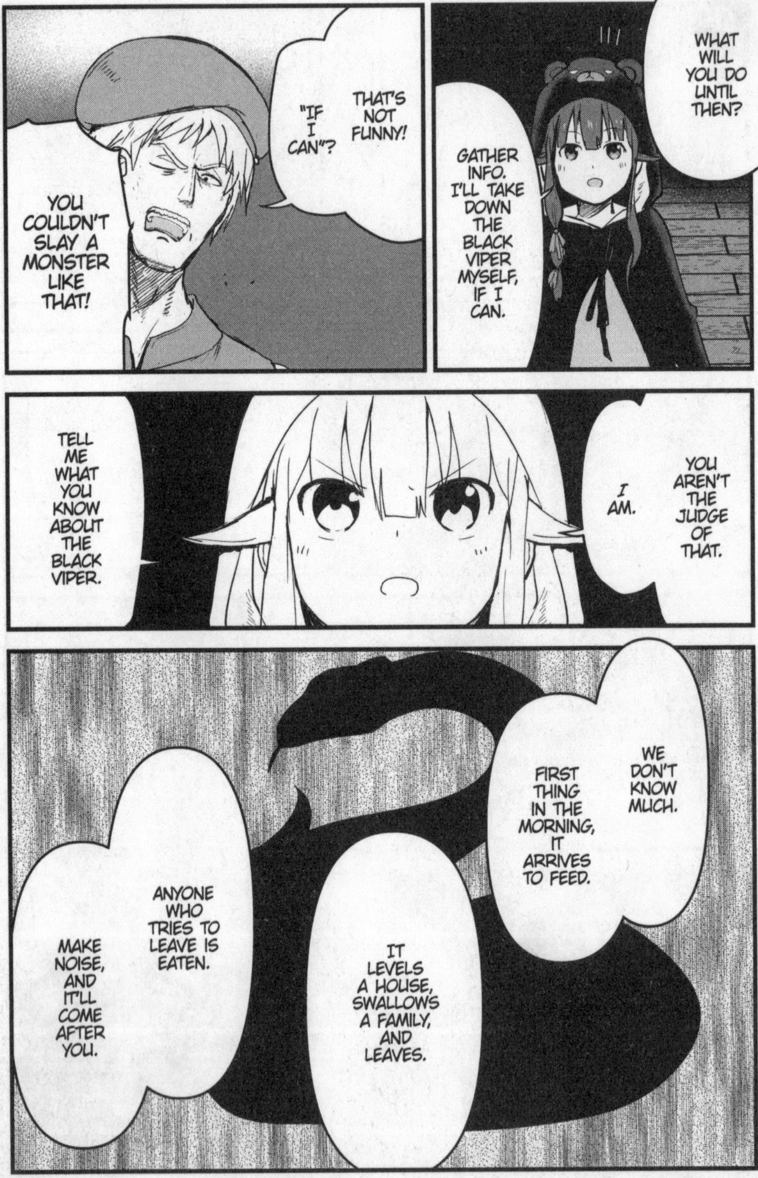
WHAT WILL YOU DO UNTIL THEN?
GATHER INFO. I'LL TAKE DOWN THE BLACK VIPER MYSELF, IF I CAN.
"IF I CAN"? THAT'S NOT FUNNY!
YOU COULDN'T SLAY A MONSTER LIKE THAT!
YOU AREN'T THE JUDGE OF THAT.
I AM.
TELL ME WHAT YOU KNOW ABOUT THE BLACK VIPER.
WE DON'T KNOW MUCH.
FIRST THING IN THE MORNING, IT ARRIVES TO FEED.
IT LEVELS A HOUSE, SWALLOWS A FAMILY, AND LEAVES.
ANYONE WHO TRIES TO LEAVE IS EATEN.
MAKE NOISE, AND IT'LL COME AFTER YOU.

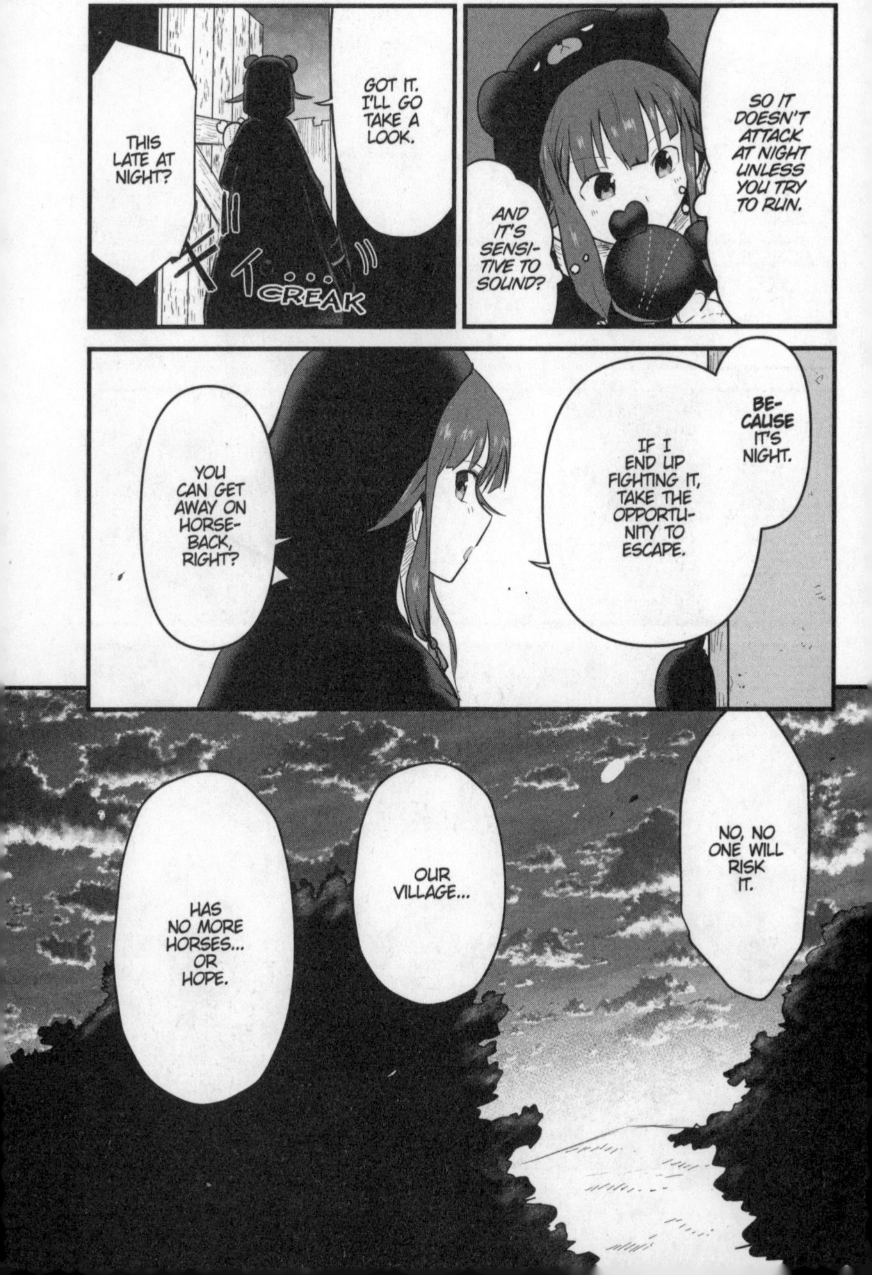
SO IT DOESN'T ATTACK AT NIGHT UNLESS YOU TRY TO RUN.
AND IT'S SENSITIVE TO SOUND?
GOT IT. I'LL GO TAKE A LOOK.
THIS LATE AT NIGHT?
CREAK
BECAUSE IT'S NIGHT.
IF I END UP FIGHTING IT, TAKE THE OPPORTUNITY TO ESCAPE.
YOU CAN GET AWAY ON HORSEBACK, RIGHT?
NO, NO ONE WILL RISK IT.
OUR VILLAGE...
HAS NO MORE HORSES... OR HOPE.

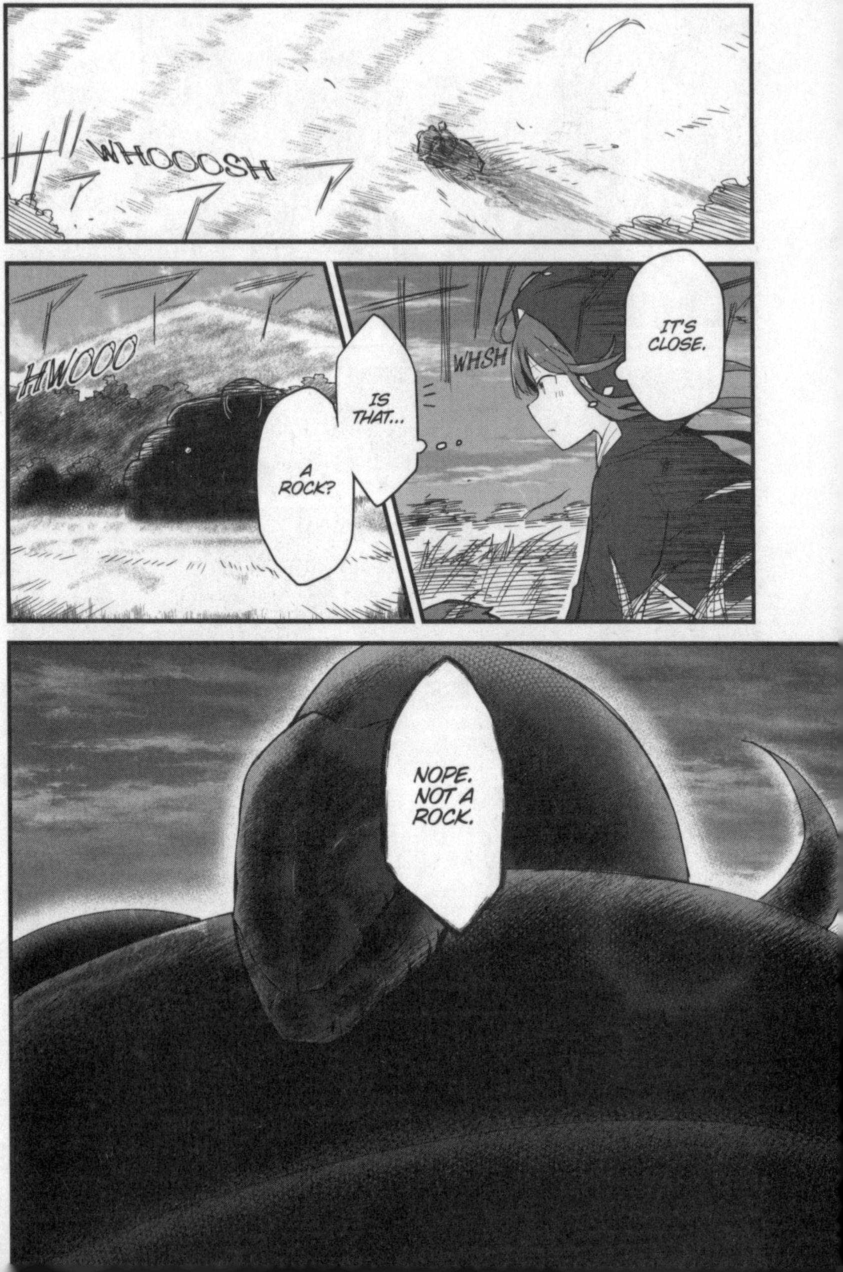
WHOOOSH
IT'S CLOSE.
WHSH
IS THAT...
A ROCK?
HWOOO
NOPE. NOT A ROCK.

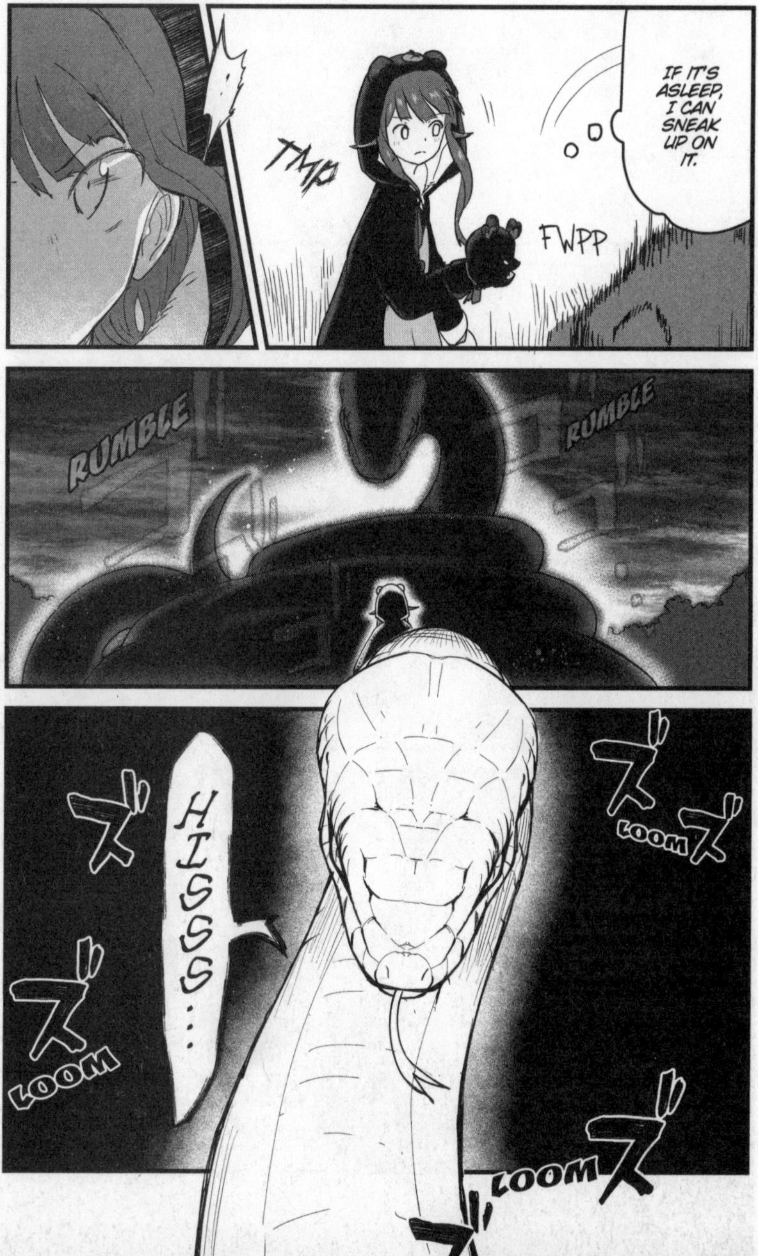
IF IT'S ASLEEP, I CAN SNEAK UP ON IT.
FWPP
TMP
RUMBLE
RUMBLE
ズ
LOOM ズ
HISSS...
ズ
ズ
LOOM
ズ
LOOM ズ

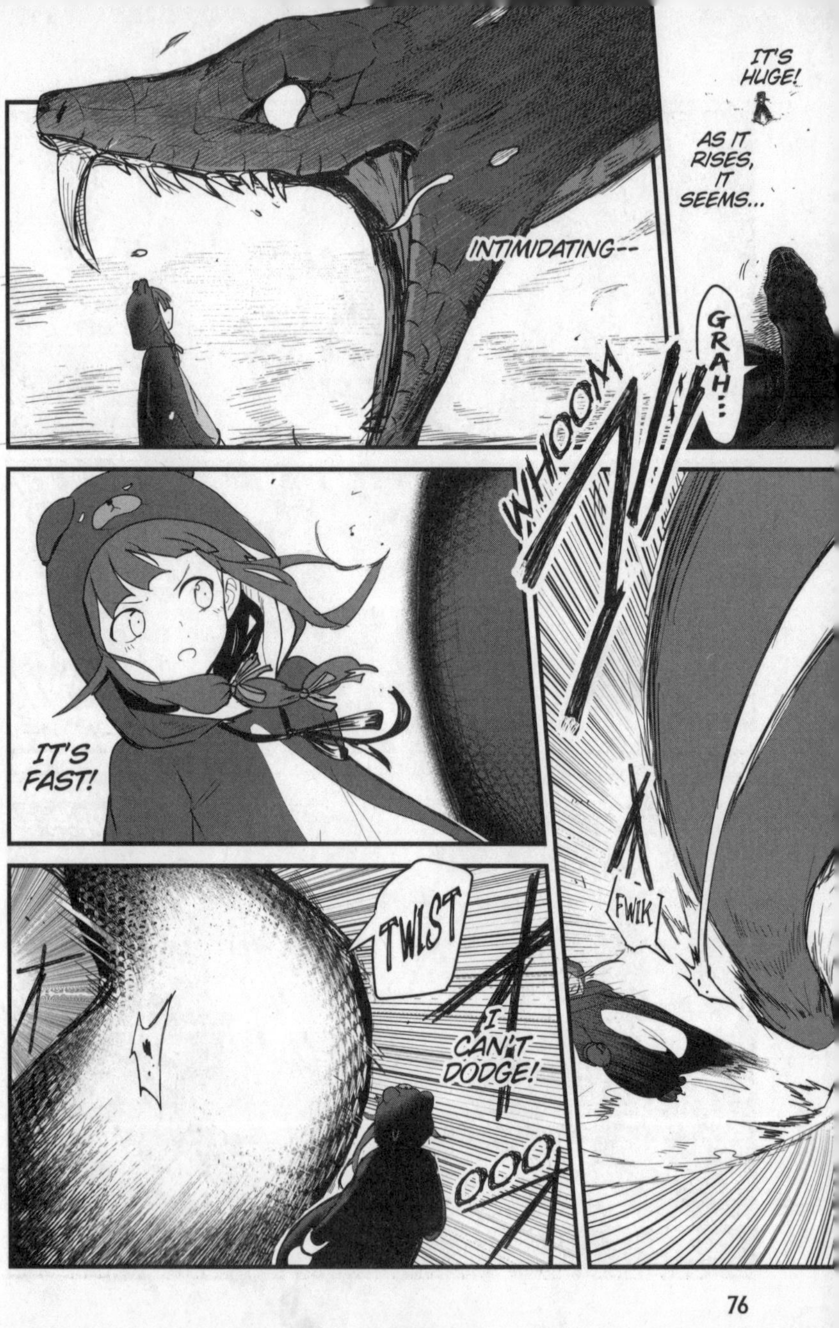
IT'S HUGE!
AS IT RISES, IT SEEMS...
INTIMIDATING--
GRAH...
WHOOM
IT'S FAST!
FWIK
TWIST
I CAN'T DODGE!
OOO

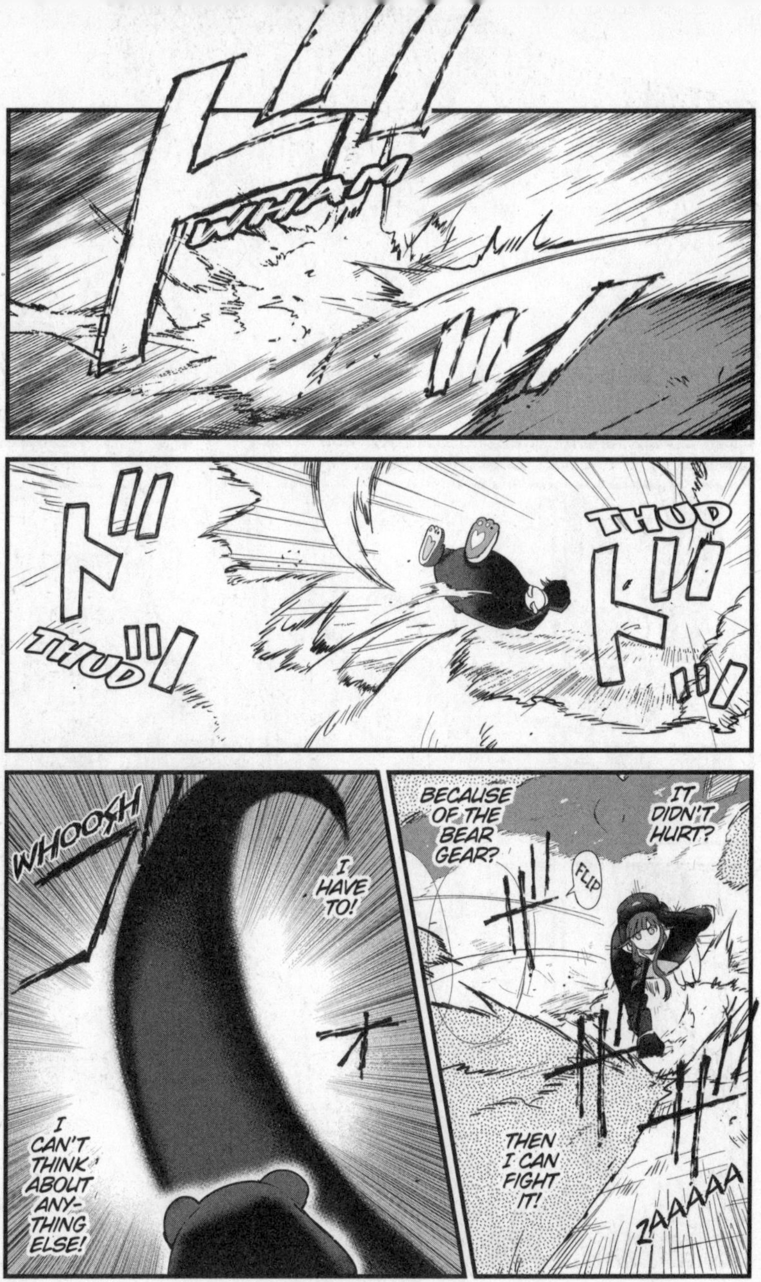
WHAM
THUD
THUD
IT DIDN'T HURT?
BECAUSE OF THE BEAR GEAR?
FLIP
THEN I CAN FIGHT IT!
ZAAAAA
WHOOSH
I HAVE TO!
I CAN'T THINK ABOUT ANY-THING ELSE!

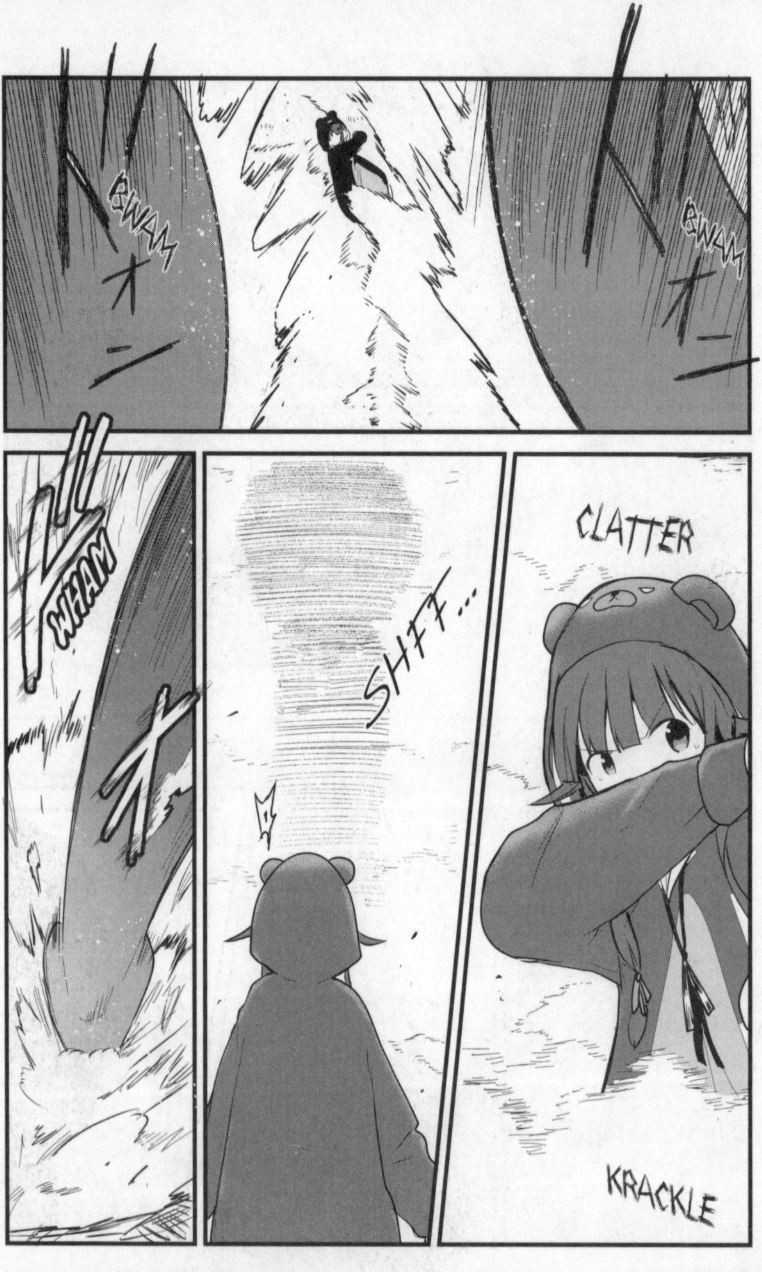
BWAM
BWAM
CLATTER
KRACKLE
SHFF...
WHAM

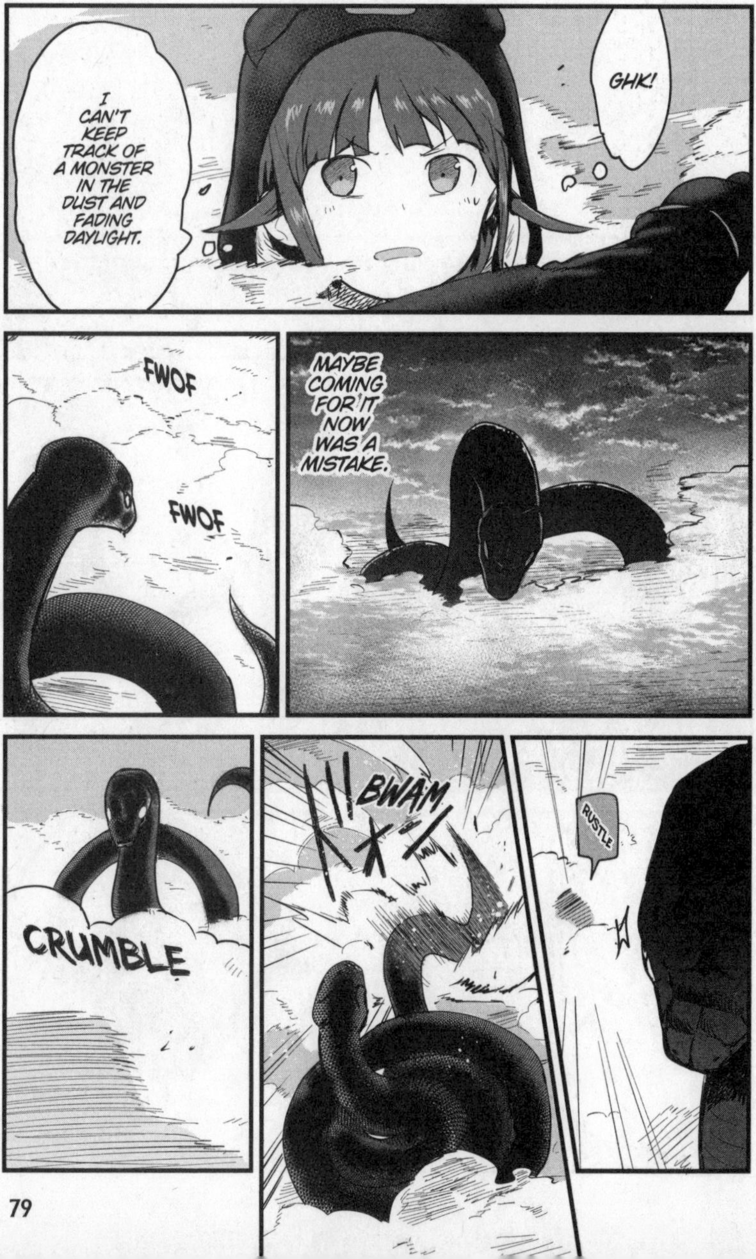
GHK!
I CAN'T KEEP TRACK OF A MONSTER IN THE DUST AND FADING DAYLIGHT.
MAYBE COMING FOR IT NOW WAS A MISTAKE.
FWOF
FWOF
RUSTLE
BWAM
CRUMBLE

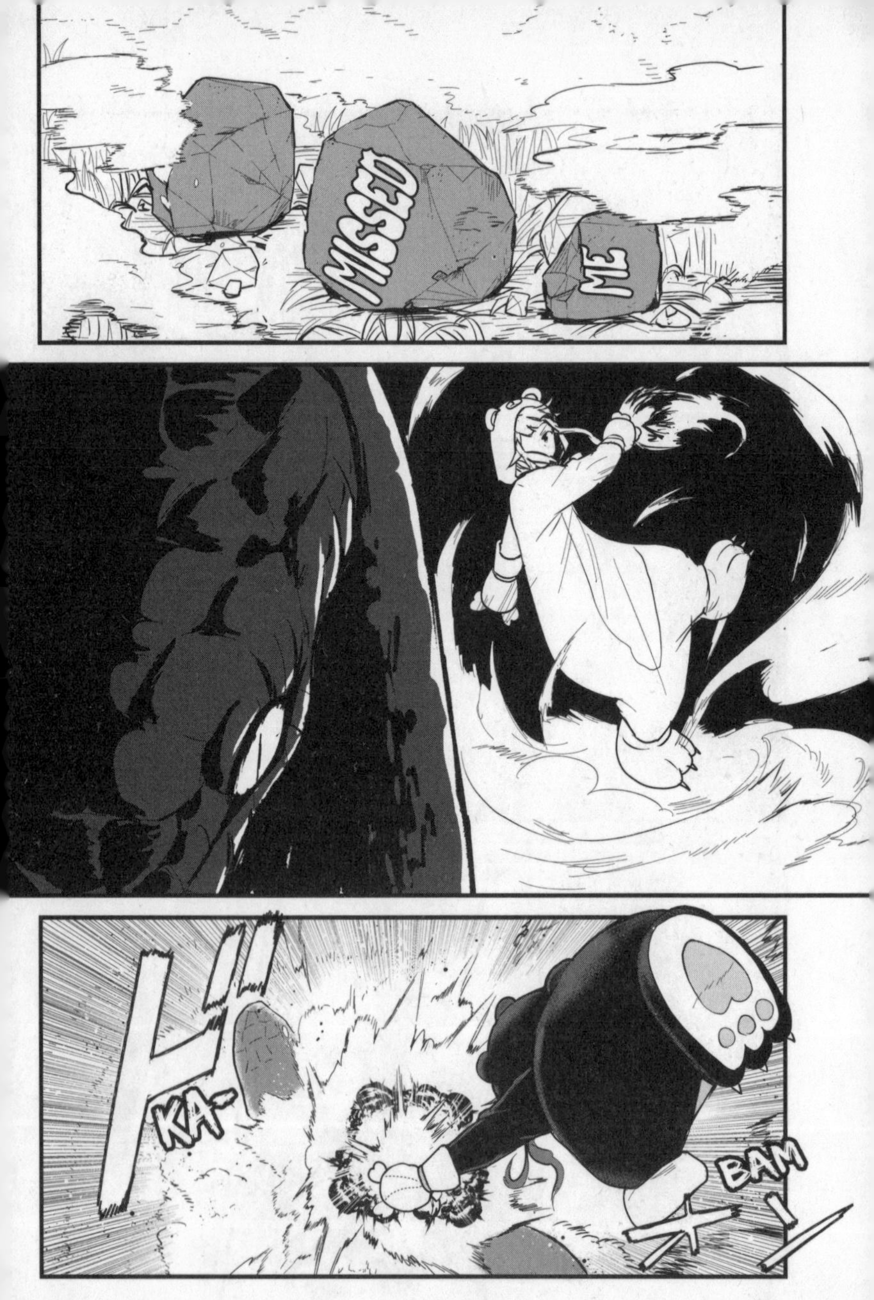
MISSED
ME
KA-
BAM

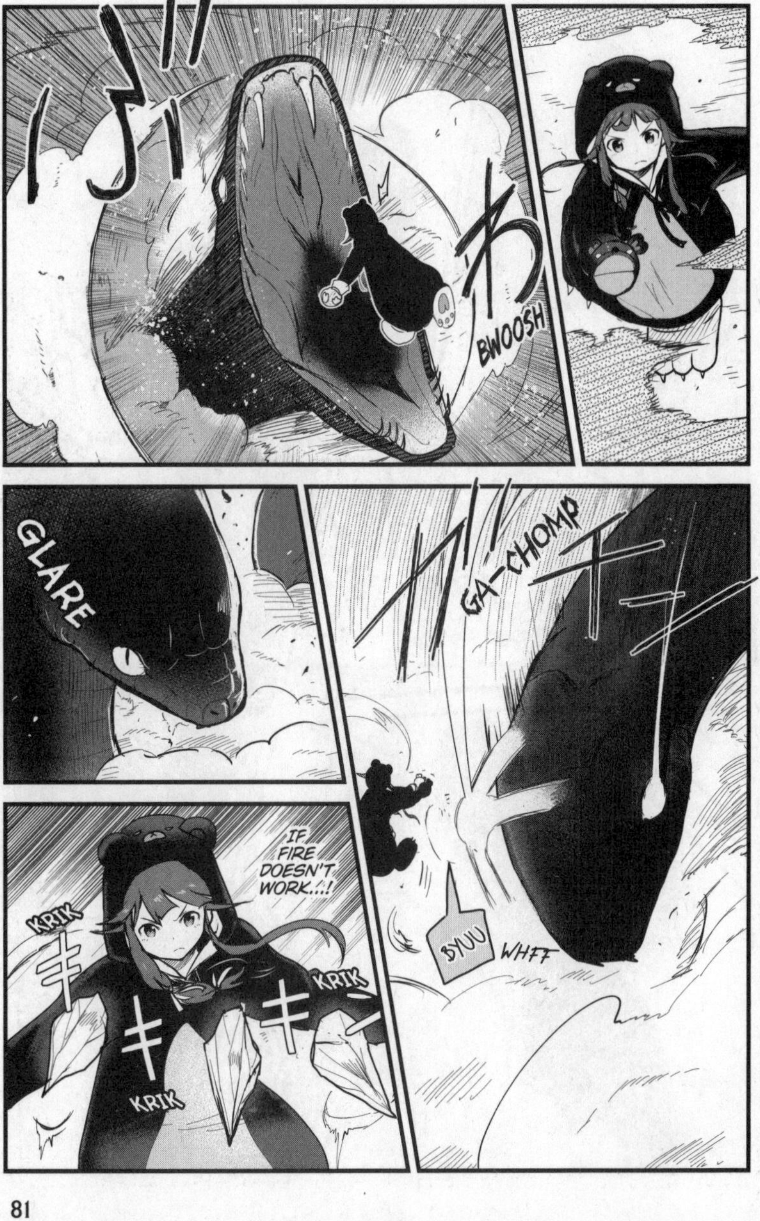
BWOOSH
GA-CHOMP
BYUU
WHFF
GLARE
IF FIRE DOESN'T WORK...!
KRIK
KRIK
KRIK

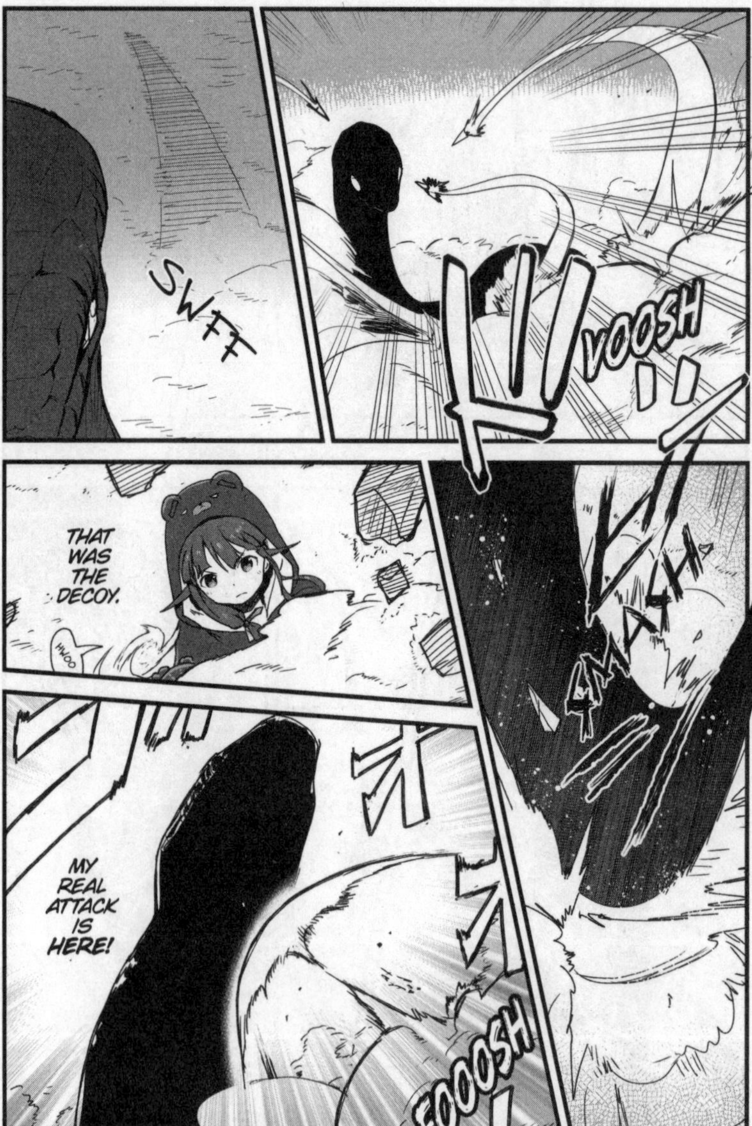
VOOSH
SWFF
SMASH
THAT WAS THE DECOY.
HWOO
MY REAL ATTACK IS HERE!
FOOOSH

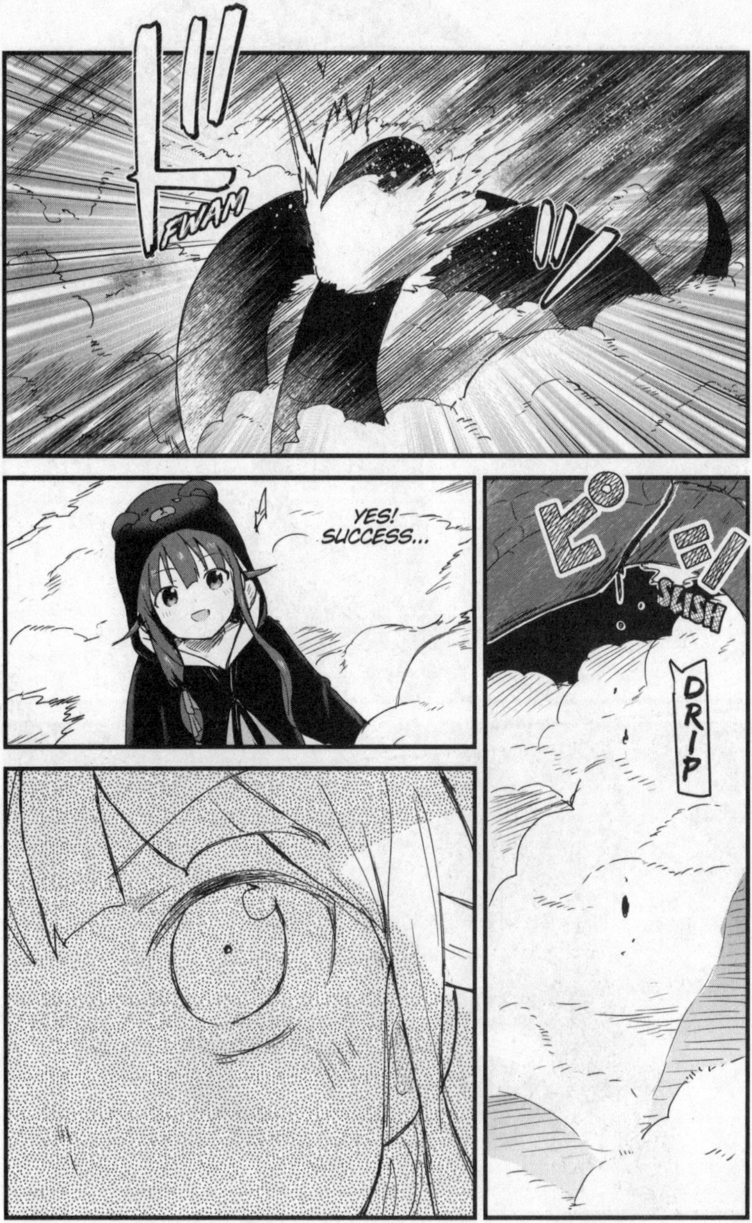
FWAM
SLISH
DRIP
YES! SUCCESS...

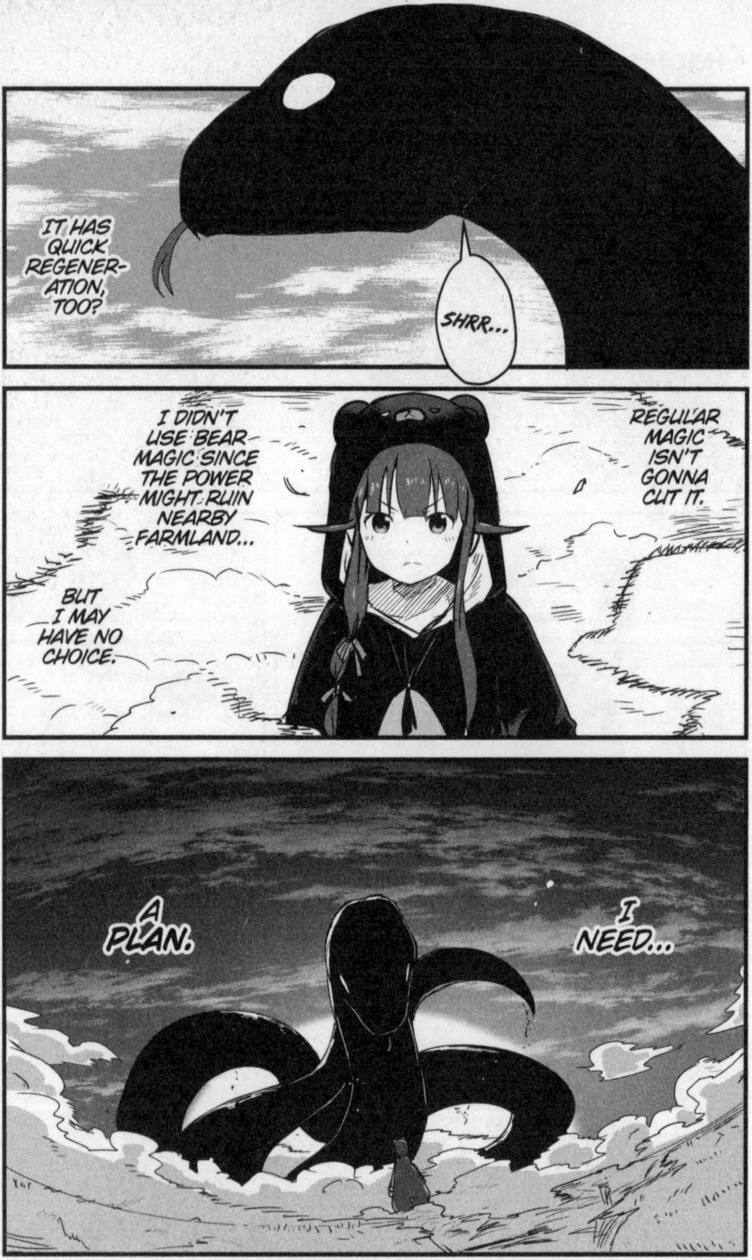
SHRR...
IT HAS QUICK REGENERATION, TOO?
REGULAR MAGIC ISN'T GONNA CUT IT.
I DIDN'T USE BEAR MAGIC SINCE THE POWER MIGHT RUIN NEARBY FARMLAND...
BUT I MAY HAVE NO CHOICE.
I NEED...
A PLAN.

Chapter 26

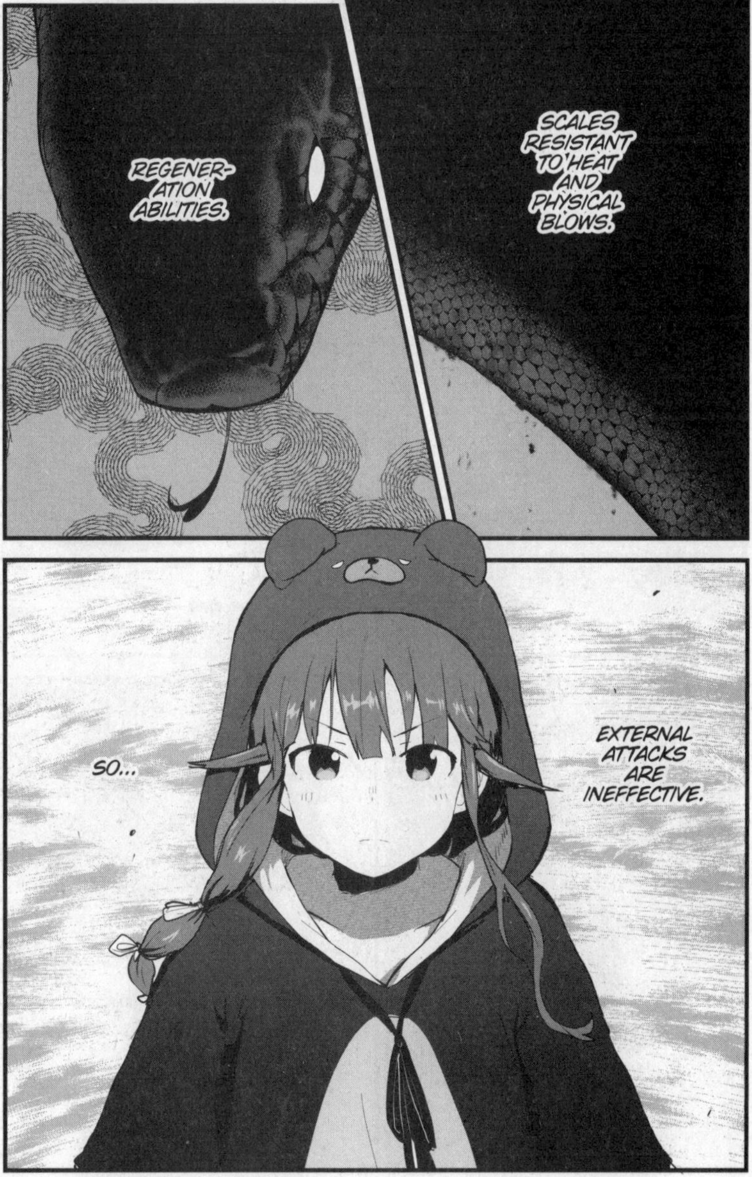
SCALES RESISTANT TO HEAT AND PHYSICAL BLOWS.
REGENER-ATION ABILITIES.
EXTERNAL ATTACKS ARE INEFFECTIVE.
SO...

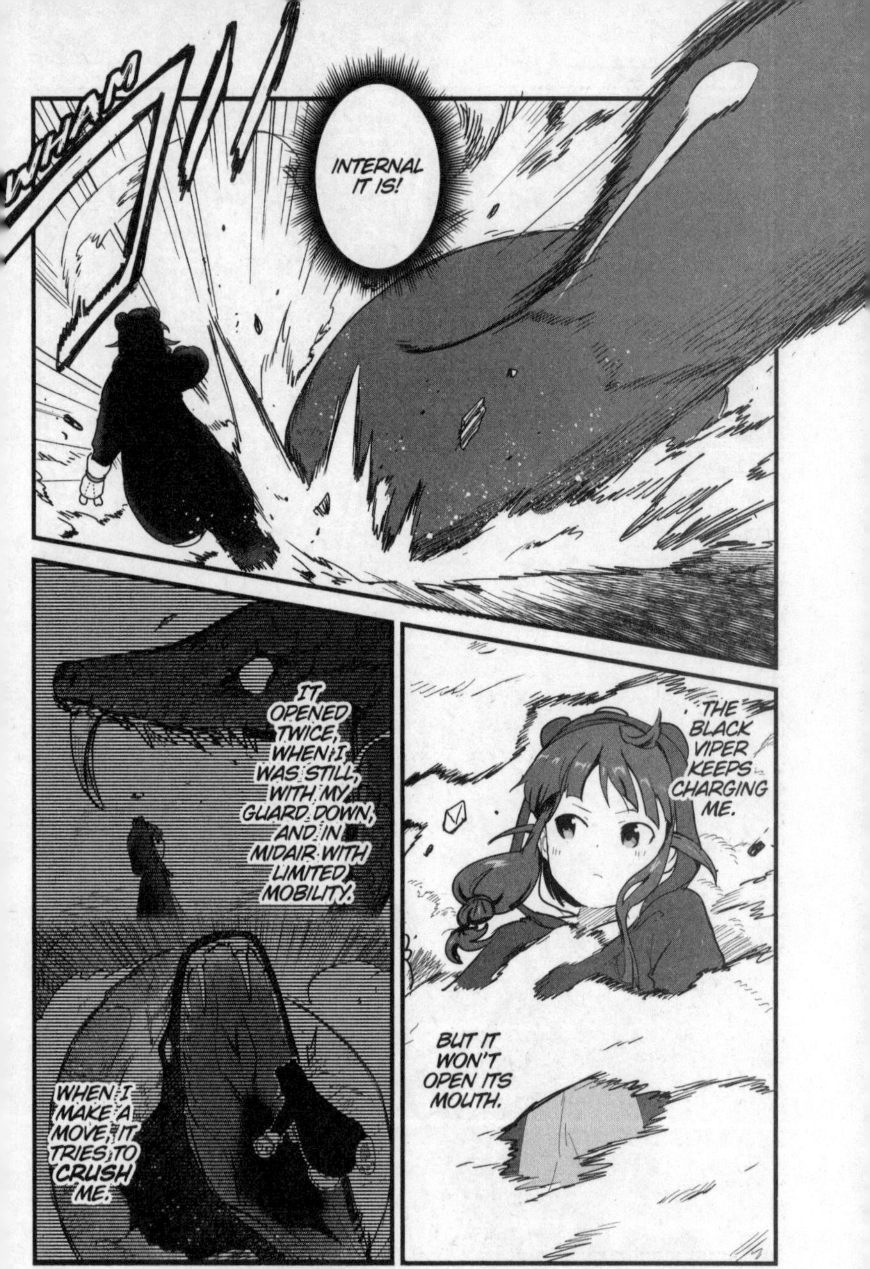
INTERNAL IT IS!
THE BLACK VIPER KEEPS CHARGING ME.
BUT IT WON'T OPEN ITS MOUTH.
IT OPENED TWICE, WHEN I WAS STILL, WITH MY GUARD DOWN, AND IN MIDAIR WITH LIMITED MOBILITY.
WHEN I MAKE A MOVE, IT TRIES TO CRUSH ME.

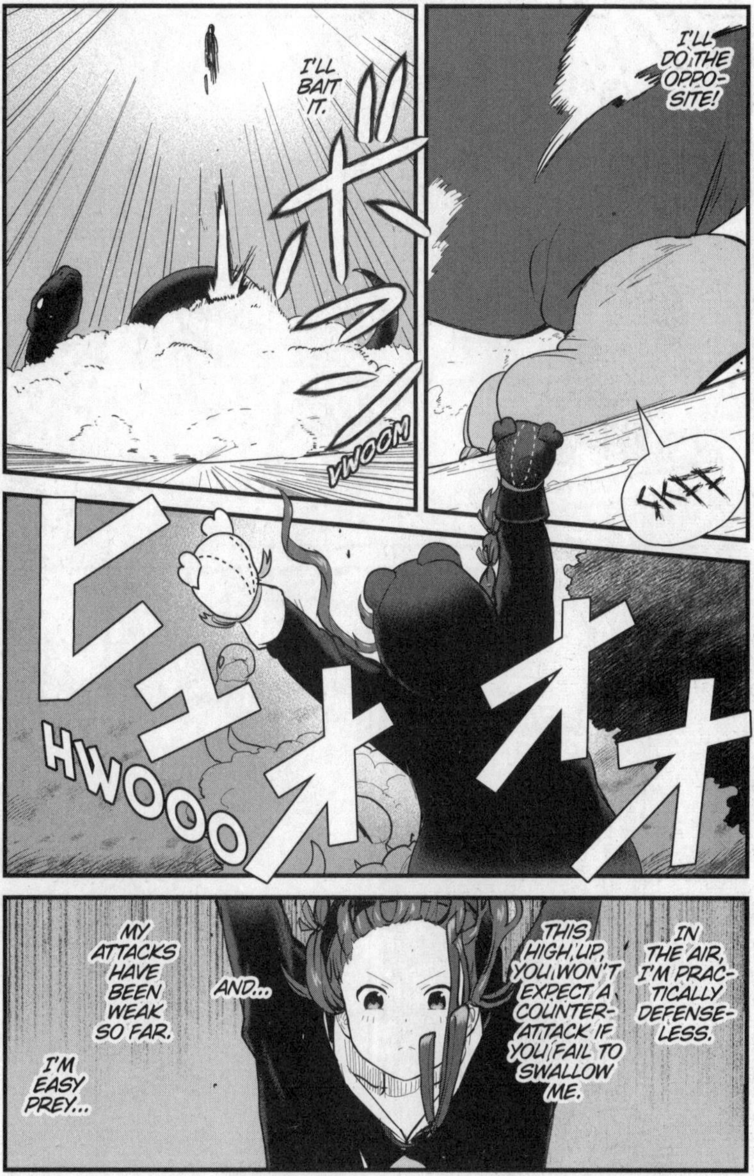
I'LL DO THE OPPO-SITE!
SKFF
I'LL BAIT IT.
VWOOM
HWOOO
IN THE AIR, I'M PRACTICALLY DEFENSE-LESS.
THIS HIGH UP, YOU WON'T EXPECT A COUNTER-ATTACK IF YOU FAIL TO SWALLOW ME.
AND...
MY ATTACKS HAVE BEEN WEAK SO FAR.
I'M EASY PREY...

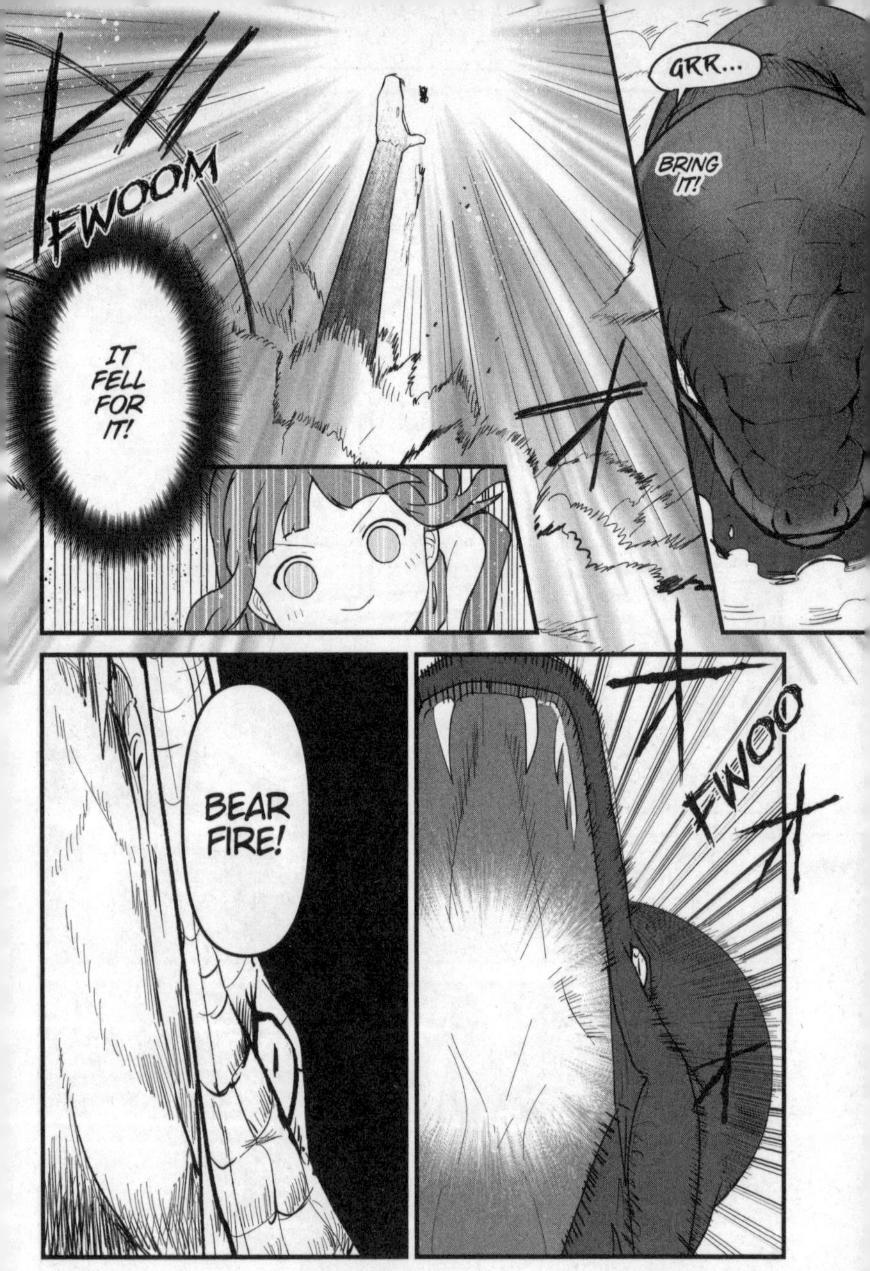
GRR...
BRING IT!
FWOOM
IT FELL FOR IT!
FWOO
BEAR FIRE!

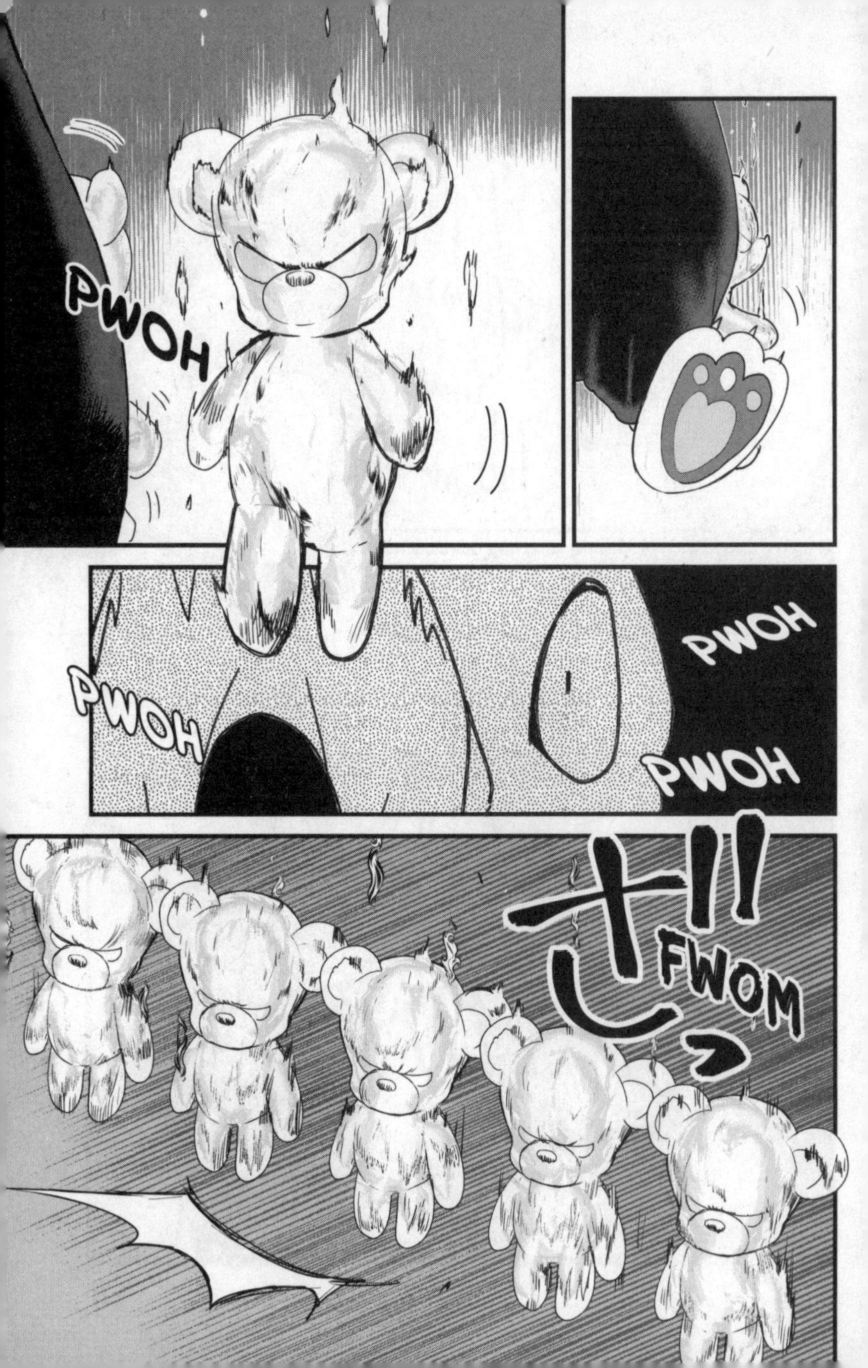
PWOH
PWOH
PWOH
PWOH
FWOM

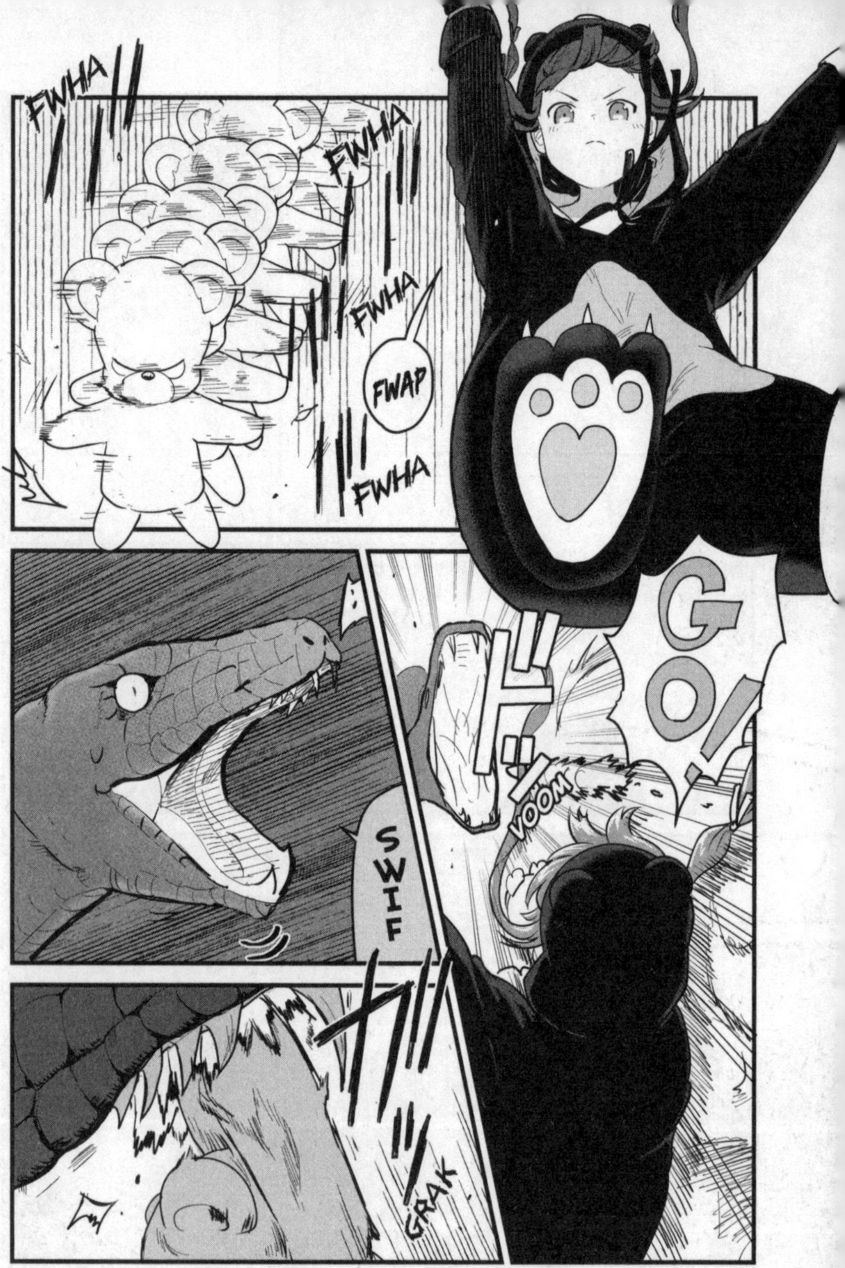
FWHA
FWHA
FWHA
FWAP
FWHA
GO!
VOOM
SWIF
GRAK

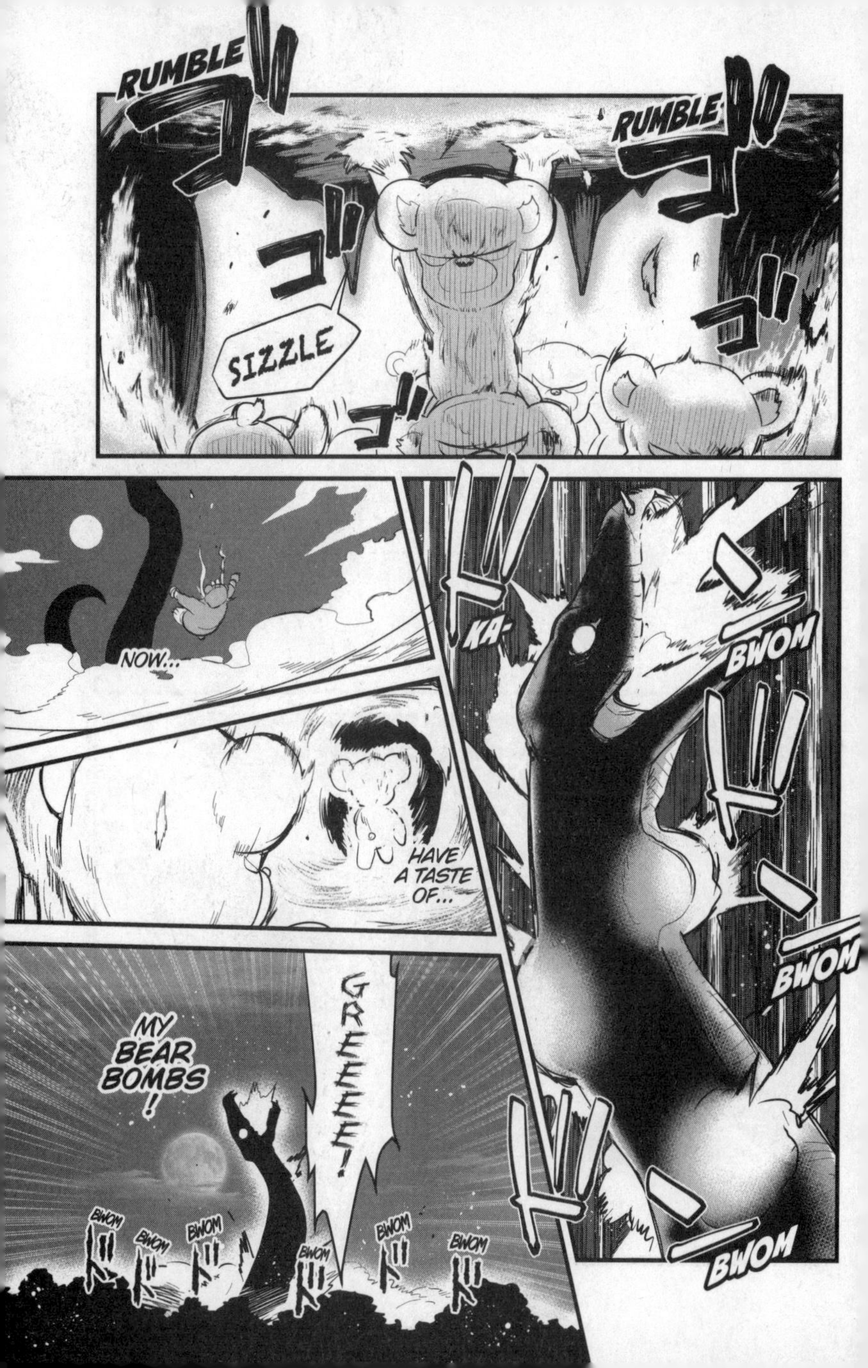
RUMBLE
RUMBLE
SIZZLE
KA-
BWOM
BWOM
BWOM
NOW...
HAVE A TASTE OF...
MY BEAR BOMBS!
GREEEEE!
BWOM
BWOM
BWOM
BWOM
BWOM
BWOM

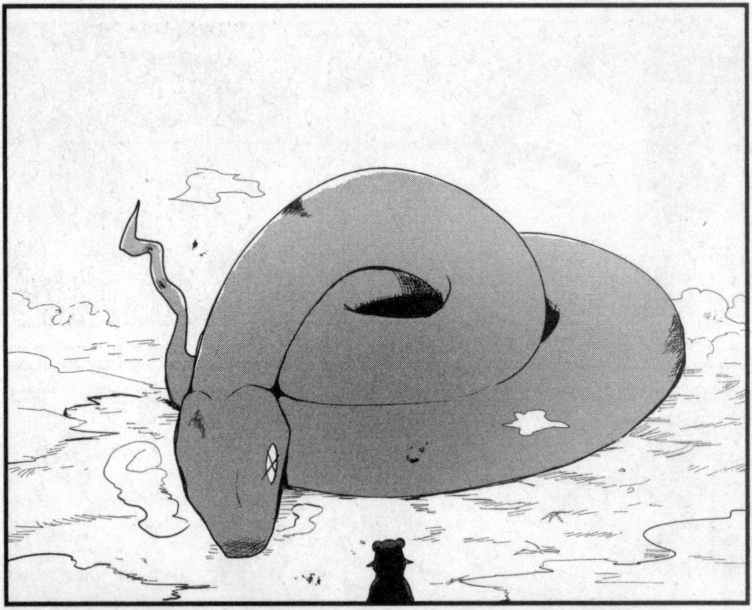

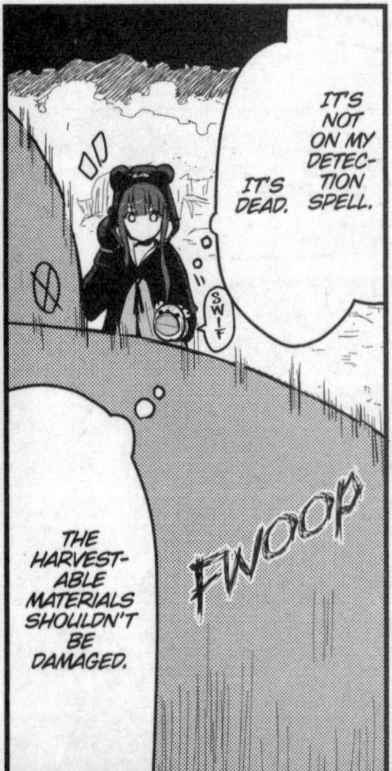
IT'S NOT ON MY DETECTION SPELL.
IT'S DEAD.
SWIF
FWOOP
THE HARVESTABLE MATERIALS SHOULDN'T BE DAMAGED.

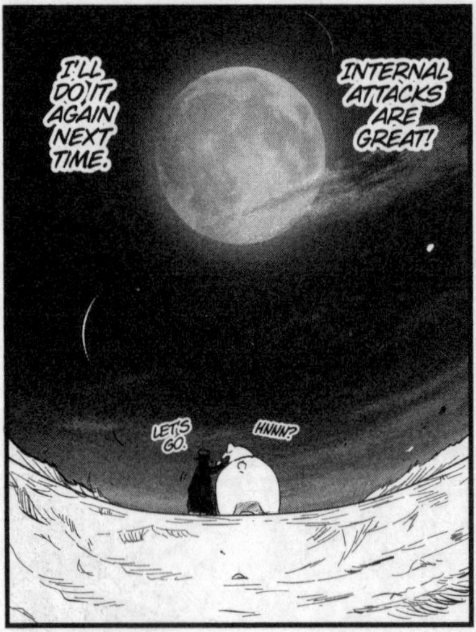
INTERNAL ATTACKS ARE GREAT!
I'LL DO IT AGAIN NEXT TIME.
HNNN?
LET'S GO.

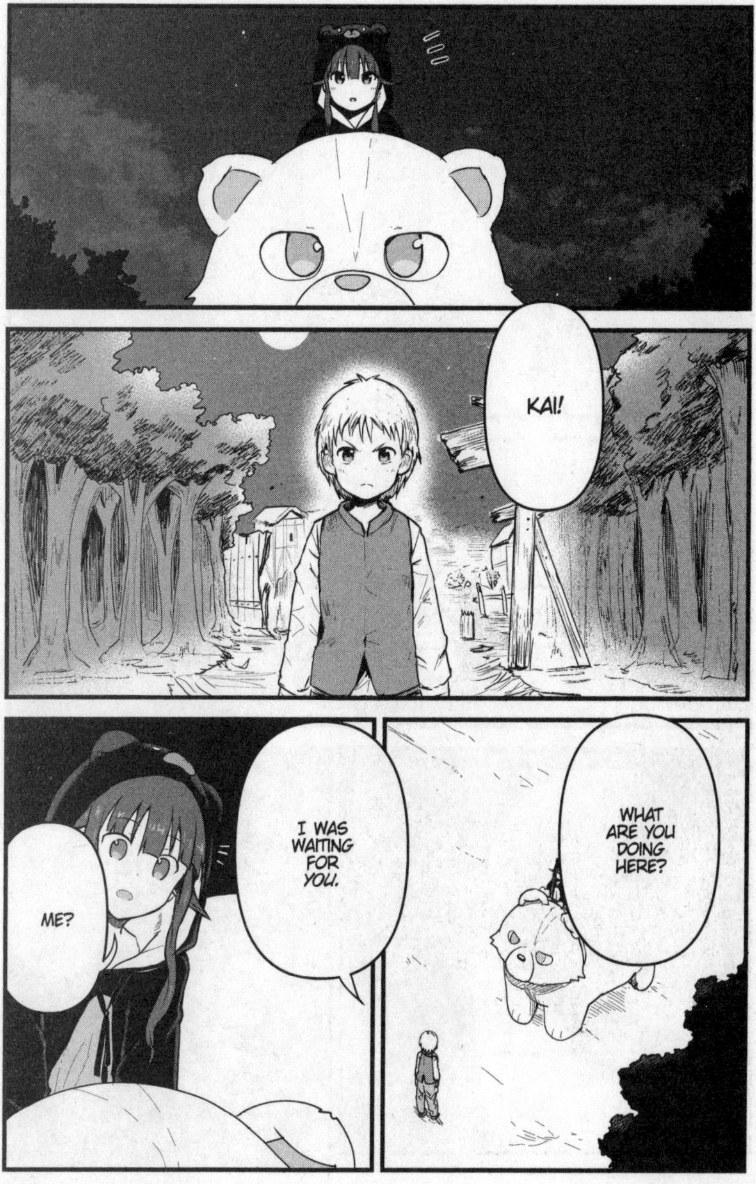
KAI!
WHAT ARE YOU DOING HERE?
I WAS WAITING FOR YOU.
ME?

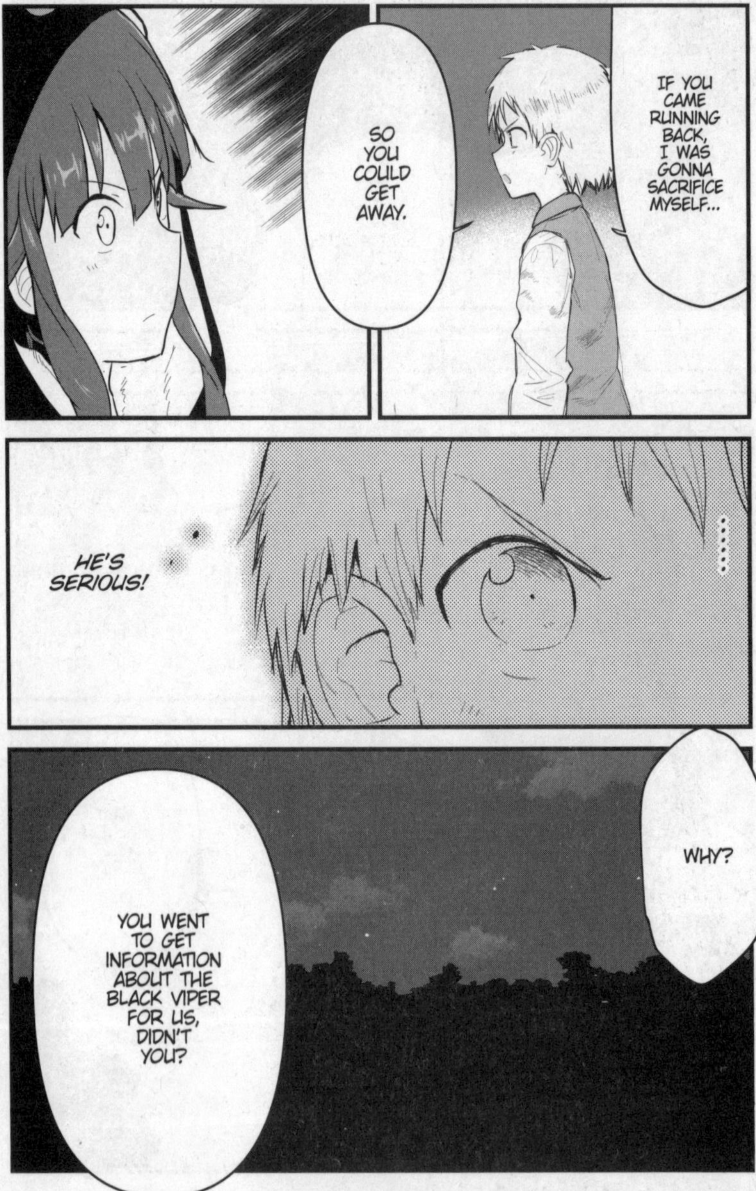
IF YOU CAME RUNNING BACK, I WAS GONNA SACRIFICE MYSELF...
SO YOU COULD GET AWAY.
......
HE'S SERIOUS!
WHY?
YOU WENT TO GET INFORMATION ABOUT THE BLACK VIPER FOR US, DIDN'T YOU?

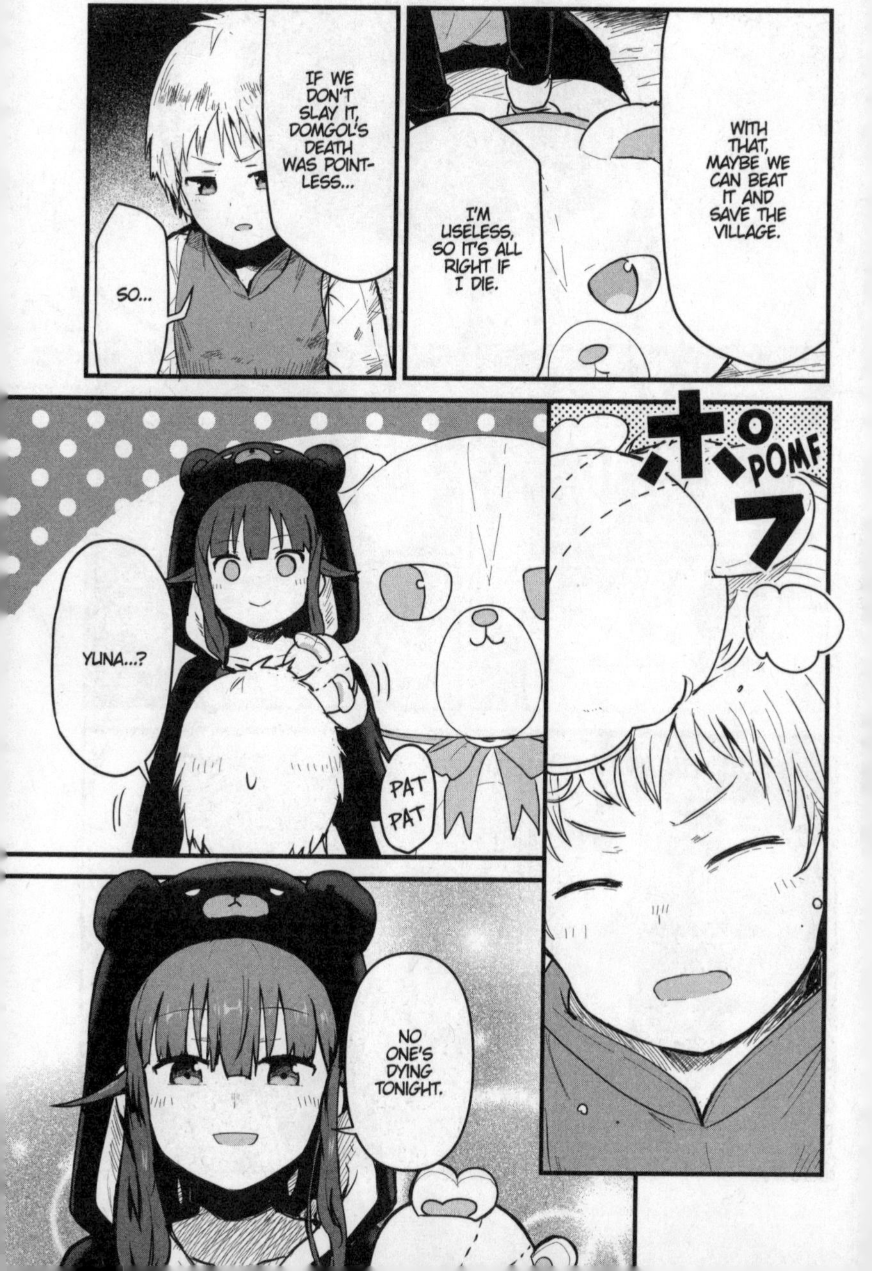
WITH THAT, MAYBE WE CAN BEAT IT AND SAVE THE VILLAGE.
I'M USELESS, SO IT'S ALL RIGHT IF I DIE.
IF WE DON'T SLAY IT, DOMGOL'S DEATH WAS POINTLESS...
SO...
POMF
YUNA...?
PAT PAT
NO ONE'S DYING TONIGHT.

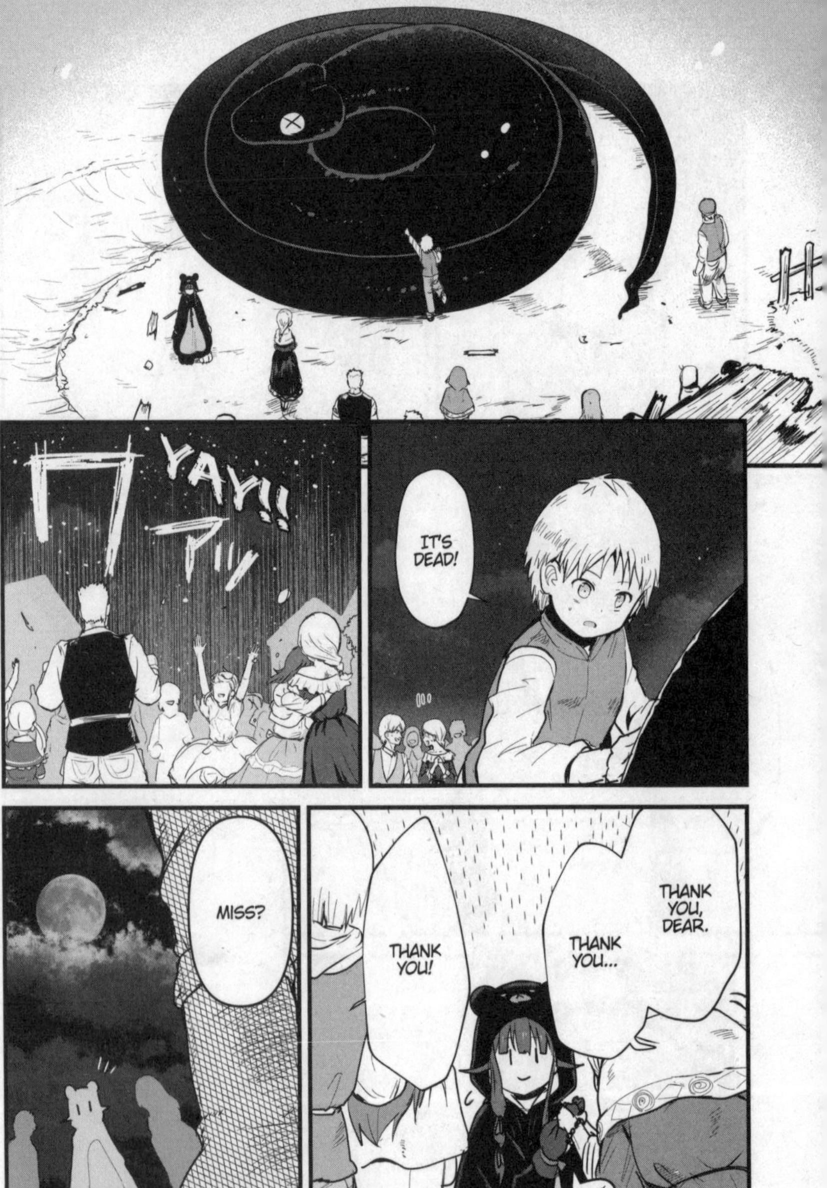
IT'S DEAD!
YAY!!
THANK YOU, DEAR.
THANK YOU...
THANK YOU!
SQUEEZE
MISS?

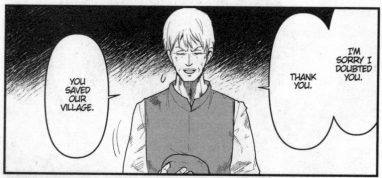

I'M SORRY I DOUBTED YOU.
THANK YOU.
YOU SAVED OUR VILLAGE.
DON'T SWEAT IT.
NO ONE WOULD EXPECT A GIRL DRESSED LIKE ME TO TAKE DOWN A MONSTER LIKE THAT.
IF THERE'S ANYTHING I CAN DO, JUST SAY THE WORD.
I'LL REPAY YOU HOWEVER I CAN.
I DON'T NEED ANY-THING.
BUT ONE THING YOU CAN DO...
PRAISE YOUR SON.
HE'S THE ONE WHO RODE TO CRIMONIA ALONE FOR HELP.

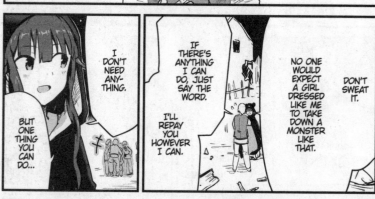

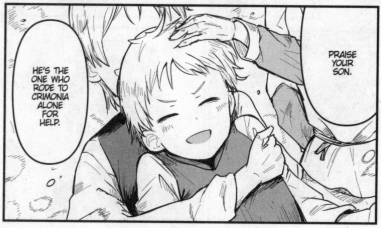

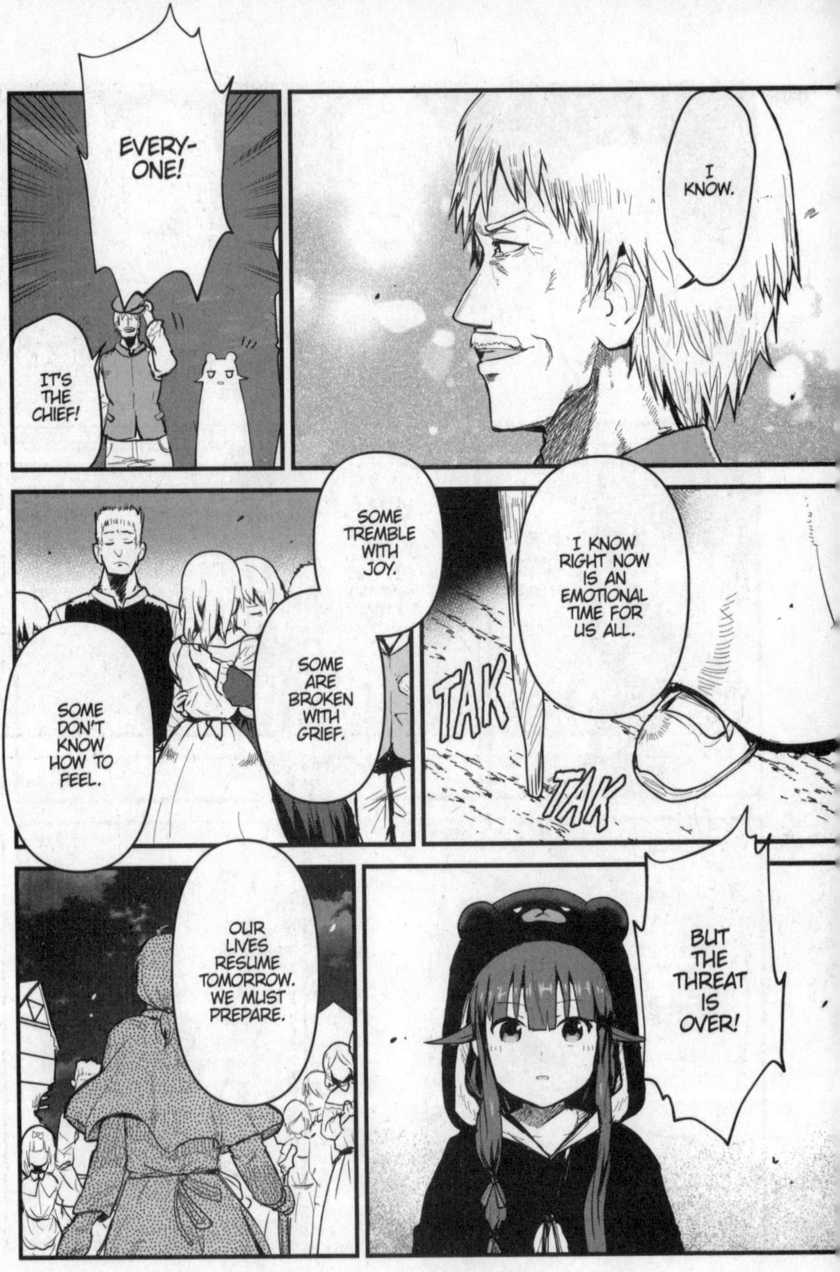
I KNOW.
EVERY-ONE!
IT'S THE CHIEF!
I KNOW RIGHT NOW IS AN EMOTIONAL TIME FOR US ALL.
TAK
TAK
SOME TREMBLE WITH JOY.
SOME ARE BROKEN WITH GRIEF.
SOME DON'T KNOW HOW TO FEEL.
BUT THE THREAT IS OVER!
OUR LIVES RESUME TOMORROW. WE MUST PREPARE.

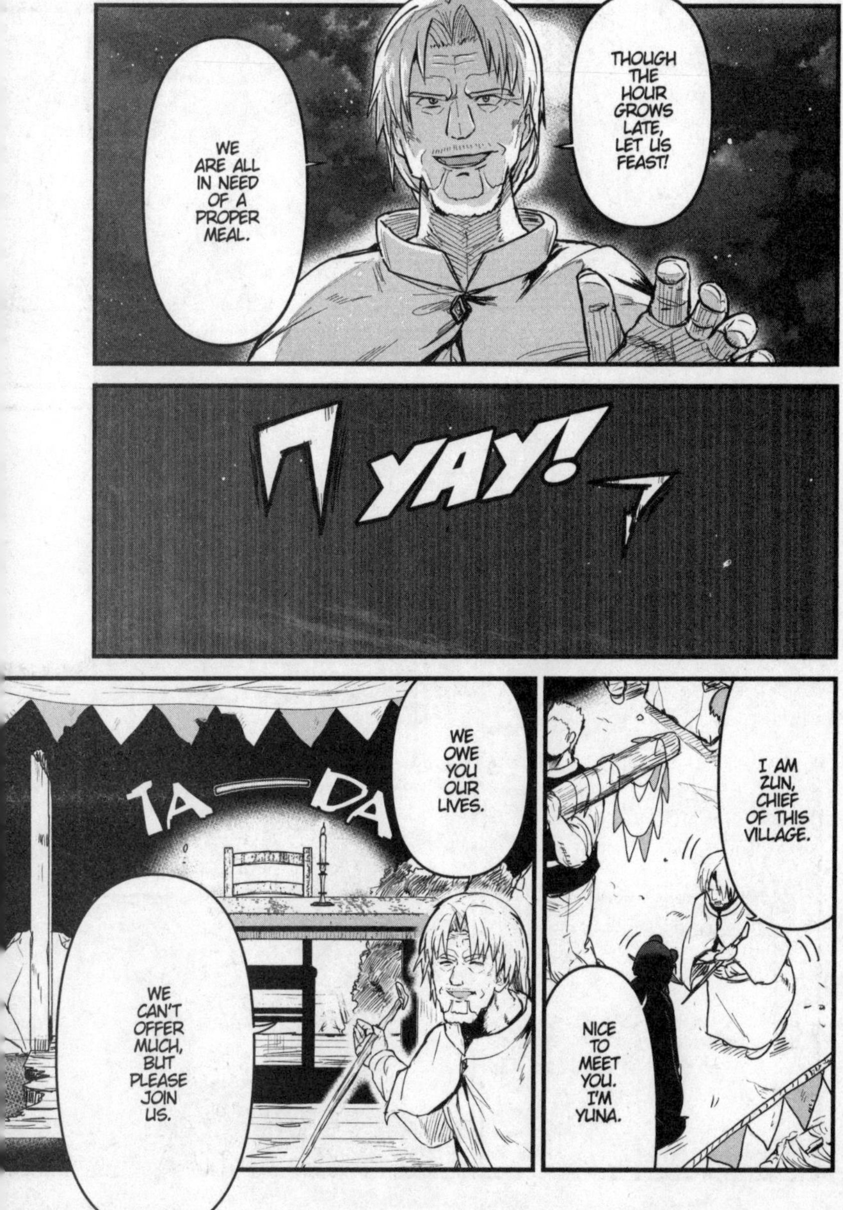
THOUGH THE HOUR GROWS LATE, LET US FEAST!
WE ARE ALL IN NEED OF A PROPER MEAL.
YAY!
I AM ZUN, CHIEF OF THIS VILLAGE.
NICE TO MEET YOU. I'M YUNA.
WE OWE YOU OUR LIVES.
TA—DA
WE CAN'T OFFER MUCH, BUT PLEASE JOIN US.

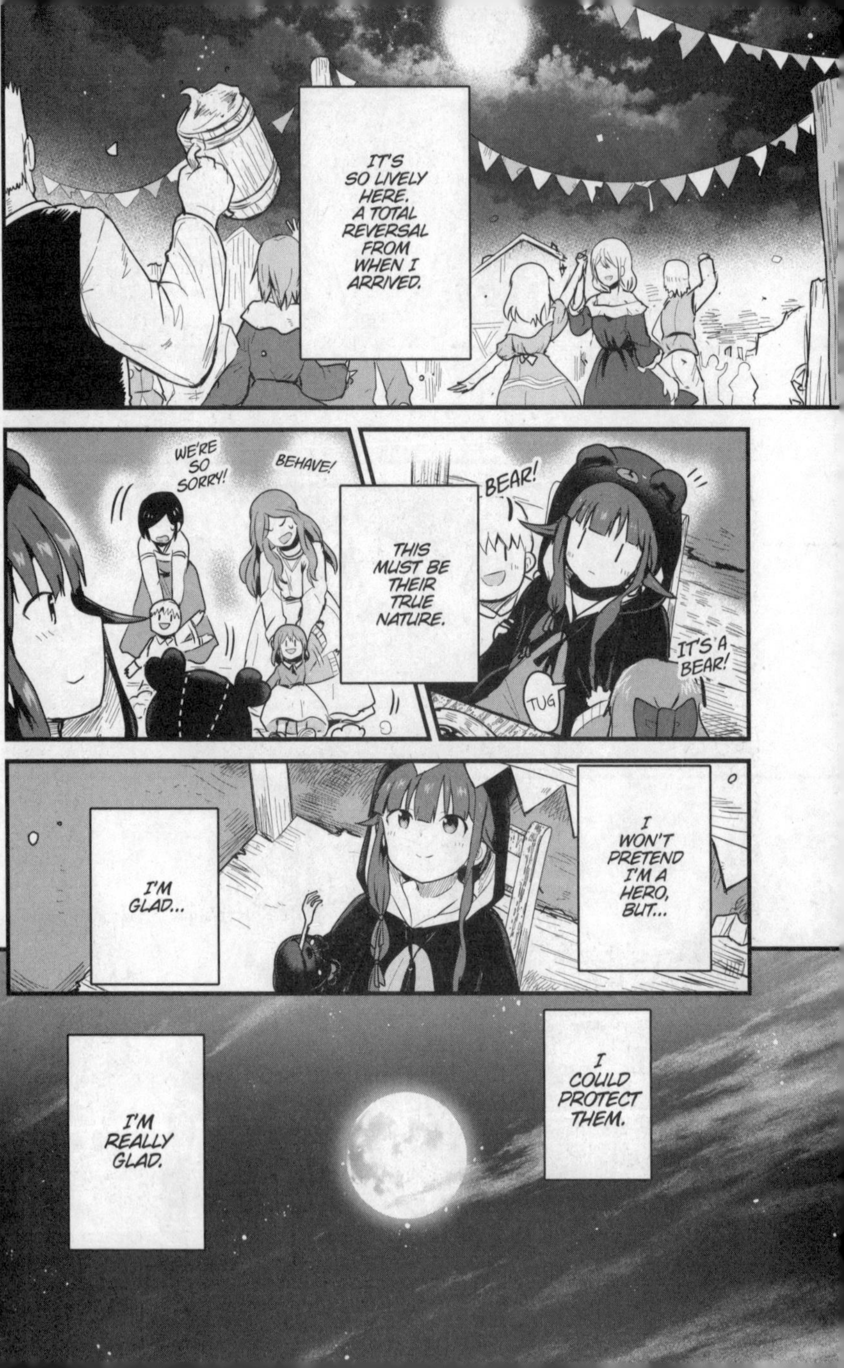
IT'S SO LIVELY HERE. A TOTAL REVERSAL FROM WHEN I ARRIVED.
BEAR!
THIS MUST BE THEIR TRUE NATURE.
IT'S A BEAR!
TUG
BEHAVE!
WE'RE SO SORRY!
I WON'T PRETEND I'M A HERO, BUT...
I'M GLAD...
I COULD PROTECT THEM.
I'M REALLY GLAD.

Chapter 27

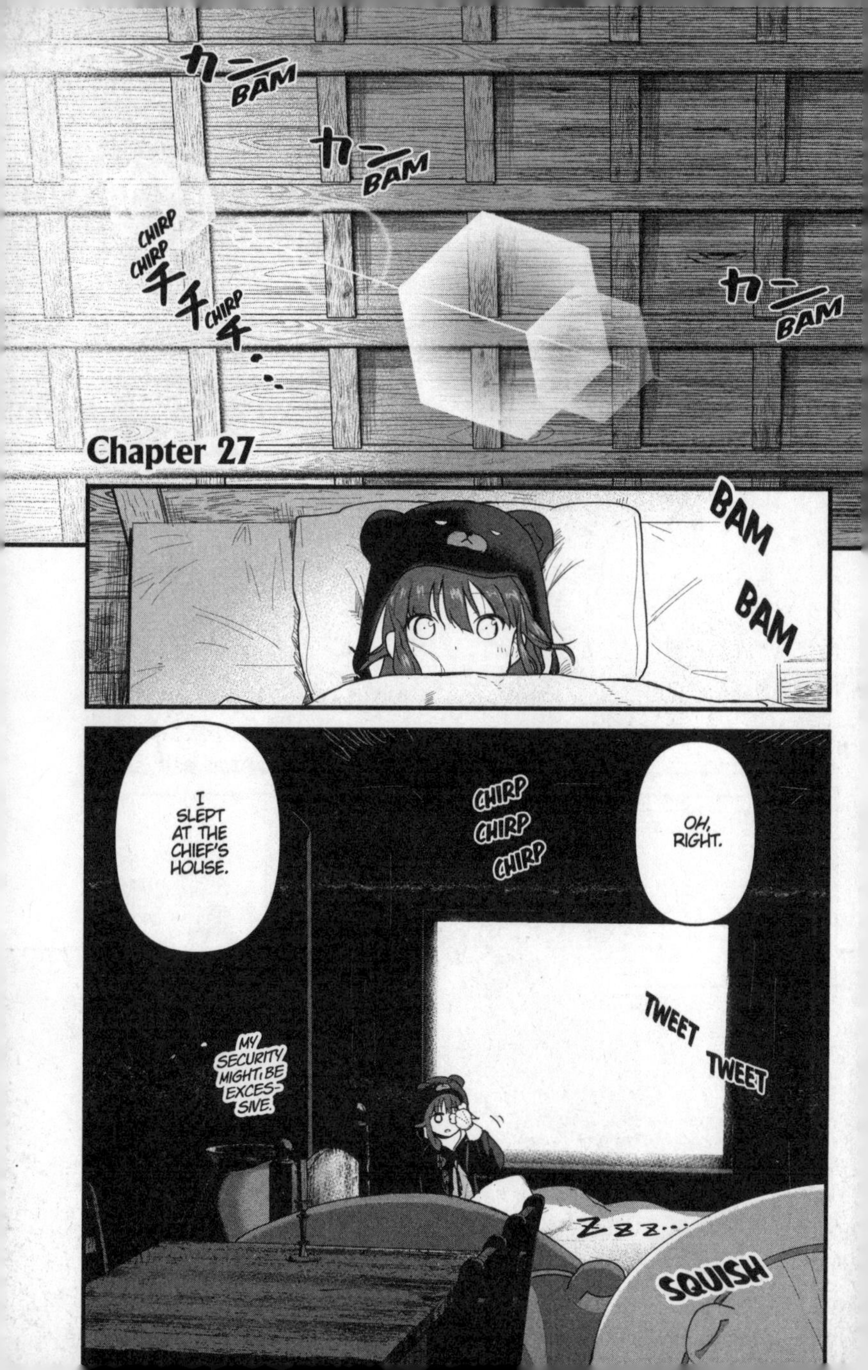
カー BAM
カー BAM
カー BAM
CHIRP CHIRP チチ CHIRP チ...
BAM BAM
OH, RIGHT.
CHIRP CHIRP CHIRP
I SLEPT AT THE CHIEF'S HOUSE.
TWEET TWEET
MY SECURITY MIGHT BE EXCES-SIVE.
Z z z...
SQUISH

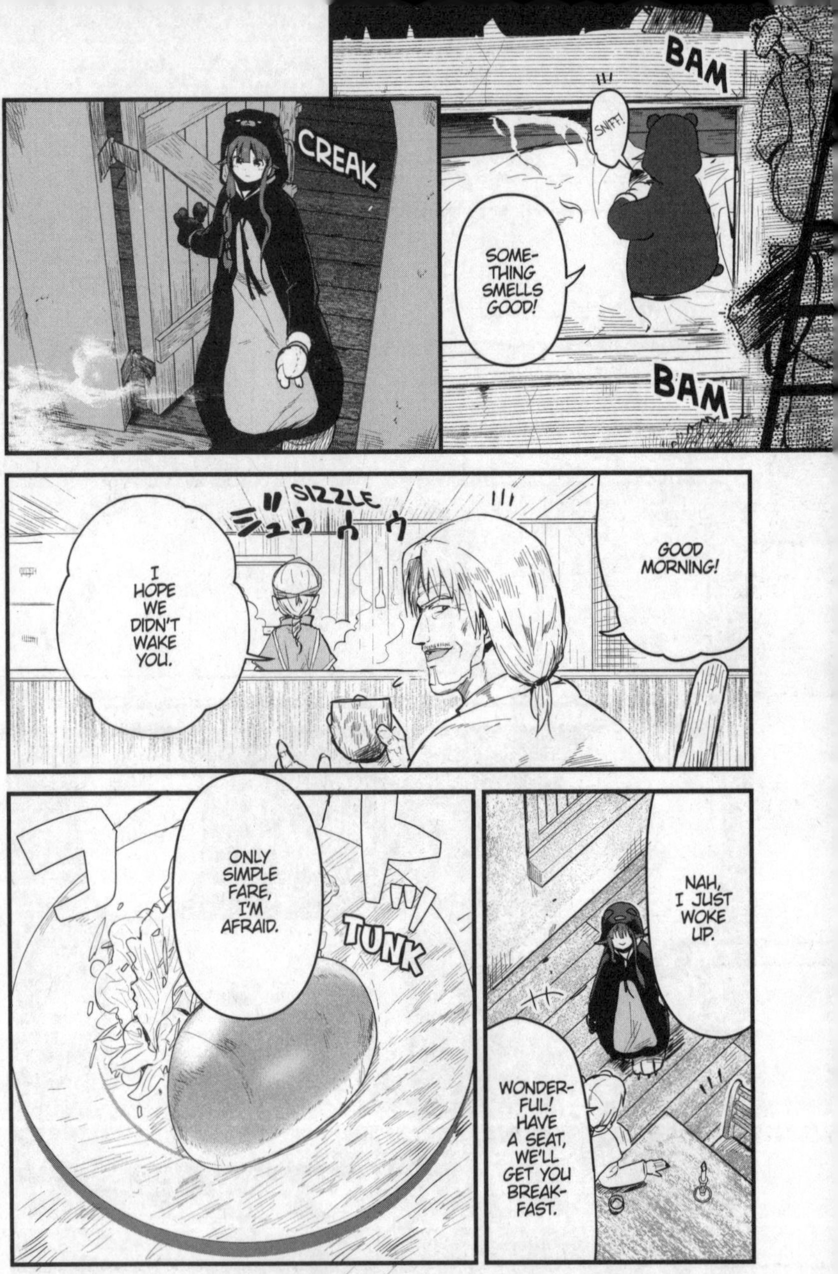
BAM
SNIFF!
SOMETHING SMELLS GOOD!
BAM
CREAK
GOOD MORNING!
SIZZLE
I HOPE WE DIDN'T WAKE YOU.
NAH, I JUST WOKE UP.
WONDERFUL! HAVE A SEAT, WE'LL GET YOU BREAKFAST.
ONLY SIMPLE FARE, I'M AFRAID.
TUNK

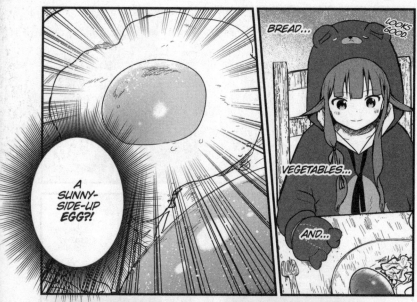

BREAD...
LOOKS GOOD.
VEGETABLES...
AND...
A SUNNY-SIDE-UP EGG?!
SORRY, BUT... WHAT'S THIS?
THAT'S A KOKEKKO EGG!
KAI'S FATHER WENT INTO THE FOREST FOR THEM THIS MORNING.
HE INSISTED YOU TRY THEM.
MM!
DELICIOUS!

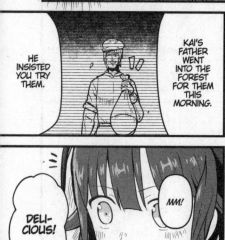

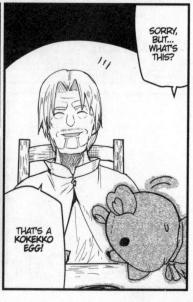

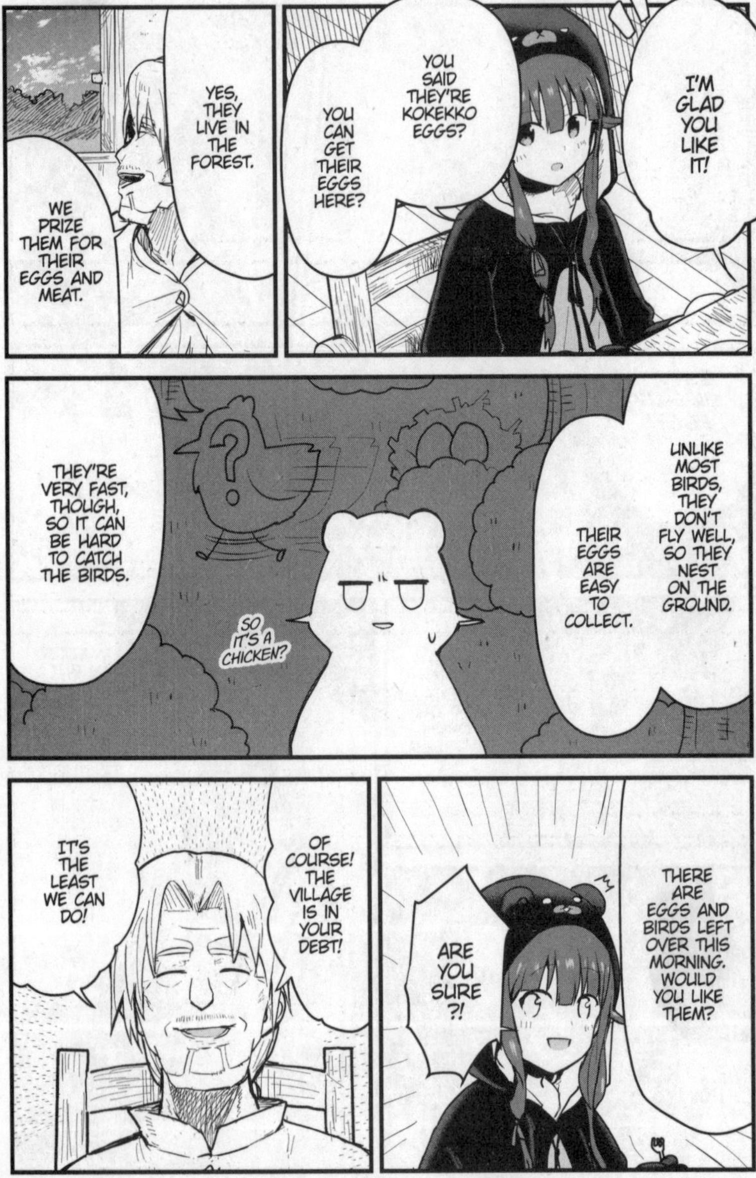
I'M GLAD YOU LIKE IT!
YOU SAID THEY'RE KOKEKKO EGGS?
YOU CAN GET THEIR EGGS HERE?
YES, THEY LIVE IN THE FOREST.
WE PRIZE THEM FOR THEIR EGGS AND MEAT.
UNLIKE MOST BIRDS, THEY DON'T FLY WELL, SO THEY NEST ON THE GROUND.
THEIR EGGS ARE EASY TO COLLECT.
SO IT'S A CHICKEN?
THEY'RE VERY FAST, THOUGH, SO IT CAN BE HARD TO CATCH THE BIRDS.
THERE ARE EGGS AND BIRDS LEFT OVER THIS MORNING. WOULD YOU LIKE THEM?
ARE YOU SURE?!
OF COURSE! THE VILLAGE IS IN YOUR DEBT!
IT'S THE LEAST WE CAN DO!

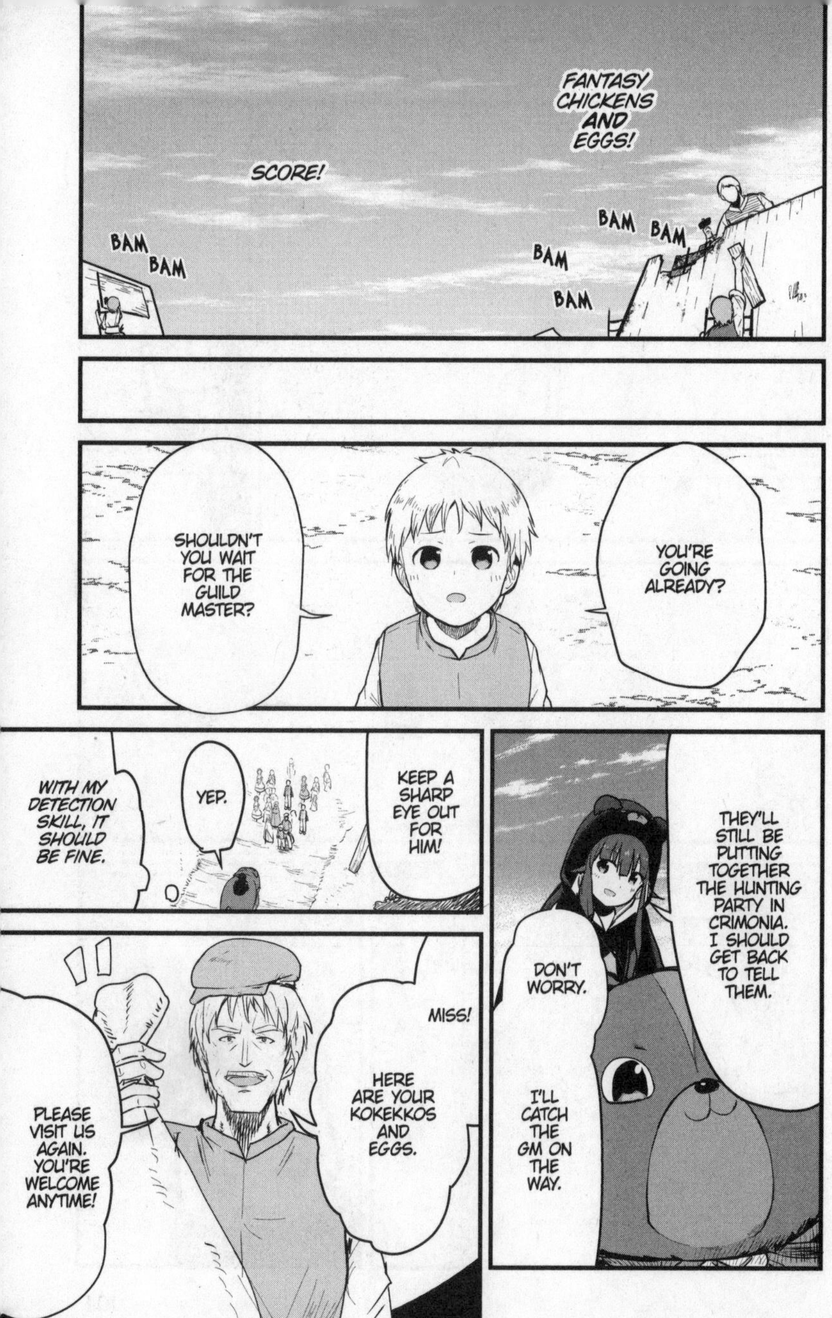
FANTASY CHICKENS AND EGGS!
BAM BAM
BAM
BAM
SCORE!
BAM BAM
YOU'RE GOING ALREADY?
SHOULDN'T YOU WAIT FOR THE GUILD MASTER?
THEY'LL STILL BE PUTTING TOGETHER THE HUNTING PARTY IN CRIMONIA. I SHOULD GET BACK TO TELL THEM.
DON'T WORRY.
I'LL CATCH THE GM ON THE WAY.
KEEP A SHARP EYE OUT FOR HIM!
YEP.
WITH MY DETECTION SKILL, IT SHOULD BE FINE.
MISS!
HERE ARE YOUR KOKEKKOS AND EGGS.
PLEASE VISIT US AGAIN. YOU'RE WELCOME ANYTIME!

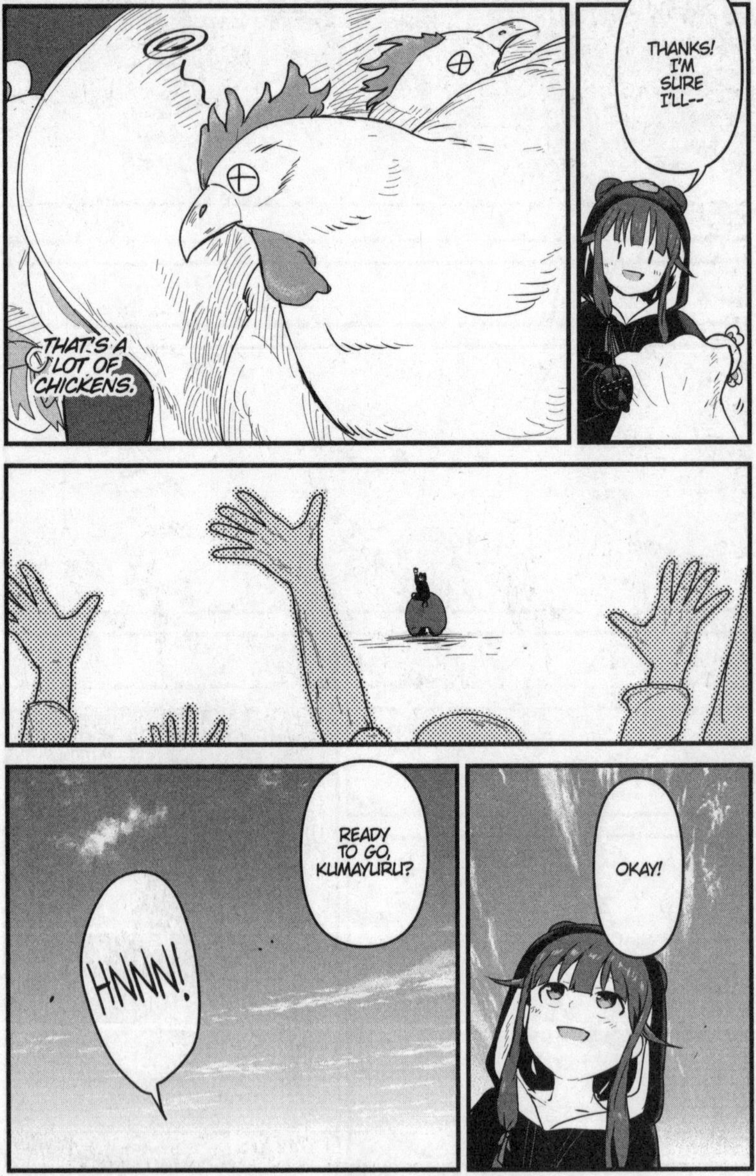
THANKS! I'M SURE I'LL--
THAT'S A LOT OF CHICKENS.
OKAY!
READY TO GO, KUMAYURU?
HNNN!

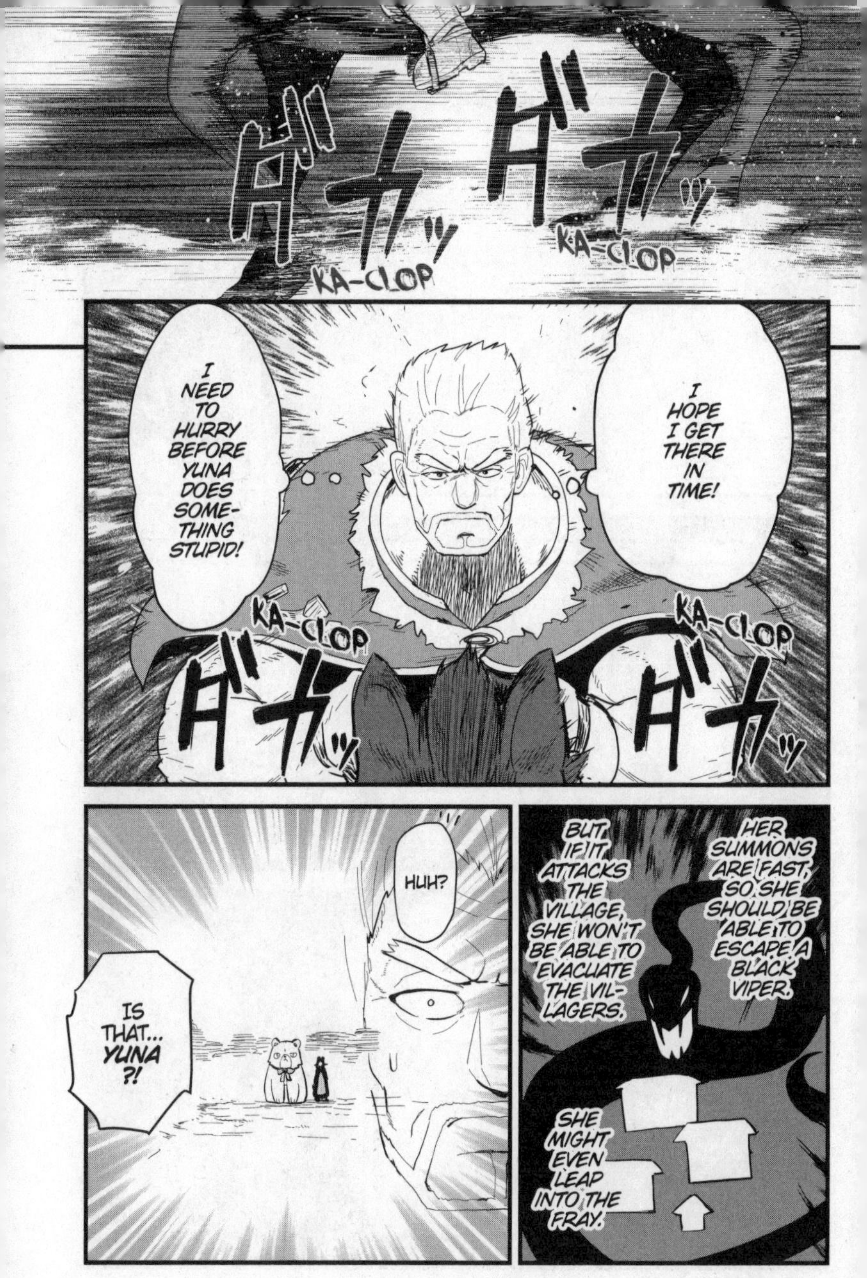
KA-CLOP
KA-CLOP
I HOPE I GET THERE IN TIME!
I NEED TO HURRY BEFORE YUNA DOES SOMETHING STUPID!
KA-CLOP
KA-CLOP
HER SUMMONS ARE FAST, SO SHE SHOULD BE ABLE TO ESCAPE A BLACK VIPER.
BUT IF IT ATTACKS THE VILLAGE, SHE WON'T BE ABLE TO EVACUATE THE VILLAGERS.
SHE MIGHT EVEN LEAP INTO THE FRAY.
HUH?
IS THAT... YUNA?!

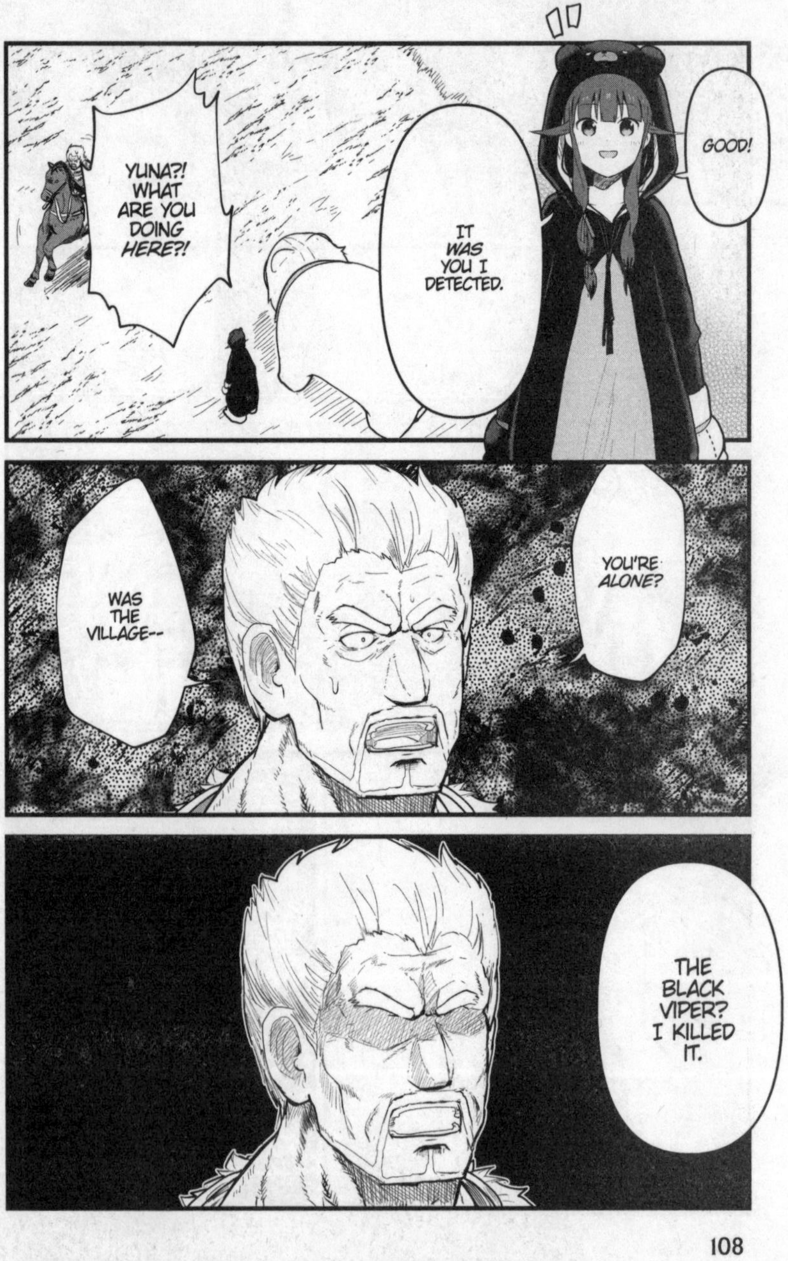
GOOD!
IT WAS YOU I DETECTED.
YUNA?! WHAT ARE YOU DOING HERE?!
YOU'RE ALONE?
WAS THE VILLAGE--
THE BLACK VIPER? I KILLED IT.

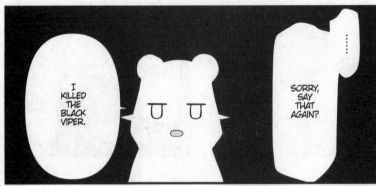

......
SORRY, SAY THAT AGAIN?
I KILLED THE BLACK VIPER.
YOU'RE JOKING!
THOMP
PAH
SEE FOR YOUR-SELF.
EXTERNAL ATTACKS WEREN'T EFFECTIVE, SO I THREW FIRE INTO ITS MOUTH AND COOKED IT FROM INSIDE.
THAT'S... IT?

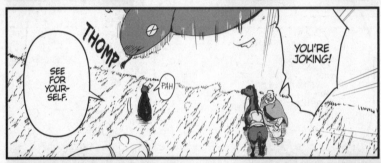

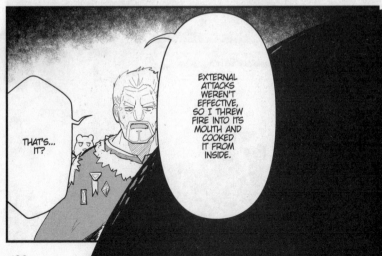

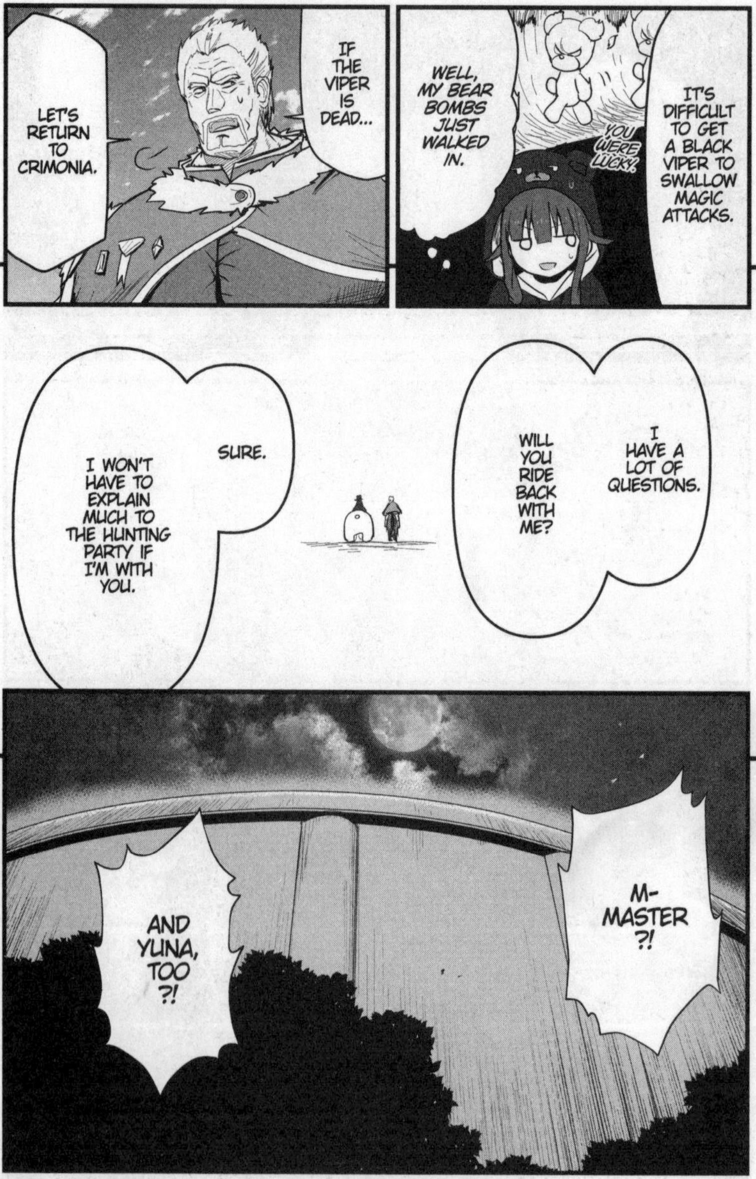
IT'S DIFFICULT TO GET A BLACK VIPER TO SWALLOW MAGIC ATTACKS.
YOU WERE LUCKY!
WELL, MY BEAR BOMBS JUST WALKED IN.
IF THE VIPER IS DEAD...
LET'S RETURN TO CRIMONIA.
I HAVE A LOT OF QUESTIONS.
WILL YOU RIDE BACK WITH ME?
SURE.
I WON'T HAVE TO EXPLAIN MUCH TO THE HUNTING PARTY IF I'M WITH YOU.
M-MASTER?!
AND YUNA, TOO?!

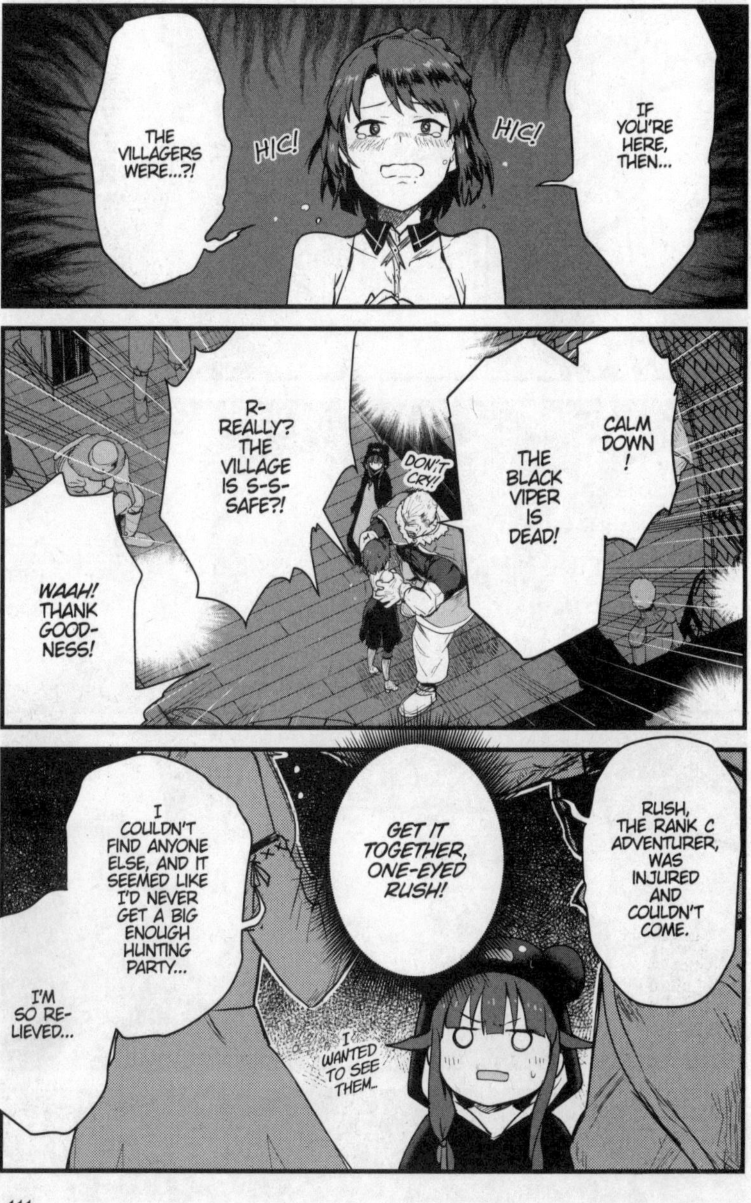
IF YOU'RE HERE, THEN...
HIC!
HIC!
THE VILLAGERS WERE...?!
CALM DOWN!
THE BLACK VIPER IS DEAD!
DON'T CRY!
R-REALLY? THE VILLAGE IS S-S-SAFE?!
WAAH! THANK GOOD-NESS!
RUSH, THE RANK C ADVENTURER, WAS INJURED AND COULDN'T COME.
GET IT TOGETHER, ONE-EYED RUSH!
I COULDN'T FIND ANYONE ELSE, AND IT SEEMED LIKE I'D NEVER GET A BIG ENOUGH HUNTING PARTY...
I WANTED TO SEE THEM...
I'M SO RE-LIEVED...

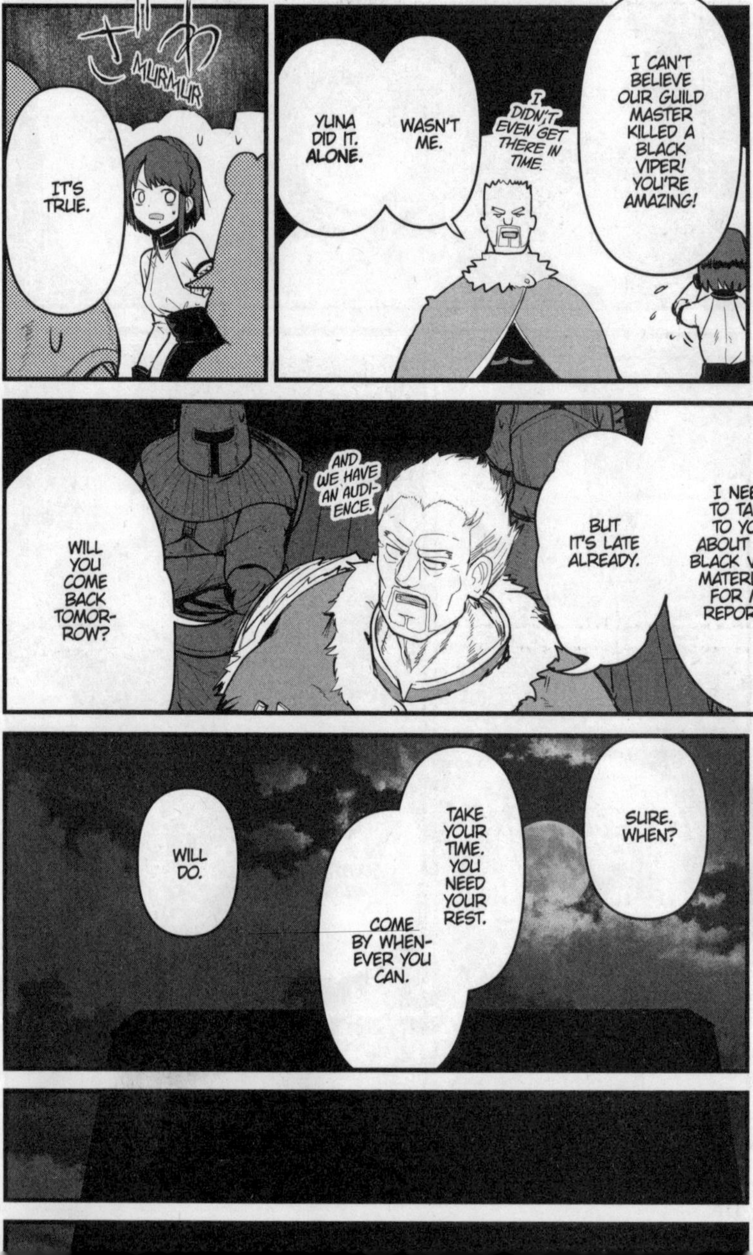
I CAN'T BELIEVE OUR GUILD MASTER KILLED A BLACK VIPER! YOU'RE AMAZING!
I DIDN'T EVEN GET THERE IN TIME.
WASN'T ME.
YUNA DID IT. ALONE.
MURMUR
IT'S TRUE.
I NEED TO TALK TO YOU ABOUT THE BLACK VIPER MATERIALS FOR MY REPORT...
BUT IT'S LATE ALREADY.
AND WE HAVE AN AUDIENCE.
WILL YOU COME BACK TOMORROW?
SURE. WHEN?
TAKE YOUR TIME. YOU NEED YOUR REST.
COME BY WHENEVER YOU CAN.
WILL DO.

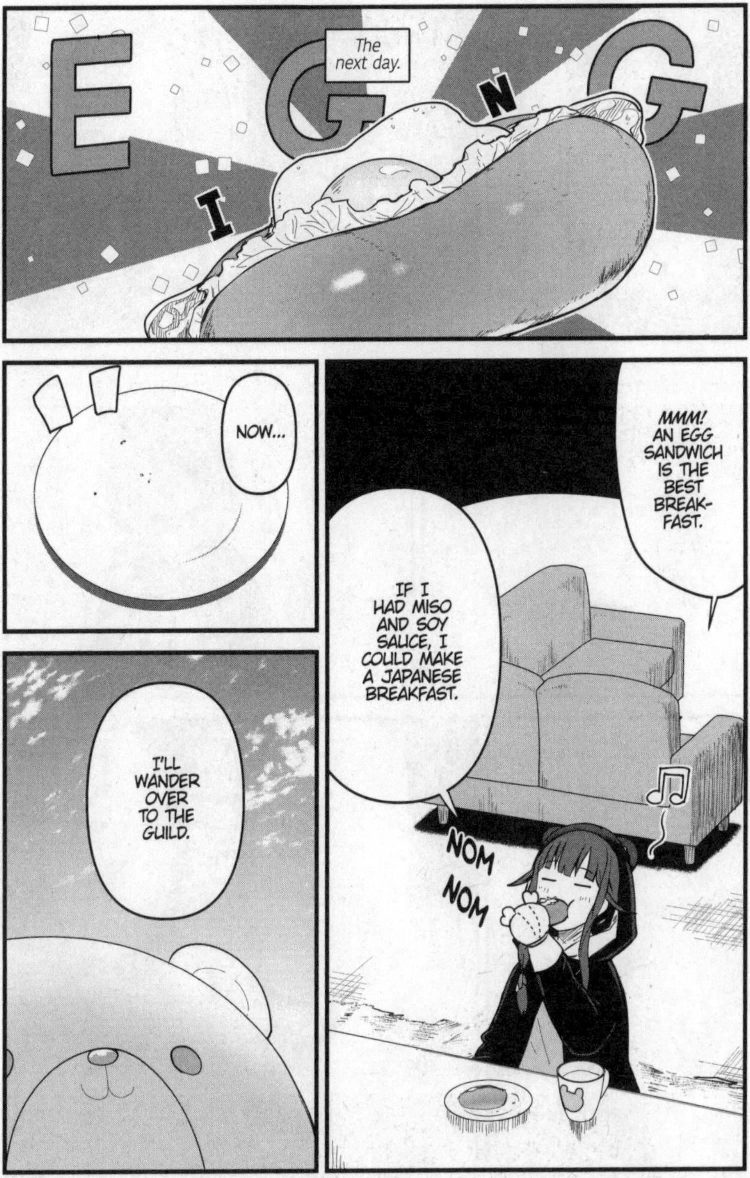
The next day.
E G I N G
MMM! AN EGG SANDWICH IS THE BEST BREAKFAST.
IF I HAD MISO AND SOY SAUCE, I COULD MAKE A JAPANESE BREAKFAST.
NOM NOM
NOW...
I'LL WANDER OVER TO THE GUILD.

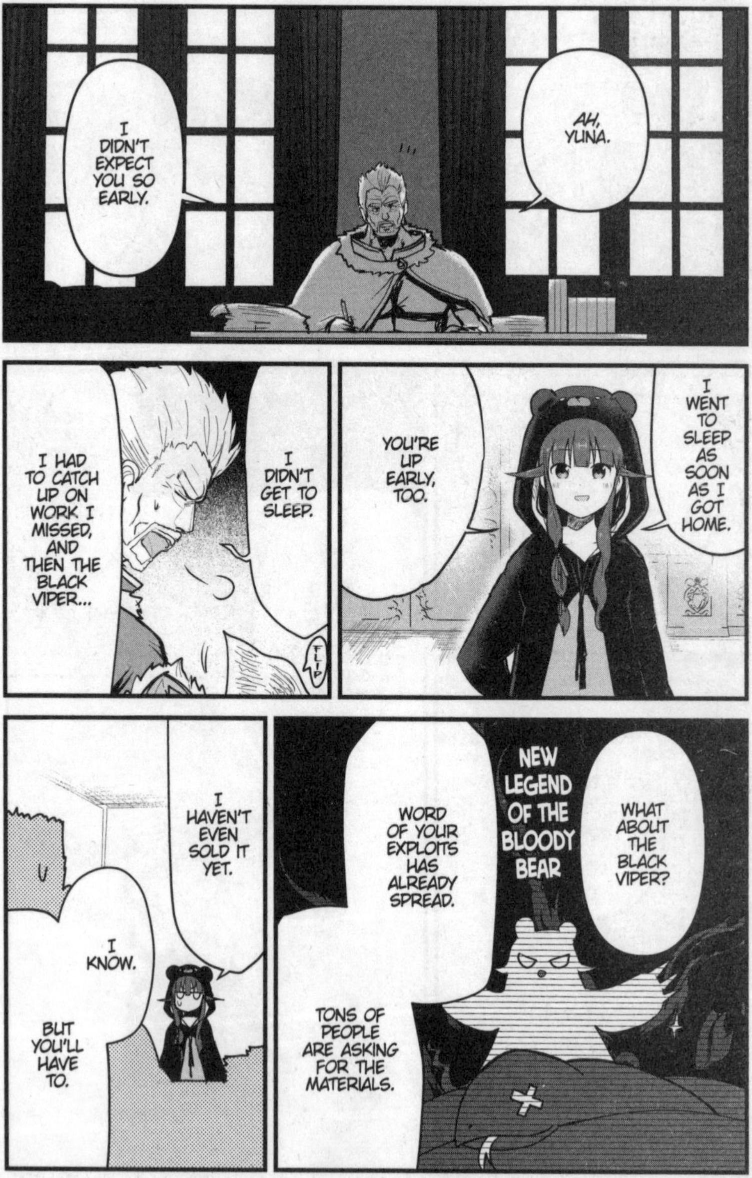
AH, YUNA.
I DIDN'T EXPECT YOU SO EARLY.
I WENT TO SLEEP AS SOON AS I GOT HOME.
YOU'RE UP EARLY, TOO.
I DIDN'T GET TO SLEEP.
I HAD TO CATCH UP ON WORK I MISSED, AND THEN THE BLACK VIPER...
FLIP
WHAT ABOUT THE BLACK VIPER?
NEW LEGEND OF THE BLOODY BEAR
WORD OF YOUR EXPLOITS HAS ALREADY SPREAD.
TONS OF PEOPLE ARE ASKING FOR THE MATERIALS.
I HAVEN'T EVEN SOLD IT YET.
I KNOW.
BUT YOU'LL HAVE TO.

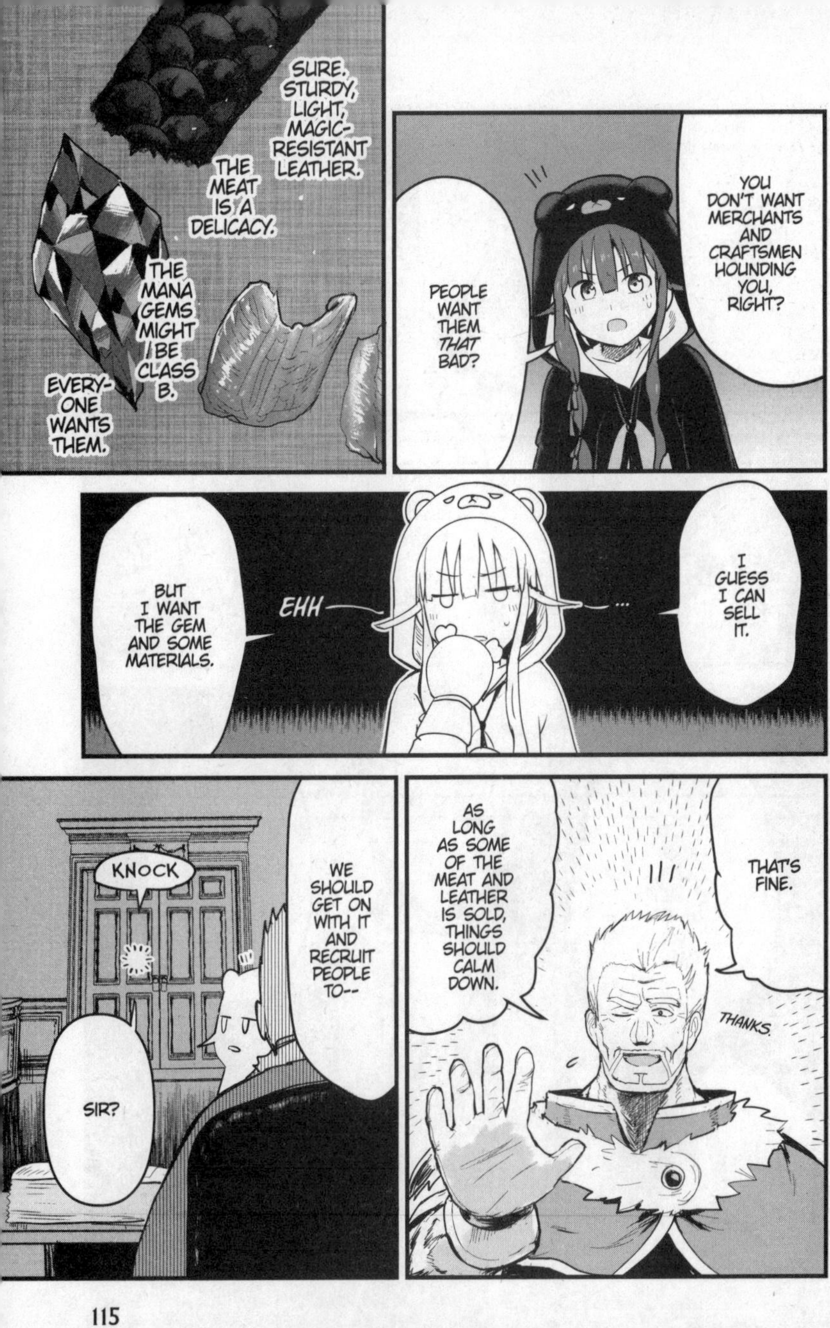
YOU DON'T WANT MERCHANTS AND CRAFTSMEN HOUNDING YOU, RIGHT?
PEOPLE WANT THEM *THAT* BAD?
SURE. STURDY, LIGHT, MAGIC-RESISTANT LEATHER.
THE MEAT IS A DELICACY.
THE MANA GEMS MIGHT BE CLASS B.
EVERY-ONE WANTS THEM.
I GUESS I CAN SELL IT.
...
EHH
BUT I WANT THE GEM AND SOME MATERIALS.
THAT'S FINE.
THANKS.
AS LONG AS SOME OF THE MEAT AND LEATHER IS SOLD, THINGS SHOULD CALM DOWN.
WE SHOULD GET ON WITH IT AND RECRUIT PEOPLE TO--
KNOCK
SIR?

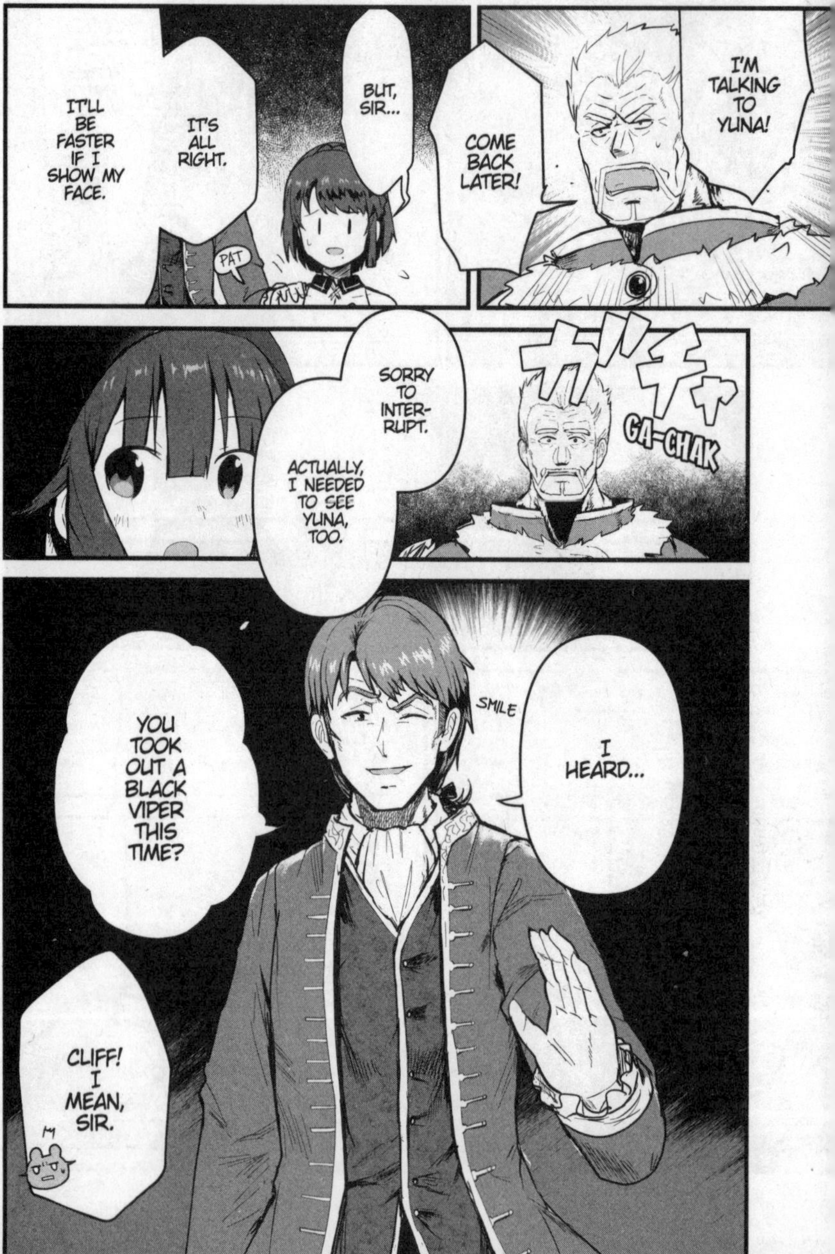
I'M TALKING TO YUNA!
COME BACK LATER!
BUT, SIR...
IT'S ALL RIGHT.
IT'LL BE FASTER IF I SHOW MY FACE.
PAT
ガチャ
GA-CHAK
SORRY TO INTER-RUPT.
ACTUALLY, I NEEDED TO SEE YUNA, TOO.
I HEARD...
SMILE
YOU TOOK OUT A BLACK VIPER THIS TIME?
CLIFF! I MEAN, SIR.

Chapter 28

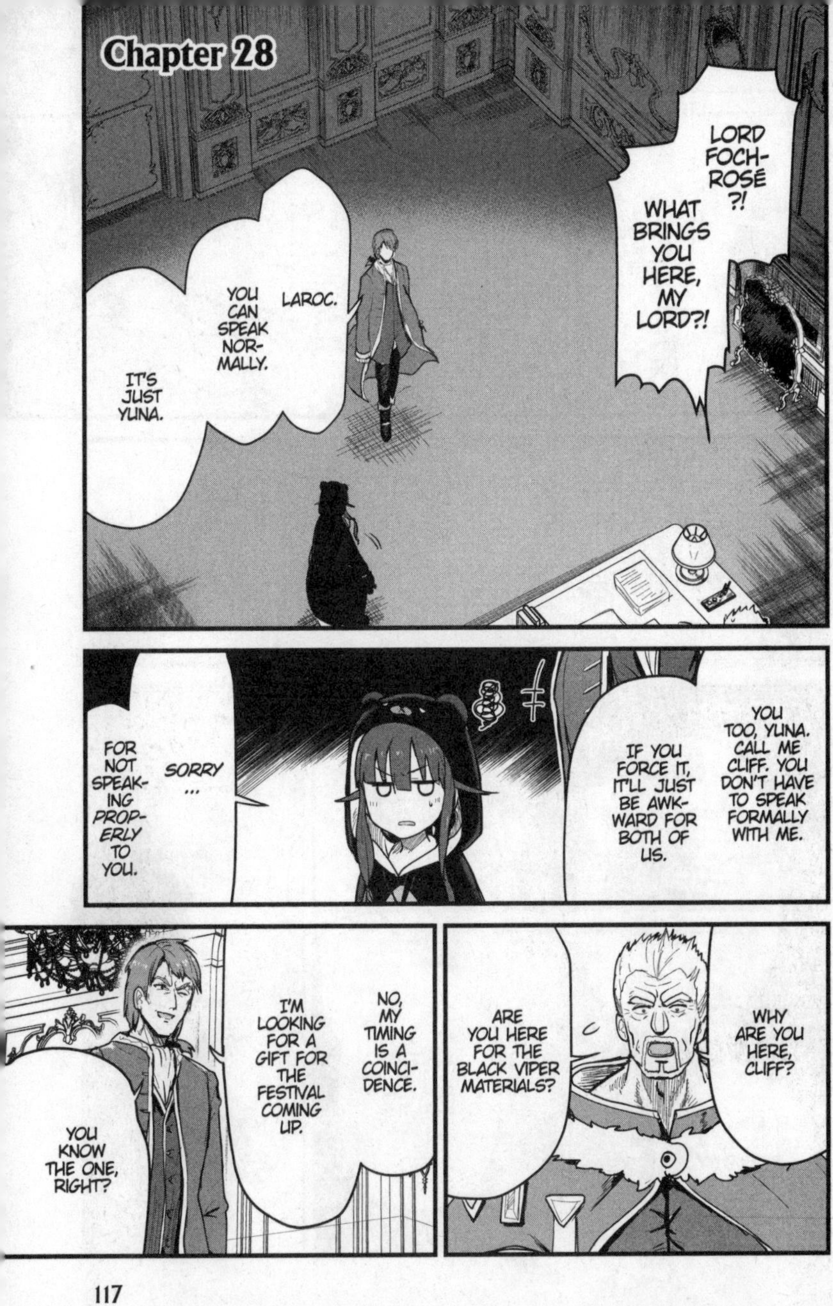
LORD FOCH-ROSÉ?!
WHAT BRINGS YOU HERE, MY LORD?!
LAROC.
YOU CAN SPEAK NORMALLY.
IT'S JUST YUNA.
YOU TOO, YUNA. CALL ME CLIFF. YOU DON'T HAVE TO SPEAK FORMALLY WITH ME.
IF YOU FORCE IT, IT'LL JUST BE AWKWARD FOR BOTH OF US.
SORRY...
FOR NOT SPEAKING PROPERLY TO YOU.
WHY ARE YOU HERE, CLIFF?
ARE YOU HERE FOR THE BLACK VIPER MATERIALS?
NO, MY TIMING IS A COINCIDENCE.
I'M LOOKING FOR A GIFT FOR THE FESTIVAL COMING UP.
YOU KNOW THE ONE, RIGHT?

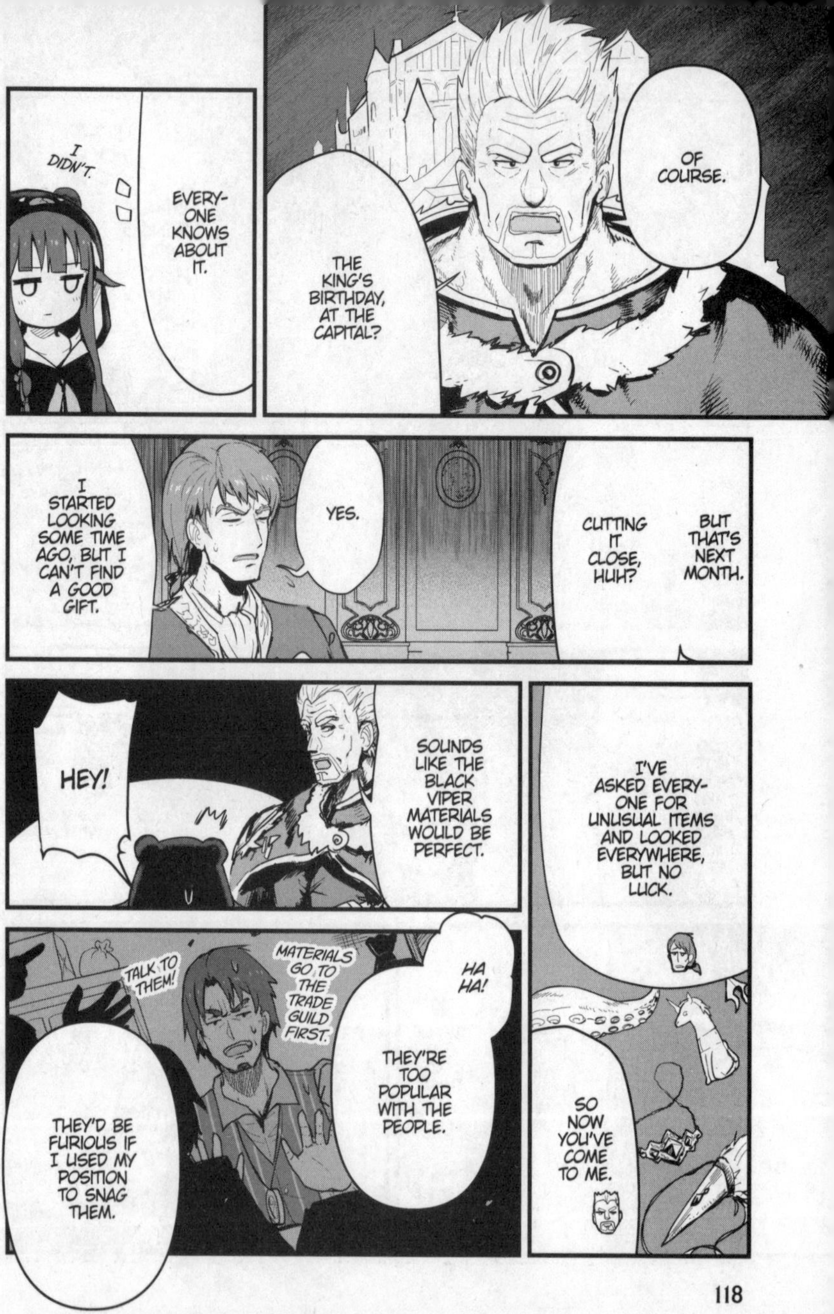

OF COURSE.
THE KING'S BIRTHDAY, AT THE CAPITAL?
EVERY-ONE KNOWS ABOUT IT.
I DIDN'T.
BUT THAT'S NEXT MONTH.
CUTTING IT CLOSE, HUH?
YES.
I STARTED LOOKING SOME TIME AGO, BUT I CAN'T FIND A GOOD GIFT.
I'VE ASKED EVERY-ONE FOR UNUSUAL ITEMS AND LOOKED EVERYWHERE, BUT NO LUCK.
SO NOW YOU'VE COME TO ME.
SOUNDS LIKE THE BLACK VIPER MATERIALS WOULD BE PERFECT.
HEY!
HA HA!
THEY'RE TOO POPULAR WITH THE PEOPLE.
MATERIALS GO TO THE TRADE GUILD FIRST.
TALK TO THEM!
THEY'D BE FURIOUS IF I USED MY POSITION TO SNAG THEM.

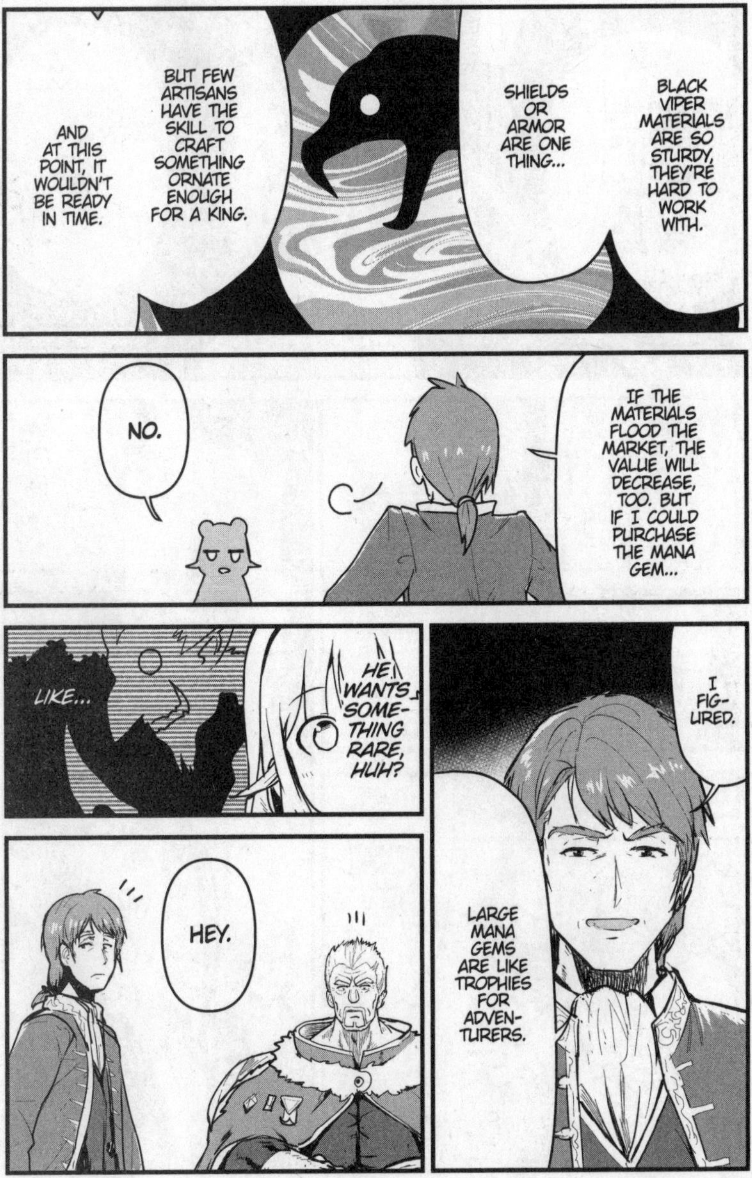
BLACK VIPER MATERIALS ARE SO STURDY, THEY'RE HARD TO WORK WITH.
SHIELDS OR ARMOR ARE ONE THING...
BUT FEW ARTISANS HAVE THE SKILL TO CRAFT SOMETHING ORNATE ENOUGH FOR A KING.
AND AT THIS POINT, IT WOULDN'T BE READY IN TIME.
IF THE MATERIALS FLOOD THE MARKET, THE VALUE WILL DECREASE, TOO. BUT IF I COULD PURCHASE THE MANA GEM...
NO.
I FIG-URED.
LARGE MANA GEMS ARE LIKE TROPHIES FOR ADVEN-TURERS.
HE WANTS SOME-THING RARE, HUH?
LIKE...
HEY.

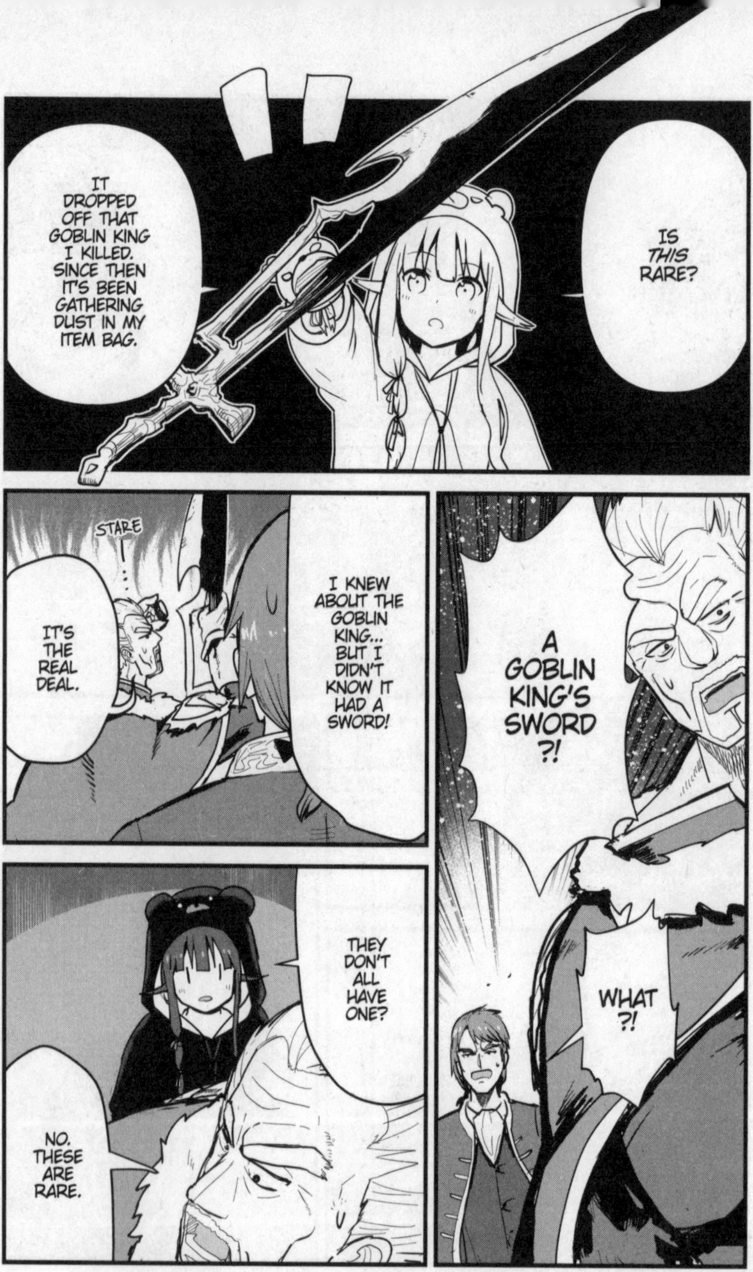
IS THIS RARE?
IT DROPPED OFF THAT GOBLIN KING I KILLED. SINCE THEN IT'S BEEN GATHERING DUST IN MY ITEM BAG.
A GOBLIN KING'S SWORD ?!
WHAT ?!
I KNEW ABOUT THE GOBLIN KING... BUT I DIDN'T KNOW IT HAD A SWORD!
STARE
IT'S THE REAL DEAL.
THEY DON'T ALL HAVE ONE?
NO. THESE ARE RARE.

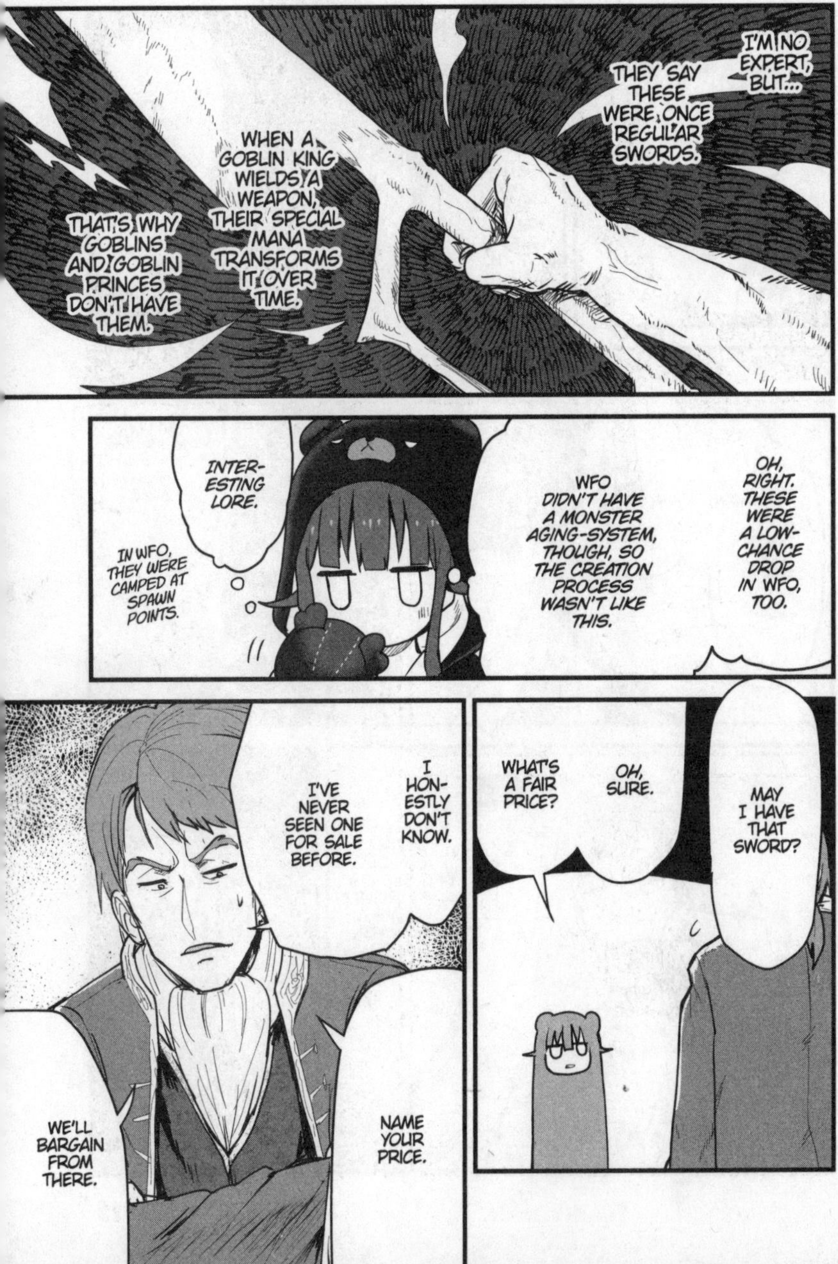
I'M NO EXPERT, BUT...
THEY SAY THESE WERE ONCE REGULAR SWORDS.
WHEN A GOBLIN KING WIELDS A WEAPON, THEIR SPECIAL MANA TRANSFORMS IT OVER TIME.
THAT'S WHY GOBLINS AND GOBLIN PRINCES DON'T HAVE THEM.
OH, RIGHT. THESE WERE A LOW-CHANCE DROP IN WFO, TOO.
WFO DIDN'T HAVE A MONSTER AGING-SYSTEM, THOUGH, SO THE CREATION PROCESS WASN'T LIKE THIS.
INTER-ESTING LORE.
IN WFO, THEY WERE CAMPED AT SPAWN POINTS.
MAY I HAVE THAT SWORD?
OH, SURE.
WHAT'S A FAIR PRICE?
I HON-ESTLY DON'T KNOW.
I'VE NEVER SEEN ONE FOR SALE BEFORE.
NAME YOUR PRICE.
WE'LL BARGAIN FROM THERE.

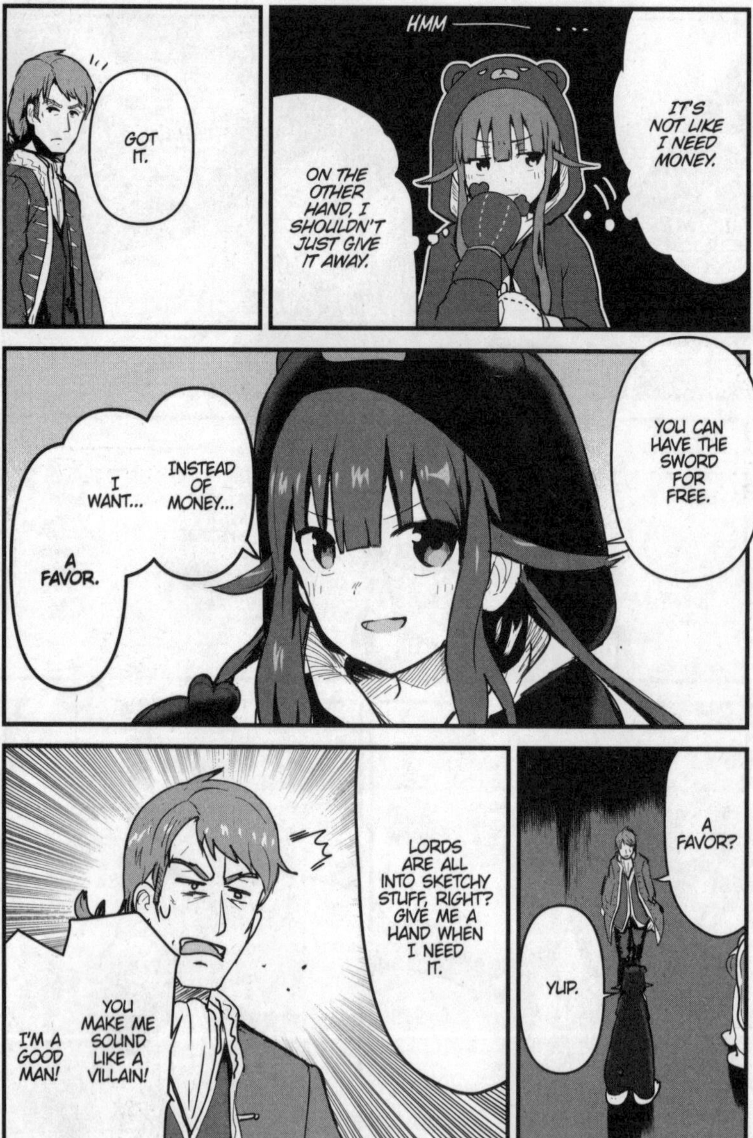
HMM ——— ...
IT'S NOT LIKE I NEED MONEY.
ON THE OTHER HAND, I SHOULDN'T JUST GIVE IT AWAY.
GOT IT.
YOU CAN HAVE THE SWORD FOR FREE.
INSTEAD OF MONEY...
I WANT...
A FAVOR.
A FAVOR?
YUP.
LORDS ARE ALL INTO SKETCHY STUFF, RIGHT? GIVE ME A HAND WHEN I NEED IT.
YOU MAKE ME SOUND LIKE A VILLAIN!
I'M A GOOD MAN!

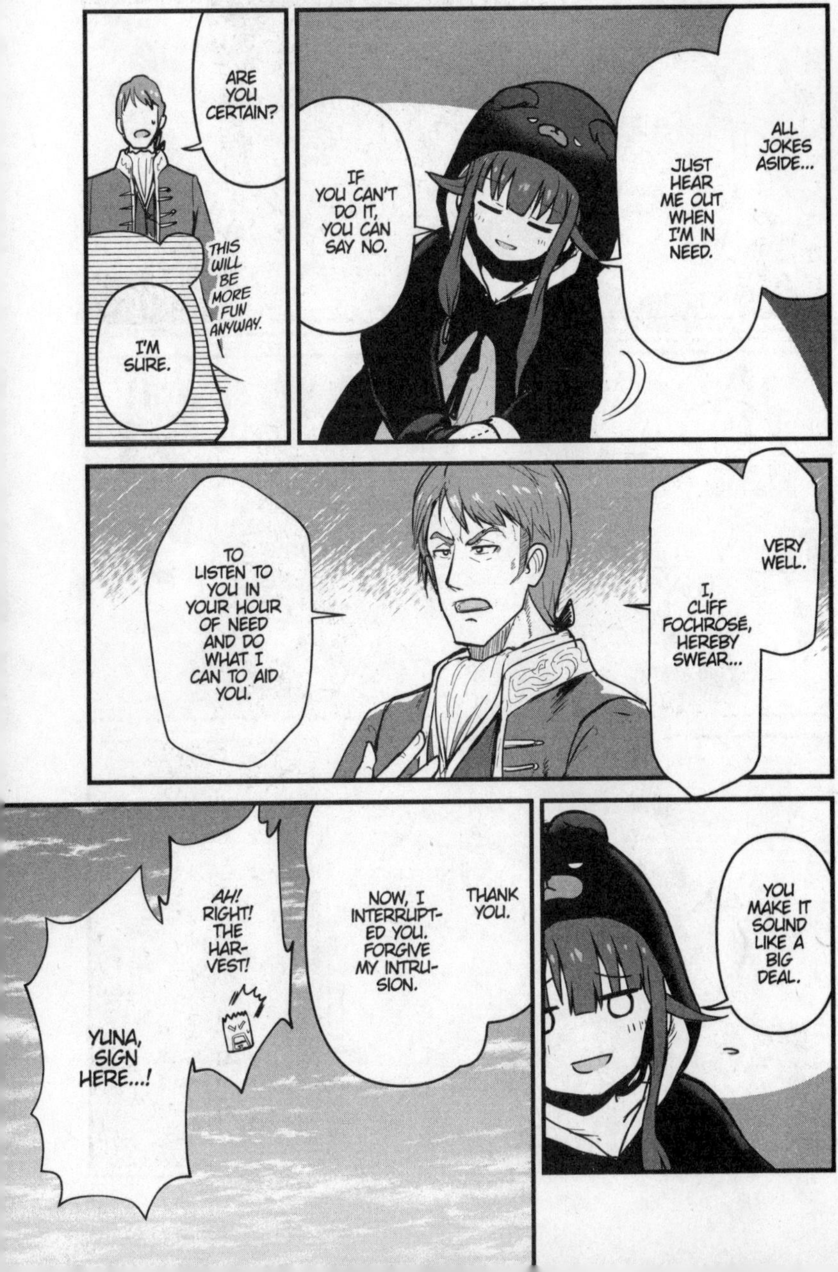
ALL JOKES ASIDE...
JUST HEAR ME OUT WHEN I'M IN NEED.
IF YOU CAN'T DO IT, YOU CAN SAY NO.
ARE YOU CERTAIN?
I'M SURE.
THIS WILL BE MORE FUN ANYWAY.
VERY WELL.
I, CLIFF FOCHROSE, HEREBY SWEAR...
TO LISTEN TO YOU IN YOUR HOUR OF NEED AND DO WHAT I CAN TO AID YOU.
YOU MAKE IT SOUND LIKE A BIG DEAL.
THANK YOU.
NOW, I INTERRUPT-ED YOU. FORGIVE MY INTRU-SION.
AH! RIGHT! THE HAR-VEST!
YUNA, SIGN HERE...!

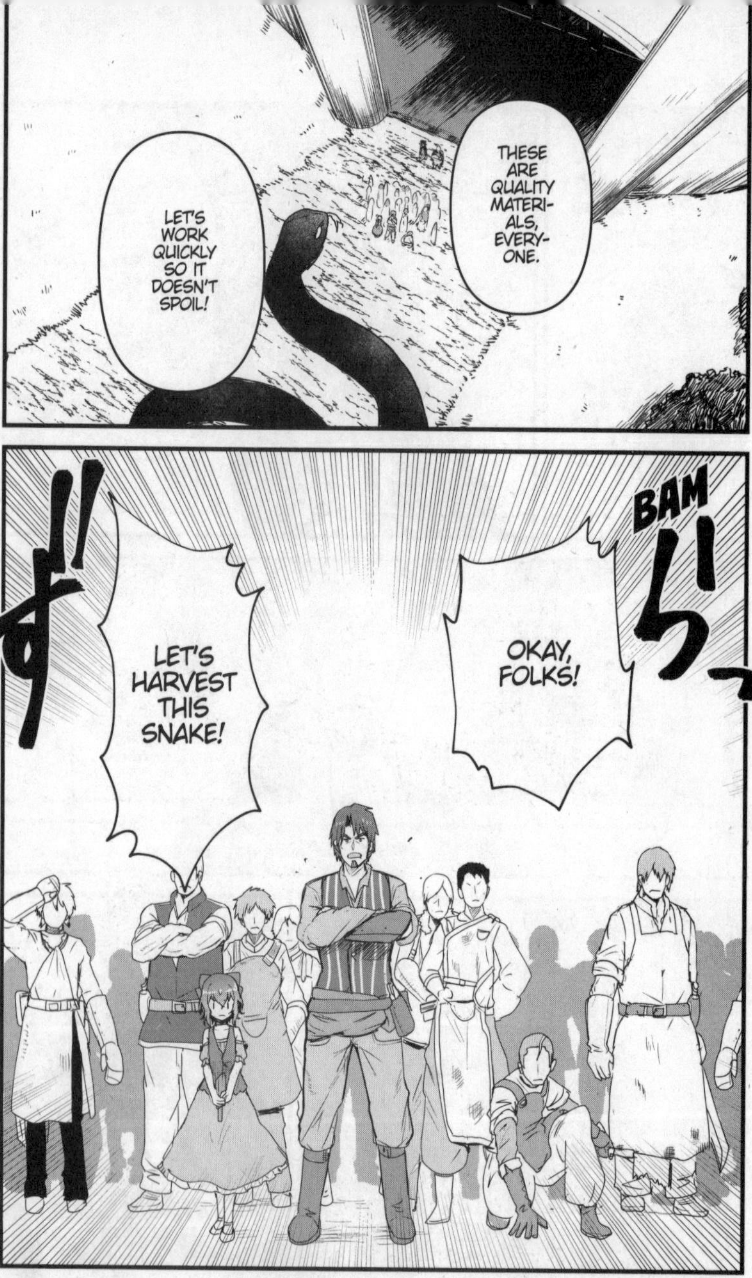
THESE ARE QUALITY MATERI-ALS, EVERY-ONE.
LET'S WORK QUICKLY SO IT DOESN'T SPOIL!
BAM
OKAY, FOLKS!
LET'S HARVEST THIS SNAKE!

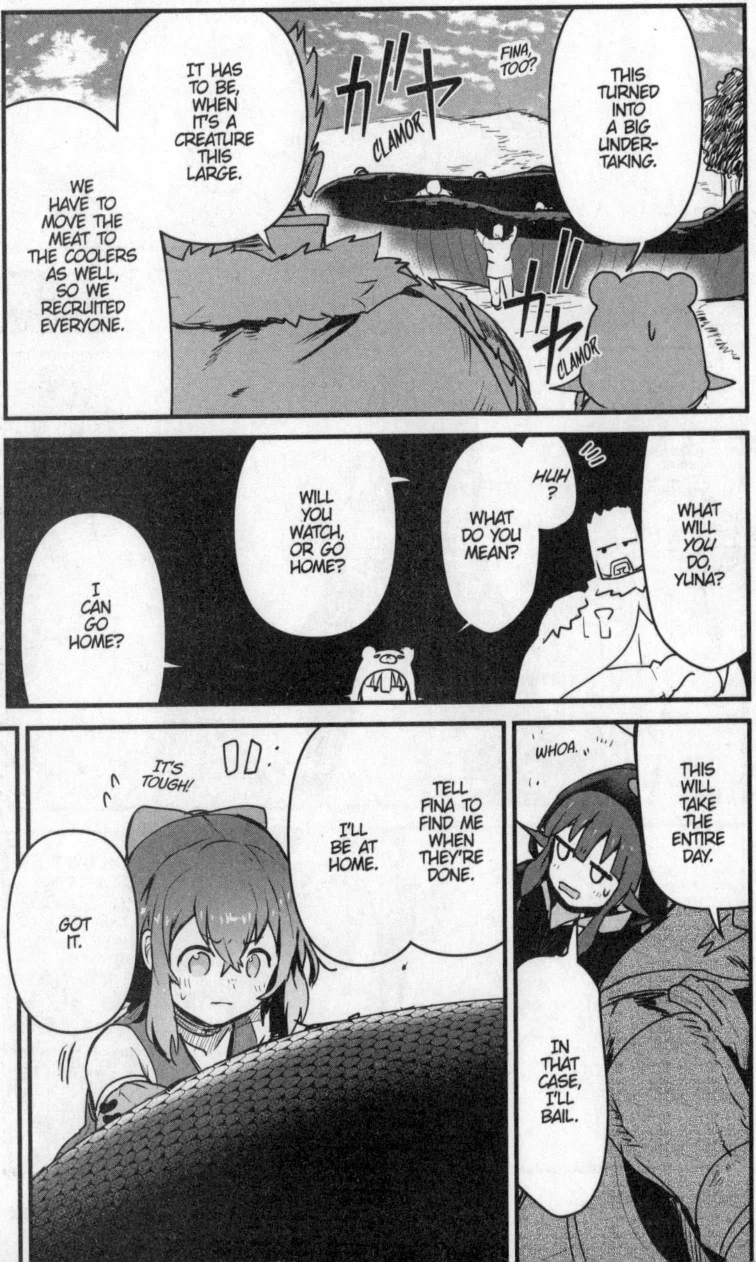
THIS TURNED INTO A BIG UNDER-TAKING.
FINA, TOO?
CLAMOR
CLAMOR
IT HAS TO BE, WHEN IT'S A CREATURE THIS LARGE.
WE HAVE TO MOVE THE MEAT TO THE COOLERS AS WELL, SO WE RECRUITED EVERYONE.
WHAT WILL YOU DO, YUNA?
HUH?
WHAT DO YOU MEAN?
WILL YOU WATCH, OR GO HOME?
I CAN GO HOME?
THIS WILL TAKE THE ENTIRE DAY.
WHOA.
IN THAT CASE, I'LL BAIL.
TELL FINA TO FIND ME WHEN THEY'RE DONE.
I'LL BE AT HOME.
IT'S TOUGH!
GOT IT.

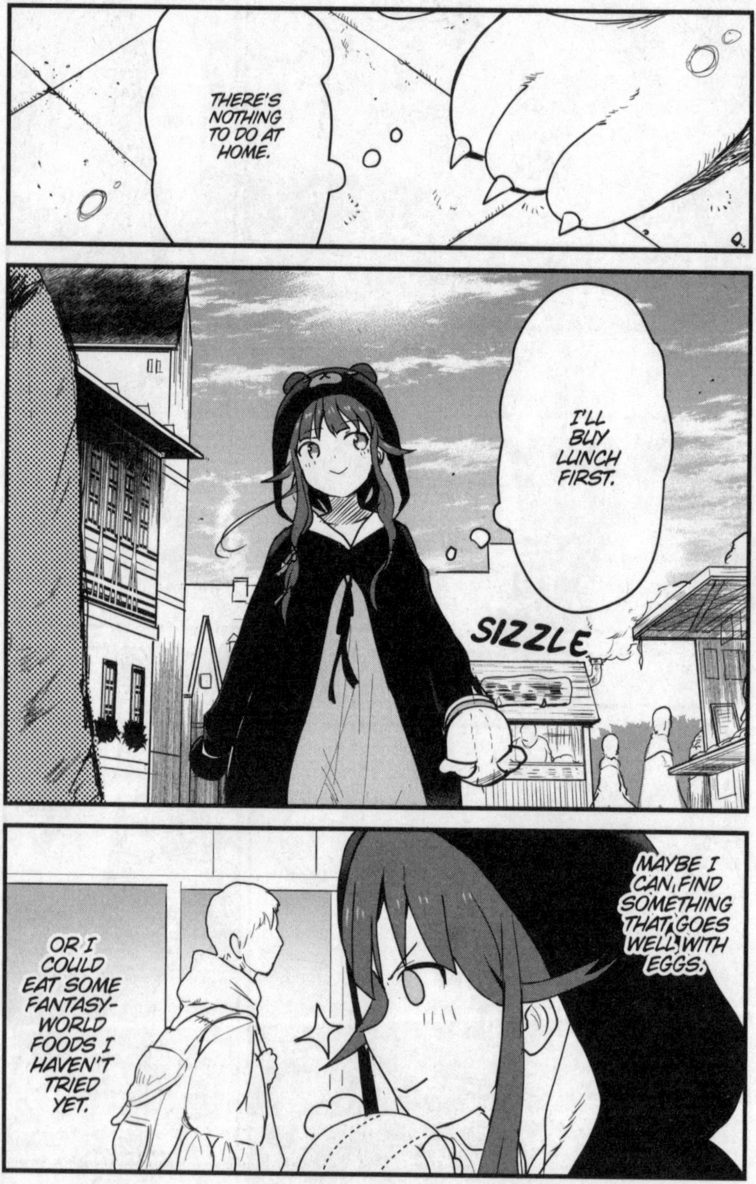
THERE'S NOTHING TO DO AT HOME.
I'LL BUY LUNCH FIRST.
SIZZLE
MAYBE I CAN FIND SOMETHING THAT GOES WELL WITH EGGS.
OR I COULD EAT SOME FANTASY-WORLD FOODS I HAVEN'T TRIED YET.

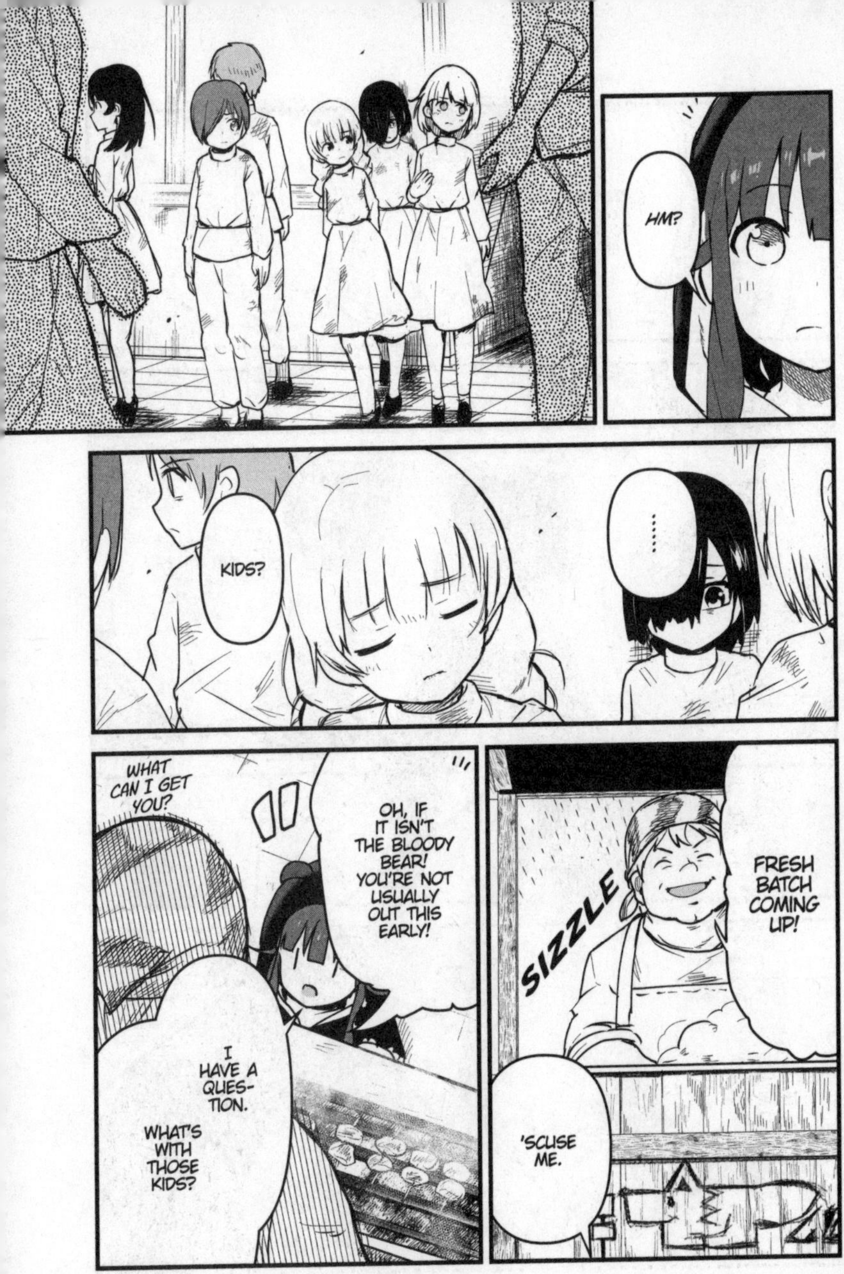
HM?
......
KIDS?
FRESH BATCH COMING UP!
SIZZLE
'SCUSE ME.
OH, IF IT ISN'T THE BLOODY BEAR! YOU'RE NOT USUALLY OUT THIS EARLY!
WHAT CAN I GET YOU?
I HAVE A QUES-TION.
WHAT'S WITH THOSE KIDS?

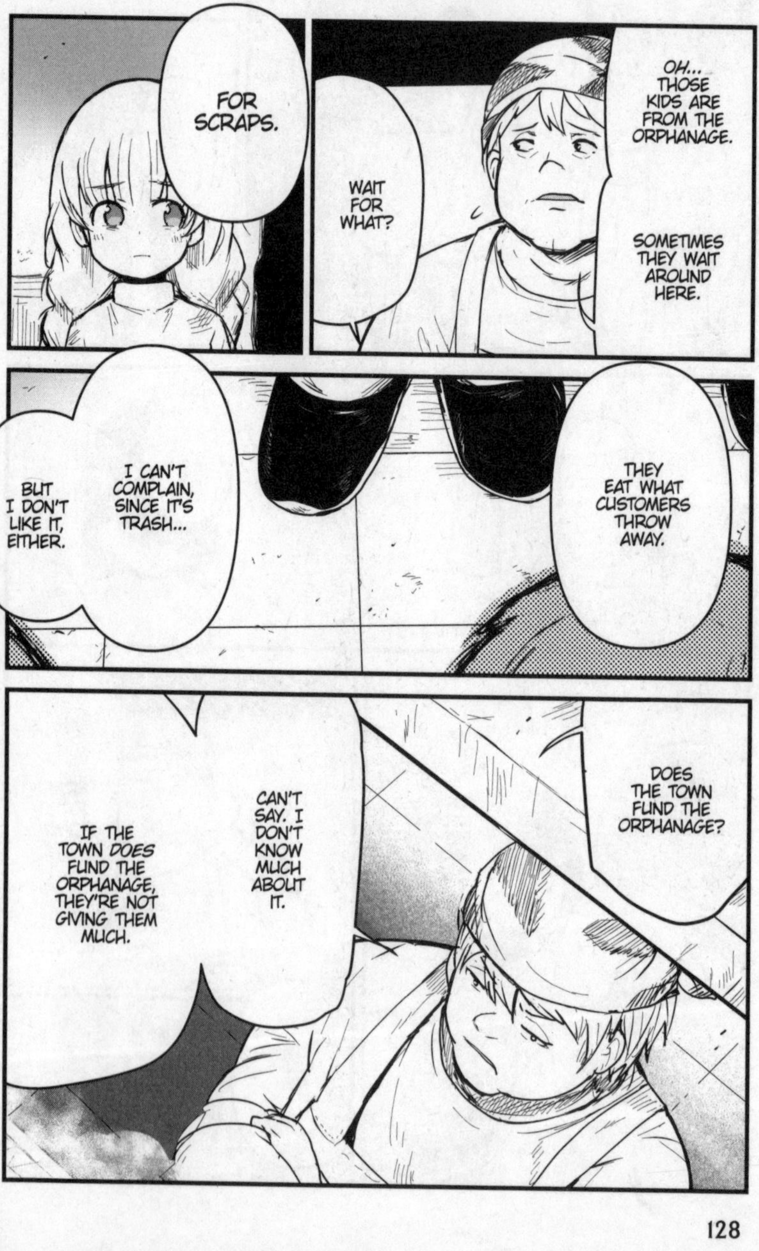
OH... THOSE KIDS ARE FROM THE ORPHANAGE.
SOMETIMES THEY WAIT AROUND HERE.
WAIT FOR WHAT?
FOR SCRAPS.
THEY EAT WHAT CUSTOMERS THROW AWAY.
I CAN'T COMPLAIN, SINCE IT'S TRASH...
BUT I DON'T LIKE IT, EITHER.
DOES THE TOWN FUND THE ORPHANAGE?
CAN'T SAY. I DON'T KNOW MUCH ABOUT IT.
IF THE TOWN *DOES* FUND THE ORPHANAGE, THEY'RE NOT GIVING THEM MUCH.

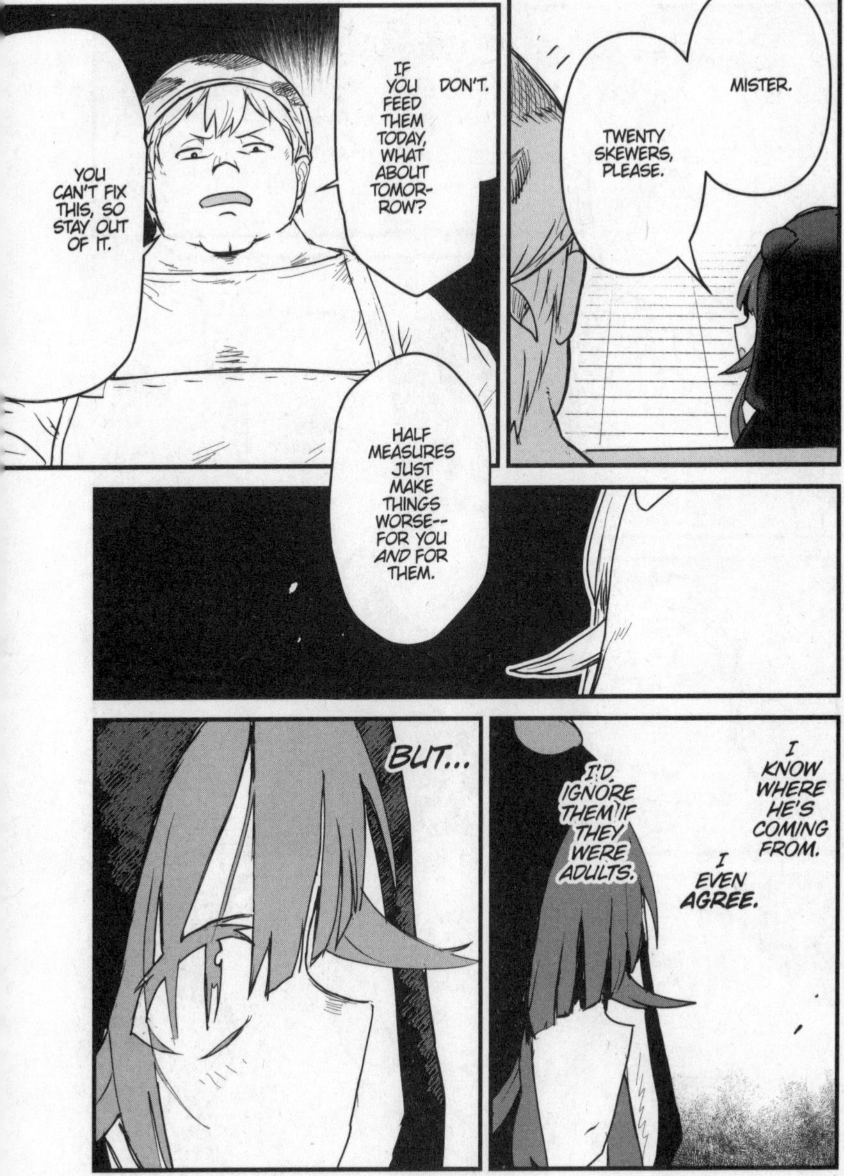
MISTER.
TWENTY SKEWERS, PLEASE.
DON'T.
IF YOU FEED THEM TODAY, WHAT ABOUT TOMORROW?
YOU CAN'T FIX THIS, SO STAY OUT OF IT.
HALF MEASURES JUST MAKE THINGS WORSE-- FOR YOU AND FOR THEM.
I KNOW WHERE HE'S COMING FROM.
I EVEN AGREE.
I'D IGNORE THEM IF THEY WERE ADULTS.
BUT...

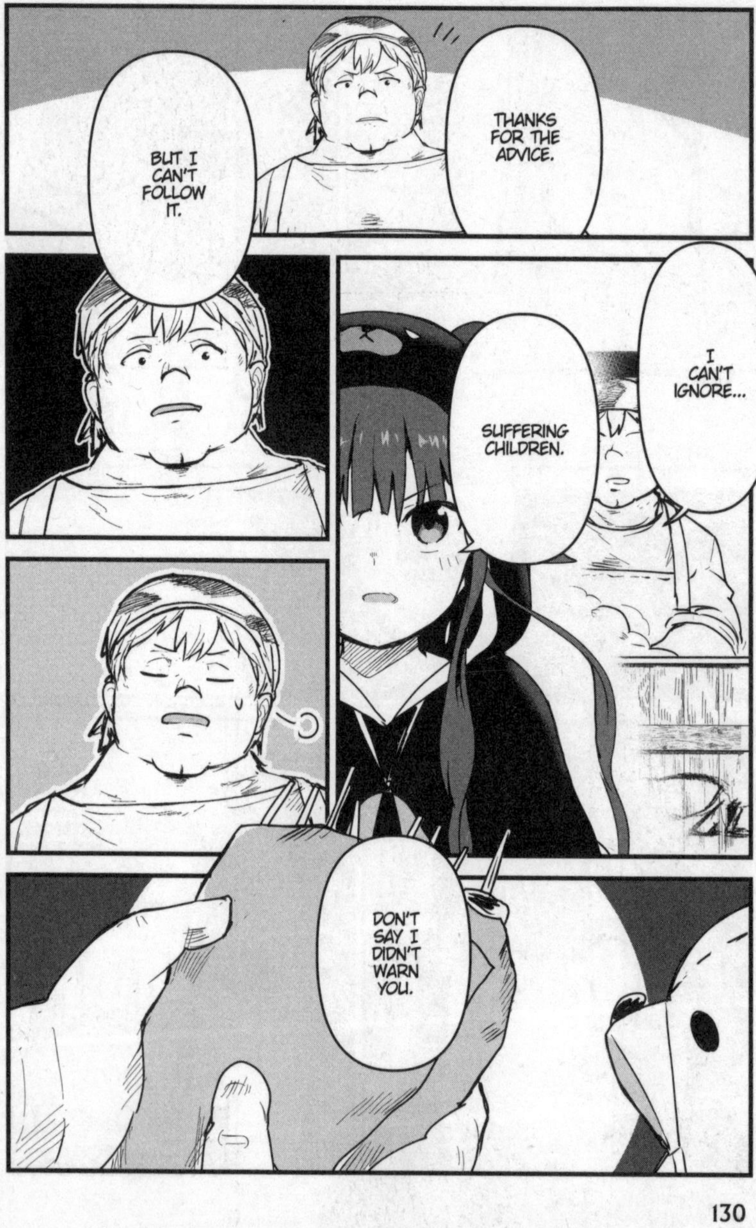
THANKS FOR THE ADVICE.
BUT I CAN'T FOLLOW IT.
I CAN'T IGNORE...
SUFFERING CHILDREN.
DON'T SAY I DIDN'T WARN YOU.

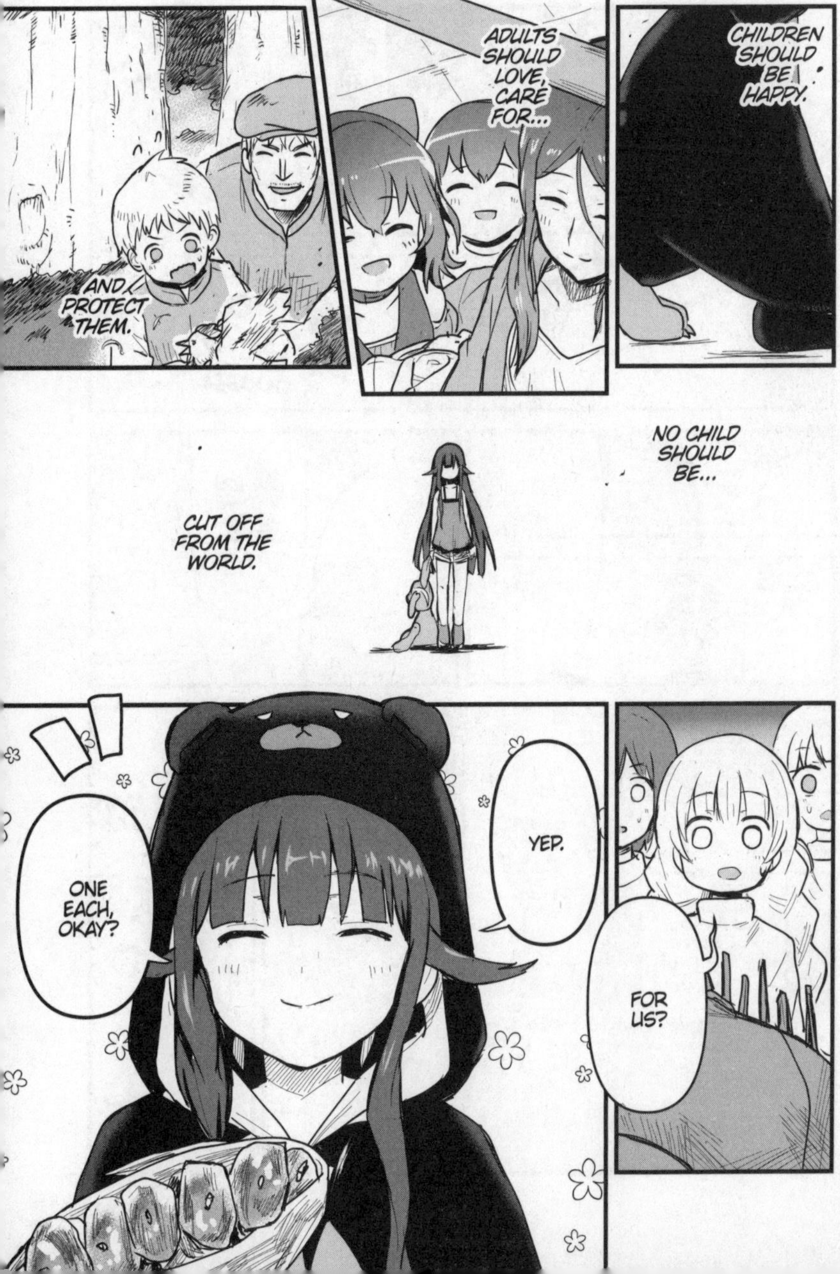
CHILDREN SHOULD BE HAPPY.
ADULTS SHOULD LOVE, CARE FOR...
AND PROTECT THEM.
NO CHILD SHOULD BE...
CUT OFF FROM THE WORLD.
FOR US?
YEP.
ONE EACH, OKAY?

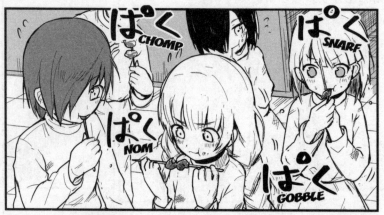

ぱく
SNARF
ぱく
CHOMP
ぱく
GOBBLE
ぱく
NOM
CAN YOU TAKE ME TO THE ORPHAN-AGE?
I HAVE MEAT, IF YOU'RE STILL HUNGRY.
X PLENTY
WE CAN EAT TOGETH-ER.
NOD NOD
THIS WAY!
I DON'T KNOW HOW MUCH GOOD I CAN DO...
BUT NOW THAT I'M INVOLVED, I'LL MEDDLE ALL I CAN.

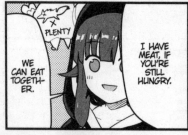

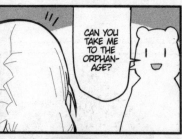

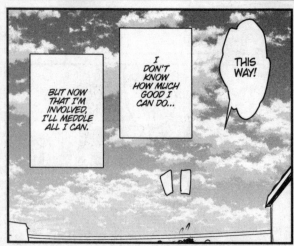

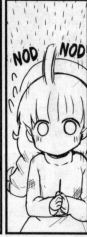

Chapter 29

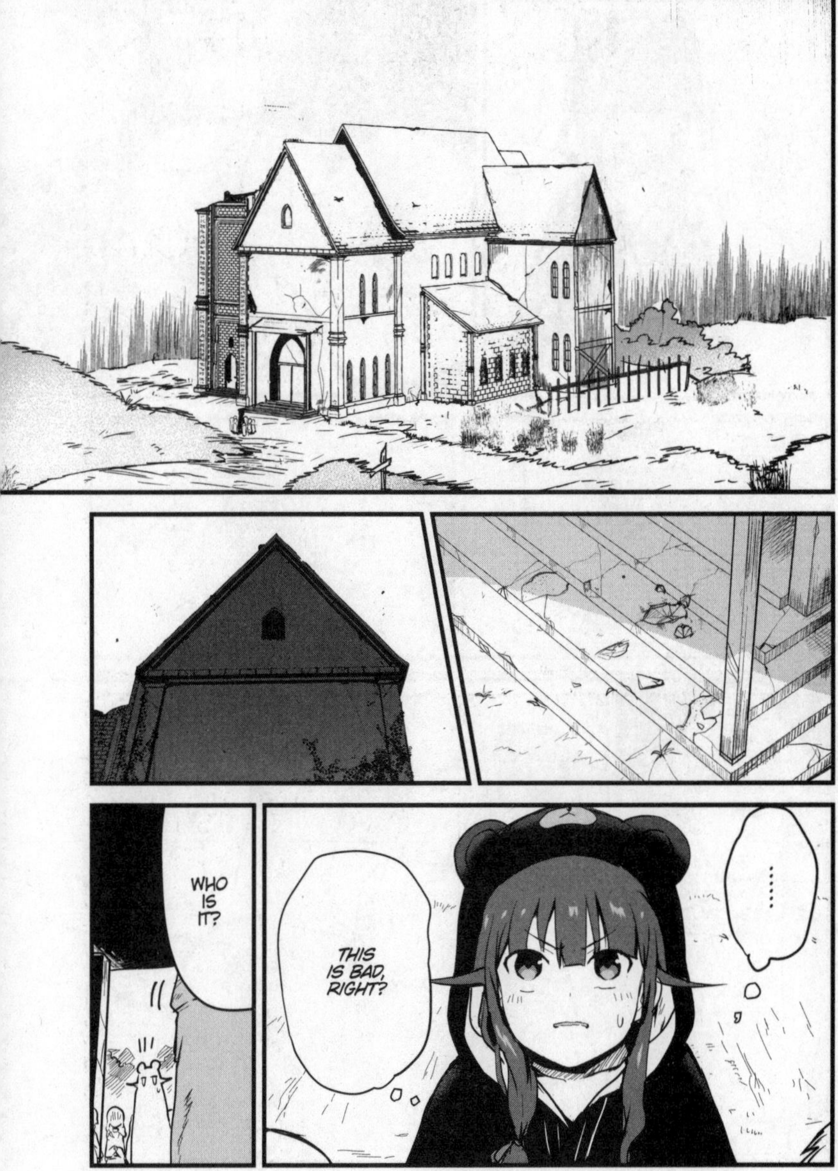
......
THIS IS BAD, RIGHT?
WHO IS IT?

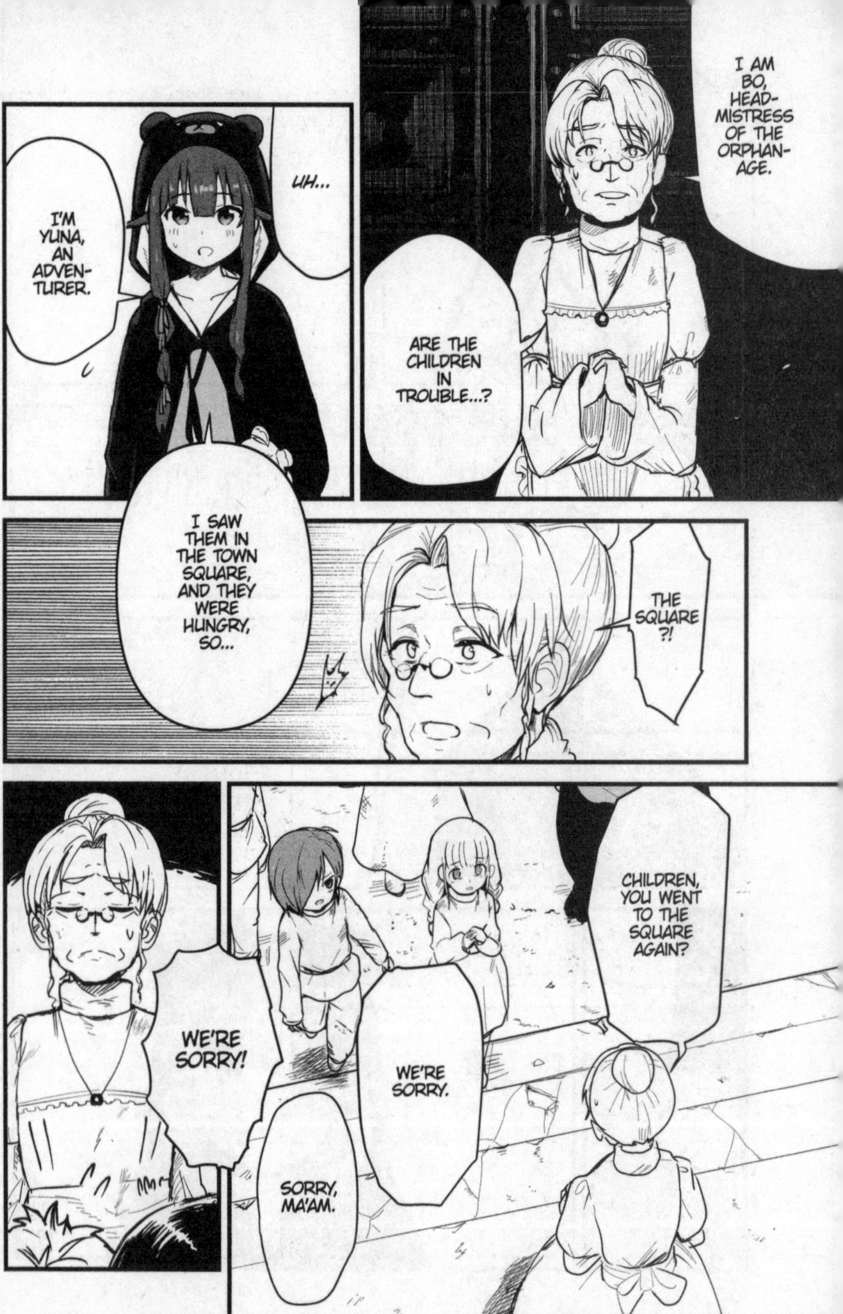
I AM BO, HEAD-MISTRESS OF THE ORPHAN-AGE.
ARE THE CHILDREN IN TROUBLE...?
UH...
I'M YUNA, AN ADVEN-TURER.
I SAW THEM IN THE TOWN SQUARE, AND THEY WERE HUNGRY, SO...
THE SQUARE ?!
CHILDREN, YOU WENT TO THE SQUARE AGAIN?
WE'RE SORRY.
SORRY, MA'AM.
WE'RE SORRY!

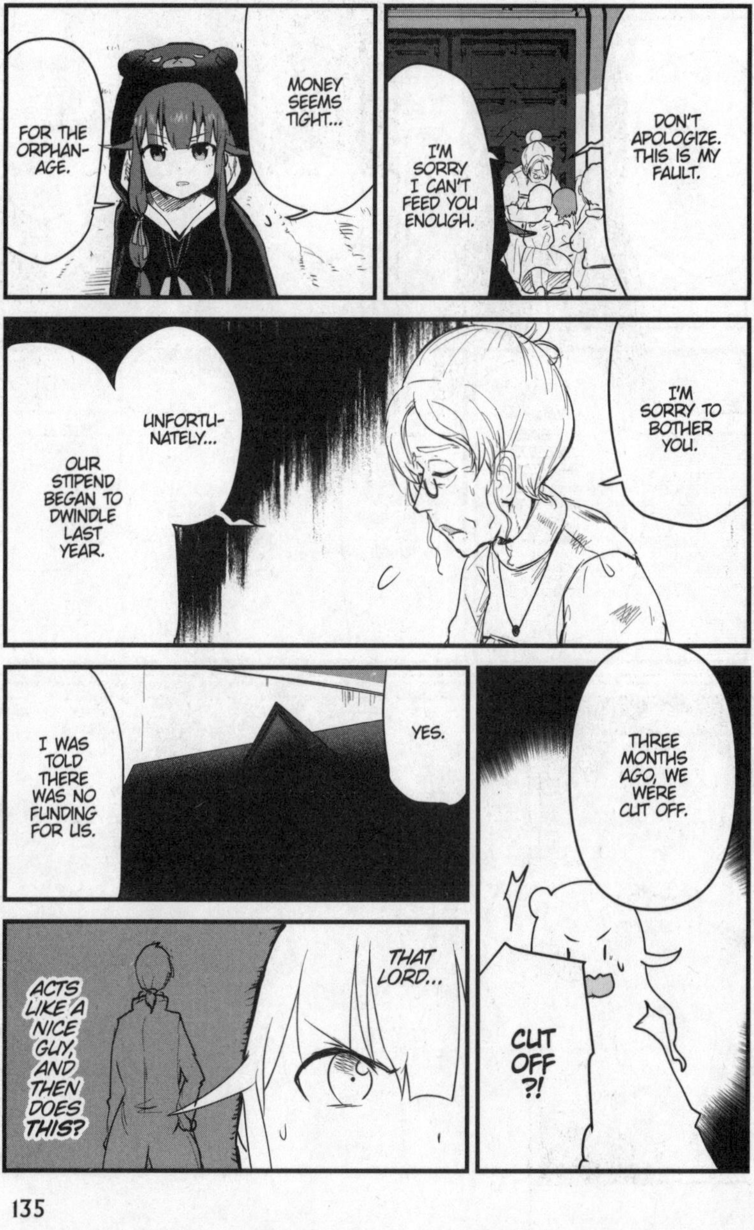
DON'T APOLOGIZE. THIS IS MY FAULT.
I'M SORRY I CAN'T FEED YOU ENOUGH.
MONEY SEEMS TIGHT...
FOR THE ORPHANAGE.
I'M SORRY TO BOTHER YOU.
UNFORTUNATELY...
OUR STIPEND BEGAN TO DWINDLE LAST YEAR.
THREE MONTHS AGO, WE WERE CUT OFF.
CUT OFF?!
YES.
I WAS TOLD THERE WAS NO FUNDING FOR US.
THAT LORD...
ACTS LIKE A NICE GUY, AND THEN DOES THIS?

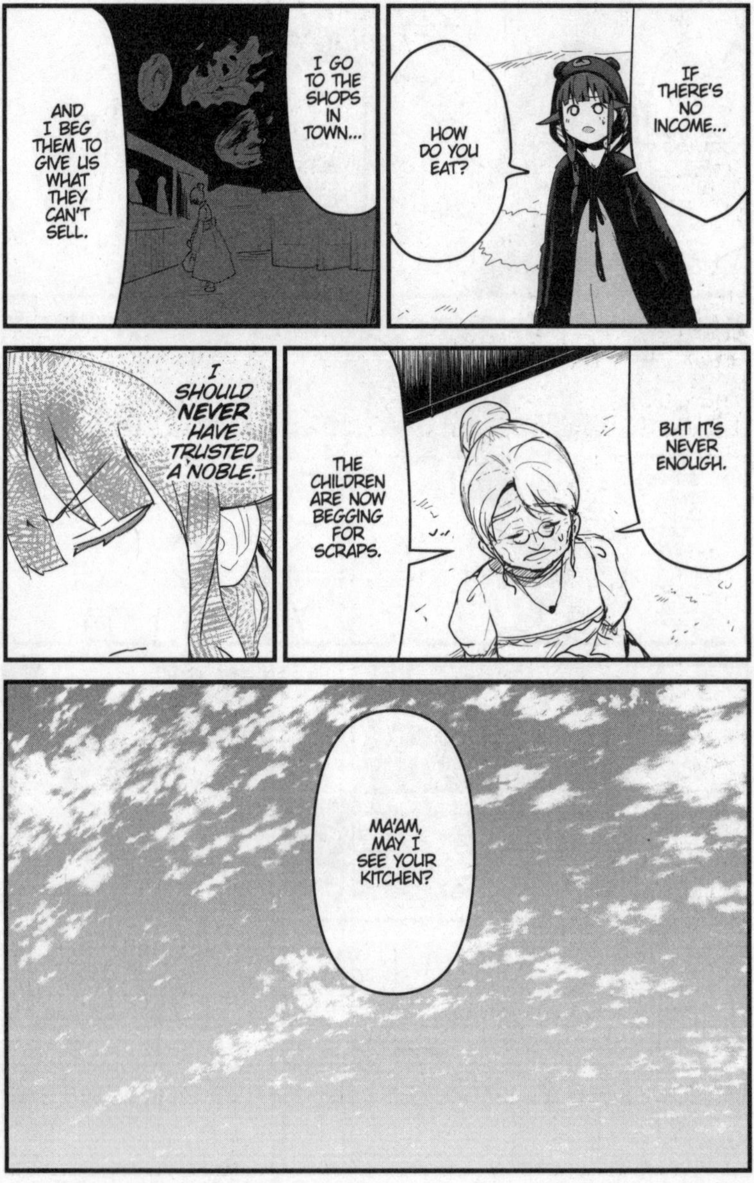
IF THERE'S NO INCOME...
HOW DO YOU EAT?
I GO TO THE SHOPS IN TOWN...
AND I BEG THEM TO GIVE US WHAT THEY CAN'T SELL.
BUT IT'S NEVER ENOUGH.
THE CHILDREN ARE NOW BEGGING FOR SCRAPS.
I SHOULD NEVER HAVE TRUSTED A NOBLE.
MA'AM, MAY I SEE YOUR KITCHEN?

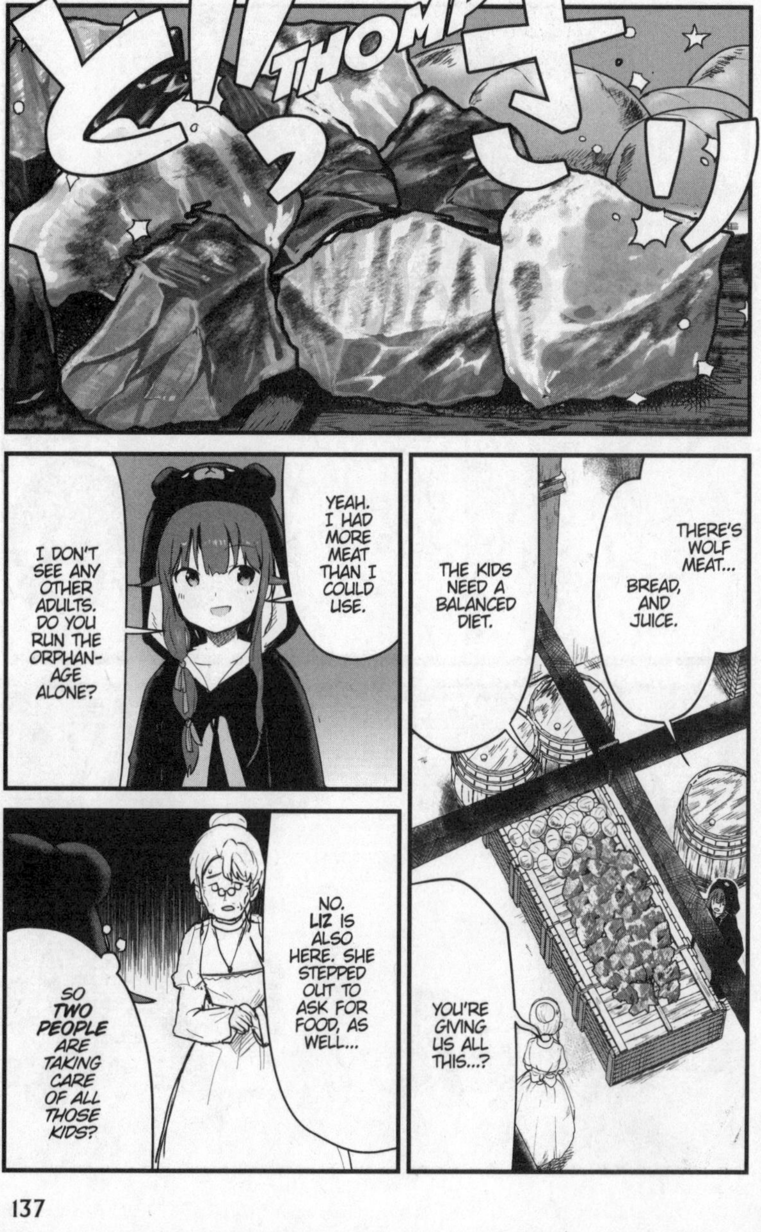
THOMP
THERE'S WOLF MEAT... BREAD, AND JUICE.
THE KIDS NEED A BALANCED DIET.
YOU'RE GIVING US ALL THIS...?
YEAH. I HAD MORE MEAT THAN I COULD USE.
I DON'T SEE ANY OTHER ADULTS. DO YOU RUN THE ORPHAN-AGE ALONE?
NO. LIZ IS ALSO HERE. SHE STEPPED OUT TO ASK FOR FOOD, AS WELL...
SO TWO PEOPLE ARE TAKING CARE OF ALL THOSE KIDS?

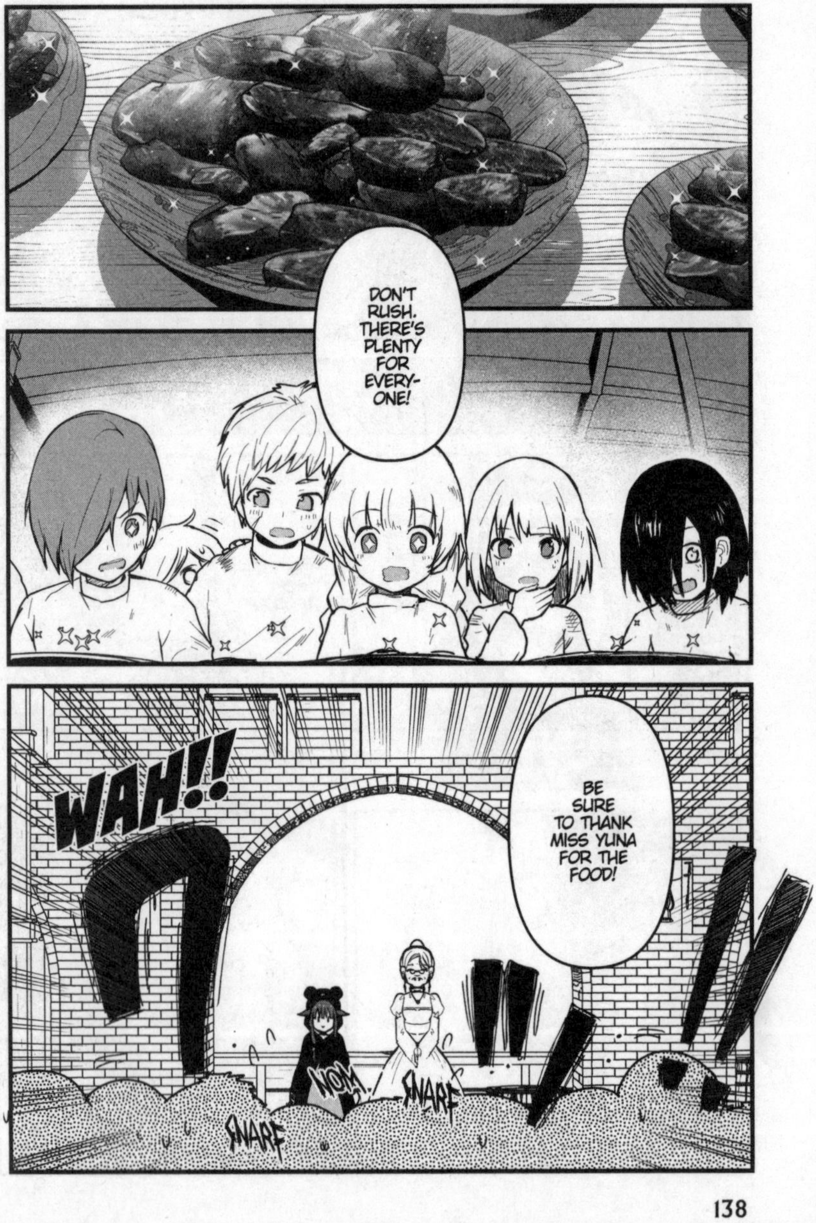
DON'T RUSH. THERE'S PLENTY FOR EVERY-ONE!
BE SURE TO THANK MISS YUNA FOR THE FOOD!
WAH!!
SNARF
NOM
SNARF

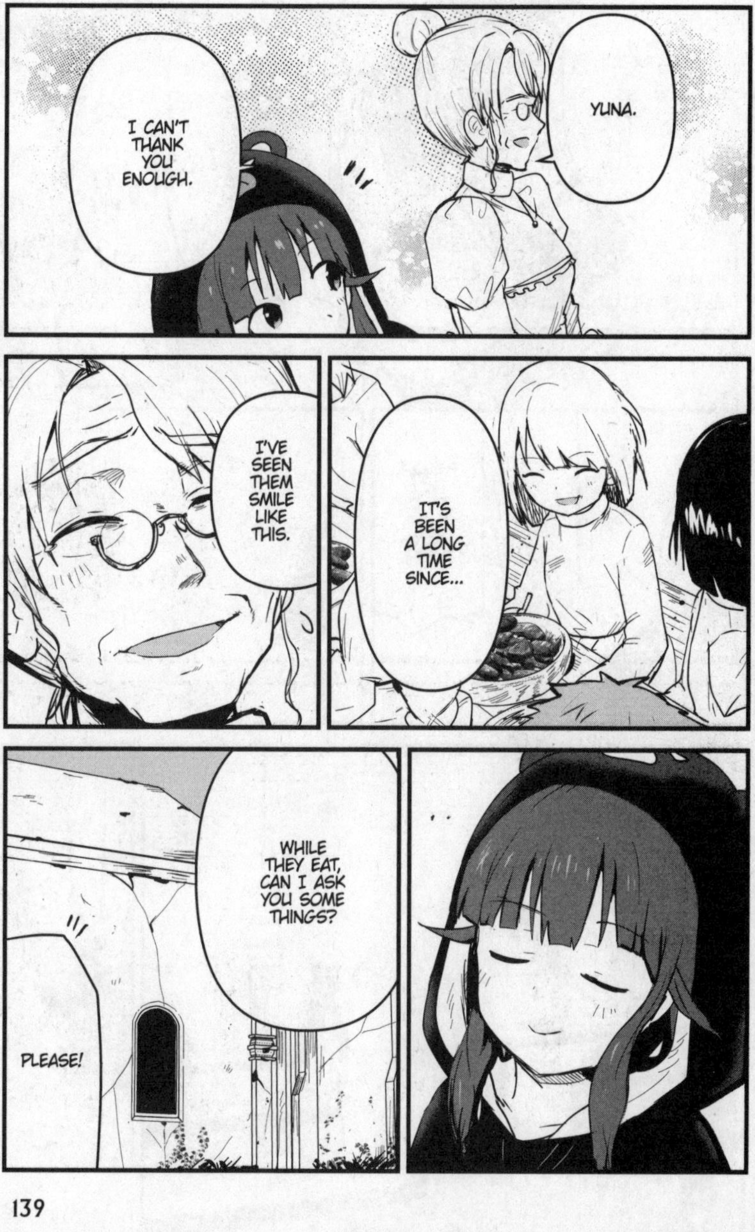
YUNA.
I CAN'T THANK YOU ENOUGH.
IT'S BEEN A LONG TIME SINCE...
I'VE SEEN THEM SMILE LIKE THIS.
WHILE THEY EAT, CAN I ASK YOU SOME THINGS?
PLEASE!

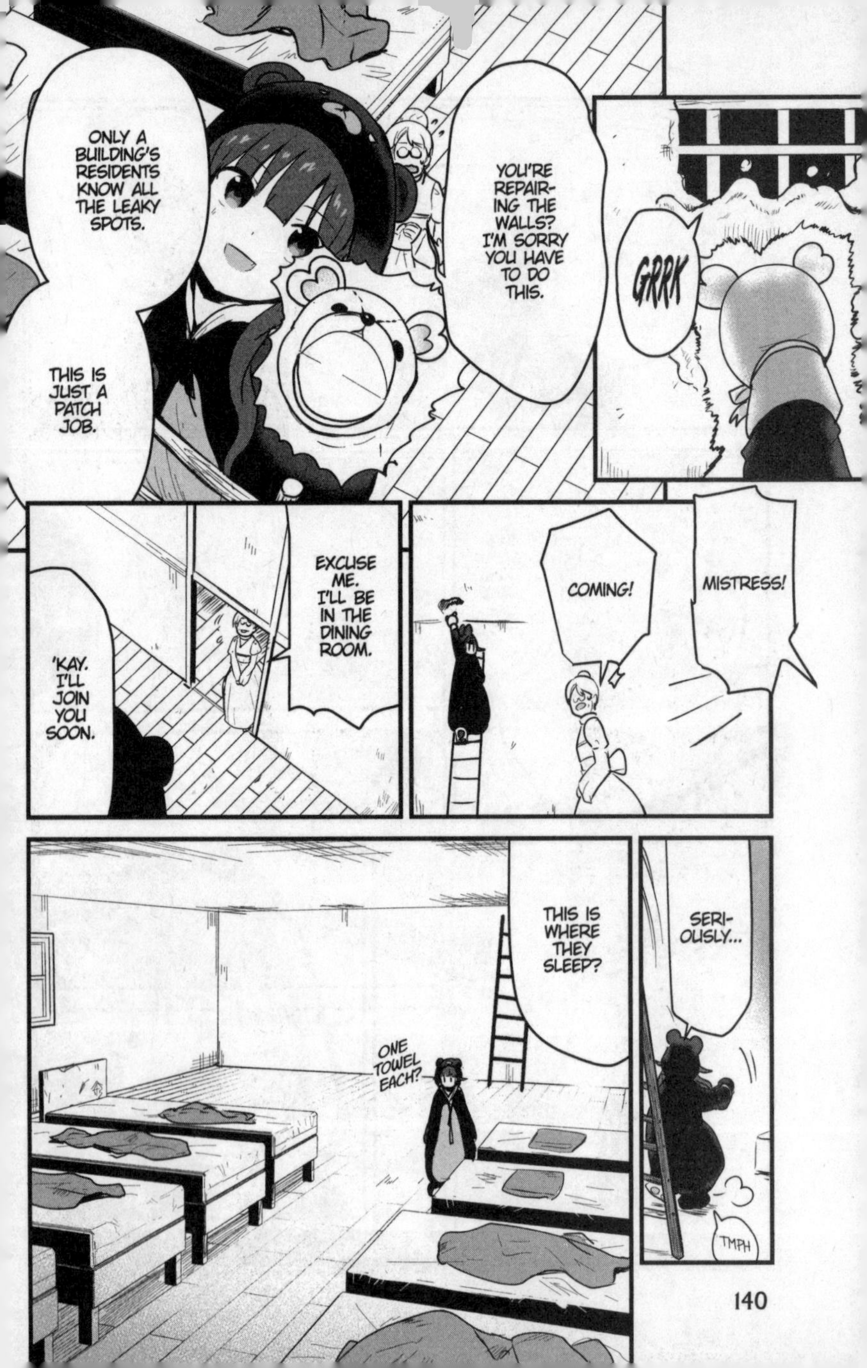
YOU'RE REPAIRING THE WALLS? I'M SORRY YOU HAVE TO DO THIS.
ONLY A BUILDING'S RESIDENTS KNOW ALL THE LEAKY SPOTS.
THIS IS JUST A PATCH JOB.
GRRK
MISTRESS!
COMING!
EXCUSE ME. I'LL BE IN THE DINING ROOM.
'KAY. I'LL JOIN YOU SOON.
SERIOUSLY...
TMPH
THIS IS WHERE THEY SLEEP?
ONE TOWEL EACH?

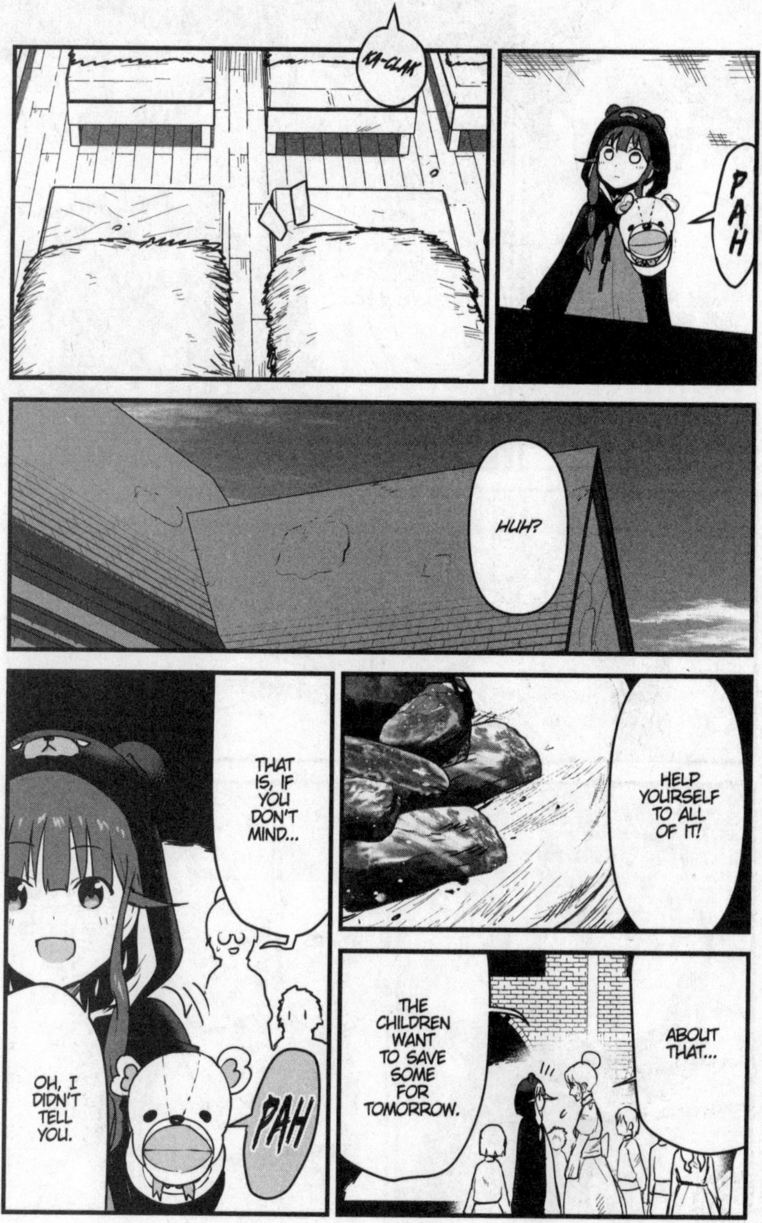
PAH
KA-CLAK
HUH?
HELP YOURSELF TO ALL OF IT!
ABOUT THAT...
THE CHILDREN WANT TO SAVE SOME FOR TOMORROW.
THAT IS, IF YOU DON'T MIND...
PAH
OH, I DIDN'T TELL YOU.

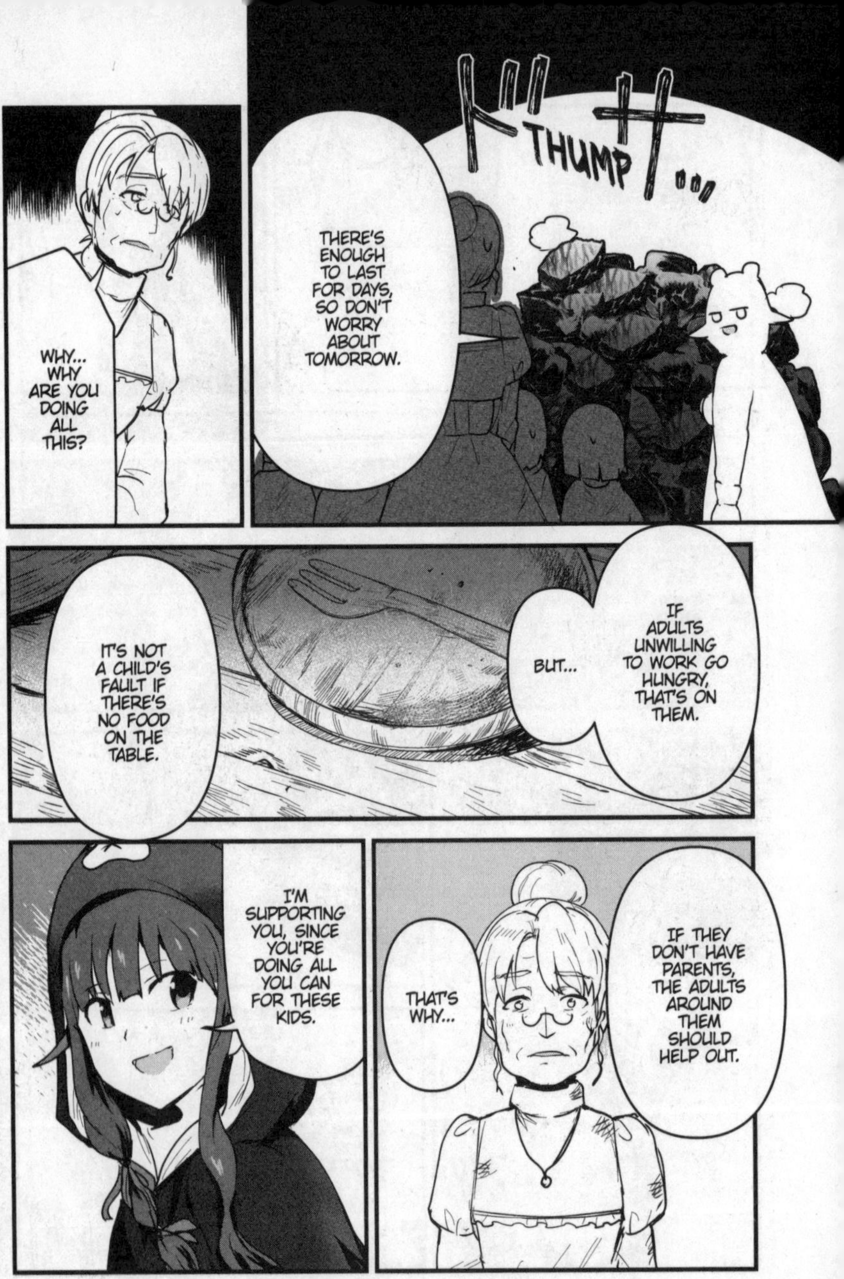
THUMP...
THERE'S ENOUGH TO LAST FOR DAYS, SO DON'T WORRY ABOUT TOMORROW.
WHY... WHY ARE YOU DOING ALL THIS?
IF ADULTS UNWILLING TO WORK GO HUNGRY, THAT'S ON THEM.
BUT...
IT'S NOT A CHILD'S FAULT IF THERE'S NO FOOD ON THE TABLE.
IF THEY DON'T HAVE PARENTS, THE ADULTS AROUND THEM SHOULD HELP OUT.
THAT'S WHY...
I'M SUPPORTING YOU, SINCE YOU'RE DOING ALL YOU CAN FOR THESE KIDS.

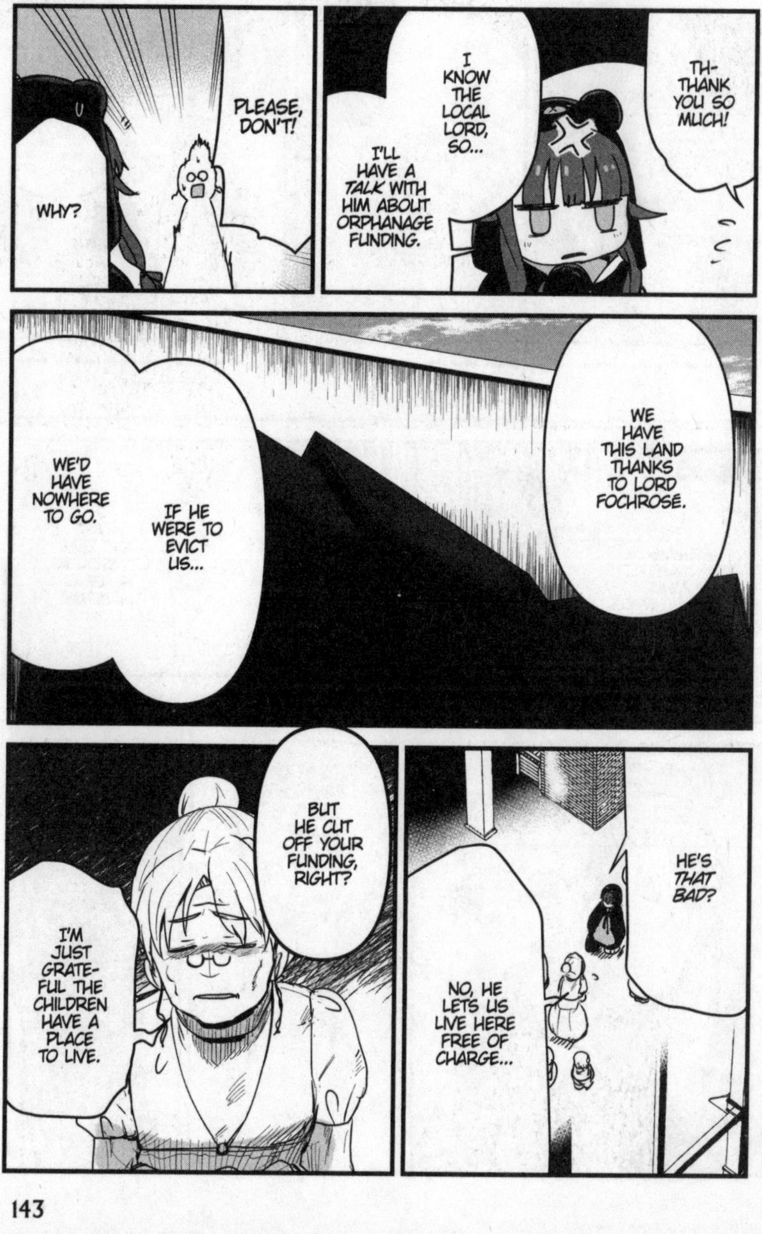
TH-THANK YOU SO MUCH!
I KNOW THE LOCAL LORD, SO...
I'LL HAVE A *TALK* WITH HIM ABOUT ORPHANAGE FUNDING.
PLEASE, DON'T!
WHY?
WE HAVE THIS LAND THANKS TO LORD FOCHROSE.
IF HE WERE TO EVICT US...
WE'D HAVE NOWHERE TO GO.
HE'S *THAT* BAD?
NO, HE LETS US LIVE HERE FREE OF CHARGE...
BUT HE CUT OFF YOUR FUNDING, RIGHT?
I'M JUST GRATEFUL THE CHILDREN HAVE A PLACE TO LIVE.

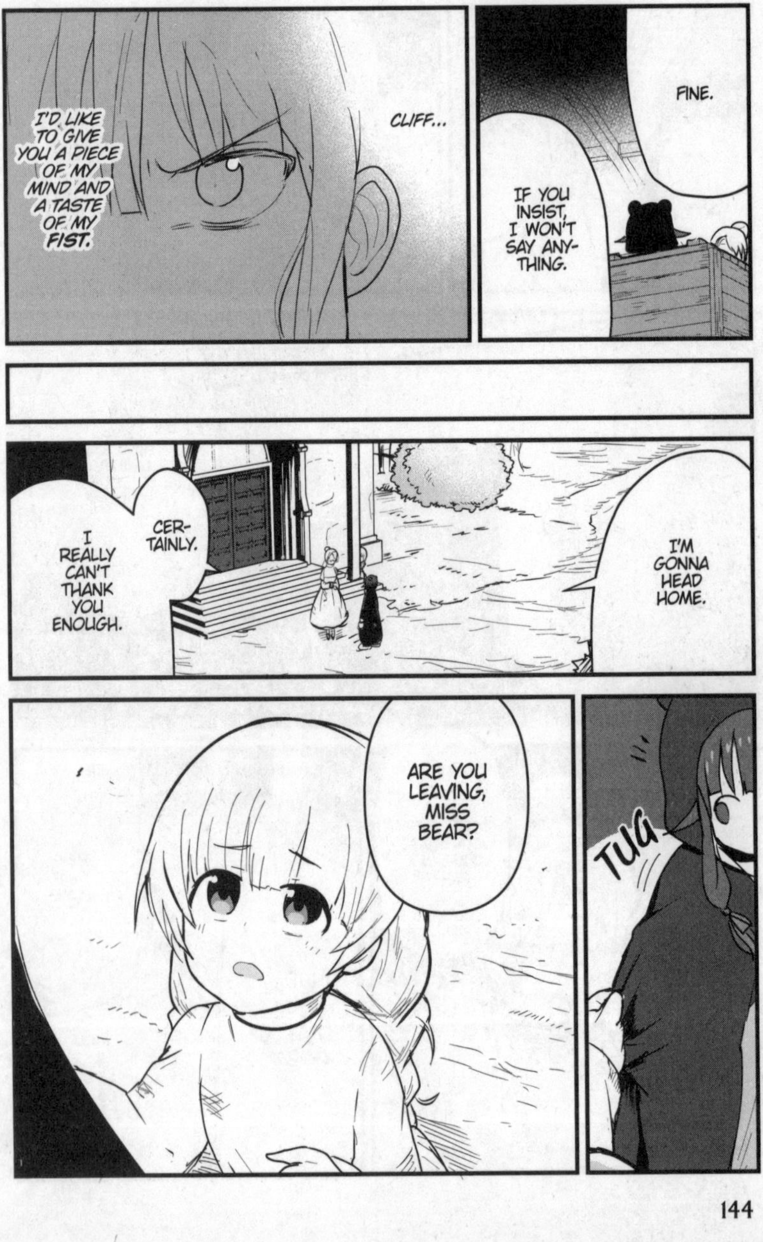
FINE.
IF YOU INSIST, I WON'T SAY ANY-THING.
CLIFF...
I'D LIKE TO GIVE YOU A PIECE OF MY MIND AND A TASTE OF MY FIST.
I'M GONNA HEAD HOME.
CER-TAINLY.
I REALLY CAN'T THANK YOU ENOUGH.
TUG
ARE YOU LEAVING, MISS BEAR?

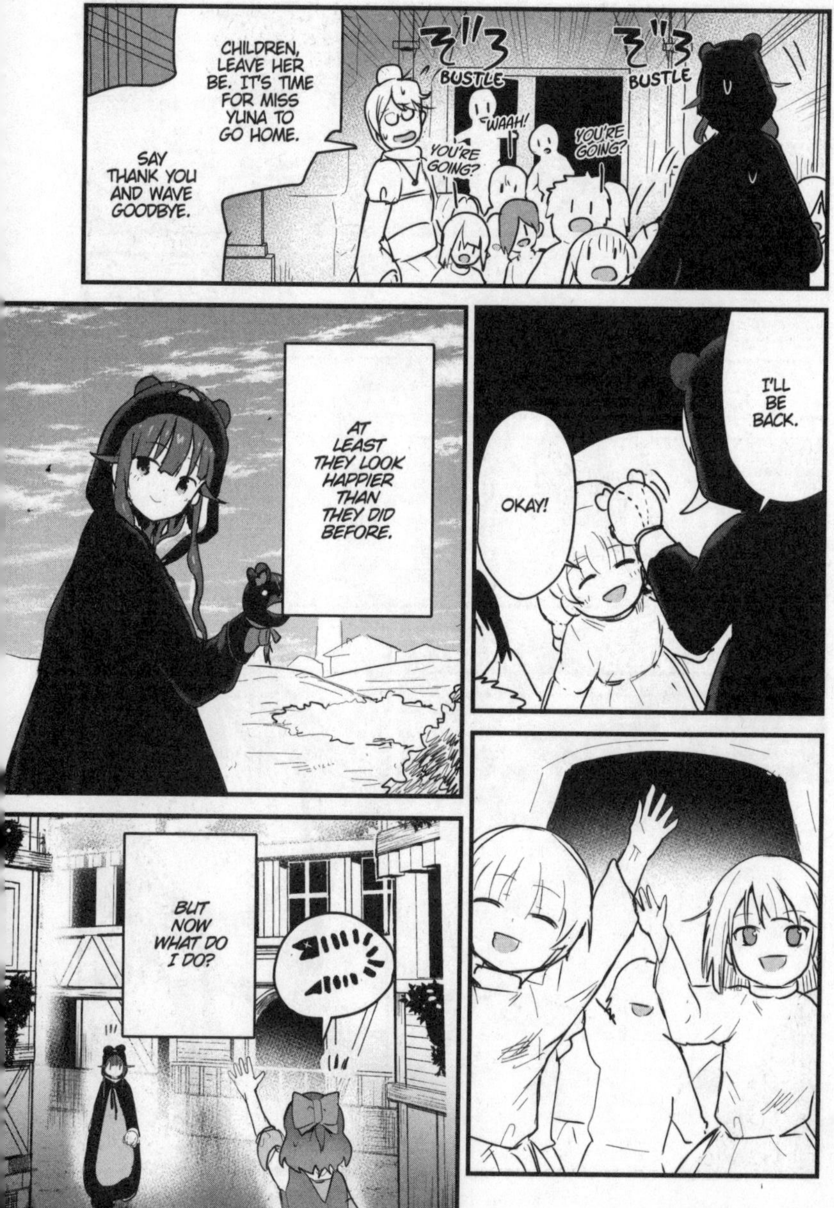
BUSTLE
BUSTLE
YOU'RE GOING?
WAAH!
YOU'RE GOING?
CHILDREN, LEAVE HER BE. IT'S TIME FOR MISS YUNA TO GO HOME.
SAY THANK YOU AND WAVE GOODBYE.
I'LL BE BACK.
OKAY!
AT LEAST THEY LOOK HAPPIER THAN THEY DID BEFORE.
BUT NOW WHAT DO I DO?

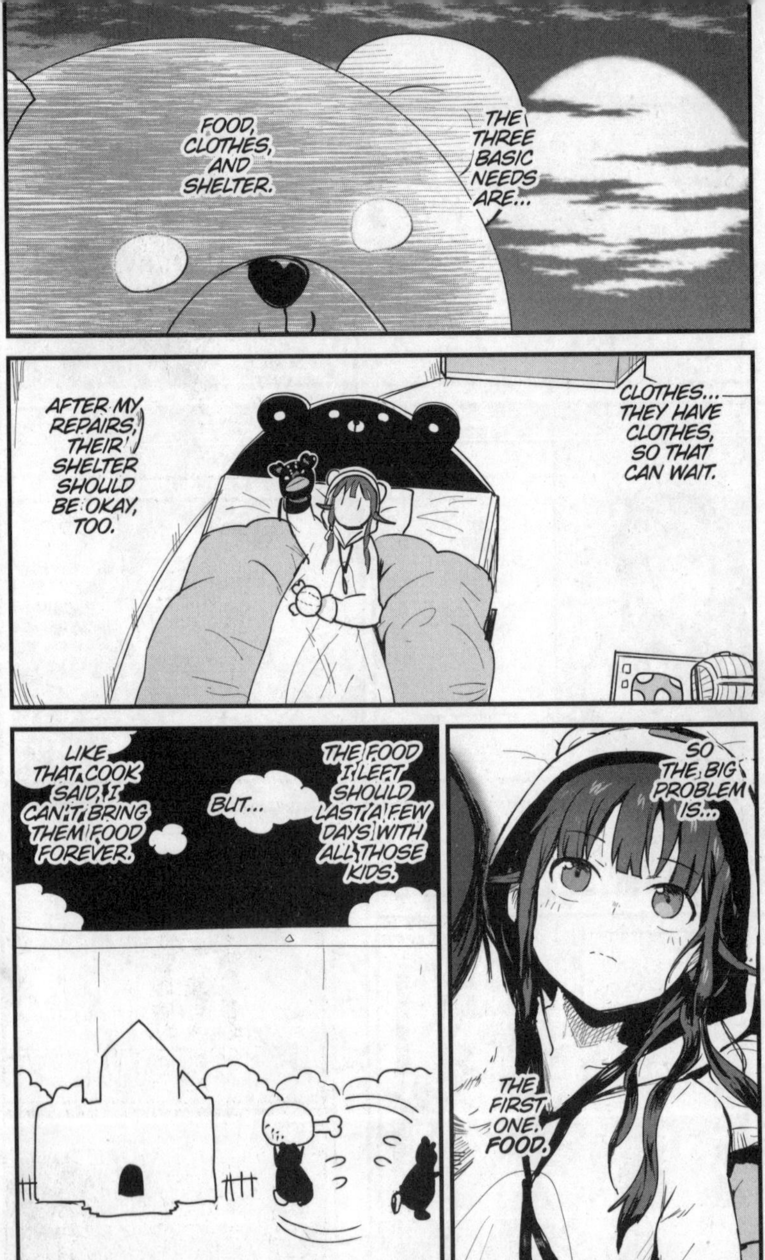
THE THREE BASIC NEEDS ARE...
FOOD, CLOTHES, AND SHELTER.
CLOTHES... THEY HAVE CLOTHES, SO THAT CAN WAIT.
AFTER MY REPAIRS, THEIR SHELTER SHOULD BE OKAY, TOO.
SO THE BIG PROBLEM IS...
THE FIRST ONE. FOOD.
THE FOOD I LEFT SHOULD LAST A FEW DAYS WITH ALL THOSE KIDS.
BUT...
LIKE THAT COOK SAID, I CAN'T BRING THEM FOOD FOREVER.

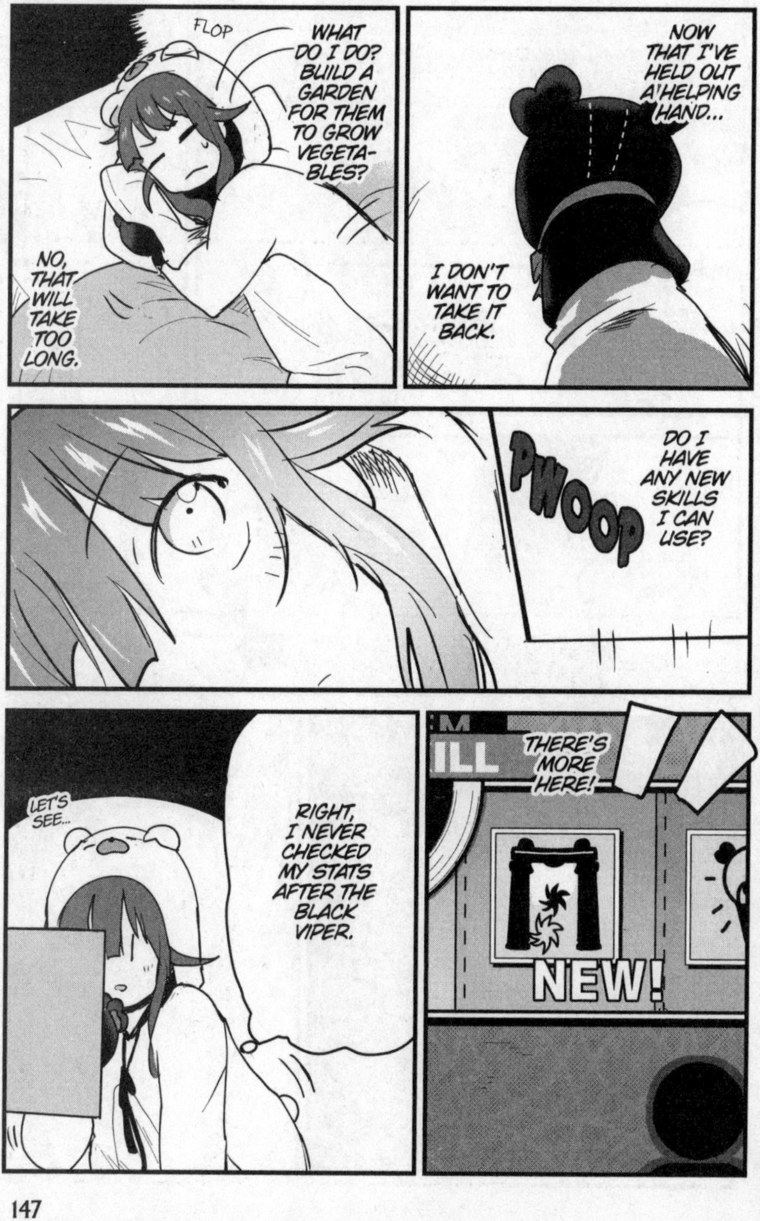
FLOP
WHAT DO I DO? BUILD A GARDEN FOR THEM TO GROW VEGETA-BLES?
NO, THAT WILL TAKE TOO LONG.
NOW THAT I'VE HELD OUT A HELPING HAND...
I DON'T WANT TO TAKE IT BACK.
PWOOP
DO I HAVE ANY NEW SKILLS I CAN USE?
LET'S SEE...
RIGHT, I NEVER CHECKED MY STATS AFTER THE BLACK VIPER.
THERE'S MORE HERE!
NEW!

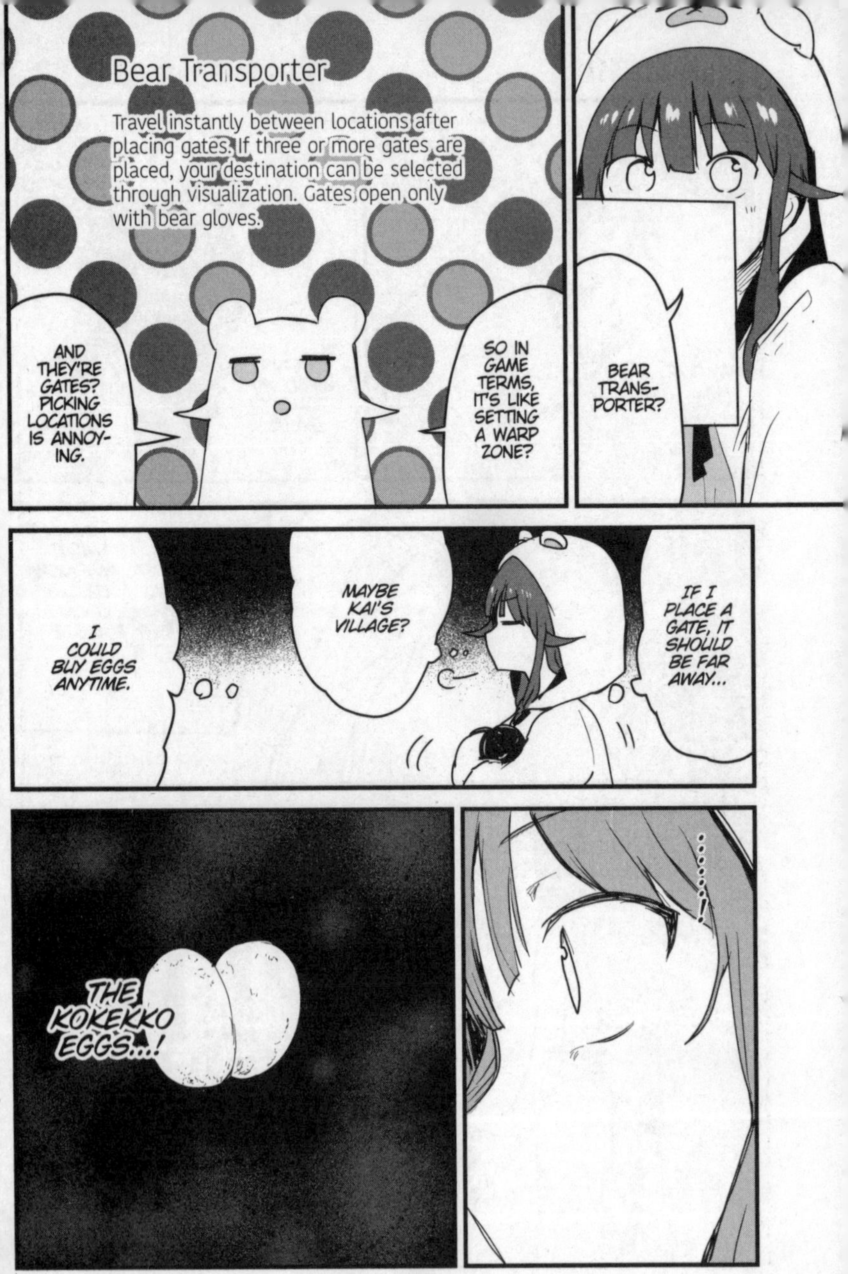
BEAR TRANS-PORTER?
Bear Transporter
Travel instantly between locations after placing gates. If three or more gates are placed, your destination can be selected through visualization. Gates open only with bear gloves.
SO IN GAME TERMS, IT'S LIKE SETTING A WARP ZONE?
AND THEY'RE GATES? PICKING LOCATIONS IS ANNOY-ING.
IF I PLACE A GATE, IT SHOULD BE FAR AWAY...
MAYBE KAI'S VILLAGE?
I COULD BUY EGGS ANYTIME.
......!
THE KOKEKKO EGGS...!

Chapter 30

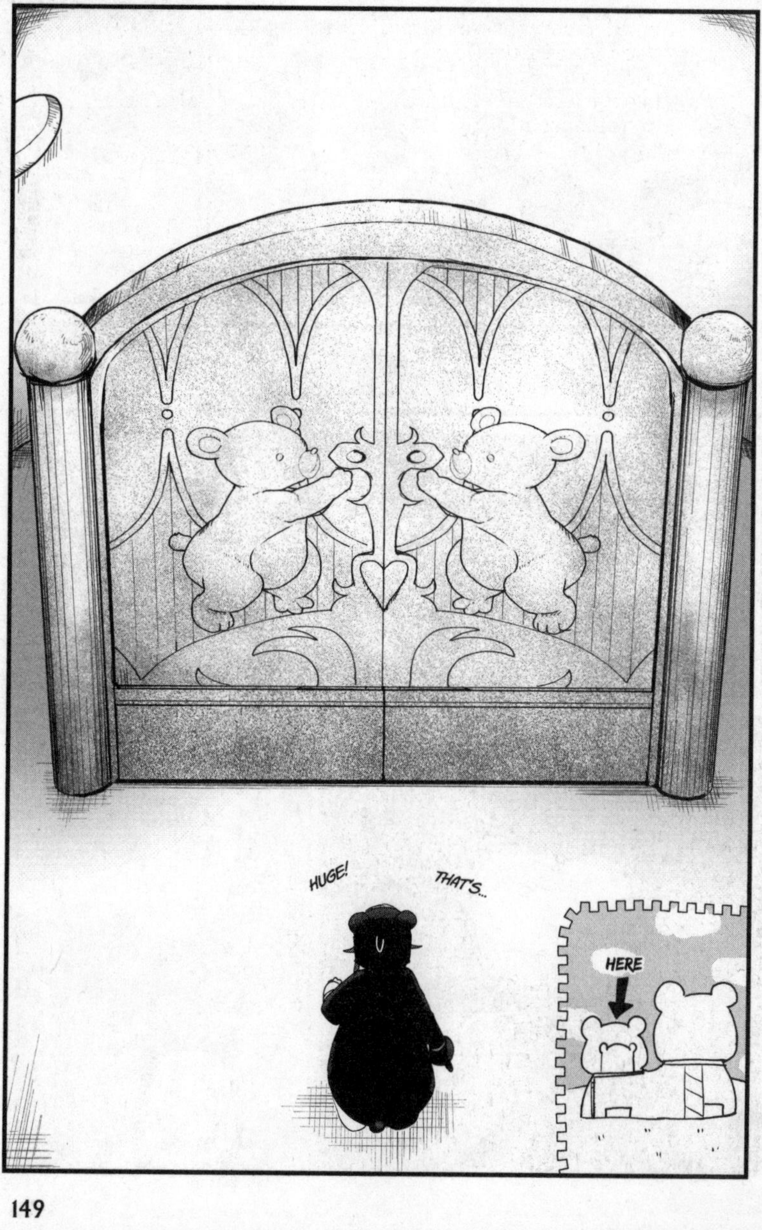
THAT'S...
HUGE!
HERE

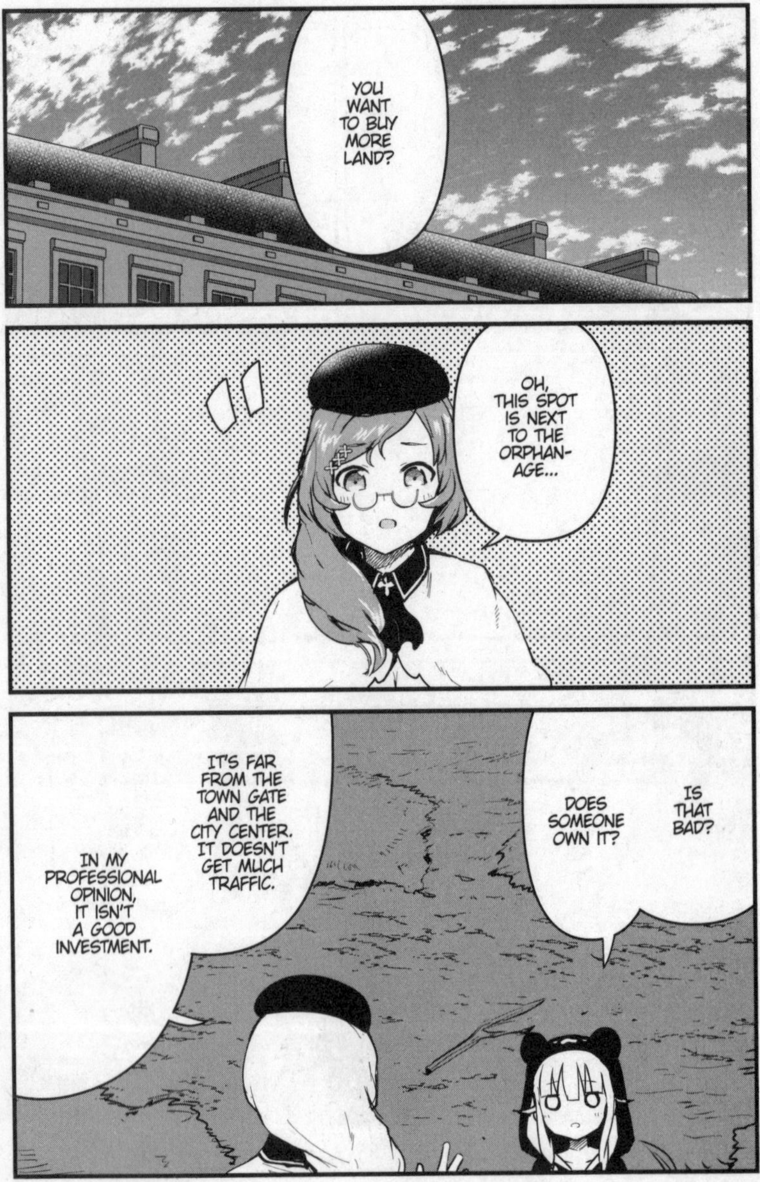
YOU WANT TO BUY MORE LAND?
OH, THIS SPOT IS NEXT TO THE ORPHAN-AGE...
IS THAT BAD?
DOES SOMEONE OWN IT?
IT'S FAR FROM THE TOWN GATE AND THE CITY CENTER. IT DOESN'T GET MUCH TRAFFIC.
IN MY PROFESSIONAL OPINION, IT ISN'T A GOOD INVESTMENT.

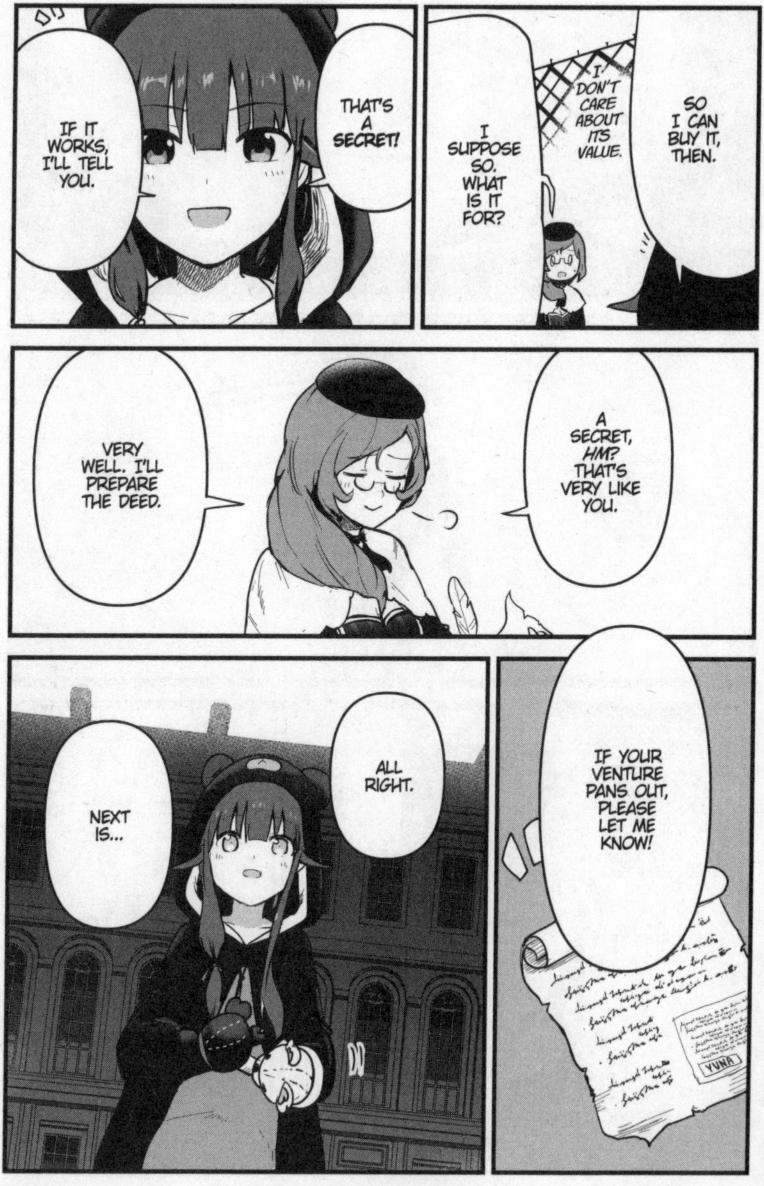
SO I CAN BUY IT, THEN.
I DON'T CARE ABOUT ITS VALUE.
I SUPPOSE SO. WHAT IS IT FOR?
THAT'S A SECRET!
IF IT WORKS, I'LL TELL YOU.
A SECRET, *HM?* THAT'S VERY LIKE YOU.
VERY WELL. I'LL PREPARE THE DEED.
IF YOUR VENTURE PANS OUT, PLEASE LET ME KNOW!
YUNA
ALL RIGHT.
NEXT IS...

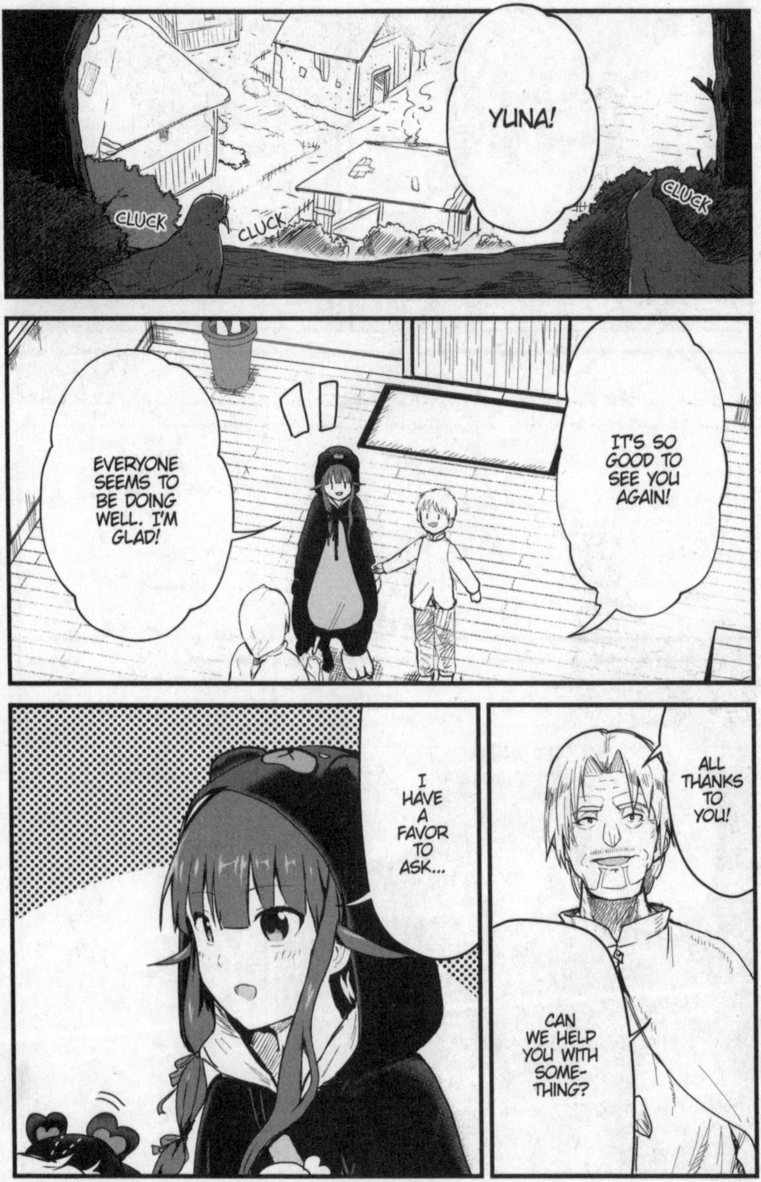
YUNA!
CLUCK
CLUCK
CLUCK
IT'S SO GOOD TO SEE YOU AGAIN!
EVERYONE SEEMS TO BE DOING WELL. I'M GLAD!
ALL THANKS TO YOU!
CAN WE HELP YOU WITH SOME-THING?
I HAVE A FAVOR TO ASK...

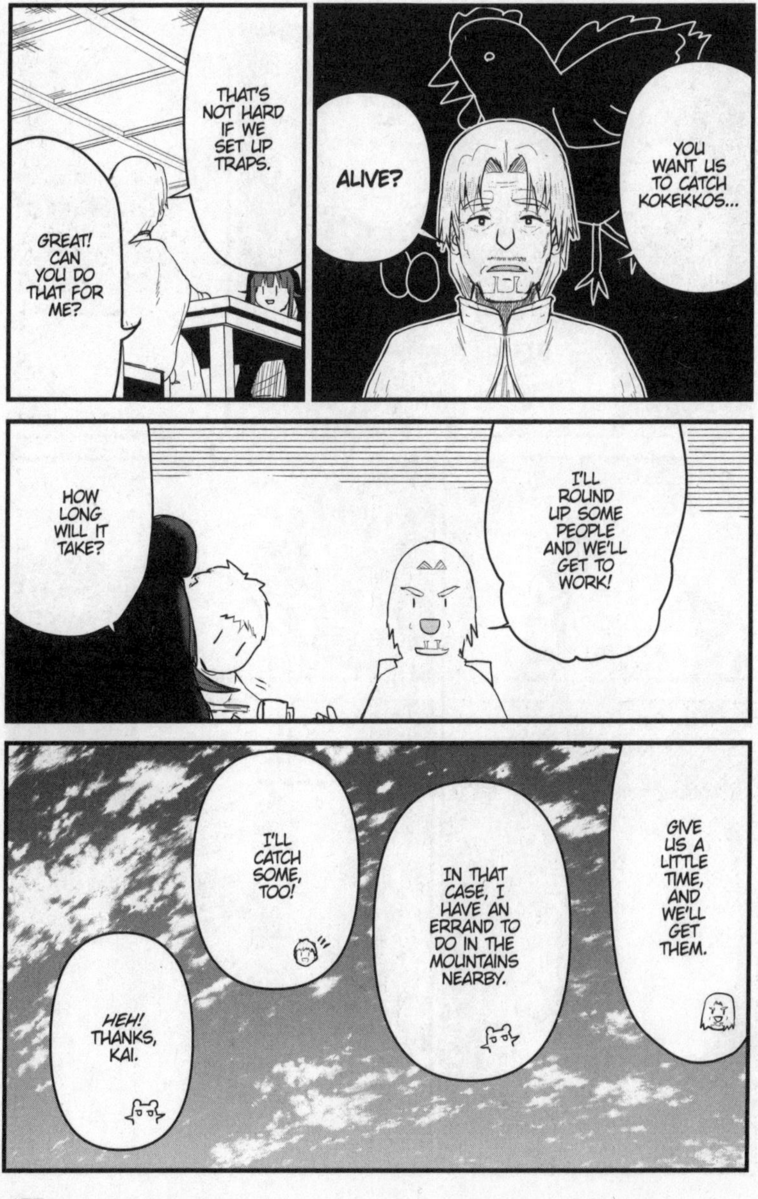
YOU WANT US TO CATCH KOKEKKOS...
ALIVE?
THAT'S NOT HARD IF WE SET UP TRAPS.
GREAT! CAN YOU DO THAT FOR ME?
I'LL ROUND UP SOME PEOPLE AND WE'LL GET TO WORK!
HOW LONG WILL IT TAKE?
GIVE US A LITTLE TIME, AND WE'LL GET THEM.
IN THAT CASE, I HAVE AN ERRAND TO DO IN THE MOUNTAINS NEARBY.
I'LL CATCH SOME, TOO!
HEH! THANKS, KAI.

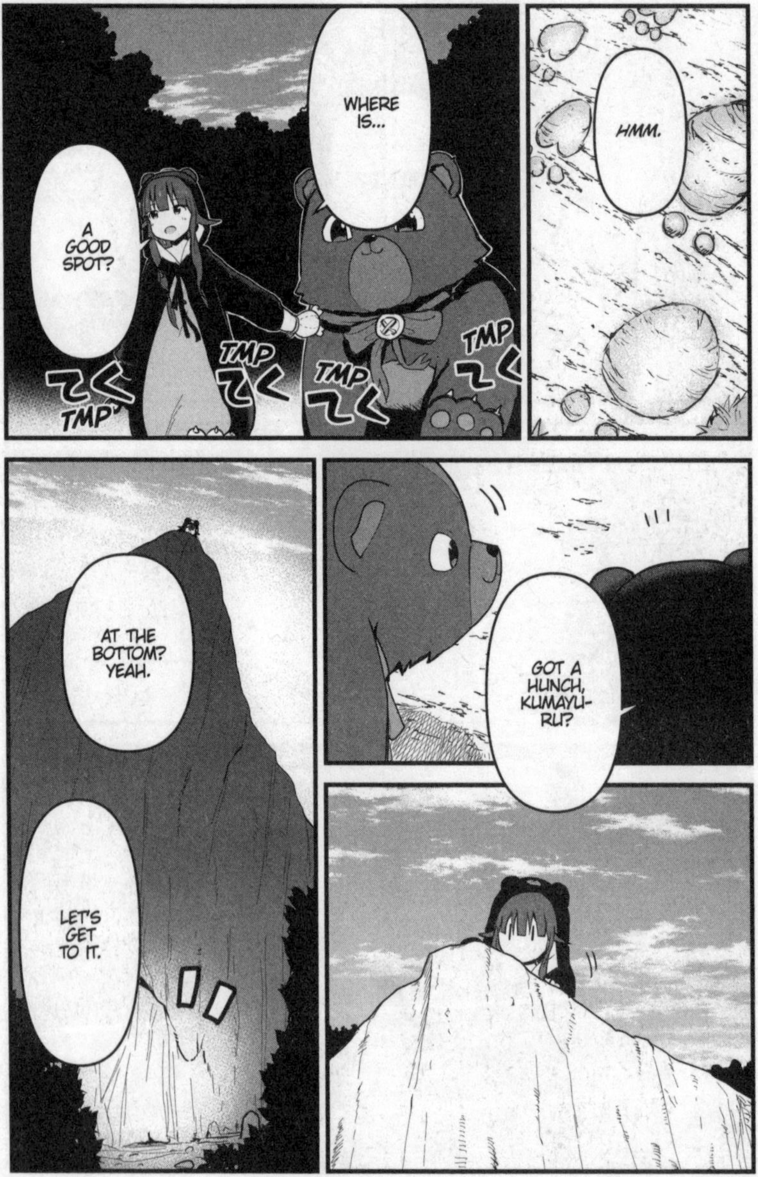
HMM.
WHERE IS...
A GOOD SPOT?
TMP
TMP
TMP
TMP
GOT A HUNCH, KUMAYURU?
AT THE BOTTOM? YEAH.
LET'S GET TO IT.

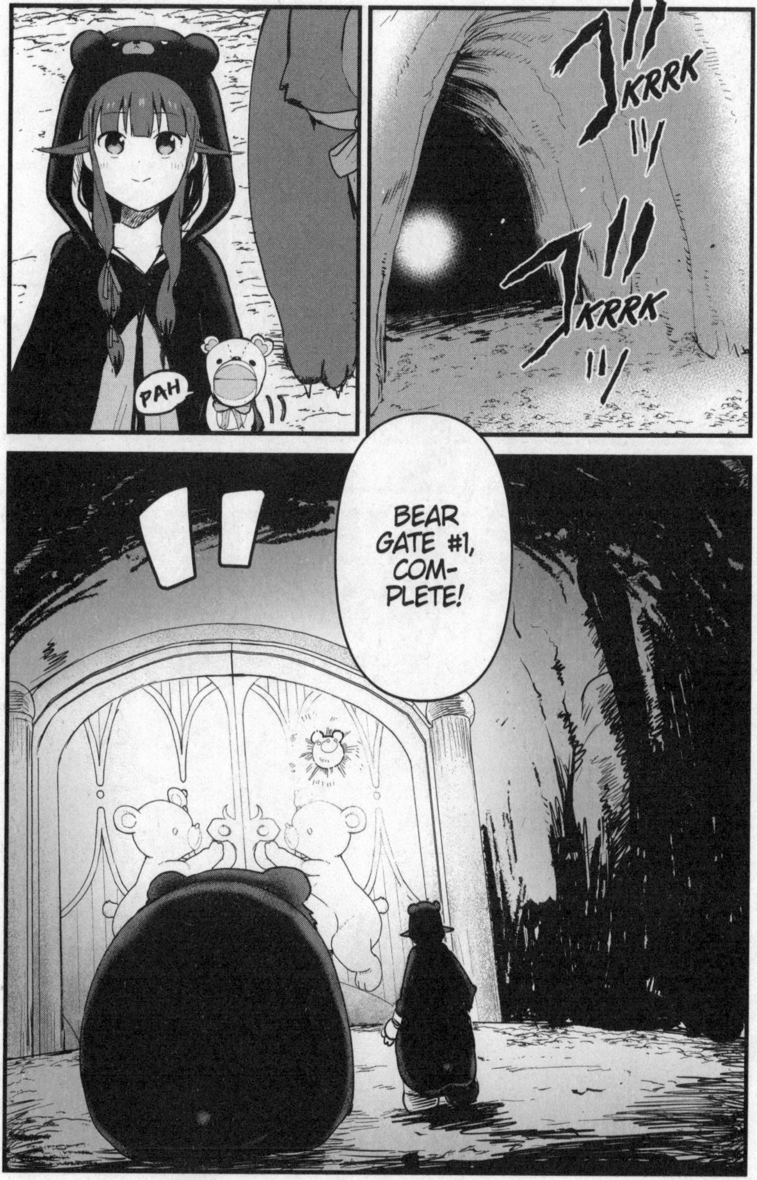
KRRK
KRRK
PAH
BEAR GATE #1, COM-PLETE!

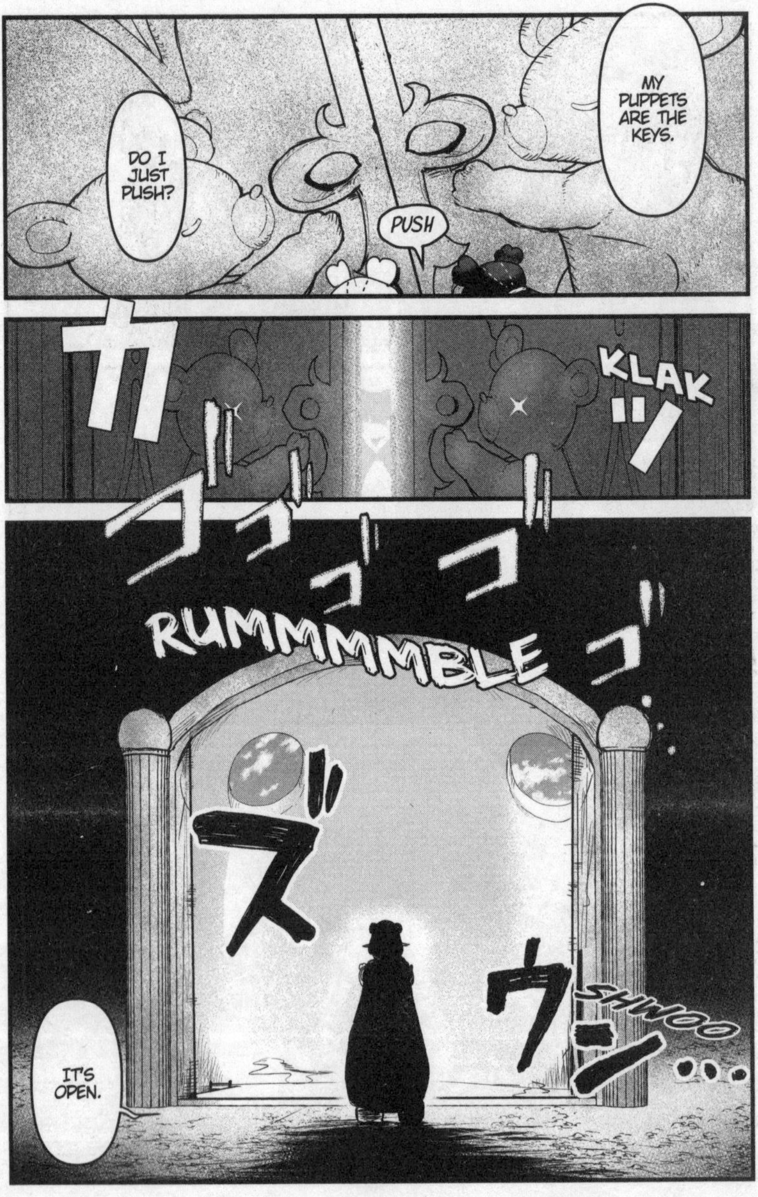

MY PUPPETS ARE THE KEYS.
DO I JUST PUSH?
PUSH
KLAK
RUMMMMBLE
SHWOO...
IT'S OPEN.

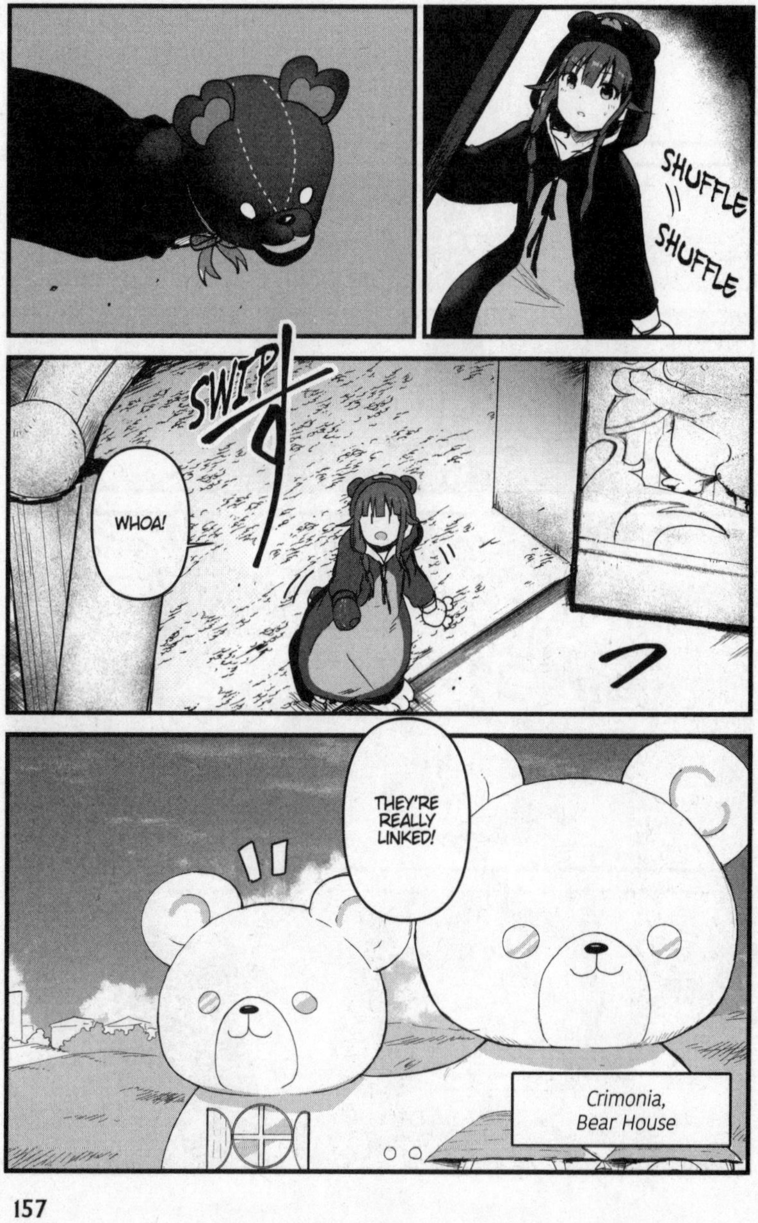
SHUFFLE SHUFFLE
SWIP!
WHOA!
THEY'RE REALLY LINKED!
Crimonia, Bear House

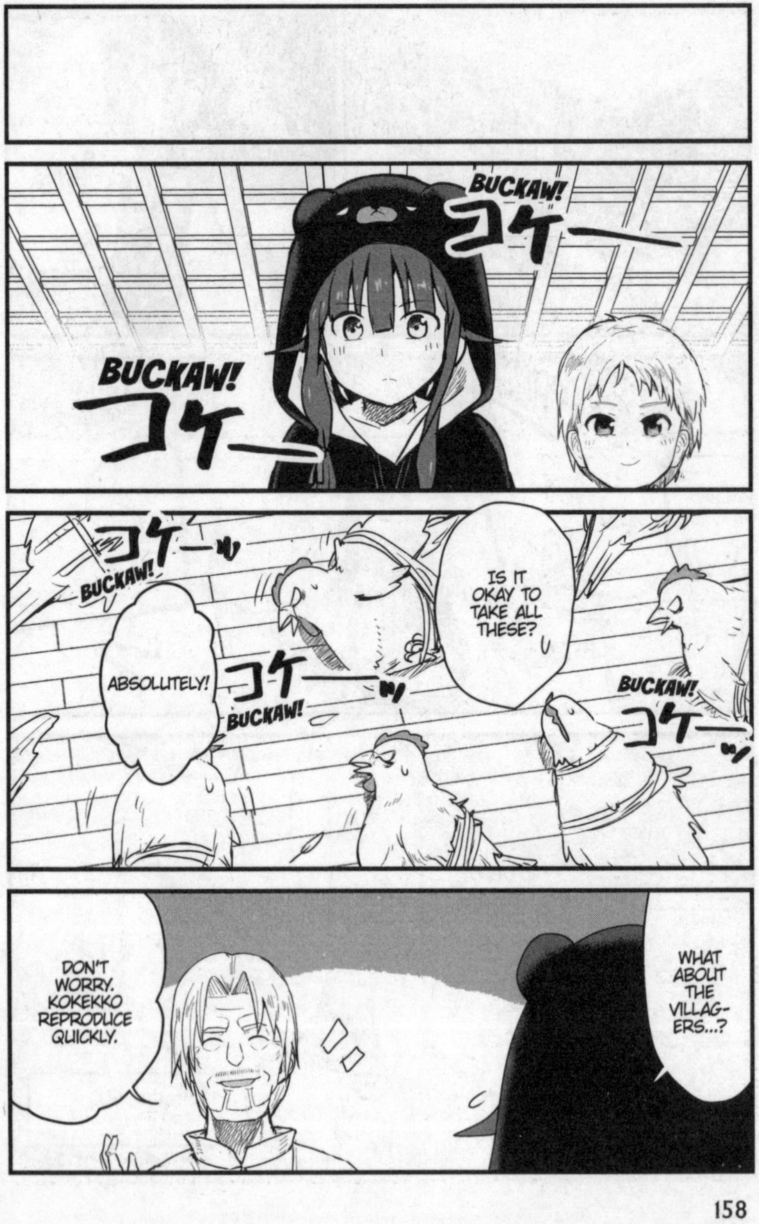
BUCKAW!
コケー
BUCKAW!
コケー
BUCKAW!
コケー
IS IT OKAY TO TAKE ALL THESE?
コケー
BUCKAW!
ABSOLUTELY!
コケー
BUCKAW!
WHAT ABOUT THE VILLAG-ERS...?
DON'T WORRY. KOKEKKO REPRODUCE QUICKLY.

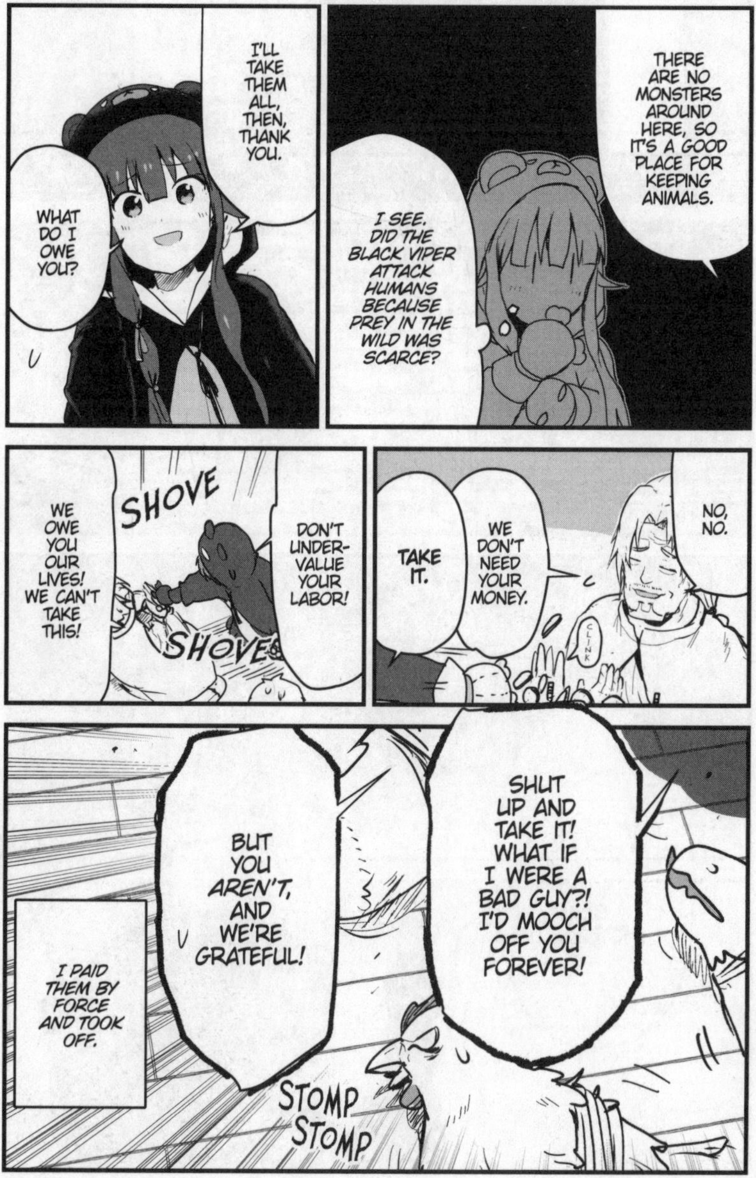
THERE ARE NO MONSTERS AROUND HERE, SO IT'S A GOOD PLACE FOR KEEPING ANIMALS.
I SEE. DID THE BLACK VIPER ATTACK HUMANS BECAUSE PREY IN THE WILD WAS SCARCE?
I'LL TAKE THEM ALL, THEN, THANK YOU.
WHAT DO I OWE YOU?
NO, NO.
WE DON'T NEED YOUR MONEY.
TAKE IT.
CLINK
DON'T UNDER-VALUE YOUR LABOR!
SHOVE
WE OWE YOU OUR LIVES! WE CAN'T TAKE THIS!
SHOVE
SHUT UP AND TAKE IT! WHAT IF I WERE A BAD GUY?! I'D MOOCH OFF YOU FOREVER!
BUT YOU AREN'T, AND WE'RE GRATEFUL!
STOMP STOMP
I PAID THEM BY FORCE AND TOOK OFF.

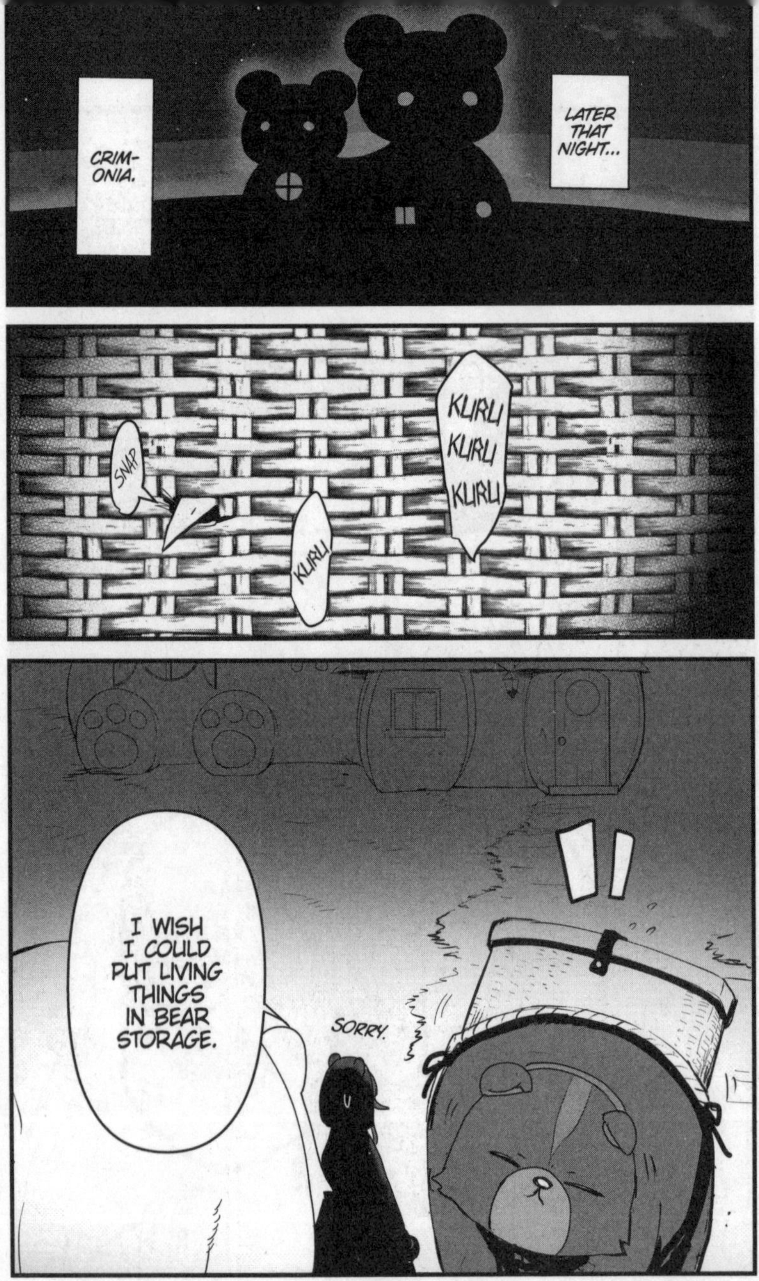
LATER THAT NIGHT...
CRIM-ONIA.
KURU KURU KURU
SNAP
KURU
!!
I WISH I COULD PUT LIVING THINGS IN BEAR STORAGE.
SORRY.

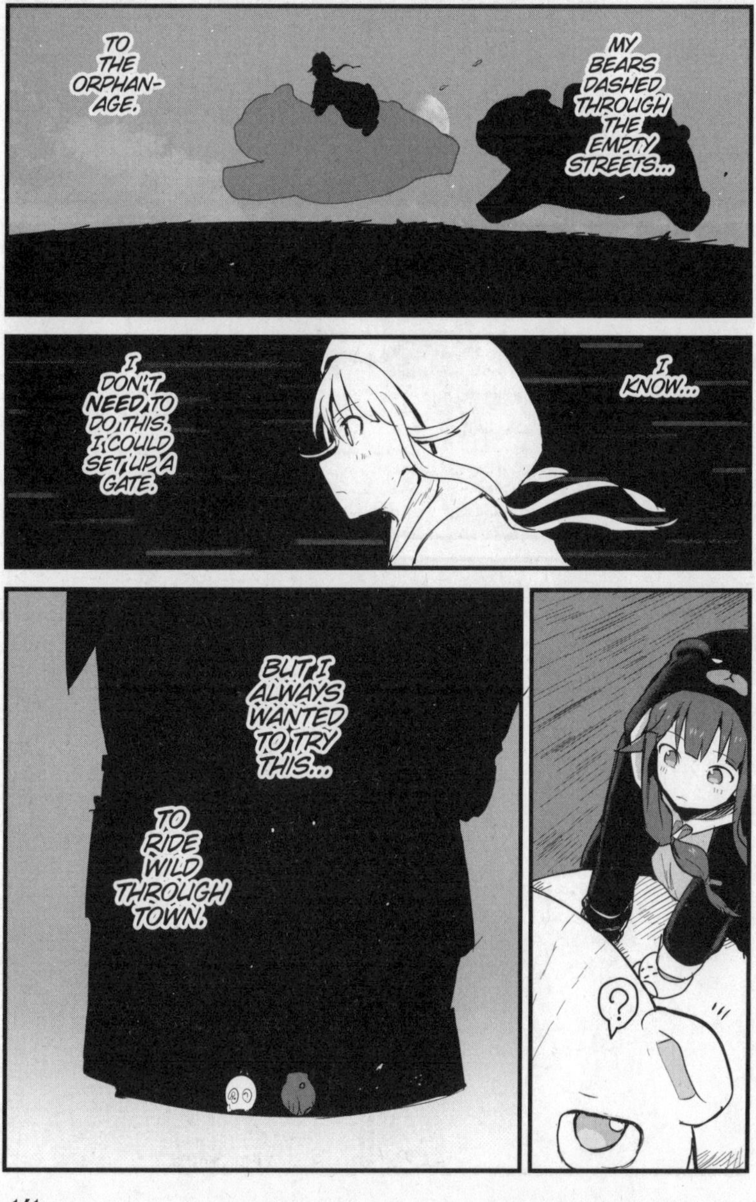
MY BEARS DASHED THROUGH THE EMPTY STREETS...
TO THE ORPHAN-AGE.
I KNOW...
I DON'T NEED TO DO THIS. I COULD SET UP A GATE.
?
BUT I ALWAYS WANTED TO TRY THIS...
TO RIDE WILD THROUGH TOWN.

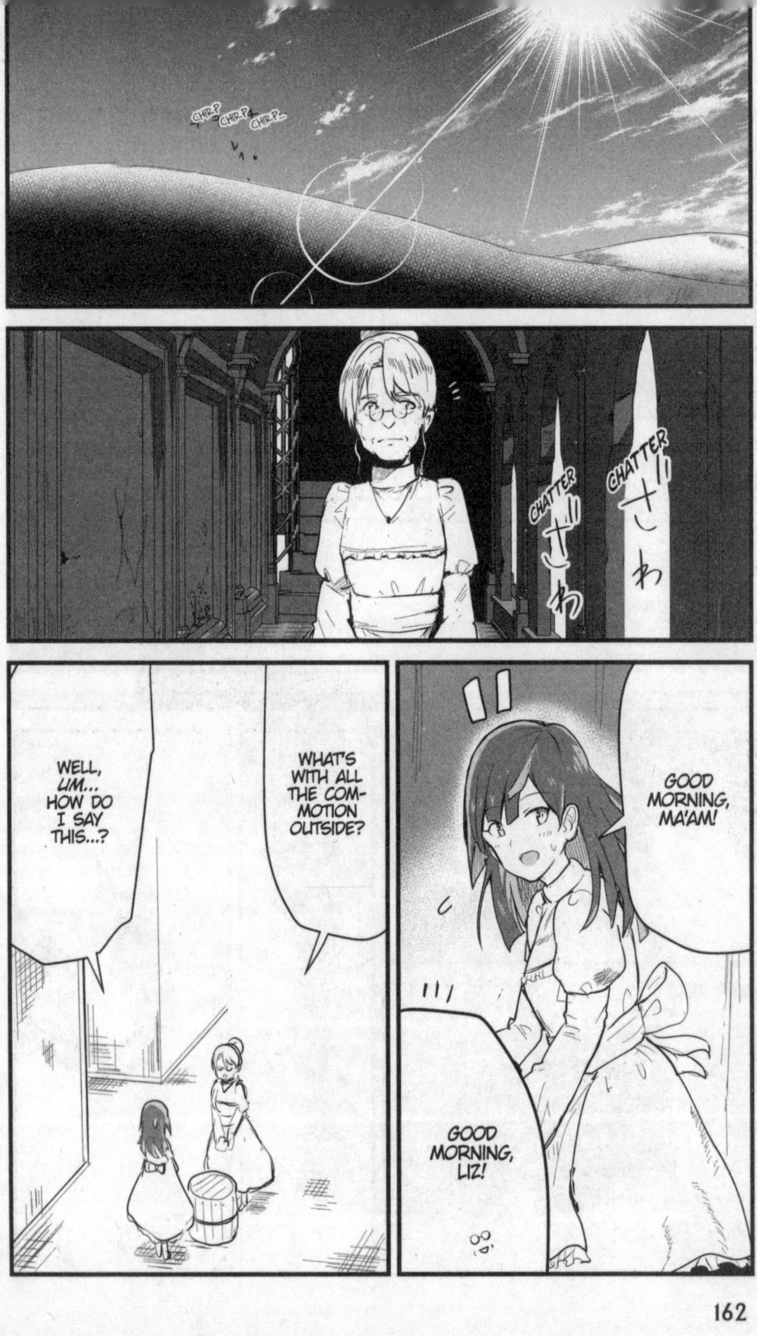
CHIRP CHIRP CHIRP...
CHATTER
ざわ
CHATTER
ざわ
GOOD MORNING, MA'AM!
GOOD MORNING, LIZ!
WHAT'S WITH ALL THE COM-MOTION OUTSIDE?
WELL, UM... HOW DO I SAY THIS...?

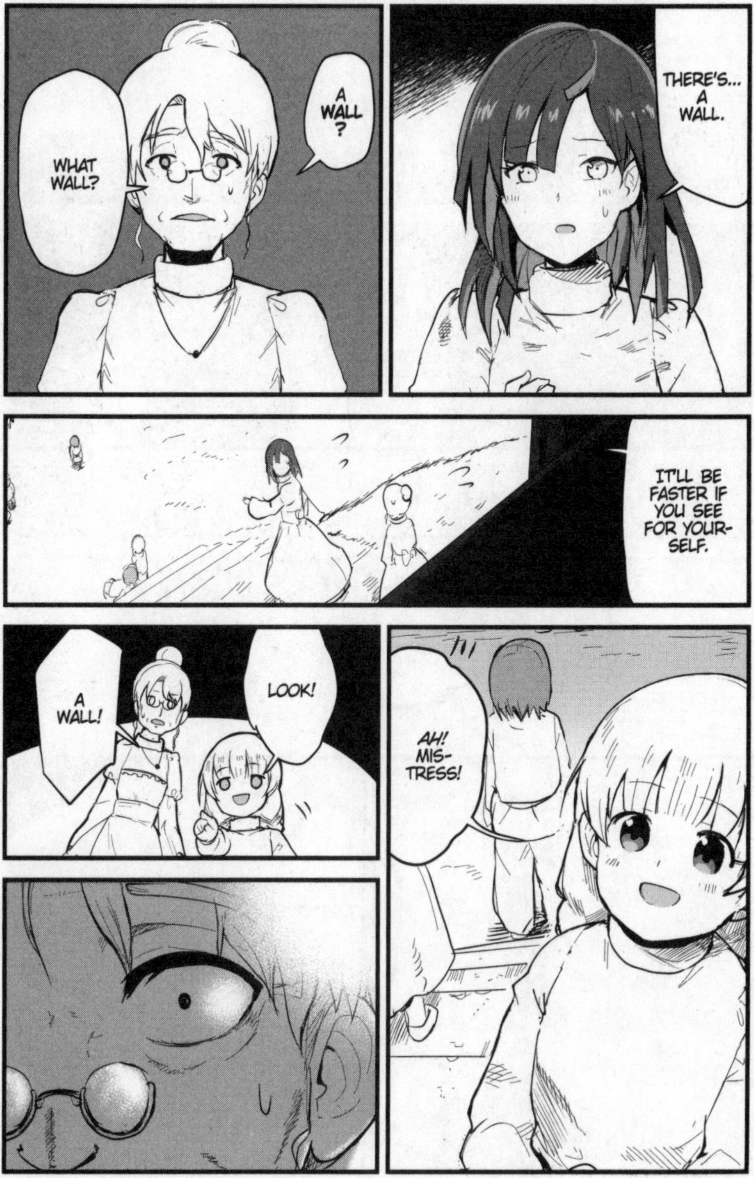
THERE'S... A WALL.
A WALL?
WHAT WALL?
IT'LL BE FASTER IF YOU SEE FOR YOUR-SELF.
AH! MIS-TRESS!
LOOK!
A WALL!

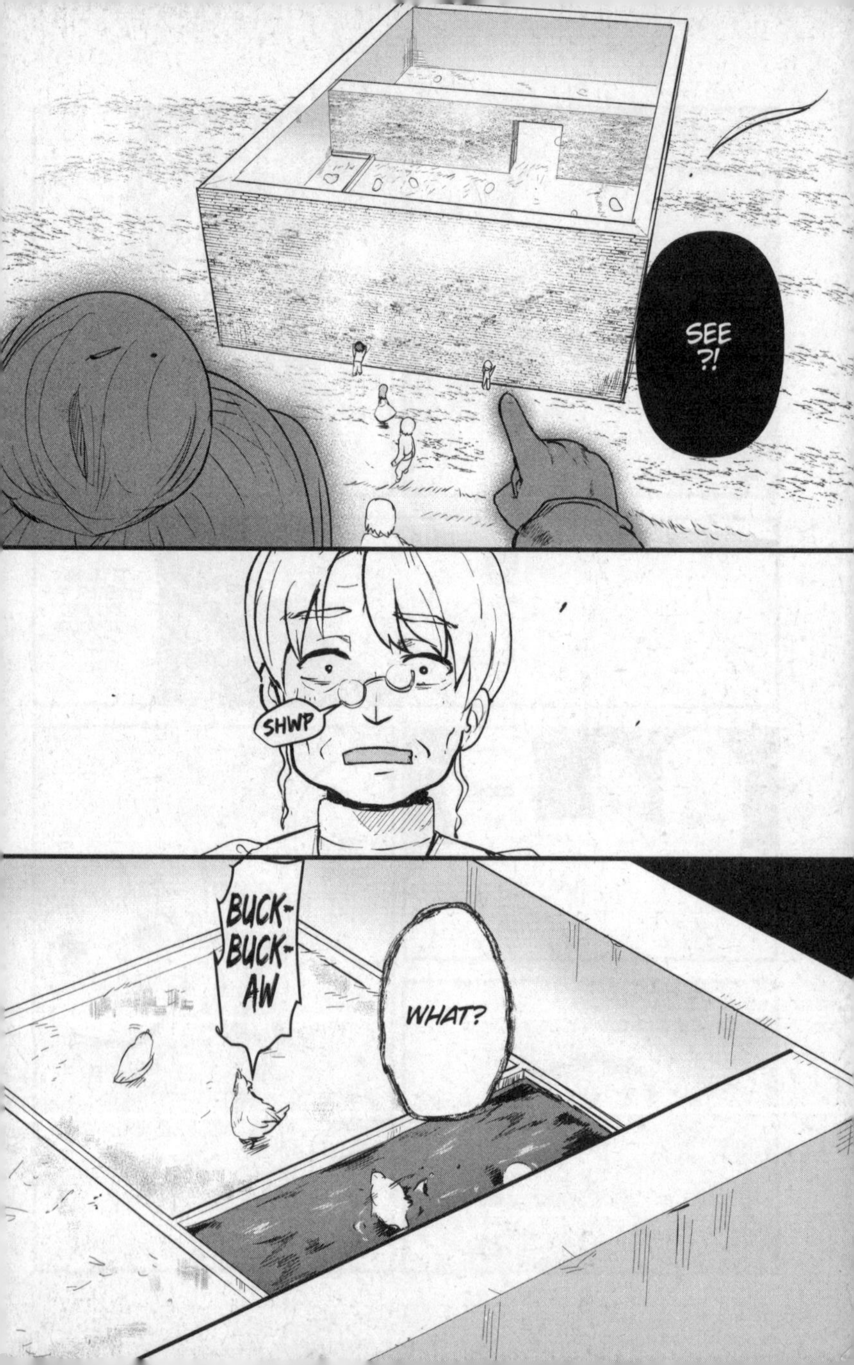
SEE ?!
SHWP
WHAT?
BUCK-BUCK-AW

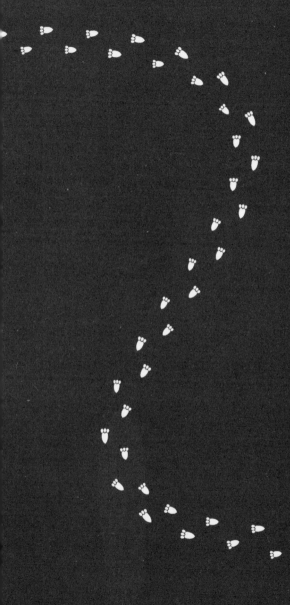

to be continued...

KUMA KUMA
KUMA BEAR
Volume.3

Bonus *Kuma Kuma Kuma Bear* Short Story

Guild Master's Bear Encounter

Written by Kumanano

I'm the guild master of the Adventurers' Guild in the town of Crimonia.

A new member recently registered with our guild: a young woman in a bear onesie. Thanks in part to her weird fashion choices, other adventurers started picking fights with her. Turns out she's stronger than you'd expect. She dropped ten adventurers, including Deboranay!

Her terms were that the adventurers she'd defeated would quit the guild, but I intervened to work out a deal. She agreed to let them off the hook if they apologized, and if the the guild would forbid further harassment and assist her with any interpersonal squabbles.

Once that was settled, the girl in the bear onesie became an adventurer.

Her name is Yuna, and she says she's only fifteen years old. She's so short that, at first, I thought she must be younger.

As I set about to work over lunch the next day, I hear shouting coming from the reception area, along with the word "bear."

Didn't I tell everyone not to start anything with Yuna? The Adventurers' Guild had a deal with her. We have to take care of any trouble she gets involved in. It's a pain, but I leave my office to check in on the commotion. Lanz, one of Deboranay's party members, is picking a fight with Yuna.

When I ask for an explanation, Lanz gripes about a quest his party accepted. Deboranay was injured by Yuna, and cannot participate, meaning their quest is in trouble.

I explain to Lanz that it was Deboranay who started the fight in the first place and that Yuna's not at fault, but he won't listen. I suggest an alternative: if Deboranay is unavailable for the quest, why not bring Yuna? She defeated Deboranay and the others in a ten-on-one fight. She'd be a fine replacement. She should be able to handle a group of goblins with the rest of the party. Lanz and his group reluctantly accept, and I return to my work.

Helen arrives in my office at sunset with an odd look.

"Something wrong?" I ask.

"It's Yuna. She killed a Goblin King."

"Come again?"

I thought I'd misheard, but according to Helen, Yuna went with Rulina as a group of two to wipe out the goblin horde. In the process, Yuna fought and defeated a Goblin King on her own.

My mind goes blank.

Goblin Kings are intelligent, strong, and formidable. Rookie adventures can't handle them! And this Goblin King was in a horde of goblins, too!

I have got to see this for myself.

I make for the harvesting workshop and see the body of a goblin so huge, it doesn't compare it to a regular goblin at all. It must be a Goblin King.

And Yuna took it out herself.

I knew she was strong, but she's stronger than I could have guessed.

Reports about Yuna come in continuously. A few days later, I hear about her defeating tigerwolves. Next, I'm told she has bear summons.

Bear summons?

According to a report, she has two bear summons, one black and one white. I've heard of black bears, but I've never seen a white bear. They say it's pure white.

And there's more. She built herself a bear-shaped house to live in. I go to see it, and it really is shaped like a bear.

That was the last bear report I receive for a while, and things are quiet. Of course, there's a reason for that.

"Guild Master?" Helen enters my office.

"What is it?"

"It's about Yuna. There's a problem. We've gotten some... *complaints*."

"Did she do something, or did another adventurer pick a fight with her?"

We've informed everyone about our Yuna policy, but not everyone has met her. I instructed Helen and the others to fill in the rest, but it's possible an adventurer who doesn't know better might start something.

"No, sir. We've been getting reports from adventurers who take monster-slaying quests, but find no monsters when they arrive on the scene."

I don't understand. Sometimes, you don't find the monsters you're looking for at a quest location. It happens.

"What does it have to do with Yuna?"

"Each report comes with a sighting of a girl dressed as a bear."

Now I get it. So, Yuna defeated all of the monsters.

"Has Yuna reported this?"

"No, sir."

An adventurer who slays monsters is obligated to report it to the guild, since those monsters might be in someone else's quest. If someone else slays them, the adventurer would get stuck looking for non-existent monsters, a loss of time and money. That's why it's required that adventurers report the monsters they exterminate in addition to their own quests.

"Got it. The next time you see Yuna, send her to me."

Yuna is sent to my office when she shows up at the Adventurers' Guild. I ask her about the monsters, and as I suspected, she wasn't aware she had to report in. I decide to let her off with a warning, since we made a mistake in not informing her.

Yuna nods her agreement and leaves.

There shouldn't be any more problems for a while, but a new problem comes from a different source.

While I'm working in my office, a receptionist comes in and tells me a black viper has appeared in a village. A boy has arrived asking for help.

Black vipers come in all sizes, but they're always a dangerous enemy.

The receptionist tells me that there are no available adventurers strong enough to face a black viper, and Helen doesn't know what to do.

I go to ask the kid for more details and I overhear Yuna offering to scout alone. She has the right idea. We should find out the black viper's size and precise location. Having that information will make the hunt go swiftly, and allow us to make a plan of attack. But we can't send Yuna out on her own, even if it's just to scout.

I leave Helen with instructions to assemble high-ranking adventurers, and I decide to go with Yuna. She has two bear summons, so she says she'll ride ahead and switch between them. It's a good idea. When she rides one the other can rest, and she can proceed to the village without breaks. It's something only she can do with her two bear summons.

I agree, but warn her not to do anything reckless.

As we leave town, Yuna summons a black bear.

So, *that's* Yuna's bear summon! I haven't seen it before. It's huge, and nuzzles up to her.

Yuna and the boy, who says he's going with her, climb onto the bear and dash off together at an incredible speed. I spur my horse into a gallop, following after, but Yuna's bear is already out of sight.

Who knew a bear could move that fast!

I make for the village, resting my horse now and then. There's no sign of Yuna anywhere. The sun sets. It's too dangerous to ride in the dark, so I make camp. I'm worried about Yuna, but I can't do anything more today.

I hope she's not doing anything crazy. Many an adventurer has ended up dead after they misjudge their own strength and take on a monster above their level. I push down my impatience and let my horse rest until sunrise. I should arrive at the village tomorrow. I pray it will stay safe until then.

I set off at sunrise, determined to meet back up with Yuna as soon as possible.

Not long after setting out, I see something white ahead. A bear? And next to a white bear, a black shape.

Could that be Yuna?

What is she doing *here?*

I rein my horse in next to her.

"You're *alone?* Was the village--"

"The black viper? I killed it."

I can't believe it. Black vipers are extremely strong. They're not easily defeated! But when I press Yuna for an explanation, she produces the black viper from her left white bear glove.

I inspect it. The black viper really is dead.

I was stunned that she had a black viper at all, and now I'm shocked that she can fit this one into an item bag. Item bags with high capacities are expensive! They aren't something newbies can afford.

Her bear onesie, her power, her item bag...so much about her is a mystery.

But it's a fact that Yuna saved that village, and as guild master, I'm grateful to her for that.

BECOMING A FATHER

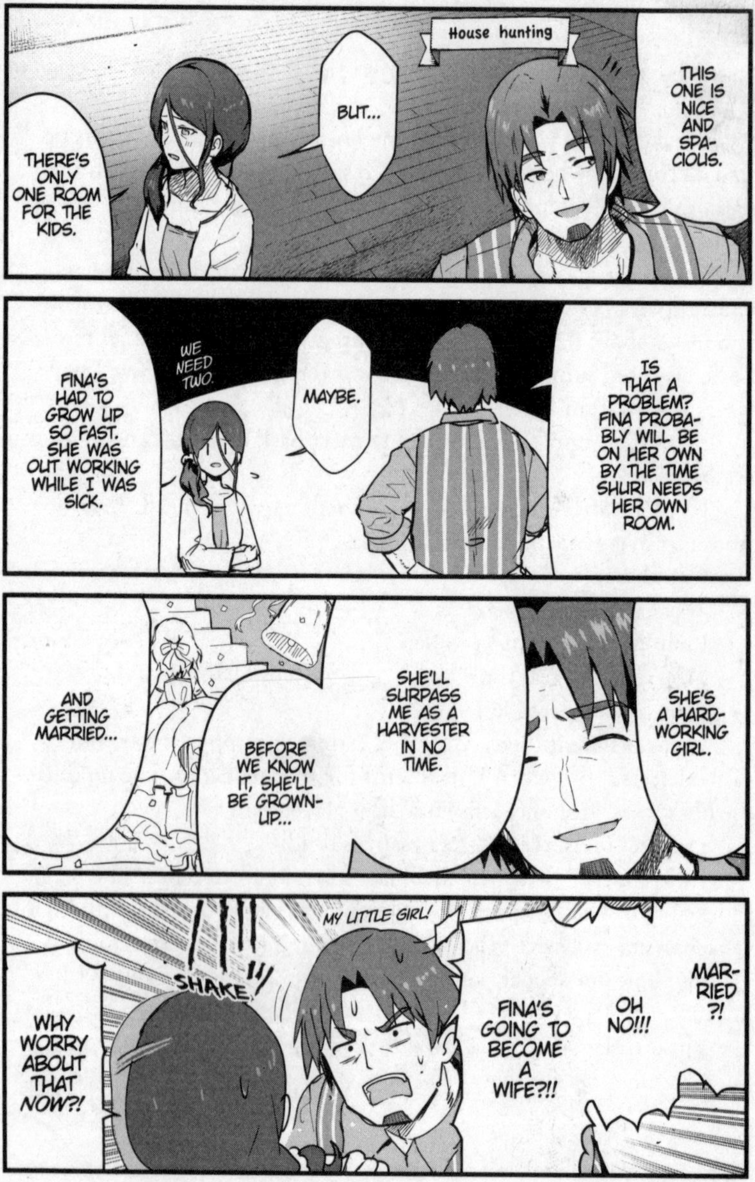
House hunting
THIS ONE IS NICE AND SPACIOUS.
BUT...
THERE'S ONLY ONE ROOM FOR THE KIDS.
IS THAT A PROBLEM? FINA PROBABLY WILL BE ON HER OWN BY THE TIME SHURI NEEDS HER OWN ROOM.
MAYBE.
WE NEED TWO.
FINA'S HAD TO GROW UP SO FAST. SHE WAS OUT WORKING WHILE I WAS SICK.
SHE'S A HARD-WORKING GIRL.
SHE'LL SURPASS ME AS A HARVESTER IN NO TIME.
BEFORE WE KNOW IT, SHE'LL BE GROWN-UP...
AND GETTING MARRIED...
MAR-RIED?!
OH NO!!!
MY LITTLE GIRL!
FINA'S GOING TO BECOME A WIFE?!!
SHAKE
WHY WORRY ABOUT THAT NOW?!

BEAR LIFE

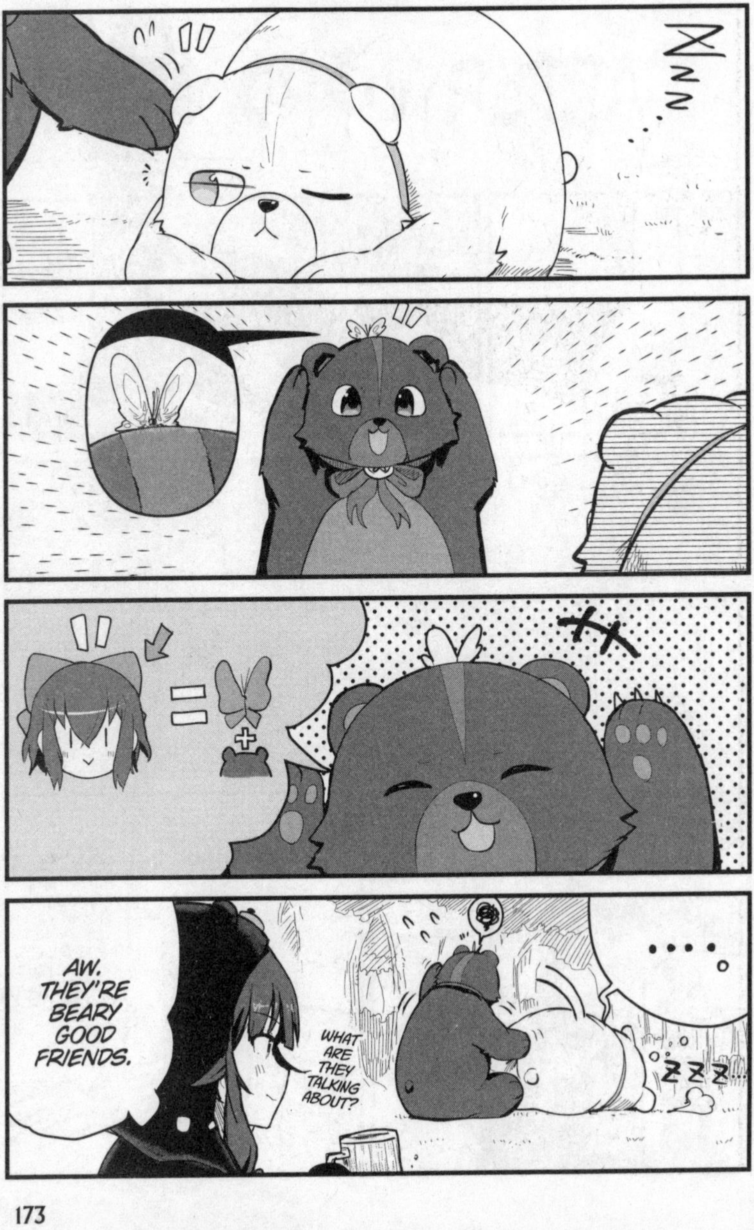
Zzz...
....
ZZZ...
WHAT ARE THEY TALKING ABOUT?
AW. THEY'RE BEARY GOOD FRIENDS.

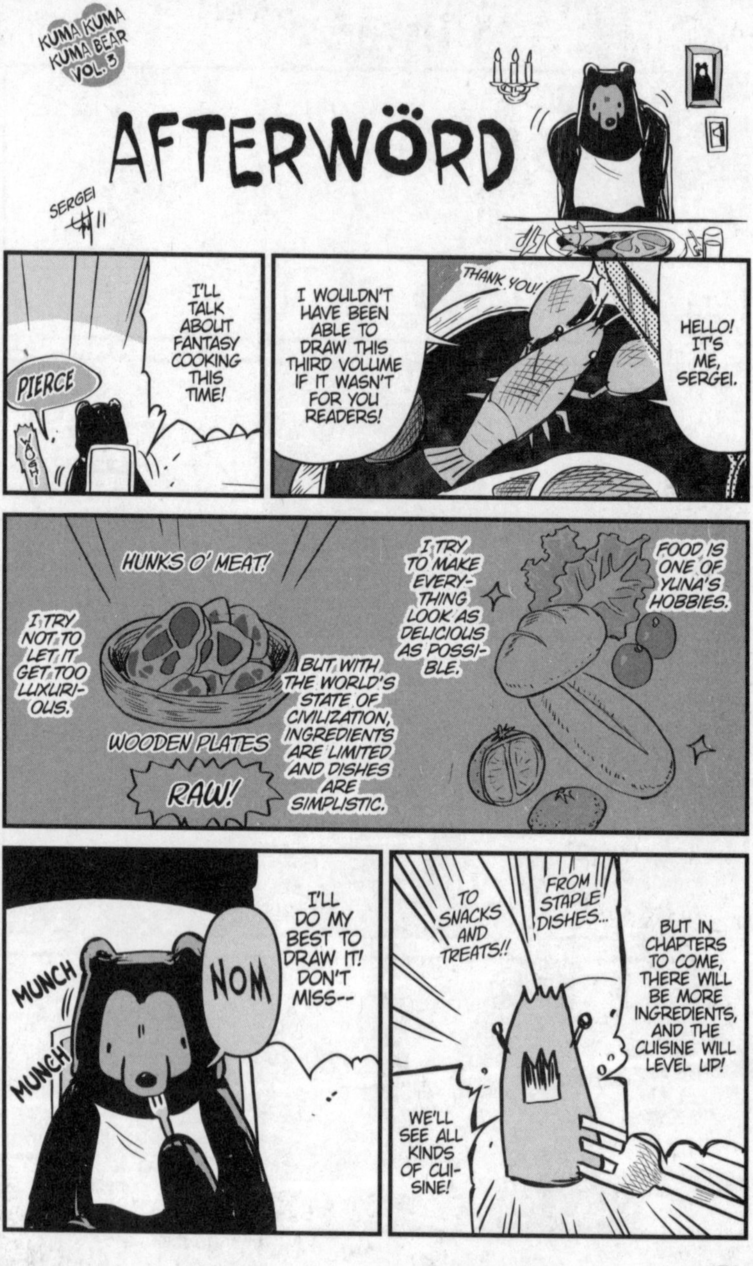
KUMA KUMA KUMA BEAR VOL. 3
AFTERWÖRD
SERGEI
HELLO! IT'S ME, SERGEI.
I WOULDN'T HAVE BEEN ABLE TO DRAW THIS THIRD VOLUME IF IT WASN'T FOR YOU READERS!
THANK YOU!
I'LL TALK ABOUT FANTASY COOKING THIS TIME!
PIERCE
WOOSH
FOOD IS ONE OF YUNA'S HOBBIES.
I TRY TO MAKE EVERYTHING LOOK AS DELICIOUS AS POSSIBLE.
BUT WITH THE WORLD'S STATE OF CIVILIZATION, INGREDIENTS ARE LIMITED AND DISHES ARE SIMPLISTIC.
HUNKS O' MEAT!
I TRY NOT TO LET IT GET TOO LUXURIOUS.
WOODEN PLATES
RAW!
BUT IN CHAPTERS TO COME, THERE WILL BE MORE INGREDIENTS, AND THE CUISINE WILL LEVEL UP!
FROM STAPLE DISHES...
TO SNACKS AND TREATS!!
WE'LL SEE ALL KINDS OF CUISINE!
I'LL DO MY BEST TO DRAW IT! DON'T MISS--
NOM
MUNCH
MUNCH

SEVEN SEAS ENTERTAINMENT PRESENTS

KUMA KUMA KUMA BEAR

story by **KUMANANO** / art by **SERGEI** / character designs by **029**

VOLUME 3

TRANSLATION
Amanda Haley

ADAPTATION
Dawn Davis

LETTERING AND RETOUCH
Laura Heo

COVER DESIGN
Kris Aubin

PROOFREADING
Kurestin Armada

EDITOR
Shannon Fay

PREPRESS TECHNICIAN
Rhiannon Rasmussen-Silverstein

PRODUCTION MANAGER
Lissa Pattillo

MANAGING EDITOR
Julie Davis

ASSOCIATE PUBLISHER
Adam Arnold

PUBLISHER
Jason DeAngelis

KUMA KUMA KUMA BEAR 3
© SERGEI   © KUMANANO 2019
Originally published in Japan in 2019 by SHUFU TO SEIKATSU SHA CO., LTD., Tokyo.
English translation rights arranged with SHUFU TO SEIKATSU SHA CO., LTD., Tokyo, through TOHAN CORPORATION, Tokyo.

Seven Seas press and purchase enquiries can be sent to Marketing Manager Lianne Sentar at press@gomanga.com. Information regarding the distribution and purchase of digital editions is available from Digital Manager CK Russell at digital@gomanga.com.

Seven Seas and the Seven Seas logo are trademarks of Seven Seas Entertainment. All rights reserved.

ISBN: 978-1-64505-778-9

Printed in Canada

First Printing: November 2020

10 9 8 7 6 5 4 3 2 1

FOLLOW US ONLINE: **www.sevenseasentertainment.com**

READING DIRECTIONS

This book reads from **right to left**, Japanese style. If this is your first time reading manga, you start reading from the top right panel on each page and take it from there. If you get lost, just follow the numbered diagram here. It may seem backwards at first, but you'll get the hang of it! Have fun!!

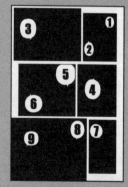